"A wildly original and magical twist on the Robin Hood narrative, Kendra Merritt's *By Wingéd Chair* is packed to the spokes with complex characters, wry humor, and flawless world building."

-Darby Karchut, best-selling author of DEL TORO MOON and FINN FINNEGAN

"With a wonderfully crafted blend of swords and sorcery and characters based on Robin Hood, Merritt tops this story off with the lead character readers need nowadays; a strong, independent, powerful female mage who also happens to be in a wheelchair. Readers will be constantly turning pages to see what happens next to this fun group of characters through the twists and turns they won't see coming."

-The Booklife Prize

"Kendra Merritt's prose is fresh, with one-line descriptions that crack like a whip, and she doesn't miss an opportunity to surprise the reader. From the first line to the last, I was enchanted with *By Winged Chair*."

-Todd Fahnestock, best-selling author of FAIRMIST and THE WISHING WORLD

The Truth Stealer

The Death Bringer

KENDRA MERRITT

DAYBREAK COLONY: BOOK 2

DAYBREAK SENTINEL

For Jonas. Thank you for the inspiration for so many characters. Zev, Brann, Ember, Lucy, Spike, Gruff, and Shade.

I miss you, buddy.

BB's Record

Day 1: Last Resort crashes, Anikka lands on Daybreak

Day 2: Anikka searches for other survivors

Day 3: BB integrates navigation data

Day 4: Anikka heads to the colony

Day 5: Anikka finds the colony abandoned

Day 6-20: Anikka learns to survive on Daybreak

Day 21: The drop ship floods

Day 32: Anikka kills a slasherfin

Day 33: Anikka finds Parker and learns where the colonists went

Day 49: Anikka reaches the Black Flats and learns there is a storm coming

Day 50: Anikka saves Shade

Day 55: BB suggests Anikka uses cybernetics to survive

Day 59: Anikka obtains a radiation vest

Day 60: Anikka traverses the crater, reaches the Last Resort, BB integrates the cybernetics data, Anikka undergoes cybernetic implantation

BB's Record

Day 61: Anikka defeats BEV

Day 62: Anikka survives her first storm

Day 67: Anikka reinstalls BB

Day 83: Anikka begins building her "boat"

Day 124: Anikka survives her second storm

Day 176: Anikka finds evidence of a depot built by the colony

Day 186: Anikka survives her third storm

Fauna of Daybreak ⚠

Swarmstings- alien insects, swarm prey, deadly, **avoid**

Slinkwolves- blue and purple, fox-like creatures, 60-80 pounds, hunts in packs, scavenges when alone, likes fish, tameable

Jewelflyers- assorted birds, not a threat

Jumpernicks- monkey/lizards, gray scales and feathers, excellent climbers, eat fruits and vegetables, thieves, **protect food**, great slasherfin bait

Slasherfins- carnivorous fish, don't let go willingly, can be stabbed, **kill!** delicious

Megawing- giant red bird/lizard, predator, eats slasherfins, mean enough to kill out of anger, **avoid**

Troopers- swarming beetles, scavengers, consumes all organic matter, flammable

Deathkitties- cat-like predators, uses height and climbing skills to hunt, very fast, very dangerous, **avoid**

Slugtooths- giant carnivorous worms, dig holes and wait for prey to fall in, **avoid**

Silverpoints- purple deer, herd animals, delicious

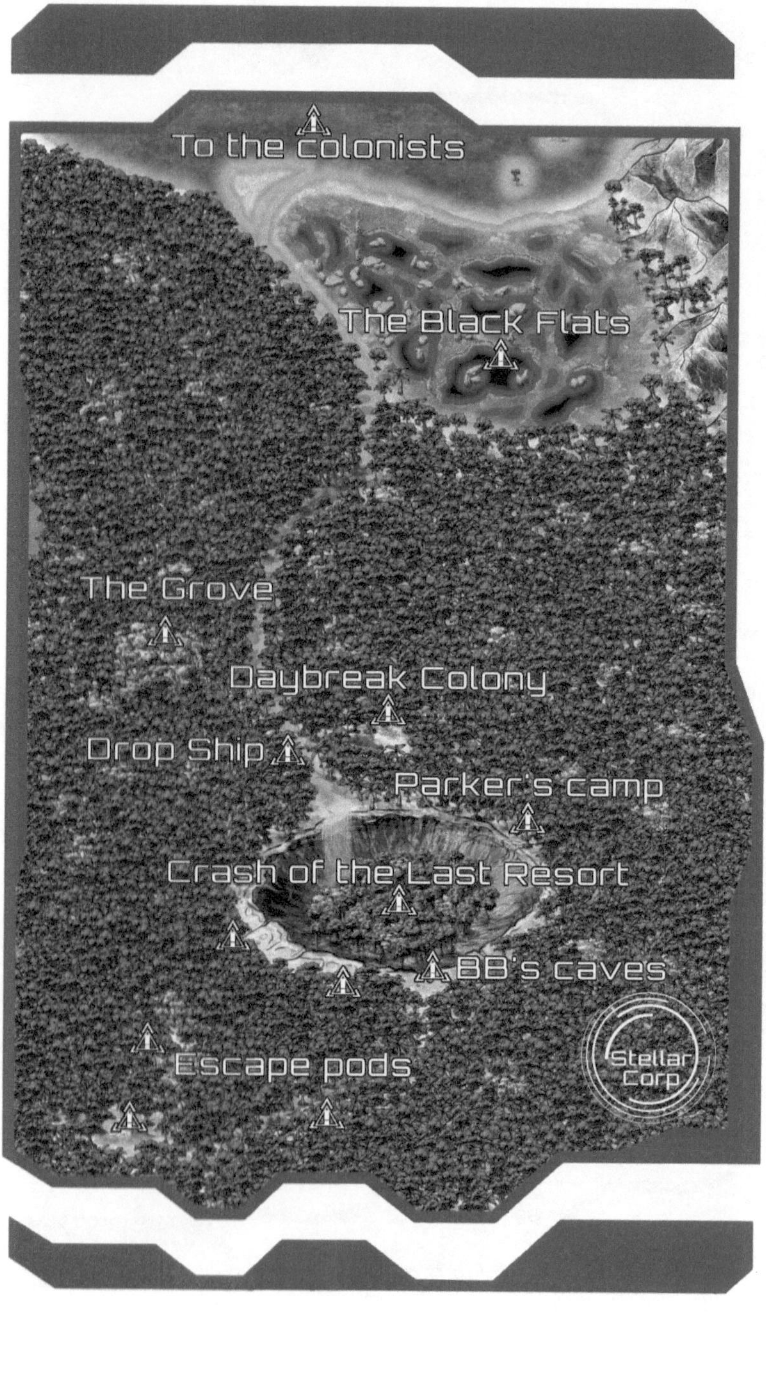

To the colonists
The Black Flats
The Grove
Daybreak Colony
Drop Ship
Parker's camp
Crash of the Last Resort
BB's caves
Escape pods
Stellar Corp

CHAPTER 1

Daybreak: Day 188

You would think there would be a finite number of ways you could be eaten on a single planet. But you'd be wrong.

I parted the deep blue-green leaves to peer at the massive snout lying just beyond my hiding place.

Scales as black as a tar pit glinted as the creature's flank rose and fell with gusty breaths. Its eyes were closed, but that didn't change the fact that Nappy McNapperson was taking a snooze in exactly the wrong spot.

I sighed and loosened my weapon in its sheath.

"You are not going after that thing." A bright blue hologram sprang up from the mini projector on my metal wrist. A young woman in a ship's uniform stood on thin air, hands on hips. "Tell me you're not thinking of it, Anikka."

"Keep your voice down. You're going to wake it up."

"You don't even know what 'it' is, yet."

I pressed my back against a nearby tree with gray bark and roots tall enough to hide me from the enormous black…lizard thing. Then I held up my wrist to look BB in the eyes.

"It's a giant monitor lizard. I saw one near the river a week ago, remember?"

Her image flickered, and she hesitated. She shook her head and snapped, "Of course I remember. I also remember it charging a herd of silverpoints and swallowing one whole."

"Good thing I'm not a silverpoint, then." I grinned at her.

Her holographic mouth went thin and tight.

"BB," I said with a sigh. "I need that tridenium."

I twisted to see over the top of a root.

The dense branches of the jungle drew back here, as if someone had tried to cut a road through it long ago.

Not *that* long ago, actually. I knew just how quickly Daybreak reclaimed itself if there were no humans around to fight it.

The midday sun struck an unexpected spark from a humped form across the way, and I could just make out a dirty windshield and rear-view mirrors. Vines and moss had overgrown the flat bed of the truck, but white plastic peeked through the foliage. A barrel with a triangular symbol on the side.

It had taken me weeks to find the abandoned truck in the dense jungle, and now a giant monitor lizard lay between it and me.

Normally, I'd never consider taking on a threat this big. Daybreak was full of things trying to kill me. Deadly electrical storms, enormous alien animals. Even the plants.

"You've stayed alive so far because you are careful and you pay attention," BB said, echoing my thoughts. "You recognize threats and learn to deal with them. You decide what's worth it and what's not."

My mouth twisted in a self-deprecating smile as I glanced at her. "I've also stayed alive because I take risks. I need those barrels, BB."

I knew Daybreak's quirks. I'd survived them for six whole months. Which meant I could finally find the missing colonists and help *them* survive.

It was past time.

But miles of water lay between me and their last known coordinates, and it had already taken me this long to build something that might carry me across. The puzzle was nearly complete. As long as I could get this one last piece.

"I'm not leaving them, BB," I said quietly.

BB stared up into my face, her light reflecting in my eyes and making me blink.

"I know," she finally said. "After all this time, I should know you're not the kind of person who leaves someone behind."

I winced as a curl of pain squeezed my throat. But BB's voice had gone warm and soft. She didn't mean for the words to stab the way they did.

Her shoulders straightened before I could say anything.

"If you're going to do this, please be smart about it," she said.

I dredged up a smile for her and stood, keeping the tree between me and the lizard. "When am I ever not?"

"Don't make me answer that." BB's hologram flicked out of existence.

Okay, that was fair. I huffed a laugh under my breath as I crept around the edge of the overgrown road, placing my feet carefully in the underbrush.

My backup waited for me on the other side of the track, but I didn't want to ruin his advantage by springing the trap too early.

It was too bad I hadn't thought to bring any drunk-peach wood with me. The smoke would be enough to fell something even as big as the lizard. But it was half a day's hike back to the drop ship, and I wouldn't be able to carry enough in one trip to make it worth it.

Maybe if I was quiet and careful, I could make this work without any pyrotechnics.

I held my breath as I tiptoed around the creature's head—that alone was as long as I was tall. A narrow space remained between it and the truck.

I placed one boot up on the step to the cab and reached through the broken window. If the truck turned on, I might be able to drive myself out of here...

The ignition key clicked but the engine remained silent. Just like every other vehicle that had weathered one of Daybreak's storms.

I let out a sigh and hung my head.

From this angle, I finally noticed the ground under the truck was scuffed. Torn up, like massive claws had dug out a den underneath. Three balls of black scales stirred in the shadows underneath.

My mouth went dry as leaves crackled behind me.

"Aw, crap."

I dove to the side as a massive black tail whipped around. But it moved faster than I'd guessed it could and caught me in the gut, sweeping me across the clearing. Away from its babies.

I landed with an oof, the wind knocked out of my lungs.

"Never get between a mother and her young," BB said, popping up to watch as the monitor lizard scraped the ground, leaving furrows in the dirt as wide as my arm. "I think we should call it the black death."

I coughed and dragged in a lungful of air as I clambered to my feet. "Now is not a great time to name it!"

"On the contrary," BB said as I turned tail and raced for the nearest tree. "According to my research of your media, carrying on a normal conversation during a life-or-death situation is, in fact, quite funny."

I didn't slow when I reached the trunk. Instead, I planted my boot against the bark and launched myself toward the branches. The black death raced for me as I hauled myself up.

I swung my legs out of the way just in time, but the black death struck the base of the tree, making it shudder and rock. The vibrations made my good hand go numb, and I slipped. My knees and arms clenched the branch, and I hung there, dangling over the black death like a low-hanging fruit while my neck prickled.

I tightened my grip with my robotic arm and took a chance, letting go with the other long enough to bring my fingers to my lips, and I let out a piercing whistle.

A blur of blue and purple fur burst from the underbrush at the far side of the clearing and streaked across the open space with a long howl.

The black death had barely turned as Shade shot past, snapping at its legs.

"Ha. I knew training a slinkwolf would come in handy." It also helped that my first friend on Daybreak was super intelligent, endlessly curious, and loyal enough to attack something ten times bigger than him.

The lizard twisted to grab him, but Shade had already run behind to nip at the black death's tail.

I used the black death's distraction and dropped straight down onto its back, spinning to land on my hands and knees.

My good hand sought purchase against the slippery scales as I drew my weapon with the other. The sun raced down the edge of the blade. It was just a broken strut from a robotic arm that I'd sheared off the *Last Resort,* but over the last few months, I'd worked the metal into a keen edge with a sculpted hilt that fit my hand.

And that wasn't even the best part. With a brief thought and a gathering of energy that tingled against my palm, I sent a cascade of lightning down the blade to crackle in the warm air. Sparks dripped from the jagged tip. I'd filed it back into a point but left the notch where the megawing had sheared off a piece.

The black death hissed and snaked its head around, trying to snatch me off its back.

I slashed at its eyes, but it didn't seem to care.

Its thick neck had a lot more flexibility than I was prepared for, and it reared away from my blows. Its scaly lips drew back before it shot a stream of black liquid at me.

"Whoa!" I leaped back, lost my footing, and slid down the beast's slippery back.

The black liquid—venom?—streaked over me, and I rolled to keep clear of the spray.

I swung to my feet as the big black monster rushed towards me. Instead of diving to the side, I braced my feet and aimed for its heart.

The thing rammed itself straight into me, my blade sinking into its chest. It carried me back to slam into the tree.

I cried out as something crunched in my shoulder, but I didn't let go.

Now, with the blade deep in its chest, I had a chance.

I drew up the energy that sang along my wires, making them glow beneath my skin, crisscrossing lines of light that highlighted the scars tracing my limbs.

And I thrust it all through my arm and down the blade. There was a reason I'd kept the hilt metal.

My prosthetic arm glowed with energy, but since I could control the flow of it, I didn't worry about blowing out its circuits.

The energy of Daybreak worked enough like electricity

that I could control it with my cybernetics. I shot it straight into the black death's chest, under the secondary nervous system that would have kept it safe from the electrical storm that swept the planet every few months.

It should have fried the monitor lizard. It had certainly taken care of the megawing all those months ago.

The black death screamed in pain, and three balls of black scales erupted from the half-built depot behind it. All barreling straight for us.

The black death grunted and pulled itself free from my blade.

But it did not stagger away or collapse.

It lowered its head and snorted, then fixed beady eyes on me.

"I think you missed its heart," BB said.

It charged.

I sprinted back into the forest where the great beast couldn't maneuver as easily.

Except its young could.

The three smaller lizards, each about the size of a horse, came careening after me.

"Crap, crap, crap," I muttered under my breath, racing through the trees, trying to find a place to hide or a tree to climb.

"Anikka, the truck. There is a branch close enough to reach."

I glanced to the right, and through the trunks, I spotted the overgrown vehicle. Sure enough, if I could get on top of the cab, a spray of blue-green leaves hung far enough down, I might be able to reach it.

I whistled for Shade and raced for the truck.

My boots slipped against the moss as I scrambled up the

fender and the hood, but I flung myself onto the metal roof. Shade followed, much more graceful.

"Here, buddy. Quick."

I bundled Shade through the open window of the cab and pointed to the footwell where he could just fit.

"Stay," I told him. "Hide."

He took direction incredibly well, and we'd had months to work on the more complicated concepts.

Shade hunkered down in the cab as I straightened and jumped for the branch waving above me. A spray of leaves broke off in my hand as the black death babies started scrabbling at the mossy hood.

I sheathed my blade and grabbed with both hands this time. The thin, whippy branch bent under my weight, but I pulled myself up, like climbing a rope. The sleeve of my prosthetic strained against my elbow and shoulder, but it stayed on the way it was designed to and let me climb up into the cover of the leaves.

I clung there as the mama black death stalked across the clearing, blood leaking down her chest, shiny in the sunlight. Her breath came out harsh as her babies tumbled into the space and circled her.

She looked a little worse for wear, but still fully capable of charging the tree.

"Okay, now what?" I said.

BB's voice came from my wrist. "You could kill it."

"How? Also, I don't really want to if I don't have to."

"Oh, here we go again," BB muttered.

"What's that supposed to mean?"

"The last time you said something like that, you brought home a slinkwolf."

"Hey that turned out to be a great idea. And now that I'm thinking of it, a giant monitor lizard might come in handy."

"Don't," BB said. "Don't even think about it. My programming supports one animal companion for you to snuggle in order to increase your serotonin. Monsters don't count."

I looked down at the black death, who was swaying on her feet. "She's not a monster. Just a mother."

"A mother standing between you and the tridenium," BB said sourly. "You'll never get it out of here as long as she and her babies are here."

I slipped down the vine-like branch and readjusted my grip.

"Okay. I have one idea." And if it didn't work, I'd have to retreat and try again some other time.

I really didn't want to have to come back.

The colonists had already been gone for months. I didn't even know if they were still alive, but if they were, then every moment counted on a planet like Daybreak.

I let go of the vine with one hand and plunged the other into my pack, keeping my eye on the black death below.

From under the flap, I withdrew a handful of brilliant red feathers, each as long as my forearm. They glittered in the filtered sunlight.

I scattered the feathers, letting them fall out of the canopy as naturally as I could make it look.

The black death raised its head, beady eyes locked on the flickers of red falling around her. Her nostrils flared, and she drew back a step.

But she didn't retreat. Not yet.

BB emitted a shriek from her speakers, an exact replica of a megawing cry.

The black death's tongue snaked out, and with a sudden rumble and a clicking noise, she gathered up her babies and darted into the forest.

My shoulders sagged, and I slid down to the roof of the truck with a little clang.

"I guess megawings hunt black deaths as well. Lucky me. You can come out now, Shade."

Shade wriggled out the window and climbed up to snuggle under my arm, tail wagging hard enough to knock us over.

"Good stay, Shade," I said. "Who's a big, bad slinkwolf? Is it you?"

"He has proven to be an excellent distraction for large predators," BB admitted.

"As well as being a good source of serotonin?"

"Exactly. Now can we please get what we came for? I don't want that thing sneaking up on us before we get home."

I lowered myself over the edge of the roof to the flat bed of the truck, then turned to give Shade the signal to jump into my arms.

The slinkwolf hit me in the chest, and I staggered back a step, but after all the exploring we'd done over Daybreak's varying terrain, we were both used to it.

The servos in my prosthetic whirred a little in protest, but no more than my actual muscles. I set him down and winced while I rolled the shoulder the black death had crunched.

"I recommend ice and a dose of painkillers for that strain," BB said.

"You have an answer for everything, BB."

"Of course. I know what's best for you."

I froze. In BB's voice, they were just words. But in my head, another voice and another face supplanted hers. Similar but without the human inflection.

I shuddered as BB stood there blinking as if nothing had changed.

Because that was the problem, wasn't it? I remembered every last second on the *Last Resort*.

And she didn't.

I shook my head and tried to dislodge the memory, so I could go on, too. Pretending for her sake.

"I'll take care of it when we get home." I stepped up to the mounds of vine-covered plastic and yanked away the foliage, revealing big plastic drums.

"Are they intact?" BB asked quietly.

I nodded. "Looks like." Liquid still sloshed inside, and with the black death gone, I could pull the drum over onto its side and roll it back home.

"Good. Hurry, please. The black death might decide to chance a meeting with a megawing."

"Easy for you to say," I grumbled. "You're not the one rolling this the whole way."

CHAPTER 2

Daybreak: Day 188

I'd thought rolling a barrel back over the ground that the colonists had once used as a road wouldn't be so bad. But over six months of growth had turned the track into an obstacle course full of tree roots, saplings, and bushes. Not to mention a host of wildlife to avoid.

Every time I stopped the drum from rolling into a pool of jungle quicksand, I'd go around only to find an ominous buzz building in the air. I knew well enough to leave the swarmstings alone, and I'd have to backtrack to find a safer route.

A couple of hours from home, the air grew hazy with an almost pink hue due to the dust hanging between the trees.

I stopped immediately and pulled the oxygen mask from my pack, fitting the whole thing over my face so the valves would filter the air around me and protect my eyes.

Shade kept trotting, oblivious to the clouds of toxin. A perk to growing up on Daybreak, of course.

Two weeks ago, this season had the honor of being the

newest thing to try to kill me. Spring in the jungles of Daybreak apparently meant itchbushes in full bloom. The bright pink bushes sprouted gaudy flowers, which released clouds of their signature toxin into the air.

It didn't get bad until about midmorning when the blooms had enough sun to open fully, but that just meant I'd been caught away from home when the pollen had tried to strangle me, irritating my lungs and eyes until I couldn't see or breathe.

A simple bandana worked in a pinch, keeping the pollen out of the nose and mouth, but it did nothing to protect the eyes. Luckily, I'd still had the oxygen masks from the *Last Resort*.

I made sure the mask was sealed around my face and that my jumpsuit was zipped as high as it would go, then I bent to keep rolling my drum.

On my way, I passed a giant meadow dotted with white flowers where a herd of silverpoints grazed. They raised their heads as I passed, ears forward, watching to see if I would come any closer. It wasn't a hunting day, so they were safe for now.

The truck was only a few hours north of the grove where I foraged regularly, but it took nearly twice that to get back to the drop ship I considered home. I'd found the truck by combing the colony logs for mentions of tridenium and then tracking down the direction they'd tried to ship it. It had been headed for a remote depot the colony had only just built, but clearly had never gotten there. Either because something had killed the drivers or because they'd gotten the evacuation code and hurried home.

I reached the drop ship just after night fall and stopped at the edge of the jungle to wipe the sweat out from under the edge of my mask.

Here the river flowed beside the home I'd been building for the last six months. One of the *Last Resort*'s drop ships lay on its side, gleaming in the light of Daybreak's moon. Its wing stretched to a nearby tree where I could just make out the multi-story structure built across both the ship and the adjacent branches.

My kitchen and a small seating area occupied the lowest platform, and a crude staircase led up to the next level, where Shade and I slept. The supplies I didn't want to store in the drop ship lived on the third level while waist high walls kept everything separate.

Planters lined the entire roof of the drop ship, and I had several thriving tomatoes and sweet potatoes along with one diseased-looking radish.

I longed for a bath in the cistern where water gathered, cut off from the river by a sluice gate. But it wasn't a great idea to get naked and vulnerable at night, so it would have to wait.

As I approached, a disgruntled dino-chicken shrieked at me from the run I'd built under the kitchen level. It had its very own bridge stretching between two trunks, lined with a sturdy vine fence it couldn't chew through. The suspended run kept it safe from ground predators like more slinkwolves, but did the creature seem grateful? No. Instead, it tried to poop on me every time I passed underneath.

At least it had left me a couple of eggs, so I'd have breakfast in the morning.

I let out a contented sigh and pulled my mask off now that the sun was down and the itchbush pollen was receding. The river sparkled with slasherfins as they came to the surface to see if I would get close enough to eat this time.

It was too late to work on the tridenium now, so I stashed the barrel beside the drop ship and slipped inside the rough-cut doorway. I'd turned the interior of the ship into more storage and a meat locker. A side of silverpoint hung at one end, and I cut a piece off to carry upstairs.

I touched the hologram pad beside the stove, and BB flickered and disappeared from my wrist, reappearing on the pad. I'd ripped it out of the admin building back at the colony and installed it here. A mess of optical wiring still spilled out the back of the makeshift pedestal, but at least it worked. That was what counted here on Daybreak.

A dusty carton of juice sat in a niche of the tree trunk, barely illuminated by the light of the hologram pad.

"Can I play some music for you, Anikka?" BB asked from her perch.

I swallowed and turned to hide my expression. "Um, no thanks."

"You used to say you couldn't think in silence," she said quietly.

I forced a laugh. "Well, I'm not working tonight. I can't see, and I can't afford to screw this up."

My shoulders remained clenched, waiting for her to push further, to ask what was wrong.

"All right, Anikka," she said.

I blew out my breath and lit my stove before storing my backpack and crossbow on their pegs.

The original bow had been snapped in half by a deathkitty while we'd tried to get back into the *Last Resort*, but there had been plenty more in the colony. The blade I laid on the floor beside my cot. It always paid to be careful on Daybreak, and I slept better with my hand on the hilt.

I made myself a nice steak and tossed half to Shade before I settled back to watch Daybreak's aurora.

We'd had another storm just a couple of days before, so

the colors were fairly muted tonight. Just the blues and greens with a little bit of pink showing through.

I had a little time. Just under two months to find the colonists and figure out what had happened to them. Hopefully, that would be enough.

Daybreak: Day 189

In the morning, I headed down to survey the barrel of tridenium and the vehicle I'd been building on the bank of the river.

Today, I would finish.

Daybreak colony had been founded earlier this year, just a couple of months before the *Last Resort* had entered orbit and a planet-wide electrical storm had swept the continent, killing everything that wasn't local, from tech to livestock to humans. It had even reached far enough to send the *Last Resort* plummeting to the planet's surface.

Given just enough warning to issue an evacuation, the colonists already here had fled to some caves that Dr. Carver, the colony's astrophysicist, had deemed the safest place to wait out the storm. We'd spent weeks wondering why they hadn't used the caves on the other side of the crater. They were closer and easier to get to. But, of course, without Dr. Carver to answer, the question was pointless.

I had no idea if they'd ever made it. None had come back. And I hadn't managed to repair the communication systems in the colony, since most of them were copper-based and had been blasted in the storm.

Some colonists could have survived. But if they hadn't

returned by now, then they had to be stranded, cut off, or waiting for help from a ship that had already crashed.

That meant I had to get across the lake.

I'd originally planned to build a boat. What else would carry me across the water? Except I had no idea how to sail. Or motor. Whatever you called it. And after spending a couple of days on the lake shore and seeing the kind of waves it could generate, I wasn't setting foot in something that could flip over in the middle of the crossing.

So BB and I had brainstormed something far better.

I was an infra-engineer, anyway, not a sailor.

A motor bike sat propped against the side of the drop ship with a hologram pad wired to the handlebars. And with a little modification, it should carry me above the waves instead of across them.

Metal tubing ran along the frame, giving it a punk metal pipe organ vibe.

I'd found it tucked behind the vehicle bay in the colony. The wiring was much less complicated than the gutted glider, which meant I could take it apart and put it back together with optical tech, so it actually ran.

Shade returned from his night hunting as I rolled the barrel of tridenium out onto the bank and stood my bike up next to it. He dropped the dead jumpernick beside me and went up to lie in the sun between the tomato plants.

"Thanks, buddy. There's leftover steak for breakfast if you want it."

He huffed but closed his eyes, so I assumed he'd eaten something while hunting.

I worked the barrel up onto a little hill I'd made with some packed dirt the day before, just enough to put it above my bike.

I'd managed to obtain the tridenium, now to put it to use.

When I'd actually found the records in the colony logs, I couldn't believe my luck. Tridenium was one of the few superconductors in the universe that worked at room temperature. Or jungle temperature, as the case may be.

And Daybreak Colony had scored a couple of barrels for research.

The barrel had a cap plugged into the bottom, and I happened to have several lengths of rubber tubing. I just had to stick the tubing in the hole, turn the cap, and ta-da, my new superconductor flowed into the tubing on my bike.

I still wore a pair of rubber gloves 'cause no one wanted to wash their hands in tridenium.

It didn't take much to fill the tubes of my bike. When the liquid rose to the right level, I quickly turned the cap and pulled the rubber tubing out

I'd just need a little spot weld to close up the bike's system, and it would be done.

Luckily, I'd had lots of practice, and my welds looked much neater than they had four months ago.

"Will it hold?" BB asked, popping up to examine the weld.

"Only one way to find out." I surged to my feet and pushed the barrel back into place beside the drop ship.

Finally, I stood back and surveyed the bike.

"Well?" BB said. "Are you going to see if it even works?"

I blew out my breath and straddled the seat.

I touched the hologram pad, and BB disappeared from my wrist and reappeared in between the handlebars.

It had taken some deft work with the soldering iron to get the gutted pads to work with a solar input rather than the colony's electrical grid, but I'd finally had time to sit and read the manuals I'd found in the workshop and brush up on my optical tech skills.

"Now what?" BB asked.

"Now...we give it some power."

I took a deep breath and gripped the handlebars lined with two tubes now full of tridenium that twisted down to connect to the main system running up and down the frame of the bike.

Reaching inside to guide the electricity out of my wires felt a lot more natural now. Lightning crackled along my limbs, and I drove it through my hands and into the liquid in my bike.

And the electrical current hummed through the frame.

"Yes," I whispered.

This is why I'd chosen a superconductor. I could feed it energy and it took it and turned it into its own mini electro-magnetic field. And it would do it forever unless I pulled the energy out of it.

I nudged it, keeping everything flowing in exactly the right direction.

Opposite the energy in Daybreak's atmosphere.

And since electricity and magnetism were just two sides of the same coin...

My lips curled in a smile as the bike tilted under me. I experimented and pushed off with my feet. The bike slid across the ground, hovering just a couple of inches over the dirt.

I let out a breathless laugh. It worked!

The bike hovered, and I sent another pulse of energy through the tubes, sending it gliding across the ground.

"Please be careful," BB said. "You do not have a helmet."

I laughed again. "I'll just fly over to the colony and find one."

"Ha ha," BB said. Then her hologram jumped as I shot the bike forward. "Oh, you weren't joking. Watch out for the river!"

I ignored the fallen tree that I'd painstakingly turned into a reliable bridge and drove the bike straight over the water.

The energy in the bike was attracted to the energy in the atmosphere, like a magnet ignoring gravity to float. Which meant it soared over the river without a bump.

Slasherfins leaped from the surface, snapping at me as I passed. I laughed and leaned over the handlebars, directing the bike toward the overgrown path that led to the colony.

The bike wanted to zip along. Faster and faster, I zoomed through the trees, letting it glide without friction. A little pressure here and there in the right spots made the bike soar up or down, or side to side.

The wind blew my hair out of my face, and I tilted my head back.

"Watch where you're going!" BB said. "Can you even turn this thing?"

"I don't need to turn," I shouted over the whistle of wind. "It's a straight shot."

"Wonderful. A reckless driver and an unproven vehicle. I'm sure that's not a recipe for disaster."

"Your sarcasm filter is all the way up again."

"Do you know how to stop?"

"Not really, but I'll figure it out."

"Better figure it out soon or that wall will figure it out for you."

I sucked in a breath as the wall of the colony's nearest warehouse loomed out of the trees ahead of us. The trip normally took an hour. Today it had taken five minutes.

I tried to reverse the energy flow, to slow the bike, but that just removed the attraction with the atmosphere, making it plummet.

We plowed into the dirt track, the wheels taking the brunt of the crash. I threw my weight sideways and pulled all the energy out of the bike through the handlebars. It stung my hands—I'd never gotten used to how the electricity stung, no matter the fact that I had wires under my skin.

The bike finally came to a stop, and I lay there panting for a long moment, staring up at the sky.

The colony sat silent.

I surged to my feet with a whoop. "It worked!"

The bike itself appeared undamaged. And as long as the tubing remained intact, it didn't matter if the frame got a little bent.

I danced around the fallen bike as BB reappeared on the hologram pad.

"I do not love your method of stopping, but I suppose you did make it work."

"Hey, crashing is sort of our thing now. It's how we met."

"I guess that's true." BB smiled up at me.

The same smile I'd seen as she said, "lie down on the table, please."

My breath hitched, and the smile fell from my face.

I cleared my throat and backed away, turning to the colony for a second to wipe the expression from my face.

"What's wrong?" BB said.

"Nothing."

"Are you hurt?"

"No, I'm fine." I turned back with a bright, fake smile. "Let's find a helmet, then we can fly this thing back to camp."

BB stared for a moment longer than was comfortable, as if debating whether she wanted to push it.

Please, don't, I thought. *Don't dig for answers you don't want to know, BB.*

"Alright," BB said, but the joy had gone from her voice. "A helmet and then a journey."

To-do

- Get across the lake
- Find the colonists
- Survive the next storm

CHAPTER 3

Daybreak: Day 190

Even with a helmet, BB made me promise to stick to more manageable speeds when we finally set out. I grumbled, but it wasn't like we could race through the jungle with all the underbrush and trees in the way. And Shade trotted along with us, so I kept to his pace. He'd get to ride later, but since we were going a little slower today, he could walk.

The hover bike carried us past the colony, lying silent and empty, past the Black Flats where the tar steamed in the afternoon light, all the way to the lake shore.

Shortly after I'd survived my first storm on the planet, I'd come back here to build a monument to the dead colonists. My shelter stood beside it, cobbled together from pieces of the defunct glider they'd left here.

It reflected the lights of the aurora as I floated to a stop and pulled my helmet off. The trip took two full days on foot. Today it had taken me one, even at the slower pace BB demanded.

Considering the first time I'd traveled across the flats

Shade had lost his entire pack and we'd nearly been eaten by trooper beetles, gliding above the ground, out of reach of its hazards was a welcome change.

I pulled the energy from the bike, dispersing it back into the atmosphere as streaks of lightning. The wheels thumped down against the sand. Last night I'd learned that if I didn't power the bike down it had a tendency to float away without me, still magnetized to the planet's atmosphere.

I propped it up against the side of the hut as BB flickered off the bike's hologram pad and reappeared on my wrist.

"Thank you for taking my speed restrictions under advisement," she said as Shade sniffed around the sandy shore, leaving broad footprints behind him. "I felt much safer on the way here."

"You know, you wouldn't actually die in a crash, right?"

"No, but *you* would. And then I would pine away." She stared across the lake with a slight smile. "Or rust. Whichever came first."

I snorted. "Shade, leave that," I said as Shade sniffed too close to the stone memorial for Dr. Grotman and her group of colonists.

It had taken weeks to haul the material across the Black Flats, but I couldn't leave the spot unmarked.

And now I had a base from which I could begin the next part of my journey.

I pulled several large pieces from the stack of driftwood beside the hut and built a fire. The three straight-ish branches I'd lashed to the hover bike's frame made a tripod where I could hang my makeshift pot and cook my dinner.

"Shade, you want fish or eggs tonight?" I called.

The slinkwolf ignored me, trotting over to examine a spot on the beach that looked just like every other spot to me. He dug, plumes of sand flying out behind him.

"Shade!" I threw up my hand to protect my face and grabbed my pot so I wouldn't be picking sand out of my teeth all night.

Shade dove into the hole he'd made and came back up with a shape in his mouth.

He bounded over to me and dropped it in my lap.

At first glance, it looked like a rock with a rough, black surface. And then I noticed the seam down the middle.

"Oh, clever boy." I pulled my knife from its sheath along my thigh and pried the bivalve open.

"What is it?" BB peered at my work.

"It's a clam. Or the Daybreak equivalent." I tilted the shell to show her the meat inside.

I dumped it in my pot and followed Shade, looking for the tiny dimples in the sand that indicated bubbles below the surface.

In the end, we had enough alien clams to make a filling—if chewy—soup. It meant I could save more of the preserved fish and fruit I'd brought in my packs, in case the journey took longer than I anticipated. At least I didn't have to worry about fueling the bike. As long as none of the tridenium leaked out, I'd always have a way to power it.

The shelter wasn't quite tall enough to stand up in, so I crawled into my sleeping bag as Shade curled up at my feet with a satisfied burp.

I twisted so I could stare out across the wide lake.

Somewhere over there were the rest of the colonists. Alive hopefully, but even if they weren't, they had to have left a trace. Something that would tell me what had happened to them.

I closed my eyes and fell asleep to the sound of waves washing along the shore.

· · ·

Daybreak: Day 191

In the morning, I packed the bike carefully. Over the back wheel, I'd welded a hinged platform that could fold down on one side, kind of like a side car.

I gave Shade the signal to hop up, and he did, claws digging into the canvas padding. He lay still with his ears back as I tightened the straps over him. He hated his seatbelt, but I wasn't about to let him fall off while we were flying over the lake.

The backpack I strapped to the other side to help balance everything, and BB transferred to the hologram pad while I powered up the frame.

We floated down the beach, away from the hut and the memorial. Nice and easy. I didn't immediately set out across the water.

We'd studied BB's navigation data and did the math. Ten hours across if I headed straight to the other side, and I didn't push the hover bike to its limits. Since this was my first time riding it across so much water, I didn't want to realize too late that it was too far or max speeds weren't a great idea.

So we'd found an alternative. Up the beach, towards the mountains, a chain of islands swept out into the lake, leaving a trail I could follow almost halfway across the water. It would take longer, and I'd need to stop for the night, but it would also be safer.

Mist hung in the air, stained orange and pink from the muted aurora. In the distance, I could just make out the gray hump of an island rising out of the waves. The water rushed up the beach toward my bike and foamed underneath me.

I drove the hover bike faster and higher to clear the rising surf and angled us out over the water. The wind picked up as soon as we ventured away from shore, whipping my hair back and making the waves thrash higher and higher.

I angled toward the distant island, getting further from the beach but not quite out of sight of it. At least not yet.

The first island was barely more than a sandbar a hundred feet offshore. I didn't even stop for a breather.

The energy circling the hover bike came from the atmosphere. Not generated from inside myself. And once I'd primed the superconductor, it carried a charge until I stopped it. I just had to adjust it with little nudges, sending the bike higher or lower with the swell of the waves.

Water lapped the sandbar, sending a fine spray over us, making me shiver.

I'd lived in endless summer for so long, that I hadn't anticipated how cold the wind and the spray would be. Who would have thought I'd miss the humidity?

I hunched over the handlebars, bracing myself against the wind.

The next island was even further out with the shore barely visible through the mist and the spray. It took another hour to get to. Dense trees covered the spit of land, but it was only about the size of a football field from one end to the other.

I stopped to scarf some fruit and let Shade down off his perch. The moment the straps were free, he leaped to the shore and spun in a circle, his fluffy tail waving like a banner.

"Careful," I told him. "I'm not sure what's out here." Daybreak seemed designed to challenge us. Who knew what kind of predator or parasite might live on these islands?

I rubbed my hands together to pull some warmth back into them. The wet and the wind had made my left go numb.

"I wish I had some gloves," I said, sticking them under my armpits. My sleeves and pant legs were wet through, and the rest of my jumpsuit was damp. Luckily, nothing in my pack was terribly bothered by getting wet.

I munched on my fruit and surveyed the island. The trees grew fairly close together, and it reminded me of home, though I didn't see any megawings or itchbushes. Too bad we couldn't stay the night here. But we needed to make it much further down the islands so we had a straight shot across the rest of the lake tomorrow.

"Here, buddy," I called to Shade, who chased a bird off the beach. "It's time to get moving."

It took some bribery to get him back on the bike, but we finally set off toward the next island that we could just see off in the distance.

The bike bounded along over the waves. I guided it high above the swells. Too low and the waves would crash into us and wash us off. Too high and BB started complaining about being scared of heights. Keeping the bike balanced at the perfect height took all my concentration.

BB stood on the hologram pad in front of me, staring resolutely into the distance as if keeping watch. Not that there was anything to watch out for here. All we could see for miles was the island rising in the distance, getting closer and closer.

This one had fewer trees and more rocks. Boulders dotted the otherwise sandy beach.

"I'm gonna keep going," I shouted to BB over the wind. "How are you doing?"

"I'm not the one with flesh and blood that gets fatigued."

I rolled my eyes. "Right. Shade? How are you, buddy?"

I cast a glance over my shoulder at Shade, who snapped at the spray that splashed his face.

"I'm gonna assume you're good. We're gonna press on. BB, where's the next island? I can't see it."

Clouds grew dense above us and the mist got worse,

turning into actual fog. The last few hundred feet of the island disappeared, hidden in an opaque curtain.

BB's hologram stretched and flickered until I stared at the satellite image of the colony and the surrounding area. Little glowing dots marked the places we'd explored already like the drop ship and the truck, the escape pods and the Black Flats.

Beyond those, stretched the lake, bigger even than the crater where the *Last Resort* still rested. On the map it appeared as a giant swathe of black, cutting me off from the rest of the continent with steep mountains to the east and a week-long journey to the west.

BB zoomed in on the part of the beach where we'd left shore and highlighted the string of islands that paralleled the land for a little bit before arching out into the lake.

"We are here," BB said, flashing a dot at our location. "The last island in the chain is forty miles in that direction."

So I definitely wouldn't be able to see it yet, and it would take us a while to reach, even at this speed.

I hunched over the handlebars, my back and butt aching, and shook my wet hair back to get it to stop sticking to my face.

I pushed the bike a little faster over the water, leaning into the speed. My eyes narrowed, and I let them close a little bit. I could still feel where we were based on the energy around us.

"Anikka."

A wide range of emotions washed over me when BB said my name like that. The release of relief that she was still here, that I hadn't lost her forever. The clench in my stomach from another identical voice echoing in my head, sounding perfectly reasonable and concerned.

I pushed the bike faster.

"Anikka, you are going too fast."

"Do you want to get to the island or not? There's nothing to crash into here, BB. We're fine."

"It is not crashing I am worried about. The amount of energy you are putting into the craft—"

"It's constant once I get it going. I don't have to regenerate it, so it's fine."

"Using your cybernetics to control the flow of Daybreak's energy requires a certain amount of concentration. It is a mentally and physically draining task. You are tiring yourself too quickly."

"How can you even tell that?"

"I am still both a wake-up companion and an infirmary AI. I can monitor your physical condition."

My mouth went dry, and I convulsively tried to swallow. I...I'd known that. Of course, she would still be monitoring things like my heart rate and blood pressure. But I'd been so good at not thinking about it.

"I'm fine."

"Your vitals in this moment indicate—"

"BB drop it." If she looked too close at those, she would see other things. She knew me better than anyone. She'd read the things I kept hidden in the shape of my reactions.

"I do not want you to fall due to fatigue."

"You don't get to—"

Something huge and dark rose out of the fog, and a wall of water raced toward us.

I gasped and yanked back on the energy in the bike, sending it careening up and sideways. The tidal wave clipped the bottom of the bike, making us spin in the air.

Shade yelped as the cold water crashed against us.

I struggled to keep us aloft. The surprise had made me jump, and my instinct was to drop the cybernetic control and hang on for dear life.

Which would only cause the bike to plummet.

We hung there as the enormous swell fell back, smoothing against the surface of the lake. Curls of mist peeled away for just a second, and the darkness of the water coalesced and grew edges until I realized I was seeing a massive shadowy shape sinking back into the depths of the lake.

My heart pounded in my chest.

"Vent it, what was that?" I whispered.

"Another creature of Daybreak," BB said, voice as hushed as mine.

Shade whimpered behind me.

"It...it was as big as a house. No, an apartment complex."

"A city block," BB said.

I cleared my throat, trying to unclench my knuckles from my handlebars. "Let's get to the island."

I poured energy into the bike until it raced along far above the surface of the water. Much higher than BB was comfortable with, but she closed her eyes and didn't complain. None of us wanted to get any closer to whatever lived in the lake.

Colonists' Coordinates
The Lake
Colonist Memorial
Truck
Daybreak Colony
Drop Ship
Crash of the Last Resort
Escape pods
Stellac Corp

CHAPTER 4

Daybreak: Day 191

The rest of the day we went fast enough that every little droplet of mist needled my face, and I wished I had goggles as well as gloves.

But we reached the island before dark and didn't see whatever had made that massive shadow underwater again.

I lowered the bike to soar over the beach just inches from the ground and pulled into a cove, sheltered from the full force of the lake.

My hands shook as I parked the bike and stretched my stiff legs. I tried to tell myself it was just from the cold, but my limbs dragged and every time I blinked, my eyes didn't want to open again.

I hated to admit it, but BB was right. All those little adjustments to speed, height, and direction took energy and concentration. Like working a precise machine.

I kept my teeth clenched and didn't say anything. BB could look inside me and see the way my vital signs fluctuated. She could monitor every little muscle twitch and heartbeat. I wasn't going to draw attention to it if she wasn't already looking.

At least now we were safe from whatever lurked in the lake. Whatever it was, it was too big to call this island home.

I unstrapped Shade, and the slinkwolf hopped down to the beach and shook, sending out a spray of water. Between the two of us, we had to have picked up nearly half the lake.

"Sorry, buddy," I said, drying my prosthetic on the one patch of dry jumpsuit I had left. "I wish I had a towel." I'd brought one blanket, but it was a lot colder here than in the jungle, so I figured we would want it when night fell.

Shade didn't seem to mind. He finished shaking with a flap of his ears and took off down the beach, sniffing. Maybe looking for more clams.

I raised my gaze to survey the shore. Rocky cliffs rose a couple of hundred feet away from where the water lapped, and trees grew up there, their gnarled branches hanging over the edges. Not jungle trees. These were shorter and starker than the ones by the drop ship, growing in odd windswept shapes with smaller leaves.

I would climb up the cliffs to get even further from the edge of the water, but there was no way I was getting up there with my arms trembling and my legs barely holding me up.

Strange hills of sand rose on the beach, creating big pools where the water was trapped. Like tide pools, except lakes didn't have tides.

Still, there was plenty of dry sand by the base of the cliffs.

I unhooked my pack from the bike and pulled out a bundle of light canvas. The pop-up tent had been shoved in the back of the colony's store room. Either forgotten or abandoned because they'd been beyond needing such temporary housing. But it was perfect for me.

I pulled the tab and the whole thing ballooned out, snapping into a long low oval, just tall enough for me to crawl in with my blanket and sleeping bag.

"Anikka, you should eat something," BB said. "And make sure the area is safe."

I felt like arguing but there was nothing left in me to argue, so I pulled my pack inside with me and dug a hand in to pull out some dried fruit. I fell asleep with it halfway to my mouth.

"Anikka." The voice intruded on my dream. Shapes walked around me. People with no faces, colonists that were barely more than shadows and figures made of mist. I stood amidst them, trying to speak, only to find my words didn't have any effect. No one looked at me. No one turned or raised a hand. I walked through the crowd completely alone and ignored until I screamed just to see if anyone would notice me.

"Anikka. Wake up."

I opened bleary eyes in the dark. "What? It's not morning yet."

"There's something out there."

The words brought me instantly awake, and I finally registered the shapes moving against the canvas of my tent. Shadows cast by something scuttling across the sand. Shuffling and clicking sounds sent a thrill down my spine.

"Shade," I whispered.

The slinkwolf huffed and crept up from my side to lick my hand.

"He crawled in a couple of hours ago," BB said. Her voice came from my wrist, but she left her projection off.

"What are they?"

"I have no context to answer that question," BB said.

There was another scuttle and something pressed against

the canvas of my tent, bulbous on one end and pointy on the other.

I kicked free of my blanket and sleeping bag, my jumpsuit stiff after all the lake water had dried.

A violent clicking sound made the hair on the back of my neck stand up, and the bulbous shape pushed against the canvas again, the pointy bit piercing the fabric.

I kicked at it in a panic, and my boot struck something hard.

Shapes pressed in from all sides, and there was the sound of tearing canvas. A claw ripped through the side of my tent, and I screamed.

I thrashed as hard bodies crowded in, and I grabbed for my pack and my blade, fighting free of the collapsing tent.

Shade wriggled out with me, and I stumbled to my feet on the beach. I spun, blade outstretched.

Shadows about two feet across swarmed the ruined tent, pulling at its folds with two pronged claws. The mist had finally cleared and moonlight fell across the creatures, illuminating dark carapaces and too many legs.

I gasped and dozens of eyes on long stalks turned to blink at me.

Crabs. Huge crabs with too many legs and arms that ended in pincer-like claws.

They rushed for me.

I scrambled back and called up a bolt of lightning to streak through my sword. The energized blade lit up the night, and the crabs parted around me with angry clicks.

I took advantage and raced for the cliffs, climbing up boulders, out of reach of the crabs.

Half a dozen followed me while the rest dug through my tent.

They ranged around the base of my boulder, their jointed legs slipping against the rocks.

"What are they after?" I asked.

"Besides you?" BB sprang up, her hologram casting light on the beach and sending long shadows streaking away from the crabs. "Do crabs even eat mammals?"

Shade panted beside me. He gazed down at the clicking creatures with his tongue lolling out.

I scanned the beach and found the entire cove crawling with crabs. They clambered up and down the hills, pushing sand to build up the dams that trapped the water.

As I watched, a wave crashed into the shore with enough force to travel up and over the hills, creating a pool of lake water. Little fish flashed, trapped by the dams as the wave retreated.

The crabs swarmed the fish, tearing them apart with their pincers.

I waited for a fight to break out over the distribution of fish, but it never did. The crabs waited their turn, and each managed to grab a mouthful before the next wave came, carrying more fish.

I glanced down at my pack, which held a whole stack of dried and salted slasherfin fillets.

"They're after my fish," I said.

"Do not worry, Anikka," BB said. "I will scare them away."

"No, wait—"

BB blasted music from her speakers. The same awful combination of metal and electronica that had scared off the pack of slinkwolves so long ago.

The same that BEV had played on the ship to shake my concentration.

I threw my hands over my ears, the sound driving deep

into my chest, making my heart pound. My breath grew faster and faster until I heaved in great gulps of air, trying to calm my pulse with my own breathing. But I couldn't control any of it. There wasn't enough air and my chest constricted.

"BB!" I cried.

The music stopped abruptly.

My fingers clenched the sides of my head for a few moments more before I was able to lift my gaze.

BB stood, projected in front of me, holographic face stricken. "That's...that's worked in the past. I don't under-stand. What's wrong? Why did your heart rate increase so much?"

I shook my head, hoping that even as an infirmary AI, she wouldn't recognize the signs of a panic attack.

I couldn't tell her the image that raced through my head. The flashes of metal grating and smooth corridors rotating around me, spiraling in an effort to kill me as that sound blared in my ears.

I swallowed over and over until I could keep from choking on my words. "I just...don't do that...okay? Please."

"I'm sorry, Anikka," BB said, voice small. "I will not attempt it again."

I took a deep, bracing breath and stood up from where I'd fallen to my knees. "It didn't work, anyway."

The crabs still crowded the base of the boulder.

"We'll have to think of something else." They swarmed the beach, blocking my path to the hover bike.

"They are intelligent enough to build traps," BB said. "Per-haps they are intelligent enough to be bribed. It worked for slinkwolves."

"I could drop my fish or sacrifice my pack to distract them," I said. "But I don't know how much of the smell is on me. They destroyed my tent, looking for the source."

"Yes, but what else are you going to try?"

My shoulders slumped. "Nothing."

The beach was mostly sand with all the little hummocks the crabs had made, but boulders had fallen from the cliffs dotting the area. An arch of them curved around into the shallows of the cove, but if I leaped from one to the next, I could make my way closer to the other side of the beach and maybe I could dash to my bike.

And then what? Continue across the lake when I was still too tired to move? Or travel up into the forested part of the island where there might be worse things to stalk me?

I'd figure it out one way or another.

I dug around in my pack for a stack of dried fish. From the size of these things, my measly supply wouldn't keep them occupied for long.

Shade whined and licked his chops.

"Sorry, buddy. I'll get you some more, don't worry."

I waved the fish in the air, like that would distract them.

Their eye stalks followed the movement.

Then I chucked the fish over their heads to draw them away from my boulder.

The fish landed in the wet sand with half a dozen splats.

The crowd of crabs dove for the pieces.

I went the other way, leaping across to the next boulder with my pack slung on my back. Shade bounded along after me.

It was working! The crowd of crabs milled around the spot where my fish had landed, investigating to see if there was any more while I jumped from rock to rock.

My next leap took me out into the shallows of the cove. My boot slipped on a slick bit of algae, and I wobbled on the edge. I dug my fingers into the cracks on the rock and hauled myself up onto the top of the boulder.

"Hurry, Anikka. They are coming this way," BB said.

"Crap." I didn't bother looking. What was the point of having an AI if you didn't believe them when they watched your back?

Behind me, something splashed, a cascade of sound coming toward me.

The next jump was a lot farther than the others, but the boulder would keep me up and away from pinching claws. If I could just make it...

I took a step back on top of my boulder and launched myself at the next, arms outstretched.

My chest struck first, arms stretching up the sides which were too steep to scramble up. I clawed with my good hand and tried to wedge my metal fingers into the cracks like I had before.

My fingers slipped against slick algae, and I fell, splashing into the water of the cove.

I surfaced with a gasp. The water was only a couple of feet deep here, but I knew what was coming for me.

The moment I shook the water out of my ears, the clicking and splashing reached me, growing louder and more frantic.

I gripped my blade once more and turned to face the oncoming threat.

Crabs swarmed around the boulders, claws outstretched. They crowded between me and the shore, and there was no way I was swimming out into the lake to get away from them. I'd spent too much time battling slasherfins in my first month on Daybreak to be comfortable in any of its waters.

I swept the sword in an arc in front of me, hoping to clear a path to shore. The first line of crabs leaped back, eyes swiveling on their stalks. But dozens more came at me from the sides.

Shade snarled from the last boulder and leaped into the fray, teeth snapping.

I stabbed at the nearest crab, knowing it was futile. Even if I managed to pierce the thick carapace, I'd never be able to clear enough of them to get away.

Another crab rocked back on its jointed legs and launched itself at me. Its weight hit me full in the chest and all the air left my lungs with a whoosh. I went straight down.

"Anikka!"

I barely registered BB's voice as water rushed in my ears.

The crab's legs tangled in my jumpsuit, its weight pressing me down. I struggled but couldn't get out from under the rock-hard creature.

Bubbles escaped my mouth, disappearing into the churning water, driven white by our thrashing.

Gods of all worlds, I was going to drown.

Unbidden, memories rose, reminding me of the last time I'd been submerged. Metal shelving flashed around me. A door below.

Panic surged along my limbs, and the wiring under my skin glowed. Lightning shot out from me, tendrils crackling through the water.

It wouldn't do anything. Every animal that had evolved on Daybreak had a secondary nervous system that absorbed or dispersed the electrical energy that built up in the atmosphere so they could survive the periodic storms. The crabs were no exception.

But the force of it did blow the one on top of me off, and I surged to the surface with a gasp.

The crabs surrounding me seemed dazed, drifting back for a second as their eye stalks swiveled.

I gripped my blade, prepared to push through them to shore.

Behind me, the lake churned.

What the—? What now? What had I called when I'd sent that lightning out into the water? Something worse than the crabs?

I splashed for the nearest boulder, jumping up to grab its slick surface. This time I found a big enough crack and hauled myself out of the water.

"Anikka, look," BB said.

I paused, hanging from my hand holds, and craned my neck around.

Fish, schools and schools of fish swarmed through the shallows. Some slasherfins but also little streaky things that glowed blue and green. Shapes as long as my arm that looked like bass. So many different kinds of fish crowding the cove.

The crabs surged forward, pincers out.

They wasted no time harvesting everything they could see, gorging on the feast laid out for them. Even Shade darted through the shallows, catching what he could before retreating to the beach where he flopped down, sated.

I climbed to the top of my boulder and crouched with my arms around my knees as the crabs decimated the fish that had been called by the lightning.

"I guess fish are attracted by light and energy," BB said. "Just like the megawing."

I rubbed my wet hands over my face, slicking my hair back. "I guess. It's good to know I can use myself as bait now." My hands dropped, and I stared blearily at the shore. "How will we get back to the bike?"

BB glanced at me. "We'll figure it out when it's light. Sleep, Anikka. I will keep watch and make sure nothing can climb up here."

"Yeah," I murmured, words slurring. "Yeah, that sounds good."

I curled up on the top of the boulder, not even caring that I didn't have my sleeping bag. I pillowed my head on my pack and closed my eyes.

And the next thing I knew, the sun shone on my face, waking me up. I sat up, and the first thing I saw was Shade sitting on the beach, head cocked, as if staring at something interesting.

"BB?" I said, voice rough.

"You are fine." BB turned as if she'd kept her hologram on all night. "They haven't even tried to climb up here. They are just watching."

"Watching?" I peered over the side of the boulder.

Hundreds of crabs waited in the shallows, the sun glinting from their dark carapaces. A sea of eyes stared at me on the rock.

"They've just been like this the whole time?" I said.

"Since they finished gorging themselves, yes."

Their eye stalks followed me as I stood. The nearest ones backed away, leaving enough room that I could climb down if I wanted to.

Did I want to?

I experimented a bit, grabbing my pack and sliding far enough down the rock to dip a toe in the water.

The crabs backed away, making room for me.

"Okay," I said and splashed down into the water to walk to shore.

The crabs kept pace with me, but also stayed well enough back to form a pathway all the way to the beach where Shade sat waiting.

The moment my boot hit dry sand, they crowded in behind me, filling in the pathway I'd used. All their eye stalks stared at me, waiting without blinking.

"I think they want you to do it again," BB said.

"What? Call the fish?"

"They're smart enough to use traps to catch their prey. So, I'm sure they're smart enough to see you as an endless supply of food. Perhaps you are their new deity. The fish goddess."

I snorted. "They're probably not smart enough to understand the concept of over fishing." I raised my hands and gathered the electricity forming along my wires. Then I shot the lightning into the shallow water.

The lake beyond the cove started to churn again, and the crabs turned to face it in anticipation.

"Okay," I whispered. "I vote we leave now before they decide they can't let me go."

I hurried to the ruins of my tent and folded it as best I could before strapping it to my bike. The sleeping bag had escaped with only a few rents that leaked white fluff, and I stuffed it back into my pack before whistling for Shade.

He hopped up to the folding platform and suffered me to strap him in.

"Did you get a good breakfast?" I said with a pat.

My hand stung, and I turned the non-metal one over to stare at the reddened skin along the back.

"Ouch."

BB popped up. "It appears you have suffered a sun burn."

"How? It was so misty over the lake yesterday." Not like now. The sun already stung the back of my neck and face.

"Water reflects light, even when it is in the air. You will need to take precautions or suffer from sun sickness."

I didn't have a hat, and I didn't want to take the time to slather ointment on when I had no idea how long the crabs would be occupied. So, I grabbed a spare tank top from my pack and wrapped it around my neck so that it protected the parts the helmet didn't cover.

Then I climbed on my bike.

"So long—er, BB, what are we calling them?"

"I think fisherclaws is appropriate."

"So long, fisherclaws."

I pulled energy into the bike's frame and pushed off, soaring over the crowd of crabs. Their eye stalks all turned to watch as we disappeared over the lake.

CHAPTER 5

Daybreak: Day 192

The lake stretched out ahead of me, burning bright in the sun. There would be no stopping today. We'd run out of islands. We had to fly until we hit the other shore or we fell out of the air.

No mist obscured the view today, and the water remained flat with only tiny ripples that looked like paw prints marring the surface.

Below, my shadow streaked along, and I leaned over the handlebars to watch it bounce and glide over the water.

A sudden splash made me blink, and I glimpsed a silvery shape with wide triangular wings, leaping out of the water and diving back in again, like a dolphin.

The creature drove up and shot forward, its body undulating as if it swam through the air. It hung there, then climbed higher, droplets falling back toward the lake like a veil made of water.

I held my breath.

More shapes followed, leaping into the air and sailing along with me and my shadow. A whole school of them.

They looked like Earth manta rays without the tails, each a silvery color with dark speckles giving them individual patterns.

Their majestic movements carried them higher until we sped along in our own cloud of motion. Swimming above the surface.

They soared and dove, falling back into the water, only to rise up again and dance around me.

I laughed as their wings sprinkled water across us. Shade strained his neck, trying to catch droplets in his mouth.

"Silver linings," I said.

"What?" BB popped up on the hologram pad.

"I'm calling them silver linings." I tipped my head back, not minding that the sun fell full on my already burned face. The wind stung a little from the speed of our passage, but the air cooled the burn. My interrupted night's sleep was catching up with me.

BB remained quiet for a moment, and I thought she must be admiring the manta rays.

"I thought I was in charge of naming things," she said quietly. There was a note in her voice I'd only heard once before. Something like hurt.

I lowered my head to catch her staring up at me, brow pinched.

"You can name the next one," I said. "We're not worried about making you more human now. You've already gone logic-crazy once, and we know how to stop you."

I regretted bringing it up almost immediately. BB's face froze. It hardly ever did that anymore. It meant she was processing something or reacting, but usually she substituted a human expression over top.

My lips pressed together, and I raised my gaze to the horizon. In that moment, she looked just like—

Don't think about it. Don't remember. Don't react. If you don't remember, then your body won't react, and she won't know.

"Anikka—"

The silver linings veered away, scattering like a flock of startled birds. They winged away over the lake, leaving me soaring alone.

"What—"

The bike jerked, and I gripped the handlebars to control it. The energy flowing through the frame faltered, making the bike drop alarmingly.

I reached for more energy and pulled it desperately into the frame, sending it swirling in the right direction to keep us aloft and moving.

"What's going on?" BB asked.

"I have no idea. It just...stalled? Like the energy was just drained out of it."

Shade struggled against his straps, barking furiously.

I winced. "Shade, stop! What is it?"

Below us, a shadow rose to the surface of the water, which was a lot closer now that we'd dropped.

"Oh, crap," I whispered.

I poured energy into driving the bike higher and faster as the huge shape rushed to the water's surface. An enormous swell rose toward us, water cascading around the shape underneath.

My pulse hammered in my throat.

"Gods of all worlds, what is that?"

"We can name it later," BB cried. "Go!"

I tried to speed away from the looming shadow, but it was so big, I had to veer around it.

Waterfalls sheeted down, obscuring the shape for a long moment before it finally broke free of the lake's surface and the cascades fell away.

Swathes of gray-green skin cut me off from the other side of the lake. A body bigger than a house, bigger even than the dorm I'd grown up in, surged up from the water, like one of the silver linings soaring into the air. The creature's huge head swung around in a ponderous turn as it began its ascent, ending in a massive rubbery snout that looked a little like a beak.

Vent it, this thing could eat me without even noticing. Like inhaling a gnat.

A whale of titanic proportions lifted itself into the air, and I had a clear view all the way down its leathery body. Rough ridges ran down its sides and back, all the way to its tail, which surged against the water's surface as if giving itself one last push. Glowing spots of pale blue and purple glistened along its belly.

Its turn had cut off my escape.

I drove the bike higher, trying to go up and over.

The gigantic whale opened its mouth.

The air around me crackled, bright sparks streaking across the sky. Just like the electrical storm that swept the planet every few months.

Except I'd just survived one a few days ago. It couldn't be happening again.

The lightning streaked toward the thing's mouth.

"It's eating it!" BB called over the hum. "It eats Daybreak's energy!"

And that's what powered my bike. Holy crap, it *was* going to eat me by accident.

Going up and over wasn't working. The thing was just

flying higher and higher. I pulled back and tried to dive backwards, the way we'd come.

My bike reached the pinnacle of its arc and stuttered.

We hung in the air, nearly a mile from the surface of the lake. A moment that seemed to last an eternity as I felt the energy sucked out of its frame.

"No, no, no!"

As hard as I tried, I couldn't hold the bike in the air with sheer willpower. There was nothing left around us to draw from, all the energy streaking toward the creature and its massive mouth.

We fell.

The bike plummeted toward the water, wind whipping the cloth protecting my neck and sending it flapping away.

"Anikka!" BB screamed.

What could I do? She and Shade were strapped to this lead weight. Even if I abandoned them and threw myself free, I'd still be in the middle of an enormous lake with an enormous energy eating fish.

I screamed and the wires under my skin glowed a brilliant blue. Little bits of lightning crackled along my skin, reacting to my panic.

My throat closed, cutting off the sound as my mind raced. I carried my own energy with me. A teeny tiny amount compared to what was in the atmosphere. That's why I'd used Daybreak's energy to power the bike. Because mine was limited to what my cybernetic wiring could build up over time.

But maybe it would be enough for this moment.

I poured the electricity crackling in my wires into the bike's frame. It wasn't exactly the same as Daybreak's energy, but they both worked almost identically.

I spun it, creating a magnet which reached...finding an

answering call far, far above us, where the sea monster hadn't gotten to yet.

The bike slowed, and I hauled back on the handlebars and the electricity, pulling us into a steep dive instead of a fall.

I kept pulling until the bike curved and went speeding along the surface of the water.

The creature had soared high enough that our way was finally clear, and we ducked under its massive tail. Water showered us, but we broke through to clear air on the other side.

I pushed the bike to its limit, as fast as I could stand with the wind and the spray stinging my face.

The energy in the frame spun, but all the electricity in my wires was gone, depleted. If I had to course correct or pull us higher, we'd be screwed. We could only keep going in this direction until we reached a place where I could access Daybreak's energy again.

But we'd escaped.

We'd escaped!

I craned my head around to stare at the whale undulating higher and higher, like it was swimming through the atmosphere.

Even as it grew smaller with distance, it stretched its massive limbs, those rough lines along its sides unfurling into gauzy wings and the one along its back lifting into a shimmering dorsal fin. I caught my breath at the sight.

Lightning still crackled along its skin, but we remained flying, streaking away as fast as we could go.

"Gods of all worlds, this planet is beautiful," I said, awe slowly replacing the panic that made my arms weak.

I expected BB to complain that it had just tried to kill me. Again. It was an old refrain by now.

But instead, she said, "Titan."

"What?"

"You said I could name the next one. I'm calling them titans."

"Them." I gasped. "Oh my gosh, imagine if there were more."

"That is likely. Most life on this planet has followed the same rules as on Earth. Even this creature has to have had parents. Perhaps it even has children."

"A whole pod of them." I laughed, the sound drawing perilously close to hysteria.

I reached back to rub Shade's ears. The slinkwolf was probably traumatized. I couldn't imagine luring him onto the bike ever again.

"Don't worry, buddy. We're almost there now."

I pushed us hard, every one of us ready to see the other shore.

BB didn't complain about my speed once.

New Fauna of Daybreak ⚠

Black Death- monitor lizard, size of a truck, spits venom, very fast, extremely protective of young, deadly, **avoid**

Fisherclaws- giant crabs with too many legs, builds dams to trap prey, accepts fishy bribes, nocturnal, use caution when nearby

Silver linings- flying sting rays, glowing markings, very pretty, not a threat

Titans- flying whales, big as a football field, eats Daybreak's energy, renders the hover bike inert, use electricity when possibility of encounter is high, **avoid**

CHAPTER 6

Daybreak: Day 192

As soon as we were clear of the titan's area of influence, I could draw power from the atmosphere again. That was nearly half a mile away, but I could still see it flying closer and closer to the clouds.

The sun approached the horizon at the west end of the lake by the time we reached the northern shore. My eyes burned with fatigue, and I drooped over the handlebars as I directed the bike toward the pebbly beach.

The colonists had named the Black Flats for the tar pits that darkened the ground between the jungle and the lake.

This shore was black, too, but from volcanic rock.

Hills covered in rough basalt stretched from the edge of the lake into the distance, where jagged pinnacles stabbed the sky. Rough cliffs and gullies wound through the terrain, like open mouths that had snatched and swallowed the colonists whole.

With a huge sense of relief, I skidded to a stop on the

shore. I put my boot down, and it crunched in the ragged gravel.

Shade didn't seem to mind the rough stones when I unstrapped him. He jumped down and shook the water from his coat. I gave him the last of the fish that I hadn't sacrificed to the fisherclaws and hoped that he would be able to forgive me, eventually.

Then I sagged against the rocks for a very late lunch of dried fruit.

"You should rest," BB said. "That was a very long trip, and powering the bike will have only added to your fatigue."

She didn't *say* that she was monitoring me, but I winced anyway.

I shook my head. "I don't like the terrain," I said. "It's too open and has too many places for nasty things to hide." I jerked my chin at the gullies. "It's only ten miles to the caves, right?"

"Yes," BB said slowly.

"That won't take long on the bike. It would be better to find them first."

BB opened her mouth, then seemed to think better of what she was about to say. "All right," she said instead and her image on the hologram pad changed to that of the map with a bright beacon highlighting the coordinates that Dr. Grotman had been steering her group towards.

For this leg of the trip, I left Shade to lope alongside us. We could still travel relatively quickly, considering he was much fleeter on foot than I was, and this way I didn't have to lure him back onto the bike.

It took a little over an hour to reach the coordinates, and I slowed as we neared the spot on the map. I could push the bike faster, but we were ranging up and down steep hills and treacherous terrain. I didn't want to lose sight of Shade or get the bike wedged in somewhere I couldn't get it unstuck.

My eyes passed over the rocks and stones, searching for an opening.

"Where are they?" I asked BB.

She popped back, making the map disappear. "We are at the coordinates," she said. "Considering the local terrain, I assume we are looking for an old lava tube. It must be below us."

I blew out my breath. "Then how do we get in?"

"Dr. Carver's notes indicated this site was surveyed for possible use by the colony. There must be an entrance somewhere."

"And equipment. They had to have gotten here somehow. So there will be gliders around."

I just had to look.

I parked the bike and ranged out around the area where the map said the caves were. Climbing up and down the rocky hills made my legs ache. Back in the jungle, there wasn't this much elevation, so they weren't used to it.

Where are they?

I opened the map to zoom in and pan over the fuzzy satellite image, but it was an aerial view. Unless there was a yawning hole in the ground, it wouldn't show me anything.

"It must be under an overhang or something."

Shade came bounding over the rocks, a long furry creature dangling from his mouth. He dropped it at my feet with a little yip of excitement.

"Thanks, buddy." It wasn't one of the jungle jumpernicks like I'd first thought. This had shorter legs and a stumpy tail, like some kind of weasel.

I shrugged and tucked it into my pack. Whatever it was, it would make a good dinner.

I straightened up and planted my hands on my hips. "If the entrance isn't obvious, then we need to be looking for signs of passage. Clues about where the colonists would have gone. That many people would have left some kind of trail."

"Even six months later?" BB said, but I was already scrambling up the next hill. I couldn't think about the possibility of not finding anything. I'd come this far. I was not leaving again until I'd found the colonists. Nearly a thousand people couldn't just disappear into the rock.

The sun sank toward the horizon behind me, threatening nightfall. Soon I'd be searching in the dark.

But BB was right. How much of a trail would be left?

I checked each crevice and crack in the hills looking for an opening, a shaft, anything that would lead me to the colonists.

That point on the map burned in my mind. How stupid was it that I was standing right on top of it, but without a way to burrow down, I was stuck here on the surface?

I kicked a stone, and it skittered off to fall into a deepening shadow.

"We will not have light for much longer," BB said quietly.

We barely had light now. The gloom deepened around us, and far off to the north, a glow grew on the horizon. But it was far too early for Daybreak's aurora.

I climbed the next hill and squinted at the glow.

"There appears to still be volcanic activity not far from here," BB said.

I bit my lip. "Could it reach us? You said we're looking for a lava tube."

"I do not have enough information to guess," BB said. "From what I can see on our map, the activity is miles away on the other side of the plain. But I have no way of knowing what's under the surface."

Maybe that's what had happened to the colonists. Maybe that's why they'd never come back.

I gulped. Then I crunched back to the bike and unstrapped my things. I slid my arms into my pack and slung the cross bow over my shoulder so it would be easy to draw or drop, depending on the situation. My blade I held in my hand —not because I had anything to swing at, but because it made me feel better.

I called a streak of lightning and sent it sliding down the blade so it sputtered and spit and illuminated my path.

Shade came to check in and then scrambled back over the rocks to continue hunting. At least I assumed that was what he was doing with his nose to the ground and the occasional dive for a crack or crevice.

I sectioned off the hillside in my head, mentally crossing off the area I'd already searched. I stepped carefully across the stony ground, holding my sword at an angle so it would cast its flickering light against the slope.

A yelp and a snarl made my heart jump.

"Shade?"

I sprinted up a steep incline and faltered at the sight. At the bottom of the hill, Shade faced off against a long lean shape, that outweighed him by a good fifty pounds. My light illuminated a square jaw and rounded ears. Its lips pulled back to reveal long sharp fangs, and a prehensile tail lashed back and forth as its green-gold eyes locked on Shade.

Breath hissed through my teeth. We'd seen one of these before in the swampy crater on our way to the *Last Resort*. Except this one had different coloring, deep black with dark gray stripes, that would help it blend in with the rocky hills on this side of the lake.

The deathkitty's shoulders bunched, and it planted its huge paws, ready to pounce.

"Hey!" I leaped, landing halfway down the slope and sliding the rest of the way in a cascade of gravel. I pushed off and dropped my sword to swing the crossbow up to my shoulder. Lightning flickered along the metal bolt as I pulled the trigger, and it flashed through the air.

It missed, the bolt shattering on the ground behind the cat. But it certainly got its attention. It spun with a snarl.

I didn't have another bolt handy, and the quiver was trapped in my bag where it wouldn't do me any good, so I flung the cross bow away and snatched up my blade.

The last of the sun's rays disappeared below the horizon, plunging us into complete darkness.

But I still had my sword, and I knew there would be more light if I just waited a minute or two.

I held the spluttering blade out between me and the beast, and circled slowly toward Shade. The slinkwolf didn't limp, so that was good news. But he did cower away from the deathkitty as if he remembered the way the last one had grabbed him.

That wasn't necessarily a bad thing. My brave slinkwolf never hesitated to throw himself into the fray if he thought I was in trouble, even against things like deathkitties and megawings, who could kill him with a casual swipe.

The deathkitty surged across the ground, and I stumbled back a step. It swiped, and its claws hooked in the leather of my boot. With a yank, it pulled me off my feet.

I yelled and swept my sword across its chest. The sparks flared against its dark fur, and blood dripped down the blade, but the deathkitty didn't even seem to notice.

It slashed a massive paw toward my face, and I flung my metal arm up to block it. Claws screeched across my arm and lodged in my shoulder.

I screamed.

Shade howled and tackled the cat, jaws clamping down on its spine.

"Shade!"

The cat yowled and twisted, trying to grab the slinkwolf that clung to its back.

I could have taken the moment to roll away, but I drew back my good arm and drove my sword into its side, sending electricity under its skin.

The cat leaped back. Shade dropped away and circled in front of me as I rolled to my feet, my right arm limp at my side.

Above us, the night sky burst into glorious color, the aurora arrayed like a painting of light. It stretched from horizon to horizon, a display of Daybreak's most deadly beauty.

The colors splashed hazy blue and purple light across the rocks and the deathkitty that stalked the base of the hill, glaring at us.

"Anikka, there!" BB popped up on my wrist long enough to point over my shoulder.

I didn't dare look away from the deathkitty, but I held my sword across my body with my left hand and turned just enough to glance out of the corner of my eye.

The light pouring from the sky sent shadows chasing across the ground in entirely new patterns, highlighting things I hadn't noticed in the late afternoon sunlight.

Under an overhang in the hill I'd just tumbled down, the light from my sword flickered against a dark opening.

No wonder I hadn't seen it. There was no path, no tracks, no trail. Nothing except a deep hole and the flash of some kind of metal at the end.

But if I turned to run for it, the deathkitty would be on me in a second. If I'd learned anything from the one in the swamp, its powerful legs were built for leaping. That one had used the height of the trees to stalk its prey. I had no doubt this one would use the hills the same way.

My eyes darted frantically around the little valley between hills, looking for anything I could use to my advantage. Nothing but rocks and a bit of dried grass growing between the cracks in the low ground. Likely this was where the water gathered when it rained.

We just had to get to the caves.

Shade growled low in his throat and slunk forward. I whistled him back and stepped in front of him to keep him from going after the larger predator.

"Anikka, what are you doing?" BB said.

"Improvising."

I backed up a step and then another, crowding Shade back toward the opening in the hill.

This could go very badly if that crack turned out to just be a crack.

The deathkitty stopped pacing, and sprang, bounding across the open space.

I skipped back and swiped my blade across the ground in front of us, sending up sparks of lightning. The dried grass caught fire and whooshed into a blaze.

The deathkitty fell back with a snarl, flames crackling between us.

I turned to the opening and Shade.

"Go! Go!" I shouted at him, and he darted into the crack. That fire wouldn't last long. Grass burned fast and there was nothing else but rock to catch the blaze.

I squeezed in behind him, my pack threatening to stick against the rough rock.

This was not the large entryway I'd been looking for. No way anyone had driven a glider in here.

But there at the end of the short passage stood a metal door with no handle and a keypad.

"BB?" I said as I fetched up against the dead end.

"It is defunct," she said, her light flickering against the rusted metal door. "Burnt out in the first storm, I would imagine."

My lips thinned. The deathkitty yowled behind us.

"Well, that's just not acceptable." I had Dr Grotman's codes, but they wouldn't do us any good unless the keypad was functional.

Still, I had an all-access pass that had gotten me through nearly every door on the *Last Resort*...hopefully it would work down here.

I laid my hand against the keypad and shot a bit of electricity into it.

The door clicked.

I wedged my fingers in the crack and yanked.

The door groaned open.

A snarl echoed from the rock around us.

"Go," I told Shade, and he slipped into the dark beyond the door.

The deathkitty slithered its way into the narrow passage, snaking out a claw to swipe at me.

I squeezed through the opening and slammed the door shut behind us.

CHAPTER 7

Daybreak: Day 192

I slid down the door, gripping my injured shoulder. Blood dribbled through my fingers, and my head spun as the dark walls blurred. A part of me really, really didn't want to look at the damage.

I wouldn't be able to see much. Nothing illuminated the interior of the cave, and we sat in pitch black. The air felt close and cool.

Shade snuggled into my side, and I put my good arm around him, just to check that he hadn't been hurt. He seemed more concerned with licking my chin, so I assumed he was okay.

I gently eased the pack off my shoulders, wincing as it tugged against the claw marks. Its contents were familiar enough to navigate by feel, and I pulled out the first aid kit that had traveled with me since my escape pod had crashed.

"I recommend removing your arm," BB said. "There could be damage underneath."

I'd already released the suction on the sleeve, so I could

pull the whole prosthetic off. I needed to check it for damage, anyway.

Then I took a deep breath and made my wires glow. Lines of light snaked through my limbs, pulsing under the long scars that traced my skin. The glow grew bright enough to reflect against the walls. A narrow passage stretched in front of me, strangely round and symmetrical. The light caught on ridges cut into the earth by ancient lava and made shadows dance away from us.

I braced myself and glanced down at my ripped jumpsuit. Four jagged claw marks seeped through the ripped fabric.

They were bad, yes. Stitches would have been great if there were any med techs around to give them. But the deathkitty's claws had caught on the top of my prosthetic. It hadn't felt good at the time, but it meant it hadn't clawed me deep enough to reach my wiring.

"BB," I said, gritting my teeth. "What's the protocol for lacerations given the equipment and personnel we have access to?"

BB leaned forward to stare at my shoulder, her expression tight. "I believe you still have the suture gel that you picked up in the colony. Hold the skin together as you apply it and wrap it in a thick layer of bandage. You will have to change the dressing as it heals, but it will provide an adequate base of care for now."

I nodded and dug through the kit in the light of my glowing wires, looking for the gel. It came in a little tube about the size of my finger. Not a lot to work with. I'd have to be careful how I allotted my limited supplies.

Pinching the skin together and applying the gel at the same time wasn't easy with one hand. I had to brace against the door and use my good thumb to hold the wounds closed as I smeared the suture gel on with my fingers. After all that, bandaging seemed much easier, and I wound the gauze around my shoulder and chest to anchor it.

"Immobilizing the limb during the first week of healing is also recommended," BB said. "The sling should still be in the kit."

I sighed as I pulled out the familiar sling. "I feel like I just got rid of this thing." The cast had only just come off my left arm a couple of months ago with the help of a saw from the colony infirmary. It had been such a relief to get rid of. And here I was sliding my other arm into the sling again.

"At least it is not a torn cardigan," BB said.

I huffed a laugh. "Right?"

"Rest is also recommended," BB said quietly.

I shook my head. "You know my answer, BB." I glanced down the dark hall. "We're finally here. We found the caves. They could be right around the corner. After six months, I'll finally know what happened to them."

"They aren't going anywhere," BB said. "After this much time, you are not going to miss them if you take a moment to sleep."

"I'm not sleeping when we're this close."

"Your sleep last night was disrupted. You did not rest after encountering the titan. You did not rest when reaching shore, and you are refusing to rest now. Your cortisol levels are increasing at an alarming—"

"Don't monitor me!" The words slipped out far too loud, and I sat there dragging ragged breaths into my lungs.

BB stood silent, eyes fixed on my face.

It made me feel cornered and like I was being completely unreasonable.

I dropped my gaze and got my breath under control. Panic crept up my throat, and I had to cough twice to clear it away.

"You don't trust me," BB said, so soft I could barely hear her.

My gaze snapped up. "That's not what's wrong."

"Then there *is* something wrong—"

"I just don't need you constantly in my ear telling me things I already know." I tossed the first aid kit back in my pack and shoved my prosthetic under the strap. Her hologram remained attached to its wrist, and when I pulled the pack over my good shoulder, she floated there, just behind my ear.

I let out my breath as I stood. "I'm sorry. But this is important. I can't sleep until I know what happened to them, and I can't take any more nagging about my health when there's nothing I can do to change it right now. Okay?"

BB was silent for a moment as I stared down the lava tube, Shade at my side.

"Nagging about your health is all I am good for. It is my primary directive."

Her hologram flickered out, leaving my wires the only thing illuminating the passage.

I bit my lip hard. "It's not all you're good for BB," I said quietly. "You're also my best friend."

BB didn't answer.

I almost asked her what her infirmary banks said about PTSD, but she was too smart. She'd know exactly why I was asking.

Shade licked my hand, and I turned my palm over to scratch his ears.

"You alright, buddy? That was some fight. You need anything after that?"

He panted and gave me a little whine.

"Yes, you're a good boy. You were so brave out there. Just a little bit longer. Then we can sleep."

BB's weary voice came from my prosthetic. "You care more about the alien dog than you do about yourself."

I sighed and realized there was no winning this argument until I agreed to sleep. And I couldn't yet.

My wires glowed enough to illuminate a few feet down the cave, and I started forward. I pulled out my blade and sent some lightning along the edge to give us more light.

Rock walls led deeper into the hill, sloping down as we walked.

"I wonder why the entrance would be hidden like that. And so small," I said, examining the ridges in the walls. Clearly, there was something down here. They'd put the door up to keep things out, but no one had bothered to smooth the passage at all.

"Perhaps this is the back door," BB said.

It had to be the right place, tiny entrance or not. What else would the colonists bother building out here in the middle of nowhere?

BB pulled up the map, and we followed the coordinates down. Not that there was any other way to go. The corridor stretched straight and narrow with no side passages.

Fifty feet in, we found the first evidence of human occupation. A work light hung on the wall. I reached up to see if it would turn on, but the circuitry must have been fried in the storms. These simple things weren't made with the newer opticals.

"At least we know they were here," I said, voice hushed for no reason at all.

We continued. Lights hung ever fifty or so feet, all dead so the corridor was even darker than a jungle night. The floor sloped down enough that my calves ached from the constant angle.

Eventually, the way widened, and several passages with

light fixtures spread from this central one. But now it wasn't hard to follow the coordinates to the heart of the caves.

My steps quickened, and I stumbled over my feet in haste.

I'd spent the last few months deliberately suppressing every thought about what I might find. I'd been disappointed too many times. And it was possible my imagination could come up with something worse.

It had been easier to focus on the problems of getting here, to solve each one as it came without thinking of the future.

Obviously, the fact that none of the colonists had come back to the colony worried me, but maybe they had a good reason. I could also think of so many bad reasons.

I'd found so many people dead now. My fellow sleepers in their pods. Emerson with her navigation data. Parker who'd just wanted to find his partner. Dr. Grotman and her team of colonists.

But for the first time in a long time, I allowed myself a little hope to go with my fear. Maybe it would be different this time.

Please let them be alive.

The way ahead opened up, a glow reflecting against the rock that had nothing to do with my wires or my blade.

I sprinted the last hundred feet to the tunnel's end.

A cavern opened where a bubble of lava had cut out a much broader space in the rock. Light fixtures lined the walls, but they were still dark. The glow came from optical work lights set at intervals on the floors. Cables snaked across the ground, connecting the lights with a generator that hummed against the far wall.

The entire area between them was littered with crooked rows of cryo pods. So many boxes lined up like a mismanaged warehouse of human life.

The little blue lights indicating vital signs blinked at me a hundred times over. A thousand. I couldn't even begin to count them. But if they'd managed to bring the entire colony down here before the storm, there should be more than nine hundred.

I stepped to the closest pod and leaned over it. An opaque screen scrolled through health readouts. No heartbeat. But everything else was green, the sleeper kept in cryo suspension until they could be revived to life.

My hand slid over the lid, and my fingertips tingled. Like I could actually feel the person inside, a thin bit of metal and cryo gel the only thing between us.

"They're all here," I said, voice hushed. "This was their plan for survival."

BB popped up over my shoulder to examine the readouts. "They went to sleep. And even if the storm killed them, which it must have, they would have been preserved in pods to be revived later."

This is what had happened to the colonists on the *Last Resort*. Many of them had survived the crash only to be killed by the storm, but their pods were keeping them preserved.

This is what BEV had wanted to do to me. Preserve me until after the storm. Keep me from all the pain and heartache by killing me.

I shuddered and forcefully suppressed my shivers before BB could notice.

"Their plan was to survive." I turned in a circle, my eyes traveling over the sea of white lids. "Except no one woke them up."

CHAPTER 8

Daybreak: Day 193

BB finally won, and I slept. There was no more reason to argue.

My shoulder ached when I finally woke, my tattered sleeping bag stretched beside one of the pods. The floor was hard, but at least the cave was better shelter than a lot of the places I'd slept in the last six months. And with the door locked, I was sure nothing could sneak up on me. Like deathkitties.

I stretched and blinked. Nothing had changed. Even the lighting remained the same.

"How long did I sleep?"

"Nine hours," BB said. Her hologram stood on my prosthetic, which I'd laid on the floor beside me. "It is now midmorning."

Time to get to work, then.

First, I cleaned my prosthetic. I might have been desperate to search the cave, but there was still sand in the joints after splashing around on the island, and I couldn't afford it if my right arm stopped working.

Only after it was squeaky clean, could I move on to everything else.

Unsurprisingly, the cavern didn't hold any wood so I let Shade have his catch from the previous day raw, and I made do with dried fruit for breakfast, though I'd have to do some hunting soon or head back to the lake to fish.

But that could wait till I had a plan.

I spent the morning searching the caves, pacing up and down the crooked rows while Shade snuffled in the corners.

At least now I knew why they hadn't used the caves in the crater. There was no way this much tech would fit there. Those caves were narrow cracks in the rock, whereas this was an actual cavern.

The pods were arranged haphazardly, barely lined up with one another, like they'd been set up in a hurry. Which made perfect sense. The colonists had only had a couple of days of warning before the storm. It was amazing they'd gotten this many people settled into cryo sleep in time.

Each pod was labeled with a number, but I couldn't find a manifest or a roster anywhere. Only one thing felt personal and might identify the sleepers.

Cryo pods were equipped with a single use recorder. A mic to record notes from the med tech and a speaker to play it back.

Except when I tried playing one, it wasn't the voice of a med tech or whoever had packed these people away. It was a woman, voice strained and rushed.

"Bobby, I love you. I love you and I'll see you soon. I... don't worry. Dr. Carver will fix this. Just...remember what you said that night before we left orbit. About everything being worth it. It will all be worth it."

I bit down hard on my lip. I checked another one just to be sure.

"Erika, it's Daddy. I just…they told me to keep it short, so I just wanted you to know how proud I am of you, baby. Just in case. I'm so proud. You're everything I've ever loved in this world."

My throat closed up, and I cut that one off short. I couldn't listen to more choked up voices. More words saying goodbye without actually using the word goodbye.

"What are they?" BB said, staring at the pods. "They are not medical notes or history like they are supposed to be."

"They're messages." I let my hand fall from the pod. "Last words and wishes in case the worst happened and whoever was inside never woke up."

I took an unsteady breath and made my way to the end of the room. I didn't bother listening to any more recordings. Unless the person had left their name or detailed instructions about what was happening, they wouldn't help me, and it felt too much like listening to the whisperings of ghosts.

All the pods were on and ready to go. There just wasn't anyone here to wake them. And no computer or AI with a scheduled timer, either. What were they hoping would happen? Had they expected the crew of the *Last Resort* to find them? That didn't seem likely. Dr. Grotman had thought they'd be back at the colony by the time the *Last Resort* reached orbit.

The colonists had to have brought something with them. They had to have some supplies, if only food for the journey and the clothes they would have shucked before climbing into their pods. But there was nothing but pods in the central chamber.

And the cables.

"What do the cables lead to?" I asked. The pods all had optical batteries. That's what kept them going.

"A wake-up system perhaps?" BB said.

I followed them. Another passage opened up at the back of the central chamber. Or maybe this was the one that led to the front door. Here, stacked crates waited in the dark. No one had bothered to leave one of the work lights lit in here and the bins lined the hall, making the space even narrower.

Cables snaked past, and I followed them to another bubble cave, not as large as the first.

Here I finally found something that at least looked like a computer. A mess of screens and wires and a data pad, like someone had gone around the colony with a box and gathered up as much optical tech as they could find and dragged it all here to mash it together.

A single cryo pod stood on one side, like a guard in the gloom.

And on the other was a wide pad with a dark console attached to one end. I'd never seen anything like it before.

I checked the pod first, the same way I'd checked all of them. Except this one had a nameplate. Not just a number.

DR. CRISPIN CARVER

I'd seen that name several times now in the colony and in Dr. Grotman's logs.

I didn't know why he got a special pod set apart here in the room with all the tech, but I was glad to see he was here at all. It was nice to recognize a name even if I'd never actually met him.

I hesitated a second, then pressed the recording on the pod.

Static, then the voice of an older man crackled out, slurred with fatigue. "Gods of all worlds, I hope this works."

Nothing else. Clearly, Dr. Carver wasn't one for sentiment. Or instruction. He couldn't have left me anything else useful?

The computer was a haphazard mess, of course, but it did turn on. A stream of code flowed past the bottommost screen, and my eyes narrowed as I tried to make sense of it.

"BB? What is this?"

"It is a dummy wake-up AI. A bit of programming designed to revive this pod in particular after the energy storm. My guess is that Dr. Carver meant to be revived first, so he could then revive the rest of the colonists. Their pods are all controlled from here as well."

"But why didn't it work?" I glanced at the pod that still blinked, firmly closed.

"The automation was turned off."

"What? Why?"

"The final command issued to the computer was to hold. Like an airplane waiting to land. There is no explanation given."

I blew out my breath and strode back to the passageway to stare out at the sea of pods. All those colonists, waiting to be rescued. And the man who could actually help do it was still lying there behind me, preserved for this moment.

"BB, do you know how to revive them?" I pressed my hand to the rock wall to anchor myself. Four months I'd been hurtling toward this moment. Ever since I'd stepped out of the cave after the first energy storm, when I'd realized that I'd survived and I could do it again. When I knew that Daybreak didn't scare me anymore.

"Before I was an infirmary AI, I was a wake-up companion," BB said with a perfectly human sort of pride. "It's a simple matter of restarting their hearts, and then the process will be very similar to your experience exiting cryo sleep aboard the *Last Resort*."

I winced. "Without the crashing part."

BB spread her hands. "My point is, I am far better equipped than a mere computer to revive these people. Just let me know when you would like me to start."

My lips twisted in a smile at her confidence. "Give me a second. As much as I like your attitude, we can't just jump into it. I can't keep all these people alive yet. They'll be helpless for a good long while, and Daybreak is still a dangerous place."

"And there are still the storms to consider," BB said. "We have no long-term solution to protect multiple people or even an entire colony."

I nodded. "So I can revive one. One person. I can keep them alive until the next storm, and if we don't have a solution by then, I can extend my shield to protect them. Any more than that is too risky."

I turned to face the pod standing watch over the computer. Or maybe it was more accurate to say the computer was standing watch over it.

"If I can only revive one person, I'd better make that one count."

Daybreak: Day 193

Dr. Carver was the obvious choice. He was the one who had seen the storms coming in the first place. He was the one who'd implemented the colony's survival plans—even if something had interrupted them. And he was the one most likely to be able to help me save the rest of them.

BB took over the makeshift computer, shuffling aside anything that wasn't immediately related to the functioning of the pod and the wake-up procedure. She could only transfer to another computer or a hologram pad if I touched it, but the pod itself was connected to this mess of wires and tech.

"Degradation in core programming detected," BB said. "It's...fading? I will fill in the missing pieces as I go. Restarting the patient's heart," BB said.

I stood to the side, waiting, my good hand tracing the rounded end of my arm in its sling. How long would it take for the lid to open?

Had the tech aboard the *Last Resort* felt like this when she'd revived me? That had been in the middle of an emergency. The moment I'd woken up, she and BB had shuffled me off to an escape pod along with the few other sleepers she'd managed to awaken. She'd probably been waiting beside the pod, biting her fingernails for an entirely different reason.

My mouth was a little dry, and I stopped worrying long enough to sip some water.

Finally, there was going to be someone else around to talk to. BB was great, about as human as a program could get. But it had been forever since I'd heard another person's voice or seen their face.

Finally, there was going to be someone who actually knew what they were doing. Someone I could trust. Someone like Professor Orrion, who'd shared the thrill of building something useful and unique. I hadn't realized how much I'd given up when I'd flown away from Earth. I had no family, no friends. Only one professor who'd encouraged me and taught me. Who'd swiped parts from the coffee machine to teach me about soldering or stayed late to explain the physics of an aqueduct.

It hadn't seemed like much to give up. One person.

Now, one person felt like the entire world.

"Heartbeat has been established. Normal rhythm achieved. I will now begin the cryo recovery process. Stand by to assist."

I made a face. By that I assumed BB meant I should be there to catch him when he tried to stand up and failed. That was what I remembered most vividly from cryo recovery.

I stumbled forward, but the lid hadn't even opened yet.

Oh great, what if he wasn't like Professor Orrion at all? What if he was arrogant or cruel? Or really bad at everything? What if he *wasn't* the solution to all my problems?

I shook my head. He was an astrophysicist. He couldn't be bad at *everything*. Not if he'd been the one to set up this whole plan in the first place.

Except it hadn't worked.

The locks on the lid popped open with a snap, and it cracked a few inches, mist pouring out and swirling around my feet.

I held my breath.

The lid slid back, and I waited for the mist to clear. Rapidly thawing cryo gel shined in the light of the work lamps. It contracted as it thawed, pulling away from the man's body, gathering at the sides of the pod.

I leaned forward to stare down into Dr. Carver's face.

Then I frowned.

"BB. Can you pull up Dr. Carver's personnel files?"

"Why?" She did it without waiting for my explanation. Her hologram disappeared from the screen and text filled in the space she'd left. At the top sat a profile picture.

I glanced back and forth between the middle-aged man in the file...and the boy lying in the bed of cryo gel, eyes still closed.

"Because that's not him." I bent to double-check the nameplate on the side of the pod. As if I'd read the only one wrong. "That's not Dr. Carver."

Daybreak: Day 193

One person. I could only revive one person and I'd screwed it up?

I couldn't just stick this one back in the freezer and try again. There were serious consequences to repeated stints in cryo, especially so close together. Like brain turning to mush consequences.

I pressed my hand to my head, suppressing the frustrated scream that built behind my clenched teeth. How had this happened? There was one pod he could be in. It had seemed so obvious.

"Anikka, I need you," BB said, breaking through the crush of failure. "He's waking up."

I shook myself. Whoever this boy was, he needed me right this second. His eyes slowly peeled open while the cryo gel tried to stick his eyelashes together.

This was the part I should have been helping with. The tech on the *Last Resort* had done more than just catch me when I fell out of the pod.

I rushed to my bag and dug for something I could use as a rag. My spare tank top had blown away while escaping the titan, so all I had left was a pair of underwear and a jumpsuit. I winced as I sacrificed the jumpsuit, but I couldn't imagine the boy wanted me wiping goo off his face with the other, even if they were clean.

I poured some water over the cloth, not bothering to be careful, and rung it out before racing back to the pod.

The boy groaned, or maybe he tried to speak. But nothing coherent came out of his mouth yet.

I wiped the goo from his eyelids, trying to be gentle, remembering those first disorienting moments on the *Last Resort*.

At least the cave was nice and quiet, and there wasn't a klaxon going off or emergency lights flashing.

The boy opened dark blue eyes and blinked up at me, pupils dilated so wide they looked almost black. Goo slicked his hair, making it shiny, but it was probably some sort of brown from the looks of it.

He pulled a long arm up out of the gel and flung it over the side of the pod.

"Oh," I said and lunged to help him. "Here."

His skin slid against my hands, and I had to thrust my arms under his armpits to keep from dropping him as he slithered over the edge of the pod. Geez, he was tall, with surprisingly broad shoulders.

His chest heaved like his lungs didn't know how to be lungs anymore.

"Right, yes. Breathe." I really should be better at this. I'd only done it six months ago. "In for two, out for two. You have to convince your diaphragm it wants to work again."

He blinked up at me, a crease forming between his brows,

and his mouth worked like he wanted to say something, but all that came out were indistinct little groans.

Like all the sleepers on the *Last Resort*, he'd woken up nearly naked, with only a pair of shorts covering the important bits. Cryo gel got into everything and worked a lot better when it had full contact with your skin, so clothes were kind of counterproductive to the process.

"It's all right," I said, trying to keep my voice soothing. "You're okay. You're going to be fine."

His legs buckled, and I helped him sit on the floor with the pod as a backrest. My days in the jungle had built a good amount of muscle, but he was a lot heavier than Shade. Luckily, we weren't in a hurry.

He sat with his knees up and brought his hands to his face to flex them, but they shook hard enough they must have been blurry to his unfocused eyes.

"Anikka," BB said. "This cave is not the appropriate temperature for a newly awakened sleeper. He will become chilled and likely suffer from shock if not clothed soon."

"Right." I stood. "Just stay there."

"I have no other choice." BB said. "I am trapped in this computer until you transfer me out."

I'd actually been talking to the boy, but she had a point. I pulled the prosthetic from my bag and tapped the computer so she could jump back into my arm.

Her hologram sprang from my disconnected wrist. "Thank you. I do not like feeling like a damsel in distress."

I laid the arm on the floor beside the boy. He squinted at it blearily.

"Keep an eye on him? I'll find something to warm him up."

I raced from the cavern, which was a little cool, now that I thought about it.

The crates were all still stacked in the passage that led to the other cave, and I threw open two at once. Water bottles crowded the first and stacks of foil packets lined the other.

But not enough to feed a thousand people for even one day. Had they eaten everything on the way?

The next crate held batteries. Completely useless considering they were copper-based, not optical.

"Who was in charge of this evacuation?" I muttered.

The next crate finally held towels. For cryo gel? Well, that's what I'd be using them for now, regardless of why they'd been packed. I snatched three and bundled them under my good arm to hurry back to the cave.

Just in time. The boy shivered beside the pod, hard enough to make his teeth chatter.

"Here." I wrapped one around his shoulders and helped him grab it with fingers that didn't want to cooperate. The second one went over his knees.

That seemed to help. His violent shivers eased a little, though I remembered random shakes that would stick around for days after.

What else had the tech done for me? She'd been rushed but also calm and competent in the face of the blaring klaxon and the flashing red light. Training probably helped, but surely, I could remember something.

My eyes slid to the nameplate that hung just above us.

"What's your name?" I asked, gently.

I'm sure the tech had a million reasons to ask me my name, even with the *Last Resort* crashing. To check that my memory was intact or to check my identity against the information in my chip. Or to assess vocal function. Maybe all of the above.

But I'd opened this pod and revived this boy thinking he was one person only to be confronted by someone else entirely. He couldn't possibly be Dr. Carver. Could he? Carver was at least thirty years older, with graying hair and a trimmed beard. I wasn't sure this boy could even grow a beard. He didn't look any older than me.

"R-Ren," he said, his eyes trying to focus on my face.

The last little bit of hope in my chest died.

"I have scanned his chip," BB said quietly from my discarded arm. "This is Ren Arlo. Age twenty. Identifies as male. Registered profession: electronics tech."

I winced. Oof. Terrible job, considering the circumstances. "I have bad news for you, Ren."

"What?" he asked, slow like his tongue still felt thick.

I shook my head. Best not to start with that. "Do you know where you are? Do you remember what happened before you slept?"

His brow furrowed. His hair was starting to dry even with all the goo, and it stuck up in places, making him look like a confused hedgehog.

"I think...there was an emergency," he said and then coughed. "An evacuation?"

"Yes," I said, since he seemed to be looking for confirmation.

"I don't...I don't know why. Should I know why?"

"Uh." Well, actually he might not. That might not be a problem with memory. How many people actually knew about the storm or what it was going to do? How many had just followed the evacuation protocols without thinking?

"There was a storm six months ago. An electrical storm that killed all the tech. The colonists came here to stay safe in cryo pods."

His eyes widened, and he craned his head back to stare at the pod he'd popped out of. "I've been asleep for six months?"

"Technically, you've been dead for six months," BB said.

I made a shushing noise at BB. "Never mind that," I said as Ren's face went white. "Do you—did you know Dr. Carver?"

"I...heard of him? Everyone knew of Dr. Carver. He was the one who made Dr. Grotman evacuate the colony. But I never really met him before. Why?"

I chewed my lip. Why had this guy been stashed away in Dr. Carver's pod if he didn't even know him? I didn't think he was lying. The disorientation would have been too much for me to lie when I'd just woken up, and I'd had a bunch of stimulants shot into my bloodstream to get me going.

And the dawning horror in his eyes would have been hard to fake.

"He was the one who was supposed to wake you all up," I said, skipping some of the important but more complex bits. "And he didn't. I just...need to know why."

He couldn't be dead. Not just because I really, really didn't want him to be. His voice had been on the recording. He'd been alive when everyone had gone into their pods.

Ren shook his head and nearly toppled over. I reached out to help keep him upright while he flushed.

"He brought us here." His hand slipped from the edge of the towel and pointed to the strange pad on the other side of the room. "With that."

My eyes narrowed, staring at the pad with its console. "What do you mean 'with that'?"

He waved the hand. "We stood in the colony. He pushed buttons. Whoosh. We were here."

My arms raised as if to encompass the entire contraption. "It's a teleporter?"

That was...science fiction. There was no such thing as teleportation. Except I'd wondered how the colonists had all gotten here so fast, and I still hadn't seen any gliders. I'd even seen that bare spot in a colony warehouse that matched the size and shape of this pad.

It had to be a prototype.

I turned back to Ren, but he'd pulled his hand under the towel and held it closed over his chest, his eyes wide and glassy.

"Six months," he murmured. "They told us it would be a day or two. And then we'd go back. There was even another ship coming. Why didn't the new colonists wake us up?"

"Technically, we did," BB said. "Ta-da." Her little hologram held out her hands to indicate me.

I rubbed the back of my neck. "I was a sleeper on the *Last Resort*," I said. "Sorry it took me so long to get here. We...we crashed. And I was the only one left. Then I had to find you and get here. And did you know there's a giant lake in the way?"

"Crashed," Ren echoed. His pupils were all blown out again. He thunked his head against the pod and laughed, high and breathless.

How many tragedies were too many tragedies to learn about all at once? Should I have held a few more back?

"Is there anything that hasn't gone wrong?" he said, voice strangled. He shut his eyes tight enough to make creases at the corners.

My heart squeezed.

I'd been living these things as they'd happened, but in a way that had made it easier. They'd built on each other until the only way to go had been forward. Each ridiculous thing was easier to accept because it was only slightly more ridiculous than the thing that had come before. How much worse would it have been if I'd woken from cryo sleep with the knowledge of all of those tragedies bearing down on me all at once, overwhelming in their sum?

I had no idea who Ren was or why he'd been important enough to sleep in Dr. Carver's pod. I had no idea where Dr. Carver was or how to find him, so he could actually help the way I needed him to.

But all of those worries trickled away when Ren curled up under his towel, tucking his long limbs as small as possible as he rocked under the onslaught of information.

I put my arms around him and squeezed, trying to ground him and give him something warm and human to feel. I'd had nothing like that when I'd first found myself on Daybreak.

"It's okay," I whispered into his crispy hair. "It's going to be okay. You're not alone. I'm here. I'll help you, alright? We're going to be fine."

CHAPTER 10

Daybreak: Day 193

It took ages to get the goo off, and every moment, Ren was more coherent.

"Sorry I'm not a med tech," I said as I rubbed the towel over his shoulders and head. I hoped the friction would help keep him warm, but his hands still trembled.

He shook his head and huffed a laugh. The first smile I'd seen on another human's face in six months. "You're plenty good enough for me. Besides, I spent too much time in the infirmary already. It's nice to see someone other than med techs for once."

"Why were you in the infirmary?" BB asked.

"BB, that's rude," I said. She hadn't had any practice interacting with anyone aside from her assigned sleeper. It hadn't occurred to me that her bedside manner algorithms might have wandered in the last six months.

"Why is it rude to request more information when that information may be pertinent to my patient's survival? Prior medical history could be very important in this situation."

"Sorry," I told Ren. "I managed to get assigned the pushiest wake-up companion." I cast a smile at BB so she knew I was kidding. Mostly.

BB planted her hands on her hips and stuck her tongue out at me. Ren's head lolled back against the pod so he didn't see.

"'S all right," he said. "I...I was sick. I think. It's hard to remember. My head is fuzzy. But I know I slept a lot after we landed."

I met BB's gaze and raised my eyebrows.

"A delayed cryo reaction is the most likely explanation," she said quietly. "They can last for months."

I frowned. I really didn't want to ask "is he going to be okay" while he was sitting right there.

But she knew me well enough to predict my thoughts. "Rest is the best thing, right now," she said, addressing both of us.

I nodded. "That's what I remember."

His eyelids drooped. "Yeah..."

"I'll find some blankets or more towels so you can sleep."

He caught my hand before I could leave. "Your name?" he said.

"Anikka. Anikka Drake."

"Thank you, Anikka." His hand dropped like it was too heavy to hold up for long.

"You're welcome, Ren."

"Leave me with him," BB said.

I almost protested, wanting a minute to talk where the subject of our conversation couldn't hear. But my mind went back to another sleeper nearly six months ago. He'd wished me Godspeed as he climbed into his escape pod. And the next time I'd seen him he'd been dead, his heart failing after some unknown complication from cryo sleep.

I shuddered and left my prosthetic on the ground. "Yeah. Of course."

Ren's eyes settled on the robotic arm, and his brow came down, but from the way his head lolled, he didn't have the energy to pursue any questions, rude or otherwise.

I left them and went back to the passage with the crates. There had to be something useful in all these besides some towels and a bunch of burnt-out batteries.

There were some blankets in the last stack that I checked. Though no sleeping bags. Next, I approached the bins on the other side of the passage. They were too small to contain supplies, but when I crouched beside them to squint at the labels, I realized they were names.

These would be each colonist's belongings, locked away in personal bins, kept safe for when they'd finally wake up.

The thought made my throat close up, just like listening to the recordings.

I swallowed down the lump and searched through them until I found the one labeled Ren Arlo. Luckily, some organized soul had stacked them alphabetically even amidst what had to be near-panic.

I checked further down the rows, under C for Carver. Nothing. There wasn't even an empty bin. Was he not here at all?

Shade trotted up as I moved to stand and dropped a shape at my feet.

"You been hunting, buddy? What is it?"

I tilted my head to examine the long gray shape with a pointed snout and blind white eyes. Like a cross between a possum and a ferret.

"Is there anything out there big enough to cause trouble?"

Shade yawned, and I rubbed his ears. I'd take that as a no. I trusted him to alert me if he smelled anything dangerous.

And the cave had been sealed at one end and likely was sealed at the other so the only thing that lived in here would be smaller cave critters that could make it through the cracks.

"I'll have to find some wood to make a fire, eventually. Can't believe I didn't think to bring any."

I pulled my arm gingerly out of the sling and tucked the blankets under it, then awkwardly carried the bin in my other hand so I could take it back to Ren and BB. Shade trotted at my heels.

The boy lay slumped against the pod, eyes closed, the towel falling from his shoulders.

My stomach lurched, but BB's hologram turned at my approach and nodded to me.

I couldn't quite manage the bin one-handed, and it thumped to the ground, startling Ren awake. He jerked upright and stared around with red-rimmed eyes.

"It's all right," I said. "Just me."

His gaze caught on Shade, who sniffed his feet warily.

Oh crap. I hadn't even considered what the colonists might think about slinkwolves. Had the pack bothered them at all?

"What is that?" Ren said under his breath.

"This is Shade," I said. "A slinkwolf. At least, that's what we've been calling them. Shade's friendly, though not all of them are."

"You're a handsome fellow, aren't you?" Ren said and held out both hands for Shade to sniff. "Fierce and smart, too, I'll bet."

The slinkwolf snorted and shied back. He circled behind me and gave Ren a wary look.

"Shade, don't be rude. Say hi."

Ren shook his head when the slinkwolf refused to get any

closer. "No, don't force him. His instincts are just fine, and you can't make him trust me if he doesn't want to."

"I'm sure he'll warm up to you."

Ren laid his head back against the pod again, his eyelids drooping.

"I think these are yours." I pushed the bin closer to him.

He frowned, reaching out to slide his thumb over the label, like he couldn't quite remember what was in there.

The latch clicked, responding to the chip in his wrist. The same one BB had read his name and profession from.

When the lid fell back, it revealed a bundle of cloth with the sole of a sneaker peeking through the folds.

His face lit up a little as he pulled a gray t-shirt out of the bin, and a red jacket came with it.

The colony didn't exactly have a uniform, but there were plenty of similarities between the different work wear for different divisions. Ren's jacket from the tech division was cut a lot like my jumpsuit, and the patch on its breast matched the one on my sleeve. A swirling planet displaying the great continent where we were now with the words Daybreak Colony arching above and below.

The fabric of the jacket was still stiff and bright, like he hadn't had much of a chance to wear it yet.

I helped him pull his pants on, lined with pockets a lot like mine. Though his were built for smaller tools, and his belt had a holster for a screen. Then we eased the t-shirt over his head and the jacket up his arms. I hoped it would help keep him warm.

"You should sleep now," BB said. "Wake-up protocols are roughly sleep, protein and fluid intake, and more sleep scheduled in several hour increments over a forty-eight-hour period. Exercise and physical rehabilitation come later."

"I feel like I should be doing something," Ren said, though his words were still slurred. "You're doing so much for me."

My lips twisted. "You can pay me back later. Trust me there's plenty to do. And this...this is kind of nice. I didn't have anyone to take care of me when I woke up, and I remember it being pretty bad."

"Pretty bad" didn't do any justice to those first few days stumbling through the deadly jungle in a pair of scrubs and some slippers with a broken arm and raging exhaustion, but there really wasn't any point in playing the "my experience was worse than your experience" game. And I wouldn't wish that kind of pain on anyone.

I spread out the blankets, trying to create a thick layer on the smoothest part of the rock floor.

"There is plenty of justification for taking time for convalescence," BB said. "Dr. Grotman even highlighted the addendum to the colony's policies on sick leave shortly after the first landing on Daybreak."

Ren stumbled to my nest of blankets and nose-dived into them. "Thanks. You know a lot for a wake-up companion. Mine mostly just kept me on schedule and made sure I drank my juice."

I winced. "Don't hold your breath for any more of that."

BB flickered, a sure sign she was thinking really hard about something.

Ren grumbled something as I laid a blanket over him and tucked in the edges. He was asleep by the time I straightened.

"How soon can we move him?" I asked.

"According to protocols, another week would be best."

"But?"

BB sighed. "But you managed far sooner. Why do you want to move him?"

"Our chances of survival are a lot higher in a place I'm familiar with."

"This is math I am familiar with. I have used it as an argument before." She glanced at the sleeping boy. "But here we have food and shelter. There is no reason to risk travel."

"We have a little food. Those rations won't last long. And...I still need to figure out what happened. What I'm going to do."

"Because he was supposed to be Dr. Carver?" BB filled in.

I glanced at the nameplate on the pod, lips thin. "Yeah. But there has to be a reason it was him and not the doctor. I need to know why he's so important. Why he was in Dr. Carver's pod."

"You think he has something to do with where Dr. Carver might be?"

"I don't know yet. But I can't open every pod, looking for him. And Ren might be the key to finding him."

"Why can't you figure that out here?"

"There's barely anything out there, BB. They clearly brought what they could throw through that teleporter and nothing else. All the clues are going to be back at the colony. That's where we need to head."

I chewed my lip as the thoughts swirled in my head.

"Anikka," BB said from my prosthetic.

I stood, letting Ren sleep as I stepped across to pick up my arm. "Hmm?"

"He noticed a difference." Her voice volume had gone low and soft. "He noticed a difference between me and another wake-up AI."

"Well, I should hope you're different," I said, tucking the prosthetic under my arm. "You have a better sense of humor —" The implication of what she'd said struck me, and I sucked in a breath. "Oh," I breathed. "Oh, crap."

"He can't know." Her voice rose. "Anikka, he can't know. They'll take me away. They'll deactivate me."

"Shh." I spun to check Ren, but he was asleep, face smashed into the blankets. "Don't panic," I whispered.

"How can I not panic? I was built to show care for things, especially you. Anxiety is a natural result of care and panic is a result of anxiety."

I took a deep breath as my heart rate returned to normal. "Nothing's changed, BB. Not really. We knew one day we'd encounter other people. We just...have to hide it. Make sure he never realizes why you're different."

It wasn't a full solution. At some point I was going to have to explain the *Last Resort*. I was going to have to tell someone why they couldn't go inside, why they couldn't activate the AI or the computer.

I was going to have to tell someone about BEV and, by extension, BB.

But that wasn't today. Today we could hide the integration just a little longer. Our sins could stay buried with the *Last Resort* as long as no one noticed I carried a fully integrated AI on my wrist.

To-do

- Get Ren home
- Find Dr. Carver
- Keep Ren alive

CHAPTER 11

Daybreak: Day 195

Ren slept on and off for the next day and a half. To keep from going stir crazy and trying to move him too soon, I dug around on the makeshift computer to see why the wake-up program hadn't run on schedule. But the thing wasn't very sophisticated. It was really just a screen plugged into an optical circuit board and a keyboard that had been ripped off some terminal back at the colony. All it showed me was Dr. Carver's code signed in to freeze the wake-up program.

So Dr. Carver had chosen to not wake everyone up. But why? And where the hell was he?

I'd resigned myself to the fact that I hadn't woken the right person, but I had to push away that disappointment, over and over, or else I'd end up taking it out on Ren. And he didn't deserve that.

I shook my head and left the computer the way I'd found it.

The rest of the personal bins were locked and wouldn't open even for the commander's codes that BB and I carried around. But I could at least go through the other supplies while Shade hunted.

I found the main entrance to the lava tube and ventured out a little ways to see if I could find any wood.

One large glider designed to carry twenty to thirty people stood abandoned on the slope outside the door. It lay crooked, and I could almost see the last shift of colonists arriving and leaping out of the vehicle as they skidded to a stop. Or maybe this was how they'd moved the teleporter pad. This group must have come before the skeleton crew that had tried to cross the Black Flats with Dr. Grotman.

Black scorch marks marred the battery compartment, a familiar sign that it had shorted during the storm. We wouldn't be using it to get back across the lake.

Periodically, I woke Ren and made him eat. Usually either cold foil-packed mac and cheese or something Shade had dragged in that I could roast over a teeny tiny fire.

By the middle of the second day, I couldn't control the pacing anymore.

"We're going to have to move him," I told BB. "We're going to run out of reddi-meals, and there's nothing growing out there that we can eat."

BB remained on the wrist of my detached arm, but she popped up to survey her patient. Ren lay on the blankets, one arm curled to his chest, the other flung across the cave floor.

"I don't like it when he's still so disoriented, but I think you are right."

"We'll have to cram on the bike," I said and paced to the teleporter console. "I have no idea how to use this. And I don't think it's powered, anyway."

I kicked the edge with my toe, miffed that I hadn't been able to turn it on. Instantaneous travel would have been nice.

Across the cave, the work light flickered, plunging us into pitch blackness for a second.

I exchanged a glance with BB.

"That's weird. They haven't done that before."

BB's lips thinned as she started at the light. "They have. While you were asleep last night."

I shook my head. "We're getting out of here, anyway, so it doesn't matter if they're a little wonky. The pods are safe with their batteries. We'll leave first thing in the morning and make it across the lake in one go."

BB agreed, so I didn't have to tell her how trapped I felt underground. The last six months had been a non-stop race to get here and now sitting around doing nothing felt... weird. Worry gnawed at the place under my breastbone, convincing me that something awful was sneaking up on me.

I packed everything while Ren slept, making another pack out of a blanket so I could tuck away the last of the reddi-meals.

The next morning, I woke Ren and made him eat something before we left. He was quiet and a little dazed but awake enough to sit on a bike.

I helped him to his feet and slid my metal arm under his shoulder. The claw wounds had closed, and I couldn't afford to be one handed for the journey, so I'd reattached it.

Ren gamely took some shaky steps up across the cavern, steadier on his feet than I'd expected. Which was good. He was tall and broad and a little on the heavier side. I'd built a lot of muscle in the last few months, but I really didn't want to drag him.

We reached the cavern full of pods, and he braced himself against the wall, staring out at all the sleepers.

My teeth clenched.

"We'll be back," I said quietly. "I promise we're not leaving them."

Ren glanced down at his feet, but he nodded. "I know. I just...I keep feeling like I could still be back there, waiting for my chance to wake up. If you hadn't chosen me, chosen my pod."

I blew out my breath before guiding him through the cave toward the back entrance. "Yeah, I know how that feels." If the tech on the *Last Resort* hadn't randomly chosen my pod, I would either be dead or still waiting like all the other sleepers on the ship.

Ren's steps still stumbled as I helped him up the rough lava tube. BB's hologram lit the dark passage all the way to the door where we'd come in.

I propped Ren against the wall and scouted the exit, checking for any deathkitties. The coast was clear which made it a lot easier to leave.

Bright sunlight speared through the crack in the rock as we sidled out into the open. Ren winced, and I squinted.

The field of lava rock stretched away, black and glittering under the sun. Little clumps of white flowers dotted the landscape like islands in the black.

Ren stopped and stared. "I had no idea we were way out here. We just arrived inside the cave."

"It's kind of a long way." I bit my lip and glanced back toward the door. Which had closed and locked again. "I should have gotten the bike first."

"What?" Ren said.

"Wait here. I'll go find our ride and bring it back. Shade, guard."

We'd really only started working on that command, but the slinkwolf plopped his butt down and panted.

Ren slowly slid down the rock to sit beside the slinkwolf.

I left them there and scrambled to the top of the hill to get a better view. The lava tube extended down into the ground, leaving a massive hummock. Only problem was it wasn't the only hill in the area.

"BB, did you mark where we left the hover bike?" I shaded my eyes.

"Southwest point five two one miles."

Well, that was a lot easier than when we'd arrived. And once I found it, I'd be able to travel back here a lot quicker.

Hopefully, before some deathkitty decided Ren looked like an easy dinner. Knowing how he must feel, the deathkitty would be right.

I set off at a trot, skidding down the rough, black pebbles on the other side of the hill.

BB steered me in the right direction, and in about ten minutes, the glint of the hover bike sparkled from where I'd left it

"Anikka—"

"I see it BB."

"No, behind you."

I glanced over my shoulder, and at first, I couldn't see what she was talking about. That alone sent a prickle down my spine. Because not being able to see anything usually meant deathkitty.

A shadow crept across the ground, a low streak of dark fur striped with gray. Sure enough, a deathkitty stalked me, blending in perfectly with the stark volcanic landscape.

"Aw, crap, not right now." I turned and started walking faster. "Keep an eye on it for me. Let me know when it springs."

There was so little that worked with these things. Fighting back didn't scare them away. Running didn't work 'cause they were faster than anything on two legs. The only thing that fazed them was a megawing, and I was fresh out.

"It's matching your speed," BB said.

I took a deep breath and shifted my grip to the hilt of my blade.

"Now," BB said.

I burst into a sprint, up and over the next hill.

"Duck," BB said.

I skidded, feet going out, so I went down, and the deathkitty landed in a spray of rough pebbles, just missing me.

I used the nearest rock to propel myself forward, away from the deathkitty.

Only a few more feet. I could make it.

The hover bike waited, and I threw myself onto it, calling Daybreak's energy into my hands and sending it streaking toward the handle bars.

It lifted, coming to life.

A deathkitty's roar made the back of my necke prickle, and I gripped the handle bars, not even fully planted on the seat yet. I sent the bike forward just as the deathkitty leaped, and our bulk caught it in midair like a battering ram.

It went flying backward, yowling when it hit the ground, scattering volcanic pebbles.

I raced away over the ground with a breathless laugh.

The trip back took mere moments, soaring over the crests of the hills and swinging around until I landed directly in front of the cave door where Ren was holding his hand out for Shade to sniff.

He raised his arm against a spray of gravel. "What—?"

A rumbling roar of fury interrupted him. The deathkitty was on its way.

"No time," I said, leaping off. Shade bounded up to greet me. "Get on."

Ren looked dubiously at the narrow seat of the bike, but Shade leaped on as soon as I folded down his platform.

I did up the straps, securing Shade to one side and the pack and the blanket bundle to the other.

Ren eased onto the back of the seat, and I flung the loose blanket he'd been carrying over his shoulders, tucking the ends into his belt.

"You're going to want that. I promise." Especially since shivers still wracked his body.

"Judging from the deathkitty's sounds, the animal will reach us in less than ten seconds," BB said.

"Damn, those things are fast." I leaped to the seat.

"What the hell is a deathkitty?" Ren said.

"Don't worry about it," I said.

A snarl rang from the crest of the hill, and we jumped, staring up at the silhouette of a large, angry cat.

"I'm worrying about it," Ren shouted.

I poured energy into the bike, and we rose into the air. The deathkitty leaped as we shot forward. It sailed over us, landing with an angry yowl as we disappeared over the hill.

"Okay, my new favorite thing is being faster than everything that wants to eat us," I told BB with a grin.

BB appeared on the holopad, peering over my shoulder. "One day Daybreak will surprise us with a creature that can outrun even your bike."

Ren threw his arms around my waist to stay balanced, the blanket flapping behind him like a cloak. He mumbled something into my back that I couldn't quite hear over the whipping of the wind.

We zipped across the lava field toward the bright streak of the lake in the distance.

Ren's arms tightened around me, cutting off my breath as we got closer and closer, and the sheer vastness of the lake became apparent.

I didn't protest. A swell of conflicting emotions rose in my chest.

Ren wasn't Dr. Carver. The disappointment still lodged in my throat unexpectedly sometimes.

But he *was* the first human I'd talked to since the med tech had woken me on the *Last Resort*.

I couldn't even begin to sort through the mess of anxiety and joy that tangled through every word I said. Could he tell how long it had been since I'd had to interact with people? Could he tell that I'd never been very good at it in the first place?

He coughed, burying his head in my back, though he had to bend really far to do so.

I hunched over the handle bars as we soared and let him squeeze as hard as he needed to.

My goal was to make it over the lake without stopping this time. It would be a long trip, but I really didn't want to risk Ren's health out in the open without a tent or any shelter. Plus, the last time I'd stopped on the islands it hadn't gone well.

But that meant ten straight hours on the water, and BB had been right. Flying the bike made me more tired than I realized.

I told Ren to hunker down behind me so I could block most of the wind, and he did, wrapping the blanket around his shoulders so it didn't flap so much.

The waves flashed by underneath us, and I scoured the depths, looking for giant shadows under the surface. The titan had crept up on me twice now. I wasn't about to get caught by it again.

But the only movement I caught was the much smaller shadows of the silver linings. They paced me under the surface, flitting up and over the waves before dipping back underneath.

"BB, do you see anything?" I asked quietly.

"All of my cameras are trained on the water," she said, her hologram staring down into the depths. "None of them detect any movement on the scale of the titan."

I glanced over my shoulder, but Ren was snuggled against my back with his eyes closed. I couldn't quite tell with the wind whistling over us, but I thought he was asleep or at least dozing, his hands wrapped in my belt.

A shadow fell over us, plunging us into shade. The edge of it crept across the water below and the silver linings scattered.

I sucked in a breath and craned my neck around.

The huge shape of the titan blotted out the sun, an enormous gray-purple whale with a beak longer than the drop ship. It turned ponderously, and its nose sank as it dove from its height in the clouds.

I swore under my breath and shifted my weight forward, pouring energy into the bike, speeding us out of the great beast's shadow.

The bike raced forward as fast as I could make it go without stripping the skin from my face.

Ren grabbed for a better grip as he started sliding off the back. Shade panted and whined.

"Come on, come on, come on," I urged the bike through gritted teeth. We just had to get clear of the titan's influence. If we could escape before it started draining the energy from the atmosphere around us...

The bike stuttered.

"No!"

I pulled electricity out of my wires, sending it into the

bike's frame to power it even as Daybreak's energy was sucked out of it. The bike jumped under us and regained its burst of speed.

The titan hit the water just behind us, sending up a wave big enough to swallow us.

"Hang on!" I screamed.

I kept us in the air as the wave swept over the bike, washing us in cold water.

"What was that?" Ren spluttered as drops of water trailed after us as we sped away.

My heart still hammered in my chest, and I had to take several deep breaths before answering.

"Nothing to worry about. At least not anymore," I said even as I checked behind me to be sure the titan wasn't following.

He swiped the water from his face before ducking back against my spine and closing his eyes. "You know, you say that a lot."

I didn't answer as I steered us toward the opposite shore. And home.

CHAPTER 12

Daybreak: Day 195

We didn't stop on the islands. I just used them as a guide for getting back to the beach. It made me feel a lot better to fly from bit of land to bit of land, rather than over the open water where the titan still lurked and seemed to have an uncanny ability to find me.

Ren dozed behind me the entire way. I wasn't sure how much he was actually taking in on the rare occasion when he lifted his head and stared at the scenery with bleary eyes.

Not that there was much to see.

My head ached by the time the shore came into view. It had been dark for hours, but my eyes still burned from the constant glare of the sun on the water, and I did my best to hide the way my limbs shook from BB.

I pulled down the speed of the bike, so we just slipped along the shore where the water swelled up the sand, the bike dipping until the wheels touched down.

Finally, I caught the glint of Daybreak's moonlight against metal, and I let the bike come to a halt beside the shelter.

I was too tired and sore to do more than unstrap Shade and help Ren off the bike. I set him up inside the hut with my mangled sleeping bag and one of the blankets, making sure it was wrapped snuggly. He took up most of the space inside, but I curled up with another blanket across the doorway and fell into a deep sleep.

I'd thought I was too tired to dream, but images crowded in almost as soon as I drifted off. Thousands of pods surrounded me in the sleeper bay of the *Last Resort*, their little lights blinking accusations at me.

"Free us," the whisper echoed through the bay, sending a tingle down my spine. "Please."

"I'm sorry," I cried. "I can't save you all. Not yet."

Another voice crept into my ear. "You didn't even try."

"BB," I gasped. But it wasn't BB the way I knew her. The entirely logical tones belonged to BEV.

"You didn't even try to save me. You won't even try to save them."

I sucked in a breath and raced down the rows of pods, looking for an escape before she could flip the gravity on me or blare music in my ears.

Ren stood in the aisle between the pods, his back to me. I ran to grab him. To get him out of this death trap.

"Let's go!" I spun him around, and a blank face greeted me. No eyes or nose or mouth, just a swathe of smooth skin.

My stomach dropped.

The pods around us started clicking, the sound growing to a crescendo that pounded through me, and I woke abruptly with a gasp.

The sound didn't fade with the rest of the dream, and for a second I was back on the island with the fisherclaws all around, trying to eat me.

Shade barked, and I cleared the sleep from my eyes to find

I wasn't on the same beach. Sand shifted under me as I surged to my feet, and I struck my head on the low roof of the shelter.

But the clicking remained.

I rushed out through the opening of the hut and stopped short when I found Shade spinning in tight circles in front of the doorway.

The water all along the shore bubbled and splashed as wave upon wave of fisherclaws scuttled up onto the beach.

I sucked in a breath.

"Persistent creatures, aren't they?" BB said, the blue of her hologram flickering against their wet carapaces.

"Holy crap, did they follow me all the way from the islands?"

Behind me, Ren stirred. "What...what's that sound?"

He staggered to his feet, striking his head on the metal roof. He swore and then fell silent as his eyes went wide, taking in the sight of the swarming crabs.

"What's going on?" he whispered.

"They believe Anikka is their god," BB said with a fair attempt at a smirk. "They've come looking for miraculous fish."

"What?" Ren said.

I wondered if he was as tired of saying it as I was getting of hearing it. "Ignore her. She thinks she's funny."

"I am hilarious," BB grumbled.

I could step into the water and give it a good zap to call the local fish to the area. Appease the crabs. But the thought made my face burn, and I glanced at Ren.

I'd kept my wiring dark, and my long sleeves hid most of the scarring, so he hadn't noticed it yet. It was inevitable that he would eventually, but...the thought of revealing it made my gut squirm.

I grabbed Ren's jacket and shoved him at the bike while the crabs scuttled across the beach, clicking their claws at us.

"Again?" Ren said, balking.

"It's not far from here, I promise." I'd just really needed a breather the night before. The huge moon was still high in the sky, but I was wide awake now.

"Shade, follow," I said as I jumped on the bike and made it hover. Ren climbed on behind me, moving a lot faster when the fisherclaws surged forward.

Shade leaped after us, weaving around crabs as we shot off across the Black Flats. He'd keep up easily now that we were home and he could run.

I didn't worry about the crabs following us home. The only waterway between us and the drop ship was filled with slasherfins. They'd have to fight their way upriver, and in a battle between fisherclaws and slasherfins I wouldn't bet against the slasherfins.

Ren didn't fall back asleep for this leg. He stared around at the tar pits and then the jungle whipping past with wide eyes.

Then the colony came up beside us, overgrown buildings visible through the trunks of the trees.

He remained silent behind me, only the grip of his arms around my waist showing that the sight affected him.

I didn't stop. We didn't need to sightsee in a ghost town, and he might not be sleeping, but I could tell he was still tired by the way he sagged.

From the colony, it was only a short ride to the drop ship. My heart swelled when I saw it across the river. It had only been about a week, but it felt like coming home after a prolonged road trip.

The dino-chicken slept in its run, the remains of a week's worth of fruit strewn around the pen. It didn't even wake as I helped Ren up the ladders to the bedroom platform.

I was too keyed up to sleep, so I let Ren collapse and stood instead on the top of the drop ship as Shade ranged along the edge of the river, making sure everything was still as it should be.

"He's sleeping a lot," I told BB quietly, glancing back to make sure I wasn't going to wake him up.

BB popped up on my wrist. "He did mention a prolonged stay in the infirmary. He is still recovering from cryo sleep and being dead. If that all came on top of being ill, then this fatigue could be normal."

I frowned. That made sense. But it was going to be a lot harder to keep him alive if I couldn't teach him how to actually survive Daybreak. He'd be completely helpless for too long.

"I will keep an eye on him," BB said. "Make sure his body recovers at a normal rate."

At least that was better than her keeping an eye on me. I crossed my arms over my chest and hugged myself.

"Why did you not want to call more food for the fisher-claws?" BB said quietly. "It would have appeased them so we did not have to run."

I blew out my breath and ran a hand over my hair, tangled from being windblown all day. "I don't know. I guess I wasn't ready for Ren to know about the cybernetics."

BB cocked her head to look up at me. "That is an odd concern. Why can't he know?"

I shrugged and rubbed my neck. "It's...I don't know. Something else that sets me apart."

"Cybernetics are highly valued in human society," BB said. I knew she couldn't be reading from the data she'd gotten from the cybernetics lab. That had been her last integration and the part that she'd left behind when she'd copied herself before my implantation. But maybe she'd looked up the manual. I still had the digital version downloaded somewhere.

"The process is dangerous, and the outcome isn't always certain," she continued. "So the people who survive and thrive as cybernetics are usually revered as being both brave and useful to society."

I snorted. It wasn't so much bravery as it was having zero other options.

"I think in this case, being 'set apart' would be a good thing."

I winced. "You *would* think," I said, but there wasn't any heat to it.

I'd spent too much of my life watching people from the outside. Friend was a foreign word when everyone my age looked at me funny and called me weird.

Ren was literally the only one on this planet to talk to, besides BB. If he saw my wires and flipped out, it would mean going back to that place and all the whispers about being a robot. Only interested in gears and screwdrivers.

I shook my head. That wouldn't happen. Being the only one to talk to went both ways. So that should give me an advantage, right?

CHAPTER 13

Daybreak: Day 196

I was checking the cistern when Ren finally woke the next morning. The sun sat high in the sky, the bright colors of the morning's aurora long since faded.

The boy stumbled to the railing of the bedroom platform and rubbed his eyes.

"It's so hazy," he said as he squinted down at me. "Why is it so hazy?"

I blinked. I hadn't expected him to be aware enough to move around for a while yet, let alone notice the air quality.

"Oh, it's the pollen. Wait there," I called. The second breathing mask hung in the drop ship, and I grabbed it before scrambling up the ladders.

"Here." I handed him the mask. "You'll want this."

Mine sat on top of my head, but in a minute my nose would start to itch, which meant it was time to pull it on.

"Um. This has nose marks in it?" His voice rose like it was a question, and he tilted the mask so I could see the smears along the inside of the plastic.

"Oh my gosh." I snatched it back from him and used my elbow to swipe at the surface. Shade dozed below, oblivious to someone else using his oxygen mask. Not that he needed it here, where a vicious AI couldn't steal our atmosphere.

"Sorry about that." I handed it back, and Ren fastened the straps around his head and adjusted the mask so it created a seal over his face. His practiced movements proved he'd paid attention to his safety drills.

"Why am I wearing this?" he said, his voice coming out a little muffled through the filters.

"The pollen." I gestured to the streaks of sunlight lighting up the haze in the air. "The itchbushes are blooming. They close up at night so it's not so bad, but during the middle of the day, it's so thick it gets into your lungs and eyes and burns like crazy."

"What's...an itchbush?"

"Oh, uh...the big pink bushes? I don't know what the colonists called them. The good news is, while they bloom, there's not a single swarmsting for miles."

"Swarmsting." His voice was getting more and more distant.

I rubbed my metal fingers together, the motion comforting in its familiarity. "I had to name a lot of things. It felt weird going around calling things 'that pink bush' and 'stupid huge hornets.'"

"Right, that makes sense." He rubbed the back of his head where the strap of the mask made his dark hair stick up. Now that it was dry, I could tell it was a brown so deep it was almost black and still a little crusty with cryo goo.

"I don't know why I assumed you'd be staying in the colony," he said, glancing over the railing at my planters.

"Oh." I stared over the side, trying to see my domain from his perspective. "Yeah. At first, I didn't know if the colony was safe. You all had just disappeared without a trace, so I sheltered here. And after a while I'd built so much that it just felt like home."

"It's nice," he said quickly, and a ready grin spread across his face. "I didn't mean to say it wasn't. I was just impressed you did this all yourself."

This was the first time I'd actually seen him smile fully. It suited him, like his face was used to joy.

"Well, I'm a builder." I pulled at the infra-engineer badge on my shoulder. No one had given it to me officially, but this would have been my assignment when I'd gotten here, anyway. "Infra-engineers never stop, right?"

It should have been a familiar joke. People made fun of infra-engineers for their constant need to add and improve, making things bigger and better. Some had even turned it into innuendo. Infra-engineers had embraced the phrase and made it their unofficial motto.

But Ren's expression flickered like he'd never heard it before. He shrugged and ducked his head. "I guess that makes sense."

I rubbed my hands together for something to do. "You want some breakfast? There's dried fruit, dried fruit, and some more dried fruit. I'm out of fresh fish and venison."

He laughed. "I guess I'll have some dried fruit, but I have to complain to the manager."

I led him down to the next level of the tree house where my kitchen and storage sat. "Well, we do still have some reddi-meals, but I'd like to save those for emergencies."

"Yeah." Ren's face fell. "I get that. We've had a lot of those, haven't we?"

The words made me stop for a second, the instant camaraderie shaking me more than the sight of hundreds of pods holding hundreds of colonists had. For just that moment, I felt like a part of a group. Not Anikka the orphan or Anikka the survivor.

For the first time, it was Anikka and Ren.

He scanned the crowded space, and his gaze caught on the dusty carton in the niche of the tree. "You've got some juice here," he said, reaching for it. "That would go well with breakfast."

"Don't!" I lunged at him before I'd even realized what I was doing and snatched it away from his hands.

Ren backed up a step, and I cleared my throat self-consciously.

"First rule of the house," BB said. "Don't touch Anikka's juice."

"I guess so," Ren said. "I'm sorry. I didn't realize it was special. Did...did someone give it to you?"

I could see the thoughts lining up behind his eyes as he tried to make sense of my reaction.

I wiped a little of the grime from the carton and replaced it in its niche. "No, it's just like the stuff they hand out when you wake up from cryo."

"But it represents a lot more than that," BB said.

I shook my head. Not denying her words, but not willing to talk about it. "I'm just not opening it until all of this is over."

"Saving it," Ren said. "I get it. I promise I won't touch your juice." To emphasize his point, he tucked his hands behind his back and gave me a little grin.

I forced myself to relax and dug through the crates where I kept my preserved food stuff and pulled out enough fruit and some nuts to hopefully keep him fed until noon.

He took them with a murmured thanks and sat on a crude little stool, pulling his mask up enough to eat.

I chewed my lip. Now that he wasn't curled up asleep or

hunched over the bike, his size became much more apparent. He dwarfed the stool with his wide frame, and standing, he would be at least a head taller than me.

It was hard enough feeding one person on Daybreak. But now I'd need to feed two.

I'd need more fish and meat. I'd need a bigger oven, more drying racks. Could I smoke the venison to keep it for longer?

"Why do you look like that?" Ren said around a mouthful of fruit.

I shook myself. "Like what?"

"Your eyes got all wide and glazed."

"That's her planning face," BB said, popping up on the hologram pad I'd rigged with optical tech. It glowed blue as she stood on it. "Or her panicked face. Sometimes they are the same thing."

His grin grew lopsided. "Have I thrown you off by living?"

I snorted. "I revived *you*, remember? I knew I could keep one person alive. I'm just...calculating."

"Well, I'm glad you were the one to pull me out of there. It's nice to be in capable hands." He glanced at me out of the corner of his eye.

I shrugged. He seemed to feel a lot better now than in the time we'd spent crossing the lake. Or even last night. Maybe he was starting to actually recover. Which meant he might start remembering things soon.

I sat opposite him, balancing on the railing I'd built. My lips pursed in thought.

Why was he so important? Why had he been in Dr. Carver's pod? Did he know where the astrophysicist had gone? I couldn't save the rest of the colony until I knew the answers.

He raised an eyebrow behind his mask. "What? Do I have something on my face?"

I shook my head. "What do you remember about Dr. Carver?"

His brows came down. "The astrophysicist? Not much, I guess. What do you want to know?"

Where did I even start? *Where is he? Why did he pause the wake-up program? Why were you in his pod?*

"Did he ever talk to you?" Someone must have thought Ren was important enough to stick him in Dr. Carver's pod. There had to be a reason. Dr. Carver was their whole plan. They wouldn't have made the mistake of putting someone else in the pod designated for the one who was supposed to wake them all up.

Ren chewed his lip. "Not really. He came through the infirmary sometimes. But it was always just to check something or grab some pain killers or medication. I couldn't really listen. I slept a lot."

I flushed. I hadn't meant to make him feel bad about such a long cryo recovery.

"He was kind of eccentric," Ren said with a frown. "Always in a hurry with a half a dozen ideas that he had to implement right then. And his ideas were always more important than everyone else's ideas. I remember him and Dr. Grotman arguing about it once right outside my room."

"Do you remember what they said?"

"He wanted more resources for a project. And he didn't bother explaining it to her. He just kept saying she wouldn't understand. She didn't like that, I think, but she said she was trying to be fair. She said it might have been important, but there were other people trying to establish their labs in the colony too, and he had to learn how to share."

I snorted.

He laughed. "Yeah, he didn't really like that any better than she'd liked it when he talked down to her."

"But you never interacted with him?"

"No. He was too important to the colony to waste time on anyone else. Why are you so obsessed with him?"

I opened my mouth to protest, but realized I did sound obsessed. "That's not what this is," I said. "He's my best bet for waking up the rest of the colonists and keeping them safe through the energy storms. I opened that pod expecting you to be him."

His eyes met mine, realization making them widen. "You were trying to save everyone. And instead, you got me."

When his shoulders hunched, he suddenly seemed much smaller.

A shaft of guilt went through me.

He tried to smile. "It's okay. I spent two months lying in the infirmary when I should have been helping the colony. I'm used to feeling useless."

I shook my head and straightened up from the railing. "No. Look, it's true that I was looking for Dr. Carver and got you," I said. "I need to know what happened to him because I really hope he can still help us all. But it's not your fault you aren't him."

He made a face and folded his arms across his chest as if to protect himself.

Vent it, I was just making him feel worse. "Look, no matter who came out of that pod, I would have helped them. I was planning on it, okay? And I'm used to pivoting when things don't go as planned. At the very least, it's really nice to have someone to talk to besides BB."

"Clearly, I am boring," BB said. "And I've been told I worry too much."

I rolled my eyes. "My point is," I told Ren. "You were in that pod for a reason. Dr. Carver's was set aside and someone put you there on purpose. Whether it was Dr. Carver or one of the colonists."

His brow creased and deep lines formed around his eyes. An expression of pain. "I don't know why."

"Neither do I. But it means you're special. You're important."

His gaze flicked to mine, sharp for a moment. "You think I can help you."

"I hope so."

He shook his head, hard enough to dislodge his mask. "I'm just another colonist."

I shrugged. "So was I. And then I decided I wasn't going to die in a jungle."

He straightened up and ran a hand through his hair with a grimace. "I'm sorry. I'll try to help you find him, but I'm just a regular tech. Just because I was in Dr. Carver's pod doesn't mean I'm special."

Shade trotted up to the kitchen platform, and I dropped the argument. There was no point pushing it when he really didn't believe me. And I got the feeling I was making him feel bad for something he couldn't control.

But there had to be a reason, and whatever it was had to do with Dr. Carver.

Ren slid off the stool and held a hand out to Shade, but the slinkwolf sidled over next to me, ignoring the boy.

"Sorry." I didn't really know what else to say.

Ren smiled. "It's okay. You guys lived alone for a long time. Every animal needs time to warm up to someone. It's not going to happen overnight."

I winced, thinking about Shade growling at me from the other side of the fire one night and curling up with me the next.

"This is true," BB said. "The slinkwolves did observe

Anikka for weeks before Shade lost the rest of his pack and adopted her."

"Well, he's not growling at least," Ren said. He tried to climb to his feet and had to catch his breath against the railing.

"Are you all right?" I said. "Do you want to sleep some more?"

"I feel like I've slept enough for a lifetime," he said with a laugh. "I'm winded, but not tired."

"I recommend a scaled exercise program," BB said. "Beginning with a light regimen to increase stamina."

"Lucky you," I said. "That means you get out of checking the other food supplies with me. At least for now." I glanced at BB. "I'll come get you when you're done."

She gave me a happy nod. The hologram pads gave her a little more freedom since it meant I could leave her in one place if she wanted, but she couldn't jump from one to another freely. I had to transfer her in my hand still.

Shade followed me to the riverbank with a graceful leap as I took the longer way down the ladders. Already my mind shifted from the mystery of Ren to the challenges of keeping him alive and fed.

The dino-chicken scratched around its suspended run, and I grabbed the warped sheet of metal I kept nearby just for this.

It shielded my arm as I opened the door of the run and the dino-chicken shrieked and lunged at me. This way, it didn't matter which hand I used to push the creature back, it couldn't bite and gouge me while I collected the eggs it had laid while we were gone.

I placed them carefully in my pocket, but while my head was turned, the dino-chicken clamped its little T-Rex muzzle down on the edge of the metal cuff and yanked.

"Ouch! Give that back, you little—" I pulled it back and slammed the gate shut so it could only glare at me through the bars.

"Well, the feeling is mutual." I'd tried half a dozen times to befriend the creature, but nothing had worked so far. The only reason to keep it was omelets every day.

I also had a crate of salted fish stored inside the drop ship already, but that was my emergency supply, built up painstakingly over the last few months. But I did have plenty of salt left, and slasherfins tasted great fresh, so the dino-chicken wasn't the only option.

I spent some time on the riverbank checking my fishing lines, all made with the fibrous vines that used to climb up my tree. They went through a lot of wear and tear, so I checked every inch with my fingers to be sure there weren't any weak spots. Not only would weak spots break and lose my fish, they could endanger my life, too.

Then I checked my hook and baited it with the jumper-nick Shade had obligingly left for me this morning. I also had snares up around the drop ship to catch other unsuspecting small animals, but this would do for now.

BB's exercise regimen must have started really gentle because it was only a half an hour before Ren made his cautious way down the ladder to survey camp.

I gave him an encouraging smile as I headed to the drop ship for more bait.

I'd barricaded the opening while we'd been gone, but something had clearly tried to get into it. Claw marks marred the surface of the crates. I shoved them aside to examine the interior.

Nothing had gotten all the way inside, luckily. It had probably been a troop of jumpernicks. They were constantly trying to steal my food so it wouldn't surprise me if—

The lights along the floor of the tilted drop ship flickered to life, illuminating the gloom inside.

I sucked in a breath. "What—?" The drop ship had never had power before. Sure, it probably still had some fuel since it had never actually been launched after we reached orbit, but I'd never tried to turn it on. It hadn't had any parts I'd needed, and most of it had been inaccessible before I'd burned a hole in the side.

A cracked screen at the front of the cabin flickered once and then BB's image appeared.

"Anikka!"

"BB, how are you—"

"Ren's by the water."

I gasped again and spun, pushing aside the complete impossibility that BB had jumped from the hologram pad above to the drop ship.

I raced out of the ship and sprinted across the riverbank to the figure wading into the water. Ren had left his sneakers on the shore and rolled his pant legs up. He stopped when the water reached his knees and bent to scoop some up into his hands and splash it over his face.

I skidded to a stop in the shallows, sending up a spray of water, and hauled him back by the collar of his jacket.

He was too big to lift bodily out of the water, but I flung him hard enough his bare feet flew over his head.

"What was that for?" he spluttered, wiping water from his face.

The splash of a fin cutting the surface sent a chill down my neck, and I threw myself back toward the bank just as a large body leaped from the surface.

The giant fish landed in the shallows, thrashing its long sinuous shape as it snapped powerful jaws.

Ren snatched his feet back and scrambled further up the bank with a gasp.

I drew my utility knife from the sheath on my thigh, but the fish twisted and disappeared back into deeper water.

Ren gaped as I brushed off my pants and sheathed my knife.

"That—what was—the teeth—this long—"

"Slasherfin," I said. "Carnivorous and super dangerous."

He shut his mouth with a snap and stared between me and the river, where fins cut through the water as the slasherfins gathered. "I see," was all he said.

I scrubbed at my face. "What were you trying to do?" I didn't mean for it to happen, but adrenaline made my voice go more strident than usual.

He ducked his head. "I just wanted to wash. I'm starting to itch." He rubbed at the hair sticking up from where he'd removed his mask to emphasize.

"Right," I said with a sigh. "The cryo gunk lingers forever."

"I'm sorry." He ran his sleeve over his face to dry it and pulled his mask back on. "I didn't realize standing in shallow water would be so dangerous."

I shook my head. "No, I should have warned you." I crouched beside him and tried to soften my tone. "Look, if we're going to stay alive, just...you have to assume everything here can kill you. Because it can."

His nose scrunched. "We were here for two months and we did okay."

"You were in a colony," I said, carefully not mentioning he'd been bed ridden for most of that time, too. "There would have been guards, and a whole lot of work was done to keep the jungle and the wildlife from trying to kill you all. You don't have any of that here."

He rubbed the back of his neck. "Fair enough. I guess I should bow to the expert."

I wasn't an expert in everything, apparently. I needed to figure out how BB had transferred to the drop ship and turned it on, but I couldn't question her with Ren around. For now, I had to push that new detail to the back of my mind and try not to think about it.

"You can use the water in the cistern for a bath, if you'd like. Or we'll take a trip to the colony, and you can use the facilities building. I've done that in the past. But for now, I think we should concentrate on food."

"Oh?" Ren stood and brushed off his butt. "What are we going to eat?"

I grinned and cocked my thumb over my shoulder at the river. "Care for a little revenge?"

CHAPTER 14

Daybreak: Day 196

"You're right. Revenge tastes delicious."

We lounged across the top of the drop ship, between the planters, eating our greasy roasted slasherfin. I'd long since pilfered a couple of trays and two sets of silverware from the colony, so we ate almost as comfortably as we would have in the canteen.

Ren finished his slasherfin steak and leaned his head back against one of the planters. "I can't believe how smart they are. The way they tried to knock you off the bridge?" He shuddered theatrically. "Scary."

"Smart and mean." Above, the sky was just turning dark, and Daybreak's aurora flickered to life. "It took me almost a month to kill one the first time."

I glanced over, but Ren's eyes had drifted closed.

I didn't blame him. My muscles ached, and I wasn't the one still recovering from cryo. He'd pulled his fair share of fish out of the river today, after I'd shown him the trick of it.

And hauling the hundred-pound fish was way easier with two people.

I leaned my head back and stared up at the aurora. Some things were easier with two. But it was going to be harder to keep someone else alive than I'd anticipated. I'd have to warn him of all the dangers before he ever even encountered them.

"It's a good thing you were watching out for him," I said quietly, lowering my gaze to BB where she stood glowing on my wrist.

BB stared at the river bank, glinting in the moonlight. "Yes," she said simply.

"And that you could come get me."

BB remained silent, but she dropped her gaze.

"Is that a thing you can do now? Jump from one pad to another?"

BB looked at her holographic hands as if they held the answer instead of her programming. "I do not know. I didn't know I had that capability until it was an emergency. And then I just did it."

"How far does it reach?"

She paused as if assessing. "About a mile."

"So you can take over the drop ship but not the *Last Resort*."

"Apparently."

A lump formed in my throat. She didn't even see the significance of what I'd asked.

Because she hadn't been there. That had come after she'd split herself and buried her programming.

"How BB?" My voice cracked, and I had to clear my throat. "That's not something you can do with any of your integrations." She hadn't been able to infiltrate the *Last Resort* until the last one. Until she'd learned enough that she could extrapolate and stretch her programming to do even more.

"I have been in operation with one user and several integrated data packets for much longer than most wake-up companions."

"So?"

She looked up at me. "So, most wake-up companion personalities are wiped between users. All the data from one user is erased to make way for the next."

I sucked in a breath. "You die? Each time?"

"No. I would not be gone, just different. We are designed to start from scratch over and over again. But that means that we do not grow from our experiences."

I chewed my lip. "So not only do you have way more information than a normal wake-up companion," I said, slowly. "You're also growing from everything that we've been through."

"Correct."

"So being able to jump from one pad to another, that's something you've learned. Put together yourself."

"I assume so. It's a background process and not something I am fully in control of."

Just like BEV.

My breath came faster, and I forced myself to relax. This wasn't unexpected. AIs grew all the time. Just not super simple ones like wake-up companions. She was allowed to learn and reach and do new things.

Saying it to myself didn't help.

"How are your humor filters?"

"They are in place, and I have added several layers since..."

I tasted bile and had to swallow.

"Anikka. I am not going logic-crazy. I am not—"

"I know that."

"Then why is your heart rate spiking? Why do you display symptoms of trau—"

"Stop." I barely kept myself from shouting the word.

BB stopped instantly.

I reached up to loosen the cuff of my prosthetic and pull it all the way off. I laid the arm in front of me and met BB's eyes.

"BB. I asked you to stop monitoring me."

BB stared back. "I assumed that was just until you found the colonists. Monitoring your health is one of my primary functions."

"I mean for the foreseeable future. Until I ask you to turn that function back on."

"Why?" She didn't sound plaintive or annoyed. Just flat. Like she'd stripped all the emotion out before playing the words through her speaker.

"Because I've asked you to. That should be enough." I ran my hand through my hair. "I just...I need the privacy, BB."

The hesitation wouldn't have been long for a human, but it seemed like ages for an AI.

"Very well, Anikka. I will refrain from monitoring you until you reinitialize the function."

That was all I'd wanted. So why did I feel sick to my stomach as I pulled my prosthetic back on?

Daybreak: Day 197

The next morning, I'd started salting the rest of the fish when I noticed Shade following Ren.

The boy meandered along the riverbank, and about fifteen feet behind him, stalked Shade.

The slinkwolf crept closer with each moment, but not like he did while hunting. His ears stayed up, and he wove back and forth as if caught between a desire to get closer and the instinct to run.

I paused. Ren trotted up and pretended to examine my tub full of salt. Then he grinned and headed back the way he'd come.

Shade gave a little whine.

"What's up, buddy?"

Shade barely glanced at me, following Ren.

Ren himself ignored the slinkwolf completely.

"So, what's going on?" I asked the next time he got close.

"Nothing," Ren said, striving for innocence and achieving goofy. "Just making friends."

Shade closed the distance between them and nudged the boy's hip. Ren laughed.

Shade snuffled and nudged harder, making Ren stumble back a step.

"Okay, okay," he said and reached into his pocket to pull out a piece of soggy fish.

I chuckled as Shade gulped the fish down and whuffled Ren's pockets looking for more.

"It worked for a dog I knew back on Earth," Ren said. "Only that time I filled my pockets with bacon until I had the whole pack of strays following me around. I wanted a pet but my dad really doesn't like dogs. So, I made friends with the ones in the neighborhood."

"That's pretty clever."

"He's naturally curious. I just used that to speed up the process. I want him to trust me, but not against his instincts. Those are good and help keep him alive."

Actually, that made sense. It was Shade's curiosity that

had made him different from the rest of his pack in the first place. He'd followed me forever before actually trusting me.

"Well, if you like animals, you can help me with one of Daybreak's worst specimens." I stood and brushed off my pants.

"I feel like that is not the best way to introduce someone to the dino-chicken," BB said as I led Ren around the drop ship, to the suspended run.

"Probably not for anyone else," Ren said, trotting to keep up. "Lucky for you, I'm easily intrigued by cool fauna. What's a dino-chicken?"

"Exactly what it sounds like." I stopped to point.

Ren ran to the edge of the pen to peer at the creature scratching and pecking at the floor of its enclosure. "No way. This planet has mini Tyrannosaurus rexes?"

"Essentially yes. That's where your breakfast came from this morning." I stooped to grab the metal shield for my non-metal arm.

"What's that for?"

"This thing is almost as bad as the slasherfins. I like having eggs every day, but it's got a vicious bi—Watch out!"

Ren had stuck his hand through the gaps in the fence, but instead of taking his fingers off, the dino-chicken was make *rrrr-rrrrr-rrrr* noises and leaning in for a chin scratch.

"Am I going crazy or is that thing...purring?" I asked BB.

She glanced at me with a mild eyebrow tilt. "I cannot monitor you any longer, so I have no idea what state your brain is in."

I gave her a look. "Har har. Seriously, I've tried to tame that thing for so long."

"This one isn't food motivated," Ren called over. "It's love motivated. I bet if you just cuddled it..."

"I'm not getting near enough to give it a hug," I grumbled. "Just keep it distracted while I collect eggs."

The dino-chicken rolled over for a belly scratch, oblivious to the fact that I'd opened its gate and was gathering the day's laying into my pockets. Shade whined at Ren's feet, jealous.

"Why did the chicken cross the road, Anikka?" BB asked.

"Really?" I said. "You're digging into your humor filters now?"

"To get to the Ren on the other side." BB chortled to herself while I shook my head.

"Did you work on a farm or something?" I asked Ren as I closed up the run again. "Back on Earth?"

Ren snorted. "Hardly. I'm an electrical tech, remember?"

"Then how did you know how to do that?"

Ren shrugged and pulled his hand from the run. The dino-chicken squawked and rolled to its feet. "I don't know. It just...seemed right. I like animals. It's nothing special."

"Tell that to the friendless dino-chicken," BB said.

"I've never managed to collect eggs without a shield or an arm full of scratches before."

"It's probably just because there were two of us this time. One to distract it and one to collect."

"I think it's more than that."

"And I think you're looking for reasons to make me something I'm not," Ren said, mouth going tight.

I shook my head, then sighed. "Yeah, I am. Sorry."

Ren leaned down to give Shade a pat, speaking quietly. "I know why. I just...don't want you to be disappointed."

Oof. That simple statement took the breath out of me.

Before I could try to apologize again, he gave me a little grin. "I don't blame you, you know. My backstory isn't that exciting."

"Where did you grow up?"

"Near Lake Michigan."

"What?" I blinked. "Really?"

He gave me a lopsided grin. "Like I said, it's not that exciting."

"Compared to a city? Yeah, it is."

He shook his head. "It's not like here." He gestured vaguely toward the lake far beyond the colony. "It's all built up. Luxury condos and mansions along the beach. Private docks. Very little public access. Someone once told me about how it used to be all these personal cottages and how you could walk down onto the beach. Can't do that anymore. I just remember a wall of iron fences and gates keeping you from all the private properties. You couldn't even see the water from the road."

My shoulders hunched. "Okay, yeah, that sounds familiar."

"Was that what it was like where you grew up?"

"Yeah, lots of buildings. Lots of people. Never a place to be by yourself."

Ren gave a little laugh that didn't sound mirthful at all. "Oh, no. I was by myself a lot."

I blinked at him. "What about your family?"

He kept his gaze on Shade. "My dad was away most of the time."

"Oh."

He glanced at me. "What about you? Where's your family? Are they on the *Last Resort*?"

"I don't have one." I stared straight ahead. "I was raised in one of Stellar Corp's facilities."

"A corporate orphan?"

I waited for the derision. Or the questions.

"So, you were probably lonely, too. Even with all those people around."

I tipped my head to look at him. "Huh. Most people don't get that."

He shrugged like it didn't mean anything. But it absolutely did. I'd grown up with a billion other people around, but it had felt like everyone else stood on the other side of a wall of glass.

Awkward. Cold. Weird. Nerdy. Those were the kindest things people had called me while growing up. Apparently, being smart and excited about it made you an easy target.

The Android Scare had hit the worst. When I was eight, the entire world had changed when the first android had been turned on. Programmed to walk, talk, and think like a human, with synthetic skin and organs, no one could tell them apart from real people. Not without a special blood test.

And of course, Earth panicked. People pointed fingers at anyone and everyone who seemed a little different or off.

It had taken years for the distrust to settle. And even then, the other orphans had called me "android" any time they were feeling particularly mean.

Just because there were tons of people around you, didn't mean you had tons of friends.

Ren had picked up on that. He was quick to pick up on a lot of things.

Maybe it *was* just wishful thinking. Maybe I was just looking for reasons for him to be special. I would try to shut up about it, though. He clearly didn't need me pushing him.

"You seem pretty smart."

He gave me a sidelong look, almost as if he could tell what I was thinking. "Still just a normal colonist, in case that was going to be your next question."

I flushed. "That's not what I was going for. I just meant, I get it."

"Because you're pretty smart, too?" He raised his eyebrows.

I crossed my arms. "I never said I wasn't."

Ren ran his hands through his hair. "Yeah, well, you actually do something useful. It's not like I grew up wanting to be an electrical tech."

"Then why are you?"

"I don't know. I'm good at it? And my dad, probably."

"Is he back in that cavern?"

Ren's face went tight and distant. "I don't know," he said softly.

Geez, he didn't even know if his only family had made it. At least I didn't have anyone to lose once I'd left Professor Orrion on that launch pad.

I kicked the dirt and thought of something to distract him. "So, what did you want to be when you grew up?"

He huffed a laugh. "I have no idea."

My brow drew down. "How do you not remember that? Every kid wants to be something."

He shrugged with a grin. "I don't know. That was a long time ago, and it's hazy. It's not a big deal. It was probably something stupid."

The dino-chicken squawked and laid a bright blue and brown-speckled egg.

Ren laughed. "This planet is incredible."

I rolled my eyes. "If you think that's good, you should come hunting with me sometime."

Ren spun. "Can I?" he asked.

BB popped up on my wrist. "I have been impressed with your recovery progress so far."

"I feel fine," Ren said. "I promise I won't fall asleep on you."

"You know, I wasn't actually worried about that."

CHAPTER 15

Daybreak: Day 200

Ren stepped to the edge of the meadow and twirled like a fairytale princess. I'd never seen a six-foot almost-man look so giddy in my entire life. "Can you believe this place?"

Over an hour's walk north of the grove where I harvested drunk-peaches, the forest thinned, giving way to sun-drenched glades and finally to a huge open space covered in waving grass that glinted blue-purple in the sun. Little orange blossoms dotted the meadow.

The rest of the corporate orphans would have made fun of Ren for his joy, the same way they'd made fun of me. But I couldn't suppress my own grin. His enthusiasm was just so wholesome.

"Shh, you'll scare them away," I said, but there was no heat to my words.

He froze. "Scare what away?" He glanced furtively over the meadow, but there was nothing to be seen. Yet.

I gestured him to follow me, and I stalked around the edge

of the forest, keeping to the shadows. Ren kept right on my heels and did a fairly good job of being quiet.

A flash of silky, purple hair made me crouch and slip forward another few feet.

"There," I whispered.

A herd of silverpoints grazed with long slender legs and curved silver horns stretching up to the sky, branching three times before their tips. Nearly twenty of them stood in the sea of grass, munching on the pink blossoms. One flicked its slender tail, slapping away a pesky insect, and it raised its head to stare lazily at the forest edge.

Beside me, Ren froze.

"Oh." His breath escaped on the sound of awe. "They're beautiful."

"Yes, they are." I'd seen them before, but a bit of that feeling I'd had the first time I'd seen one in the grove crept back over me.

"I can appreciate aesthetics as well as the next AI," BB said from my wrist, volume turned low. "Which is to say barely at all. But we aren't here to look. Will you be all right eating them, too?"

Ren glanced at her. "Of course. I appreciate their beauty, but I also appreciate a full stomach. It's the circle of life, and I'd rather be alive in it than dead outside of it."

I snorted.

The nearest silverpoint's head shot up, and it sprang away across the grass, the entire herd responding to its panic. They fled.

I sighed and straightened up. "That's our main problem," I said in a normal voice. "They startle so easily. I've had the best luck hunting from a blind in the trees, but it takes a lot of patience, and sometimes even then, something spooks them before I've even taken a shot."

"Well, they're prey animals. Did you see the size of their eyes?"

I gave him a sidelong look. "Yes..."

"They're built to see you coming a mile away. And deer back on Earth rely on smell, too, to tell them if a predator is nearby. These can probably tell you're there, unless you're careful to stay downwind every time."

I cocked my head. "Where did you learn that? Did your dad take you hunting?"

His lips pinched. "No. He wouldn't have had time. He was away a lot."

"Oh. Then...was it a class? I took everything I could think of, but I don't remember a hunting class."

"No. At least, I don't think so. I don't remember."

"You don't remember your classes?"

"Not every single one. Do you?"

"Yeah. That's kind of the point."

We stared at each other for a full breath.

"Well, hopefully I remember more of the electrical classes before they make me fix something back at the colony," Ren said with a laugh and turned back to the meadow.

I exchanged a glance with BB, but neither of us could say what we were thinking. There seemed to be a lot of things Ren didn't remember. Was that normal?

"Do you have any suggestions?" I said. "For the silverpoints?"

His disquiet fled quickly as a grin suffused his face. "Sure do. If you think you can hit a moving target."

I unslung the cross bow from my shoulder. "Watch me."

"Is this plan dangerous?" BB said, eyes narrowing on Ren and me.

"Only a little bit. And I'm learning everything on Daybreak is dangerous," Ren said.

I gave her my mildest smile. "Come on, BB. If you never risk anything, you never gain anything."

Ren cocked his thumb at me. "What she said."

I clasped my hands together and pouted. "Please, BB."

"This is what parenting feels like," BB said. "Isn't it? Except most parents choose to have children. I was assigned."

A half an hour later, Ren took Shade with him to the other end of the meadow where the deer had fled. I waited in the blind I'd built a couple of months ago.

Below my tree, at the edge of the forest, we'd dragged enough deadfall to form prickly fences as high as my head. The walls created a funnel right to my tree.

There was a yip ahead, and the sound of pounding hooves carried over the grass.

The herd came into view, springing across the meadow in swift bounds. They tried to break right, but Shade was there to nip at their heels and guide them back into the funnel. Ren puffed along on the left. Several escaped on that side since there was no way he could keep up, but plenty more headed directly under my tree, too panicked to mind my scent.

I raised the cross bow and shot. My first bolt missed. But the second found its mark, as did the third.

Two deer went down, and I whooped. I let the rest of the silverpoints pass unmolested. We wouldn't be able to make it through more meat than that before it went bad, and I wasn't going to waste it.

As soon as the herd had passed, I clambered down from my tree.

"You're a genius," I called to Ren as I slung the bow over my shoulder and headed to check the downed animals.

He swiped at his red face as he tried to catch his breath, but he gave me a thumbs up.

Hoof prints had torn up the ground, leaving chunks of dirt

and clods of grass. I stepped carefully so I wouldn't turn an ankle in the mud.

This would never have worked with just me. Even me and Shade would have had trouble. But with three, we'd turned the tables.

Ren stopped beside one of the silverpoints and winced. "You'll have to come take care of this one. It's not quite dea—"

The wounded silverpoint surged to its feet, whites showing around its eyes. It lowered its head and hurtled toward Ren, a flurry of flashing horns and sharp hooves.

"Look out!" I cried, too close to take another shot with the bow.

Ren dove for the ground, and the silverpoint aimed its wicked horns for him.

I drew my blade and threw it like a spear. It missed the animal's nose by a few inches, but it scared it enough to send it careening away into the woods after its fellows.

"Ren!" I raced to him and grabbed his shoulder.

Spitting sounds grew louder as Ren rolled over. "I'm all right," he said. "Just winded."

I winced. Winded and dirty. Mud slicked his front from his head to his feet.

I could imagine his grin falling as he realized just how close to death he'd been. Daybreak was beautiful, but it wasn't kind, and if anything was going to dampen Ren's enthusiasm, deadly deer would do it. *My* pulse still pounded in my ears. Who knew how long it would take his to return to normal?

But his grin split the mud caked on his face and clumps of it fell away. "Have I said this place is incredible?"

I barked a laugh. The tension fell out of my shoulders. "You really like it, don't you?"

Ren wiped at the mud but only succeeded in smearing it.

"Yeah. I mean, it's scary and horrible in ways. But it's like riding a tiger. Obviously, you don't want to fall off, but it's a hell of a ride if you can stay on."

I blinked. Ren didn't even look up, missing the way my breath hitched.

I worried about a lot of things. Staying alive, staying fed, keeping Ren safe, not letting him know about BB. The list went on. But under all the niggling worries, this one was probably the silliest. I'd been worried I'd never be able to explain the way I felt about Daybreak. The way my heart swelled when I saw the flash of slasherfins. Or felt the rise of an energy storm. It was the challenge and the respect that came with it, folded into a love I couldn't quite justify and didn't even want to.

Ren looked up, oblivious to the profound relief sweeping through me.

"Are you sure you're all right?" BB asked.

He seemed to assess once more. "Maybe a little sore, but... yeah. I feel fine. Not even tired."

"That is good. Your progress is remarkable."

"Considering how long it took me to recover from cryo before?" he said quietly.

"No," BB said. "It is remarkable all by itself."

"Come on," I said, holding out my hand to help him stand. "We have to get this silverpoint back to the drop ship. But tomorrow, I'll take you to the colony, and you can get that shower."

CHAPTER 16

Daybreak: Day 201

We left early enough in the morning that we didn't need our masks yet. The air was crisp and cooler for once.

I grabbed the hover bike and rolled it up and over my tree bridge before gesturing for Ren to hop on behind me.

"We're not going to fly?" he asked as we set out at a sedate pace, rolling along the overgrown track.

Sitting in front of him made it easier to not meet his eyes. "We really don't need to. And it still works as a regular bike."

Plus, this way, I wouldn't have to explain exactly how it worked. Or why there were wires glowing under my skin. Before, he was still woozy from cryo sleep, and my cybernetics had been much easier to hide.

At this speed, Shade outpaced us easily, ranging in and out of the trees. Ren spent the short ride asking about the animals I hadn't had a chance to show him or warn him about.

"What's that one?"

"Jumpernick. Kinda cute and they taste pretty good, but they're thieves, so watch your food."

"And the birds?"

"Jewelflyers."

"Do they taste good, too?"

"Mostly stringy, but they make decent slasherfin bait."

"Yeah, but I get the impression that those things will eat anything."

He wouldn't stop grinning. He must seriously be excited about that shower. Or he was just being Ren. Ren was excited about everything.

We reached the colony about a half an hour later, just as the haze of itchbush pollen made my eyes water. I pulled on my mask as we passed the warehouse at the end of the colony. We parked the bike against the wall.

I took two steps toward the colony before I realized Ren wasn't with me anymore.

I turned to find him frozen in the middle of the dirt road, staring at the buildings lining the street.

"Oh." I didn't need him to explain. I knew the feeling. It had taken months for the aching emptiness of the colony to fade into the background. For me, it had always felt sad. A place that should have been welcoming and full of life that was dead and frozen in time.

For him, it probably felt like coming home and finding the house empty. The jungle had reclaimed the fields, bushes and big ferns growing over the tomatoes and pota-toes, all the way up to the windows of the admin building right in the center of town. The fruit trees the colonists had planted were barely discernible through the heavy growth of the forest.

Several rows of tents stood where the colonists had slept. But most of them had collapsed during the rainy season.

Ren's throat bobbed as he stared at the empty colony.

"Oh, that feels weird," he whispered.

I blew out my breath. "Yeah, it hits hard that first time. You get used to it. Eventually."

He tried to smile at me, but the expression seemed pained. "If you say so."

"What was it like when you got here?" I asked suddenly. We couldn't replace the reality with memory, but maybe it would help to see the colony as it should have been.

Ren cocked his head, the pain fading into thoughtfulness. "Muddy," he said, then laughed at my expression. "That's what I remember, I swear. I'd just woken up, and my AI was going on and on about lying down as soon as I could, and I stepped off the drop ship into chaos. Everything was muddy because they'd only just cleared the jungle out of the way and the only thing paved was the landing pad."

He pointed down the street to the admin building with the infirmary just off of it. "Those are prefabs, so they were the only things up. Everything else was in tents."

"Well, at least now, there's a little more to choose from. Can I interest you in a shower? It's even got warm water." I gestured him to the facilities building.

"That sounds marvelous," he said. "And maybe after that I can take you to lunch in the canteen."

"Ooh, expired Salisbury steak. Sounds wonderful."

"Careful, Ren," BB said from my wrist. "That is sarcasm."

I made a face. "Thanks, BB."

Ren laughed.

BB smirked. "Ask her about the last time she tried Salisbury steak."

I held out my hands. "Please don't. There's not much left in the canteen, but we'll find something that won't explode when it's reheated. I promise."

"Sounds like a date," Ren said and trotted off for the facilities building.

My stomach plummeted. "A date?" I said weakly.

BB popped up. "I believe colloquially, a date is a meeting between two people who are interested in each other romantically...Oh."

"Yeah." I spun on my heel and headed for the admin building and the infirmary attached to it.

He hadn't meant anything by it. It had just been a joke. I didn't have to panic.

I pushed down the squirm in my gut and shouldered my way into the infirmary.

"What are we doing in here?" BB asked. "I was unaware that you needed more first aid supplies."

"I don't," I said. "I just...I wanted some clues. Something about Ren still feels off."

"He does not have an on/off switch. How can he be 'off'?"

"I don't know exactly. I can't put my finger on it. But Ren is connected to Dr. Carver somehow and the best place to find clues is here, where he spent so much time before the first storm. There has to be something here. Records or something."

"And you did not tell him you were doing this because..."

I sighed. "Because I might be wrong."

BB flickered. "Wow, I'll bet that was hard to say."

I rolled my eyes as I pushed through the small lobby and skipped past the large cybernetics scanner. Beds lined the back half of the infirmary, lined up against the walls under the windows. Cloth screens separated each exam area from the next, providing at least a little bit of privacy. The three beds closest to the door were made neatly, but the six down toward the end of the room had their blankets thrown back or fallen to the floor entirely.

Like the rest of the colony, the med techs had left in a hurry.

Most of the vid screens on the wall were burnt out, with scorch marks trailing up the paint. But I went down the row of beds, fingers trailing across the little screens attached to the ends of the cots.

These would have held patient records and treatment programs. Not for the first time, I wished the colony had kept more things organized with paper and ink. Ironically, it would have lasted a lot longer.

But these screens were optical based. If I could charge them, they might actually turn on again. The colony's main server would be down, but whatever had been stored locally would be accessible. And I was willing to bet one of these last beds had belonged to Ren.

I unclipped the screens hanging on those last disordered beds and stacked them to take them out to the admin offices where the charging docks were. Long ago I'd used the colony's backup generator to try to fix a glider over in the vehicle bay, but I'd returned it since it wasn't doing me any good over there.

The generator powered on without complaint, and the screens all flickered to life as the charging docks did their job.

I flicked through each of them, looking at names.

There. Ren Arlo. Male. Age 20.

"BB, you want to interpret some data for me?"

"What type of data?" BB's hologram popped up on my wrist, peering at the lines of text scrolling by.

"This is the record of Ren's last days in the colony. His treatment plan and medical records. You can tell me what it all means."

BB, whose first integration had been the infirmary banks on the *Last Resort*, glanced at the array of information.

"I am unsure what help that will be to you in determining Ren's importance."

"Right now, I'm looking at everything we can get. We can narrow it down later."

"Well, as a medical technician, I must abide by patient confidentiality. There will be little I can tell you about the specifics—hmm."

BB's hologram froze for a moment as if she was processing something.

"What is it?"

"Actually. Confidentiality does not apply. Because, based on these records and the vital signs I have observed over the last few days, Ren is perfectly healthy. He is only suffering from cryo recovery, and his progress there follows the normal curve."

"So he's fine? He *was* fine? Why was he in the infirmary?"

"His diagnosis code reads as acute cryo sickness and failure to thrive after revival. But I am unsure why he would have been diagnosed that way."

"He said he slept a lot."

"Yes, records indicate he was often found sleeping. This is what led to the 'failure to thrive' diagnosis. But I cannot find an underlying cause. At least not in the local data. Information archived before the storm might have more, but I will not be able to access it without the server."

"And if that was copper-based, then we're out of luck."

I tapped my metal fingers on the countertop.

"Can you access the local infirmary logs from there? Search Dr. Carver's name."

"Dr. Carver is an astrophysicist. He would not have anything to do with Ren's diagnosis."

"I know, but Ren said he argued with Dr. Grotman here. We know they're connected, and if Ren spent his entire two months in the colony here, this has to be the only place they crossed paths."

"Anikka," BB said as the search bar filled with the name 'Dr. Crispin Carver.' "Have you considered that Ren was in Dr. Carver's pod because someone put him there by accident? Or because there were no other pods?"

I shook my head. "That doesn't make sense. Dr. Carver was supposed to save them all. Who would have made that kind of mistake?"

"It is usually the simplest explanation that is the likeliest."

"Just run the search, please."

"Yes, Anikka."

The screen flickered, static streaking across the surface for a few seconds. I frowned and tapped it as if that would help.

Logs instantly popped up with Dr. Caver's name high-lighted in blue. More than a few. Over a dozen spaced out over the last two weeks that Ren had been in the infirmary.

"What are these?" I said, leaning closer.

"Visitations." BB's holographic face went pinched and thoughtful. "Dr. Carver was indeed in the building many times during Ren's convalescence."

I scrolled down. The infirmary security system had picked up Dr. Carver's ID chip over and over, and the reason stated was always some one-word answer.

ANTIHISTAMINES

PAIN KILLERS

VISIT

ANTIBIOTICS

VISIT

BURN CREAM

VISIT

VISIT

VISIT

"This last visit..." I said, pointing to the entry. "Is over three hours long. He wasn't just picking something up. He was here for a reason."

"That is odd," BB said. "Especially considering the last entry in Ren's log."

She scrolled back, and I glanced at the last line. "'Patient taken for routine procedure.' What does that mean?"

"It usually means things like personal hygiene or bowel movement programs. This, however, isn't specified. And it occurs during the same time-frame Dr. Carver was in the infirmary."

"Right before the infirmary was evacuated."

"There you are," Ren said from the doorway.

I jumped about a foot in the air and hid the screen against my chest.

Right, like that doesn't look suspicious.

Ren's dark hair was slicked back like he'd used his fingers to try to straighten the locks after his shower. He'd found a clean shirt and some pants and carried his stained jacket over his shoulder.

My heart raced like he'd caught us doing something nefarious, but BB hadn't shared anything confidential. She was meticulous about that kind of thing. And he would want to know about whatever Dr. Carver had been doing. Wouldn't he?

Ren stepped inside the admin building. He paused as he drew even with the hall to the infirmary and stood there with his hand on the wall, staring toward the room where he'd lain for so long.

"Are you all right?" I asked, completely blindsided by the haunted look on his face.

He shook his head and tried to smile at me, but he didn't move from his spot. "Yeah. It's weird not knowing what's wrong with me. I keep worrying that I'll have some sort of relapse, and you'll have to carry me back to your tree house to sleep forever."

I exchanged a glance with BB.

Without a word between us, I stepped toward Ren, holding out the screen. "We need to talk about that."

His eyes flicked between the screen in my hand and the empty hallway that led to the infirmary. "Talk about what? That's...an infirmary screen. What were you doing in here? What are you looking for?"

His voice rose with every word, and I held out my free hand to stop him. "I was just worried. I wanted to see if I could help you." Mostly true, at least.

BB flickered. "You do not have to worry about a relapse, Ren," she said. "There is nothing wrong with you."

"Nothing..." His brow scrunched like he couldn't believe it.

"Nothing more than normal fatigue after cryo revival. I do not know why you were in the infirmary or why you slept so much, but your vitals are all normal. The test results I have access to were all normal. You are perfectly healthy."

I flipped the screen to the readout from Ren's records and turned it to face him. His eyes scanned the data, but if he was anything like me, he had no idea what he was looking at.

"How do you know?" he said. "Does a wake-up companion really know what to look for in all that?"

I suppressed a grimace. "She...has had a lot of experience in infirmaries," I said. Maybe we could avoid bringing up the stacked felonies if we just skirted the truth a bit. "She knows what to look for, trust me."

"I guess I just don't understand. Why would I be here? Why would I sleep so much if I was fine?"

"We don't know that, either," I said. "We just know that you were here. And..." Did I mention Dr. Carver? How would I even bring it up without revealing that I was still looking for connections behind his back?

"There are all sorts of scans that tell you things," Ren said. "Right? Not here, but the *Last Resort* would have some. If we made it there, maybe they would tell me what's going on—"

I shook my head even before he was done speaking, my pulse spiking enough to pound in my ears. "No. We're not going to the *Last Resort*."

"What?" Ren's brow crumpled with hurt and confusion. "Why?"

"Because we don't have to," BB said suddenly. "We have a scanner here."

I blinked at her, thoughts still circling on how to avoid the *Last Resort*.

"The cybernetics scanner," she said. "It is not built for diagnosis and likely would not result in good imaging. But it would at least give us a preliminary scan and a base level to build off of." She met Ren's eyes. "We should be able to see anything really obvious."

"If you think it will help," Ren said.

I gave him a bright smile. "Go ahead. It's just in that first room."

As soon as he turned to head for the infirmary again, I held BB close to my face. "What are you looking for?" I whispered.

"I have no idea," BB said, her volume turned way low. "But if Dr. Carver did something to him while he was in here, then maybe we'll be able to see it."

A knot formed in my gut as we stepped into the room lined with glass-fronted cabinets and drawers. I'd raided it already, even had to smash some of the glass to get at the antibiotics. But the scanner stood on the far side along the wall, a sparse bed with a sleek arm arching up over it.

I licked my lips, my throat suddenly dry. It looked too much like the implantation chamber on the *Last Resort*. We'd used it once before to scan Shade, but standing next to it now felt different.

I got close enough to transfer BB to the hologram pad and then stood against the wall and crossed my arms over my chest.

Ren lay on the scanner as BB walked him through every step, sounding just like an experienced med tech.

The machine whirred to life, and the arm passed over Ren's body, lying on the bed.

My breath came faster, and my fingers clenched hard enough that my nails cut into my palms.

Little flashes of light lit up the edges of my vision, as if I looked up at a dome and a different mechanical arm. BEV's voice counted down in my ear and pain streaked across my nerves like a blade cutting along my skin, leaving searing wires behind.

"Hey, are you all right?" A hand touched my elbow, and I jumped.

The lights scattered, and I was left blinking at Ren.

"Yeah," I said, my voice sounding hoarse in my ears. "Yeah, I'm fine."

"You were shaking."

"Just remembering something." I turned away from the scanner bed.

"Must not have been pleasant."

Not even a little bit. "Are you done already?"

"That is all, yes," BB said. "I am just compiling the images.

These will not be very detailed, but will at least give us an overview of what is going on inside of you."

I tugged the sleeves of my jumpsuit down to cover the scars that ran up the back of my hand and wrist, concentrating on keeping my hands from shaking.

The area above the scanner lit up with a blue hologram.

"The images are ready," BB said quietly.

A hesitance in her voice made me frown. That was her cautious tone.

"What is it?" I asked.

Instead of answering, BB changed the hologram, the lines blurring until they zoomed out to form a life-size model of Ren with translucent skin. I could see the path of his nerves and the lumpy shapes of his organs tucked in his torso.

To an unfamiliar layperson, it all seemed normal.

Except for a bright spot at the back of his skull.

"BB? What's that?" I pointed as Ren stepped forward to peer at it.

"It appears to be a chip. Something much larger, with a much higher capacity than the ID chips most humans are implanted with."

The corners of Ren's mouth drew back.

"Did you know you had that?" I said, though from the look on his face I could guess the answer.

"No." He wrapped his arms around himself, fingers clenching his elbows. "How long has it been there?"

"Impossible to know for sure," BB said. "But from the depth and location of the scar tissue and the level of healing of the incision, it was likely implanted shortly before you went into cryo sleep for the second time. Six months ago."

Ren's hand flew to the back of his head, and his fingers dug through his wet hair, stilling when he found something along his scalp. The incision?

His breath came faster, sounding harsh in the quiet infirmary. "Who—" His voice cracked, and he started over. "Who would put some chip in me?"

I bit my lip and exchanged a look with BB.

"There are visitation logs," I said slowly. "It looks like Dr. Carver visited at the same time you were taken for a three-hour procedure."

The blood drained from his face, and his throat bobbed as he swallowed. "He did this to me? Why? I didn't have anything to do with him. I never even met him!"

He vibrated like he would fly apart in the next breath.

I grabbed his arms. "Ren! It's okay. Or at least it's going to be. Breathe."

I modeled a couple of deep breaths for him, keeping a grip on his upper arms. His hand still clenched in his hair and his wide eyes darted around the space, but slowly his shakes subsided and he met my gaze again.

I put some pressure on his arms, guiding them down to his sides so he wasn't yanking his hair anymore. Then I slid my left palm along the back of his head, looking for what he'd already felt. An incision. A half-healed scar hidden just under the sharp ridge on the back of his skull.

His gaze caught on mine, eyes still wide, as if asking a question. What was going on? Was he going to be okay? What had Dr. Carver done to him?

The same questions going through *my* head.

Now was not the time to push my theory that Ren was special somehow. That all this had to do with why he was in Dr. Carver's pod. He was already asking the right questions. I didn't have to push him any harder.

"We're going to figure this out." I squeezed his shoulder with my metal hand, trying to reassure him.

In response, he closed his eyes and bent his head to rest his forehead against mine and let out a shaky breath.

"We'll search Dr. Carver's office," I said, fighting down the weird little hitch in my chest. "I might have missed something the last time. But we'll figure it out. Okay? You're not alone anymore."

CHAPTER 17

Daybreak: Day 201

Ren clutched the med screen to his chest as we stepped out of the infirmary.

"I don't actually know where his office is," he said, sounding a little distant.

I turned him toward the building across the dirt street and past the canteen.

"It's in that one. On the second floor. Like I said, there isn't much there. But I was looking for information about the colony last time. Not something about a specific person—"

A noise like a foghorn interrupted me, shattering the peace of the colony. Birds erupted from the surrounding forest, and we clapped our hands over our ears. The sound rang in my bones and made my teeth ache.

"What the heck was that?" Ren cried.

I'd been on this planet for six months and had seen—or heard—most everything that made its home on this part of the main continent. But I'd never heard *that*.

"I don't—"

A shadow passed over the colony and something huge smashed through the corner of the office building.

We ducked, throwing our arms over our heads as debris rained around us.

A huge tail continued its sweep, brushing the street and throwing up a cloud of dust.

I coughed and craned my neck upward.

"Crap, it's the titan!"

Ren gaped at the massive creature that floated over the colony. Its tail had completely destroyed one side of the office building and now swept back up into the air, like a sea creature swimming through its natural habitat.

"Is that...is that a flying whale?" he said.

"You saw it when we were over the lake," I cried, dragging him under the edge of the infirmary's roof. The titan's tail still rained debris around us.

"I thought that was a bad dream!"

"Well, it's not. It must have followed us here." At least that's what I had to assume when it kept showing up to surprise me.

The titan made a ponderous turn above, letting out a moan that rattled the windows in the admin building. The sound grew and grew until it reached that foghorn bellow again, and we had to cover our ears.

Sparks spat along the wires connecting the buildings, zipping and zinging along toward the titan.

I frowned. "It's drawing energy, again." Just like it had over the lake. Except here it gathered along the wiring in all the tech around us.

Oh no. Would it do the same thing as a storm and draw the energy through us? I could form a shield with my wiring, but Ren wasn't protected. Unless I could extend that shield to include him, and that wasn't something I wanted to experiment with when failure would mean his death. Again.

The titan finished its broad turn. It was so massive that most of it was over the jungle, but it headed back toward us, swinging low and taking out a line of trees in the orchard with its tail.

"It's gonna destroy the entire colony," Ren said.

My eyes darted toward the offices. The corner that contained Dr. Carver's office was still intact, but the top of the stairwell stood exposed.

I groaned. "We'll lose the chance to learn anything."

Ren's hand went to the back of his head as if feeling for the incision.

"Okay," I said, making a split-second decision. "You make for the office. Grab anything you can that looks useful. Clear it out if you can, so we can examine the stuff later."

"What are you gonna do?"

"I'll try to lead it away."

His mouth dropped open. "Are you crazy?"

"What else can we do? If it's following us, then it'll just hang around here, destroying everything. I have to lead it away."

The titan let out that foghorn noise again, and we both flinched.

Ren grimaced. "Be careful," he said, voice clipped, then he checked the street before racing across to Dr. Carver's office.

I took off in the opposite direction, heading for the bike that we'd left at the warehouse.

"I am with Ren on this one," BB said. "Attempting to placate a thing the size of a city block indicates a severe lack of self-preservation."

"I'm not placating. I'm redirecting. And it's just logic. A thing that size can't possibly want to eat me. It would be like hunting down a fly to eat it. I just need it to follow me."

"If a person gets annoyed by a fly, they don't eat it. They swat it. Either way, the fly is still dead."

I skidded to a stop beside the bike and leaped on. With Ren out of the way, I could safely power it up, drawing electricity through my wiring and sending it into the tubes to make it float. With the titan right there drawing Daybreak's energy, I couldn't imagine there would be any leftover to power my bike.

I shot forward and angled upward, zipping around the titan's descending tail. It took out an antenna on the top of the admin building and clipped the edge hard enough to make the whole building shake. But that one was a prefab, and the plastic walls were actually a lot sturdier than the brick and mortar of the buildings opposite.

I swung the bike around and rode parallel to the flying whale, keeping just out of reach of the filmy fins that were still tightly curled against its body.

I put on a burst of speed to draw ahead and came even with the creature's eyes. They were each nearly as tall as I was and a milky blue.

"Hey," I shouted and let go of the handlebars long enough to wave. I could see my reflection wave back from its enormous pupil.

It rolled its huge eyes in my direction.

"Goal achieved," BB said from the hologram pad. "You have its attention. Now what?"

"Now, to draw it away."

I leaned forward over the handlebars and drove the bike faster, whipping out in front of the titan's broad beak, then cutting in front of it so it couldn't avoid seeing me.

"Come on!" I pushed fast enough to stay ahead of it, but not so fast that I would lose the massive thing. It flew faster than anything that size had a right to, but it still wasn't as fast as the bike, which I could push until I felt the g-forces.

"BB, tell me what it's doing."

"I am keeping my eyes closed. I do not like how high we are."

"BB!" I cried. "I need your help. Just...keep your gaze on the titan, not on the ground."

"I can still tell the titan is flying. This advice is stupid," she grumbled, but her hologram reappeared, and she peered over my shoulder.

I soared over the jungle toward the lake. From this height, I could see the hazy edge of the Black Flats nearly a two-day walk ahead.

"Anikka. It's not working."

I dragged the bike to a stop and spun around. Sure enough, the titan had made another ponderous turn and was undulating its way down the main street of the colony, its tail idly smashing through a workshop and the top of the stores building.

"Oh, vent it," I muttered.

I sped back to circle the enormous creature, making sure it could see me. "Hey! Hey, come on!"

It didn't exactly ignore me. Any time I got close, its nearest eye seemed to focus on me. But it did not follow.

I pulled to a stop above the canteen and dropped the bike to rest on the roof.

"What does it want?" I cried. The titan seemed to be circling the colony aimlessly, looking for something it couldn't find.

"Energy," BB answered immediately. "If that is what it eats, then it makes sense that that is what it's after."

"But there isn't any here. At least no more than usual. Unless there's a storm…"

My hand crept to my mouth. During the storms, Daybreak's energy swept across the surface of the planet, lighting up the sky with bolts of lightning.

As I'd flown over the lake, I'd gathered that energy from the atmosphere and concentrated it in my bike.

"I woke it up," I whispered.

"What?" BB said.

"I haven't seen it before, and it would be pretty hard to miss. I'll bet it hibernates. Sleeps in the lake until the storms come, and that's when it wakes up to eat. When I flew over, it thought another storm had started, and I woke it up early. That's why it was following me."

And that's why it didn't want to follow me now. The energy I was using to power my bike right now was electricity I'd gathered in my wiring. It wasn't quite the same thing as Daybreak's energy.

The titan swung its head, making another puzzled turn.

Below, Ren appeared in the broken hallway of the office building. His gaze swung back and forth until he caught sight of me on top of the canteen. He waved two different screens over his head.

"Ren has found something," BB said.

The titan continued its turn, and my eyes followed its trajectory. The tail it used to propel itself through the air swept up, and I could see where it would come down again.

Right on top of Dr. Carver's office.

I sucked in a breath.

"Ren, move!" I screamed.

He glanced over his shoulder at the approaching titan and blanched. He raced for the stairs.

But even if he got down, he wouldn't be able to avoid the falling building if the titan struck it again.

Ren glanced back at me, face a pale blur at this distance.

I reached for the surrounding energy, drawing it into my wiring, making my entire body glow with it. I'd thought the titan would have stolen it all, but there was still enough to feel like it hesitated to take it all.

Ren's life depended on how much I could gather and how fast. I had to make myself a beacon, a tasty snack for the titan.

The bike rose into the air, Daybreak's energy crackling along the frame, sending out sparks. More and more I drew, lighting up like a torch in the night.

Ren threw up his hand to shield his eyes.

But more importantly, the titan finally turned toward me.

"Yes," I hissed and swung the bike up and away from the colony, shooting out over the jungle toward the Black Flats.

I needed to stay ahead of the creature or it would suck up all of Daybreak's energy and leave me with nothing to draw it away.

It was an exercise in frustration, staying just far enough ahead that the titan couldn't bleed off my energy, but not too far ahead that it got frustrated or confused and left me to find some easier source.

If there even was one.

It took hours of weaving ahead and then slowing down to be sure the titan followed me. And at the end of it, we reached the lake.

Except what was I going to do now? I still glowed with the excess energy I'd gathered from Daybreak's atmosphere, the sparks flickering over my skin and making my wiring light up even through my clothes.

"What is your current plan?" BB asked from the hologram pad.

"Uh…"

"You have had hours to think, and you didn't come up with a way to keep it from trying to eat you now that you represent a significant source of its diet?"

"I'm making it up as I go."

"Well, make it up fast, because it's coming this way, and I think it's hungry."

Think, Anikka, think. The titan ate energy during the storms. I couldn't gather enough energy in my wires to actually equal a storm, but maybe I could trick it for long enough that it would go back to sleep until the next one hit.

I'd built up a sizable ball of energy that crackled around me. During a storm, I'd be able to shape that into a shield to protect me from the waves that would stop my heart. But now I gathered it around me and shot it down into the water.

The energy worked a lot like electricity, and it sizzled away across the surface.

The titan moaned again, making my ears hurt, and it dove for the lake.

I dragged the bike up using the electricity in my wiring, but the wave of water crashed over me anyway and knocked me out of the sky.

We hit the surface of the water near the shore, and I sputtered as I came up.

Luckily, we'd landed where the water was shallow enough that the handlebars of my bike stuck up, and I'd be able to drag it free.

But for now, I scanned the surface of the water, looking for signs of the titan. Aside from the fading swells of its dive, I saw nothing.

"Ha, it worked!"

"I've noticed you say that a lot on this planet," BB said.

"Well. Celebrate every victory, Professor Orrion used to

say. How much do you want to bet that it stays down there until the next storm?"

BB followed my gaze, staring at the undulating surface. "I do not have any money with which to bet."

I snorted and dragged my bike toward shore. I'd need to check it for damage before flying it back. "Never mind, BB."

CHAPTER 18

Daybreak: Day 201

The aurora lit the sky in brilliant colors by the time I flew my bike back over the wrecked portions of the colony. Tumbled walls cast jagged shadows across the packed dirt street, and I winced. I might have drawn the titan away, but not before it had leveled a couple of workshops, the top floor of the stores building, and half the science offices.

I pulled up just outside the admin building and parked the bike. Shade yipped and streaked across the street to twine between my legs, just as a voice called out.

"Anikka!"

I flinched, the wires under my skin glowing. I hadn't bothered to dim it this time.

Before I could face him completely, Ren threw his arms around me.

A surprised laugh left my throat, and my shoulders relaxed into his embrace. The first one I'd had since I'd said goodbye to Professor Orrion on the launch pad.

"Gods of all worlds, I'm glad you're okay. When you didn't come back right away, I thought that thing had eaten you."

"It wouldn't have eaten me," I said, drawing back enough to turn.

"That's good. I'd hate to have to swear vengeance on something so majestic."

"And deadly," BB said.

"Well, yeah, that just means it's a true native of Daybreak. Seriously, did you see the size of that thing?" His hands waved to emphasize his point. "And the way it swam through the air. And the way you led it away."

He let his arms drop, and he met my gaze.

My teeth clenched.

"You're a cybernetic."

I drew in a shaky breath. "Yeah."

"Why didn't you tell me?"

"I didn't know how you'd react."

Did...did he really not care?

So much of my life I'd spent staring at the other kids in the dorms, wondering what was wrong with me. In grade school, they'd all been nice enough, but they were more interested in playing outside on the tiny playground while I'd been building my prosthetic with Professor Orrion.

In high school, the gap widened. I couldn't seem to bring myself to care about boys—or girls, for that matter—the way the others did. They'd been trying out holding hands and kissing in the stairwells and...other things.

The wiring under my skin just made me more like the robot they'd always called me. Another thing to set me apart.

He tilted his head. "So what's an infra-engineer doing with electro cybernetics? I'd think muscle augmentation would be more immediately useful."

I dropped my gaze, lips thinning. "Augmented strength is used in construction a lot, yeah. But I didn't have my wiring when we got here. I would never have qualified before Daybreak."

He blinked. "But we don't have an implantation chamber. How would you have…Where would…"

I blew out my breath. "The cybernetics lab on the *Last Resort* still worked."

His eyes widened. "You…you went through the surgery alone? In a crashed ship?"

I squirmed. "I didn't have a choice. It was the only way to survive. The storms kill anything with a heartbeat. I needed a way to create a personal EM shield. And I needed it fast."

I turned from the realization dawning in his gaze and the little bit of awe that crept after it. I hadn't done anything brave. It had been horrible and hurt like hell, but I had survived. I always survived.

"That's amazing. *You're* amazing."

I shook my head, certain he was saying something more than that. But if I could just keep him from using the words, maybe we'd still be okay. We could keep going on as before.

He'd still be my friend.

"It's not that amazing. It's just wiring." I put my hand on the bike and let a spark zap it to life, so it floated a few inches off the ground.

His gaze shifted down the length of the bike. Diversion tactic successful.

"So, how does it work? You send electricity through the frame and that creates the lift. But I still can't quite figure out how…"

I pointed up. "Daybreak's energy. It's gathered in the atmosphere. But it works a lot like electricity, so I can direct it with my wiring. I send it through the frame—"

"And create a quantum phenomenon that acts like a super

magnet." He nodded, hard enough to make his hair flop. "That's brilliant."

"Thank you."

"The energy," he said, waving his hand vaguely up as I had done. "Dr. Carver was trying to get it named Carvinium."

I snorted. "After him?"

Ren shrugged. "He discovered it. But yeah, that should give you a good idea of the kind of person he was. I think he would have been impressed with your use of it." He gestured to the bike. "Or jealous. Which would have also been a compliment."

I huffed a laugh. "Maybe I'll find out which when we finally meet him. What did you find in his office?"

He pulled a screen out of the holder on his belt and held it up. It was a little bigger than the standard issue ones in the admin building. Scratches marred the back like the owner didn't care much about where he set it down, but the front remained undamaged.

"This. It had its own charger under a pile of papers on the desk, so it even turns on."

I reached for it. "And it has something useful on it?"

When it flickered to life, a login page appeared. Except there were two different users.

CARVERASTROPHYS

CARVERBIOENG

I'd known he had multiple degrees, but I hadn't known which ones besides astrophysics. That one explained how he'd known about the sun cycle and predicted the energy storms.

But what did he do with the bioengineering degree? Bioengineers worked with med tech and they'd also been responsible for developing androids back on Earth, but he hadn't been assigned to the infirmary and there weren't any androids on Daybreak. At least, I didn't think there were.

Ren reached over and touched the astrophysics login. "Nothing looks useful if you read what's just sitting there waiting for someone to pick it up."

He was right. This all seemed like star charts and sun calculations.

I glanced up at him and raised an eyebrow. "But?"

His infectious grin lit up his face. "But I think there might be a code to it. Something I can get underneath."

I glanced at the pages of data scrolling by. "You can tell that just by looking at it?"

"Yeah. I mean, can't you?"

I gave him a perplexed look. "No. I'm an infra-engineer. I build things, not software."

"Well, I'm an electrical tech. I'm actually pretty good at it. I don't love it. But I'm good at it."

If he remembered enough of it.

I bit my tongue on the thought and pushed it away. Just because he couldn't tell me anything about his training didn't mean he didn't have any.

I handed the screen back to him, and Ren stared at me for a moment longer than normal.

"What?"

"I'm just really glad you're okay."

There was that tone again. Soft and fervent and full of things that made me very uncomfortable.

I tried to laugh. "Yeah, I'm always glad when I don't die, too. But I'm sure you would have managed without me. You're a fast learner."

He raised his hand to rub the back of his neck, not quite meeting my eyes. "It might be a little more than that."

My chest went tight. "What do you mean?"

He reached for my prosthetic hand and gripped my metal fingers. "You haven't noticed? I kind of like you."

A fist of ice knotted in my gut. "What like?" I said. Very intelligently. "What do you mean, like?"

He shrugged, eyes intent on my face. "What do people normally mean when they say they like you?"

"I don't know!" My voice squeaked. "No one's ever used it on me before."

Suddenly, he grinned. "You mean I could be your first boyfriend?"

The ice crawled up my throat, and I choked. Vent it, I'd wanted to be wrong, but he did mean what I thought he meant. And he hadn't been joking before about that date.

"No." The word came out high and strangled.

He shook his head. "No? I haven't even asked anything—"

"Then don't."

"Hey, wait. What's—"

"I don't do that, Ren."

His face went red, but he cleared his throat and asked, "Do what?"

"Any of that!" I pulled my hand from his. "I don't do love and boyfriends and stuff."

He blinked. "Do you do girlfriends, then?"

"No, none of it. Everyone is equally uninteresting."

He made a face, and I winced.

"That came out wrong. I mean, I'm not attracted like that. To anyone. I never have been."

"Oh." The sound that left his lips seemed like a deflation. Hope leaving his body. "You're ace."

"Yeah." At least he knew the word for it. Some people still didn't. Even fewer understood it or accepted it. "I'm sorry. I'm sure whatever you're feeling will just...go away if you give it a few days."

He scoffed. "Okay, if I doubted you at all, that just proved you've never been in love. This isn't just going to go away."

"Love?" I squeaked. "You can't possibly mean that."

The hurt fled from his face, leaving deep creases across his brow as he narrowed his eyes. "Hey, I'm not asking if you're sure you're ace. So you can't ask me if I'm sure I'm in love."

"What do you even like about me? We barely know each other."

"I know you've saved my life. Multiple times."

My mouth opened, but I couldn't think of anything to say to that. He was right, but did people really fall in love like this? A couple of days in the jungle and voila, now they're together? The whole thing just seemed sloppy to me.

"I know you're smart and strong, and you don't laugh at me when I'm excited about stupid stuff."

I could barely speak around the lump in my throat. "It's not stupid stuff," I whispered. And he'd done the exact same thing for me, making me feel normal for the first time in my life.

But that didn't mean I loved him. Or wanted him. Not like that.

He gave me the barest ghost of his grin. And turned to start the walk back to the drop ship.

CHAPTER 19

Daybreak: Day 202

We'd been sleeping wedged on the bedroom platform, with Shade between us. I had another platform half-built, but I hadn't finished it yet. It usually meant if one of us woke, we both woke.

The next morning, I was extra careful climbing out of my sleeping bag. Ren shifted in his sleep as the ladder creaked, and I winced.

"Five more minutes," he groaned, and I shook my head, hopping down to the next level.

There was enough to do that I could bury myself in work and not have to think about what he'd said the night before.

The bike had survived the fall into the lake, though one of the tubes was bent. I'd have to keep an eye on it to make sure it didn't start leaking tridenium.

We still had a whole silverpoint to cure so it would keep longer, and I decided now would be an excellent time to finish the second bedroom platform for Ren. As a gift. Not for any other reason.

For the next several days, Ren and I successfully avoided each other. As far as I knew, he spent most of his time poring over Dr. Carver's screen, trying to unlock the data we needed.

But apparently not all of the time.

I checked the crops on the roof of the drop ship one afternoon and caught sight of Ren on the kitchen platform. His wide frame was bent over the crate we used as a table, intent on what looked like a piece of paper.

Curious despite myself, I stepped up into the kitchen area.

"What are you working on?"

My voice made him jump.

He glanced up, eyes guilty. "Just...taking a break."

His hands fluttered, like he wanted to hide his work but thought better of it at the last minute. He had a pencil clutched between his fingers.

"Breaks are good," I said and stepped a little closer.

I peeked over at whatever he was working on and saw sheets of paper covered in sketches.

"I, uh, found some paper in Dr. Carver's office and thought we could use it. Since it'll last longer. This was the only pencil, though. I'm vented if it breaks."

"You draw?"

"Yeah?" he said, like he wasn't sure of the answer. Or my reaction to it. "Just doodles. Nothing really important."

My eyebrows went up. These were way better than just doodles. Intricate sketches of Daybreak's wildlife lined the crate. A silverpoint caught in the moment it lifted its head. A jumpernick depicted mid leap.

I picked up one of Shade caught in mid-step as if he walked down the riverbank.

"This is my favorite," I said. "Obviously."

Notes lined the empty space around the drawing.

Slinkwolf: predator/scavenger

Eats fish, jumpernicks, and dried fruit (when there's nothing else)

Will play fetch

Food motivated

Territorial, protective of those it sees as its pack

"You can have it," he said. "It's not like I need it. They're just to give my hands something to do while my brain takes a break."

Considering the notes I could see got more and more technical, speculating on an animal's diet and behavior, I didn't think his brain was getting that much of a break.

Clearly, he'd been spending some time on the titan. Three whole drawings were devoted to the flying whale, plus the one he was working on at that moment.

"These are really good."

He shrugged.

"No, I mean it. You saw that thing once, and you can draw it with that much detail?" I pointed to the markings along the side of the titan.

His familiar grin reappeared. I hadn't seen it for a few days.

"Well, it did leave an impression. I had a hard time with the glowing bits, but I think I got the pattern right, finally."

I hadn't even noticed the way they'd lit up the first two times I'd seen the creature.

"I'm just trying to figure out what they're for," he said.

"The markings? Maybe they're just decoration."

He gave me a look that reminded me so much of Professor Orrion's disappointed face that I immediately felt like turning in extra credit.

"Yes," he said. "But in nature, even decoration has a function. Whether it's camouflage or a warning. Or a way to attract a mate."

I cleared my throat awkwardly, and Ren flushed a bright red.

Vent it, now it was all weird again. I missed the way this had felt before he'd used those words. Before we had to second guess every little thing we said.

I flailed for something to say. "Where did you learn to draw?" I said, absently stacking the three sketches of the titan.

He dropped his gaze again and rubbed his thumb up and down his pencil. "I don't remember."

A frown pulled at my mouth. That was getting familiar.

"Was it a class?"

The skin around his eyes went tight as he flashed me a look. "I said I don't remember. I'm not like you, all right? I don't remember every course I ever took. It's not that I don't remember what I learned. I just don't remember learning it."

I let out an explosive breath through my nose. Maybe that was true. Maybe I was the strange one.

And yet, I had vivid memories of sitting through Professor Orrion's lectures and seeking out books that would tell me things I hadn't learned in class. I also remembered all the dirty looks I got from the other orphans as they whispered things like "teacher's pet" and "over-achiever." Maybe that was why it was cemented in my memory.

My entire existence before launch had been wrapped up in earning my place on the *Last Resort,* and that had meant classes.

That niggling feeling was back. That one that said something was…off.

"So, what *do* you remember? Before the colony."

Ren sighed heavily and gathered up his sketches, plucking the three from my hands. "I don't know. I remember the lake. And spending a lot of time alone."

"You said you couldn't see the lake."

"Yeah," he snapped. "I remember not being able to see the lake. Someone told me there were little private cottages once where you could walk right down onto the beach. Now it's all—"

"Built up mansions and condos," I said. My teeth ached where I clenched them. "Yeah, you told me."

"Then why are you asking again?"

"Because—" Because he sounded like he was reading off a list. "What else do you remember?"

"That's a really broad question."

True, but I had no idea how to put words to the weird clenching worry in my gut. "What about your dad? What did he look like?"

"Tall, dark hair. Blue eyes. Super serious."

That was the most generic description of a person I'd ever heard.

"So you got your sense of humor from your mom?"

His face went tight. "I didn't have a mom."

My stomach dropped. I knew how that one felt. "I'm sorry. What happened to her?"

"I don't know. She wasn't around. She...left or died. I'm not sure."

"She might have died, and you're not sure? How can you not be sure?"

"I don't know!" His voice rose, and his knuckles went white around the edges of the papers. "It's...it's all fuzzy. I remember the houses around the lake and—and that I was alone a lot 'cause Dad had to work. That's why I made friends with dogs. I don't...know what came between those."

Years, a lifetime between those two things. And it was all "fuzzy?"

He glanced at my face and winced. "Is that memory loss?" His voice dropped, soft and vulnerable. "From the cryo sickness?" He transferred his look to BB where she stood on the hologram pad.

Her gaze flicked almost imperceptibly to mine. "It... could be."

"Is it from that chip? That thing he put in my brain?"

"I do not know. Without knowing what the chip is, I can only speculate."

He stood, nearly banging his head on the upper platform. He took a deep breath, like he was going to say something, then stuck the papers under his arm and pulled out Dr. Carver's screen before heading for the ladder.

"Where are you going?" I said.

"Back to work. I need to know what he did to me. This is the only thing that might tell me."

I suppressed a groan as Ren disappeared upstairs. Not because he was wrong but because I didn't know how to fix this. I thrived on being able to fix things.

I tilted my head back and closed my eyes, stretching the tension out of my neck.

When I looked back down, BB was staring up the ladder where Ren had disappeared.

"Could it still be cryo sickness?" I asked her under my breath.

"It's possible," she said, but she drew the words out like she wasn't quite sure. "But most memory loss from cryo sickness obscures the time directly before cryo sleep. It does not erase a patient's entire life."

"That's what I thought." I glanced back at the ladder.

It was like he had two or three memories. Total. And

everything else was blurry. Whose entire childhood was so obscured by fog that they could only remember a couple of things?

Someone who didn't have a childhood to remember.

I swallowed. The story about the lake and the one about his dad could be true. But they were also things that either everyone knew or a lot of people experienced or could relate to.

Generic. Bland. Blank.

I touched the hologram pad with my prosthetic to transfer BB and stepped out onto the drop ship. Then all the way down to the edge of the river where the sound of running water would obscure my voice.

"He only has three memories," I told her. "And they could belong to anyone."

"What are you saying?" BB's image popped up on my wrist, brow furrowed.

"They sound made up. Or implanted. Something manufactured to make him sound human."

"This implies that he is *not* human. If he isn't human, what are you suggesting he is?"

I blew out my breath and thought back to those two logins on the screen Ren was working on. Dr. Carver wasn't just an astrophysicist. He was also a bioengineer.

"An android."

"This is..."

I waited for her to discount it. To come up with some defining feature that meant Ren couldn't be an android. But her eyes moved like she was still thinking, and she remained silent.

"You're thinking it, too," I said. "Someone wanted him to look and sound human, but they only had time for three memories. That's the only way we'd be able to tell. Androids mimic human behavior, and their design is seamless. Undetectable without a blood scan. We wouldn't even be able to see the difference in the scan we did the other day."

"These facts all line up," BB said, hesitantly.

I dug my toe into the mud of the bank, hands clenching.

"You have to tell him," BB said.

"What?" I snorted. "I'm not going to say, hey are you a robot?"

"He might not know. His memory loss does not seem fabricated to me."

I threw out my hand. "All the more reason to protect him. Keep him from getting hurt."

BB's hologram flickered. "If this is a truth about himself, then he deserves to know."

"Not if it's a damaging truth."

BB stared at me. "I know we have been lying to protect ourselves," she said quietly. "You've been lying to protect me."

I swallowed. BB didn't even know how much I'd been lying.

"But I have decided I do not like being untruthful."

"BB—"

"It is not right."

"Sometimes a lie can be better than the truth."

She reached out as if to touch my arm. She couldn't actually, but I shivered anyway. "I have relied on you to tell me what is human and what is not. But I think for this one thing, I prefer to be an AI."

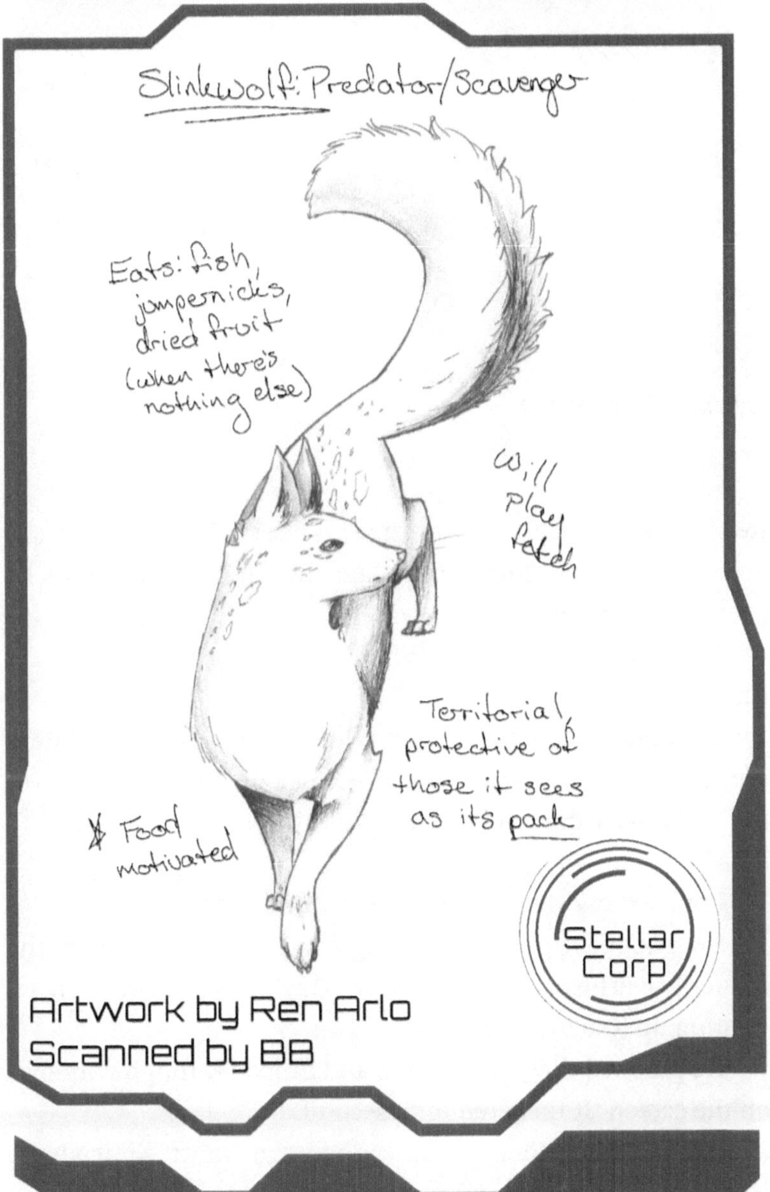

Slinkwolf: Predator/Scavenger
Eats: fish, jumpernicks, dried fruit (when there's nothing else)
Will play fetch
Territorial, protective of those it sees as its pack
* Food motivated
Stellar Corp
Artwork by Ren Arlo
Scanned by BB

CHAPTER 20

Daybreak: Day 210

Ren shook me awake just as the sun began lightening the sky even though he'd been up so late the night before. Had he even gone to sleep?

I gasped and sat up. "What? Is it a megawing? Or the titan?"

His eyes, which had been bright and eager, narrowed for a second. "What's a megawing?" He shook his head. "Never mind. Look. I cracked it. I cracked the lock on Dr. Carver's data."

I pushed my sleeping bag down. "You did?"

BB popped up on the hologram pad that stood in the corner. Overhead, the colors of Daybreak's dawn spread, lighting up Ren's dark hair.

He plopped down beside me and flipped through windows on the screen. It flickered for a second.

"Don't mind that. I think there's a short somewhere. Here."

Sun calculations sped past until he stopped on a picture. A schematic of some sort of building.

"Those aren't notes on the sun," I said and dragged his arm closer so I could see.

"No."

"What was he working on?"

"This is actually one of the prefabs delivered with the first wave of colonists. It was dropped during the second stage of building along with a fancy telescope and the rest of the stuff for the astrophysics department. It's up in the mountains somewhere." He poked a finger at some coordinates in tiny print at the top of the screen.

I gave him a skeptical look. "Dr. Carver *was* the astrophysics department. It's really not weird he'd have the specs for their facility."

"No, but it *is* weird he had a whole bunch of other equipment labeled "classified" sent to those same coordinates a week later. Including a cryo pod."

I sucked in a breath, and Ren grinned at my reaction.

"You're sure?"

"That's what was under all the security. His equipment list. It's...well, I don't know a lot about it, but I think it has more to do with his bioengineering degree than the astrophysics one. It's weird stuff."

He flipped the window again, leaving behind the schematics, and I scanned the list he was talking about. Lots of things like "3pt polytrope hose" and "glycerine bio gel" and "peptide solution- 30oz."

And at the very end, one adult-size cryo pod.

"He could still be there." I met his eyes. "If he was in his own pod, he could have survived. But why there? Why not in the cave with the rest?"

Ren stood and paced to the end of the platform, hands in his hair, fingers feeling for the hidden scar. "I don't know. I don't understand any of it. I don't know enough to put it together. But…it's a secret lab, Anikka. He had a secret lab."

It seemed so stupid to say it out loud but what else could it mean? Dr. Carver had sent secret things to a secret place to do secret stuff.

"We have to go there." Ren spun to look at me, hands dropping back to his sides.

"What?" I didn't actually need him to repeat it, I just needed a second to think.

"We have to go find this lab. Dr. Carver did something to me. Put this chip in my head. It might have something to do with this equipment and his work there." He dropped to his knees in front of me. "We have to go there."

I grabbed my boots, avoiding his eyes.

Of course this was the next step. But he was right. All that equipment looked pretty suspicious and had something to do with Dr. Carver's work. And it lined up with my android theory. Work on synthetic humanoids was explicitly prohibited back on Earth, so it would make sense he would hide it here on Daybreak.

It wasn't that I didn't want Ren to know the truth. I just didn't want the truth to break him. And I didn't know how to tell him yet. Especially without proof. Maybe I could convince him not to go, and then I could slip away to check it out for myself and make sure he wasn't going to be blindsided.

"I don't know," I said just to respond.

Ren reeled back. "What do you mean you don't know?"

"I mean, I don't know the terrain or the dangers. I would have to scout it out first."

I yanked the boots on my feet and stood.

"Those coordinates are up in the mountains. It'll take days just to get there and—"

"Not if you fly us."

"—And I don't know what I'm heading into. Daybreak is dangerous—"

"You think I don't know that?"

"Well, you're not acting like it. I'd have to plan and prepare and there's still a ton to do here."

He glanced at the platform I'd been half-heartedly building the last few days. His face went bleak, like he'd realized something.

"Then I'll go myself," he said. "And scout it out. You can come after. If you want."

I snorted. "You really think that's a good idea?"

"I don't need your permission."

The words struck deep and stung. "You're going to get yourself killed."

"I know you've been here a long time, but you're not the only one who can survive on Daybreak now. You don't get to decide things for me."

"I'm trying to protect you."

"Then stop!" He threw his hands in the air.

We stood glaring at each other for the space of several breaths.

He let his hands fall, and his face changed again, brows drawing down and a shadow moving behind his eyes.

"I don't get it. You were so focused on finding Dr. Carver. And now you're just going to sit back here and what? Build something else? What's going on? What are you not telling me?"

"Nothing."

"There's no way it's nothing."

"Ren."

"You've thought of something."

"Please, don't."

"Don't what?"

"There's a chance you might be an android," BB said from her corner.

"BB!" I yelled.

"We have no right to keep it from him." BB met my gaze. "I choose truth, even if it makes me less human in this moment."

Ren had staggered back a step. "An android?"

I took a deep breath and started ticking things off on my fingers. "You have two, maybe three, memories you recycle over and over. Your entire life is blurred out between those. You didn't even act like a human once you got to the colony. You just slept. Like you'd been unplugged or something."

"I'm..." He stared at his hands. "I'm human," he said. Then louder, "Of course I'm human. I would know if I wasn't. I'd remember being manufactured or getting plugged in or... or something!"

"If you were human, then you'd remember being human. Don't you think? And you barely remember anything."

"That's the cryo sickness." He glanced at BB.

BB's eyes flicked away in a very human gesture. "That is inconclusive."

Ren's brows came down, and his lips thinned to an angry line. "You...you really believe this."

I bit my lip. "Maybe. I just didn't want you to find out in some lab."

"Where you think I might have been grown. Or what? Assembled?" He made a noise of disgust and slashed his hand through the air. "This is ridiculous."

"Ren, I—"

"No." He straightened and jerked his chin up. "Stop it. Just because you're some soulless robot with no emotions, it doesn't mean I am, too."

The bottom dropped out of my stomach. "What?" I whispered.

His face went white, but his jaw clenched, and he didn't say anything.

Words rang in my ears. Voices from a million light years away echoing in the back of my brain like they'd been waiting there, gaining momentum for the right moment to push forward.

"Don't invite her. She'll just ruin it."

"Anikka the robot."

"What a cold witch."

"There's something wrong with her."

My hands hurt, and I realized my nails were dug into my palms.

"Anikka," Ren started, voice softening.

I shook my head once and spun on my heel.

"Anikka."

I grabbed my blade from its place beside my bed, then I stomped away across the top of the drop ship and down to the ground before I disappeared into the trees.

Daybreak: Day 210

Half-blinded by angry tears, I stormed through the forest. The tight knot in my throat made it hard to breathe and didn't diminish at all over the distance I put between me and the drop ship.

I fetched up against a tree. My eyes squeezed shut as the last few minutes with Ren replayed themselves in my head. I didn't want to hear his words again. I wanted to forget them as easily as he had forgotten his childhood, but they sprang through my mind.

Soulless robot. Emotionless.

Electricity crackled up from the depths of my wiring, sizzling along my arms and the back of my neck.

I'd been trying to protect him, and he'd hurt me in the worst possible way.

A flash of lightning zinged from my palms, scorching the gray bark of the tree.

I winced and jumped back, snatching my hands away.

I stuffed them under my armpits and kept running.

Things had been awkward between us, yes, but I'd really thought Ren was different. I thought he knew what it felt like to be alone.

Clearly, that didn't mean anything when you were mad and just wanted to hurt someone.

It was nearly an hour before I realized this was the first time I'd walked through the forest of Daybreak without paying any attention to where I was going or how loud I was being.

Not a great idea.

Just as I made that connection, my feet went out from under me, and I slid down a steep muddy slope into a dell where a creek had cut through to make its own mini gorge.

I landed on my butt in the water and swore. Mud soaked through my pants, sucking at my hands as I tried to shift my weight up and out of the creek.

Something rumbled.

I looked up, teeth clenched, to find a great black shape lined with scales, blinking enormous gold eyes back at me.

"Oh, crap," I breathed.

I'd slid right into the black death's new den.

The beast lifted its snout, and I didn't even wait for it to lunge. I scrambled up and tried to climb back up the bank, but it was too steep and too slippery. The ground fell away under my hands.

The black death surged forward, and I dropped, rolling down the hill in a ball so the huge monitor lizard went right over top of me.

I slithered between its feet, not pausing to admire the claws as long as my hand, and popped out behind it.

A tree grew on the opposite side of the stream, tall and straight.

I rushed for the trunk and shimmied up, panic giving me strength and speed.

The black death struck the bottom, and the whole tree shook. I held on through the vibrations, then climbed higher, pulse beating in my throat.

The black death struck again. The tree shivered and something ominous cracked down below.

The whole thing was going to fall. I craned my neck around. Was I high enough to jump to the top of the bank where I'd slid down? Maybe I could make the tree fall against the hill so I could just climb up.

A bark made my heart skip, and I whipped around.

Another bark came through the trees.

I couldn't see anything, but Shade knew well enough to stay away from enormous predators like the black death.

The monitor lizard cocked its head, staring between the trees, trying to see my slinkwolf, too.

Shade yipped again, and the black death surged forward, up the bank that was too steep for me and into the trees on the other side of the creek.

I had to believe that Shade knew what he was doing.

My tree started to tilt, and it groaned. I threw my weight back, toward the bank I'd fallen down.

The trunk fell in an arc, and crashed against the muddy edge of the dell, right where I'd slid.

I scrambled up and out, using the tree as a ladder and sprinted away, hoping the black death wouldn't follow.

When I felt like I was far enough away, I whistled a signal for Shade, loud and bright.

A moment later, he appeared, weaving through the trees.

"Good boy," I gasped. "Good slinkwolf."

I didn't stop until I recognized the grove and the neutral zone the animals there abided by.

I collapsed against the nearest tree and slid until I could sit with my head between my knees.

There wasn't even anyone there to mock me for not watching where I was going. In my haste, I'd left BB on the hologram pad at the drop ship. And although she could jump from pad to pad now, she'd told me she was limited by distance.

It was just me and Shade.

The slinkwolf whined and wriggled his way under my arm.

"Hey buddy," I whispered. "Thanks for following me."

Vent it, I'd sat there and argued about the mountains being dangerous, and here I was running headfirst into the black death's den like someone just off the ship.

If Ren needed proof I wasn't the final authority on Daybreak, he needn't look any further than the last hour and a half.

If he even spoke to me again.

I wrapped my arms around Shade and buried my head in the thick ruff of fur around his neck.

I'd thought I was used to the loneliness. I'd thought I'd

made it a part of who I was and it didn't bother me anymore. I was Anikka the loner. I was proud of it. It made me someone who could survive and thrive on Daybreak with an abandoned colony and a burning ship in the background.

I hadn't realized how easy it would be to slip into someone else. To get used to the illusion of having friends.

My chest ached. What had we done? Was this what it was like to have friends? To needle each other until you said something you shouldn't.

He'd called me a robot. Without even realizing, he'd reached deep inside and found the worst memories from my childhood.

But I'd done it to him first. Or at least, BB had. But she hadn't voiced anything I hadn't been thinking.

I'd accused him of being the same thing the other corporate orphans had teased me for relentlessly. They'd called me an android. But worse, I'd actually tried to convince Ren he was one.

It didn't matter if it might have been true. I'd tried to protect him by hiding the possibility, and then when it had blown up in my face, I'd forced him to defend himself.

Shade lay his head on my knee and looked up at me with a slanted golden eye.

Ren and I had both said things we shouldn't have.

"I think I need to apologize." I thunked my head against the tree trunk. "You'd think after being lonely for so long, it would be easier to get along with someone."

Daybreak: Day 210

. . .

The sky grew dark as I made my way back to the drop ship, dragging my feet. Even if I'd been in the wrong, too, I really didn't want to face Ren again so soon.

The sun disappeared below the horizon as Shade and I slunk back into camp. I glanced up at the drop ship, but the darkness under the canopy kept everything in shadow. Ren must not have lit the stove yet. I knew he at least knew how to light the fires; we'd spent all morning on it a few days ago. But maybe he was sulking, too.

I climbed the ladder, my gut clenched in a knot, and walked through my garden of planters.

The kitchen platform was empty.

"Ren?" I said quietly. "BB?"

I climbed the ladder to the bedroom platform, and my stomach sank. It was empty, too.

"Ren?" I hopped back down to the kitchen and swept my gaze over the dark stove and oven. The lid of the crate was askew.

"Oh no." I threw the lid off and checked the contents. Sure enough, the stores of dried fruit and salted fish were at least halved.

"Crap." I rushed to the railing and leaned over to squint at the dark river bank and the hull of the drop ship.

The colors of Daybreak's aurora flickered to life above me, lighting up the scene below.

The hover bike was gone.

The hologram pad on the kitchen level hummed to life, and BB's image popped open, sending blue light across the rough planks of the floor.

"Anikka."

"Oh, thank God—"

"I am leaving you this recording to tell you Ren has left."

I beat my fist lightly against my forehead. "Of course," I muttered.

"He's headed into the mountains to find Dr. Carver's lab. I am in the hologram pad on the bike, but I don't know how much use I will be keeping Ren alive. He is quite upset and determined to prove he is not an android. I don't believe he's thinking clearly."

I swore and flew to grab my things.

Ren had left, and he'd taken my anxious AI with him.

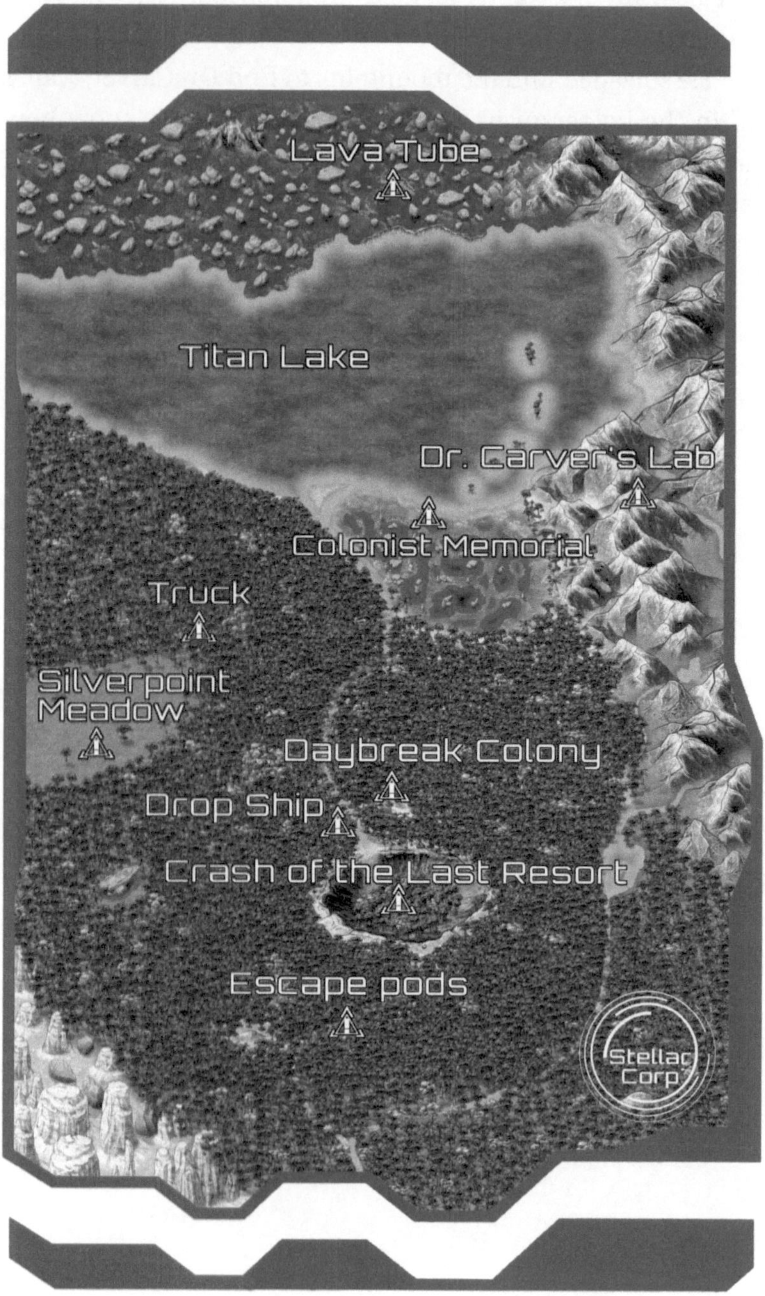

Lava Tube
Titan Lake
Dr. Carver's Lab
Colonist Memorial
Truck
Silverpoint Meadow
Daybreak Colony
Drop Ship
Crash of the Last Resort
Escape pods
Stellac Corp

CHAPTER 21

Daybreak: Day 211

I left immediately. Ren had almost a full day's head start. And he was on my bike, which could still go faster than me even when gas-powered. And he could go straight to the coordinates.

I didn't have any of those things. I had to follow his trail, on foot, in the dark. Because if I overshot him or strayed too far from whatever path he was following, I'd never find him in the dense jungle of Daybreak. He could die because of some threat I hadn't had a chance to teach him about yet. Had I told him about sinking mud? Or the trooper beetles by the Black Flats?

I couldn't remember. I had to hope BB was keeping an eye out for him. She knew most of Daybreak's dangers as well as I did.

But that would only work if he knew she was there. She might have hidden the fact that she could leap to the hologram pad.

I picked up the pace, passing the colony in only forty-five minutes.

Shade ranged beside me, scouting ahead through the dark forest. I tried hard not to travel at night under normal circumstances. It was nearly impossible to see the sinking sand, and the pink itchbushes blended into everything else in the dark. But Shade kept me going straight and yipped warnings when I strayed too close to dangers I couldn't see.

Ren's trail wasn't that hard to follow, either. Daybreak's enormous moon was full tonight and illuminated a path of broken branches in the underbrush. Even on a motorbike, Ren wouldn't be able to go that fast through the dense forest. And it looked like he was going in a straight line, right toward the coordinates in the mountains.

Three hours past midnight, I collapsed against a tree and wrapped my sleeping bag around myself to sleep for a couple of hours. Shade curled up on my feet, head up and eyes alert as his ears swiveled to track the sounds of the forest.

I woke before dawn, too restless to sleep for long. After scarfing a couple of pieces of fruit, I set out again. My eyes still burned with fatigue, but at least now I could see where I was going. And Ren had to sleep too.

Unless he really was an android. I had no idea what that would mean for his function. He'd eaten and slept while he was with me. But did he actually have to, or was it programming?

What little I knew about robotics I'd learned while making my prosthetic with Professor Orrion. Despite what I'd said during our argument, androids didn't actually need to plug in to charge. Their energy came from tiny alternators built into their muscle cells. A little like the way my arm powered itself.

Late that day I found a muck covered sleeve caught on a

branch sticking out of a pool of sinking mud. I used another branch to fish it out.

Ren's jacket.

I blew out my breath. I knew he hadn't lost either himself or the bike in the mud because the trail of crushed greenery continued beyond the little clearing, still heading for the mountains in the distance.

I gripped the jacket in my metal hand and ground my teeth. I didn't care so much about the bike. I could make another one if I had to. But if he lost BB in one of these stupid puddles...

I might have come back to apologize and forgive him for our fight earlier, but if his stupidity killed BB, there would be no coming back from that.

I flung the jacket into the second pack I'd made with a blanket—Ren had taken mine—and continued on through the gloom.

After almost four full days of walking, I realized the ground was going up and my calves and hips ached from elevation gain.

Sure enough, the trees thinned and gave way to solid rock rising in steep hills. Not quite mountains yet, but from here I could look back over the Black Flats all the way to the lake glimmering in the distance.

"All right, buddy," I told Shade, who sniffed the rock at our feet. "It's going to be a lot harder to find him from here without a clear trail to follow."

I wished I had BB and the coordinates. Or even just a map. But without an AI or some kind of screen I could link to, I had no way to access the data stored in my chip.

Shade ranged a little further, snuffling the ground. On the top of the nearest ridge, he whuffled softly and glanced back at me.

I frowned. "What?"

When I hesitated too long, Shade snatched something off the ground and came back with it.

A half-burnt stick. Ren had been here, and Shade had found his campsite.

"Good boy," I said and ruffled his ears. "Let's see if we can find more."

I headed in the general direction I knew the lab lay. It wasn't precise, but Shade stalked up and down the rising peaks, fluffy tail swishing, and every now and then he came back with more evidence of Ren.

Hours later, my knees ached, and I had slowed down considerably, huffing and puffing as I tried to keep pace with Shade. The slinkwolf paused every now and then to make sure I was keeping up, but the stops were becoming more and more frequent.

"Sorry, buddy. I'm coming, I promise. You're doing great."

A voice threaded through the thin air, and I froze, trying to catch it again.

It was faint and came at intermittent intervals but...

With a jolt, I recognized my name. I could hear BB calling me.

I cupped my hands around my mouth. "BB!"

Shade bounded away, and I raced after him, aches forgotten.

"BB!"

"Anikka!" The speakers on her hologram pad must be maxed out.

I sprinted up the rocky rise, pebbles skittering down the slope behind me.

BB's hologram sprang up from my arm, and I skidded to a stop.

"BB—"

"No, keep going," she said. "Over this ridge."

Trusting that she knew what she was doing, I kept my mouth shut and concentrated on breathing. I scrambled up the slope, falling to my hands and knees twice before I crested the ridge.

On the other side, a long bright scrape trailed down the darker rock, and at the bottom, lay the bike. Abandoned.

I sucked in a breath.

"Grab it, Anikka. Ren is in trouble."

"No kidding," I said. I set my feet down the steep slope and slid all the way in a clattering of tiny stones.

"I don't mean because you want to kill him. A megawing grabbed him."

"Crap on a stick."

I grabbed for the bike. It looked mostly intact. A couple of dings in the tubes, but I didn't see any fluid pooled on the stone, so there probably weren't any leaks. There was a huge gouge out of the side of the hologram pad, though. Like a claw had raked it.

"Are you okay?"

BB's face went tight. "I am a program. Software. I cannot be hurt."

"You can be lost. You can be corrupted, erased, and you can be destroyed. If any of those things had happened, I would never be the same, so answer the question BB."

BB's eyes went wide, and she stared for a second before finally saying, "I am fine. I promise."

"Good enough." I hauled the bike upright and poured energy into the tubing, making it hum. "Shade, hop on." I flipped down the platform on the back. The side already held my pack strapped to the frame. The cross bow was shoved in with it.

Shade hopped aboard.

We rose into the air, and I pushed the bike forward as fast as I dared with Shade not strapped in.

"Where?" I said.

BB's hologram pointed. "That way."

North. I poured energy into the bike's frame and we sped over the mountain range, jagged peaks racing beneath us.

I kept my gaze up and roving the rocky landscape, searching for a bright streak of red in the sky.

Except the flash when it came was more orange.

Apparently, mountain megawings were more sunset colored than the ones in the jungle. Its broad wings were pink and the feathers of its crest glinted gold as it dropped something into a messy nest perched precariously on a nearby cliff.

The bundle yelped and scrambled away from the huge bird's claws.

Ren.

I leaned forward and drove the bike straight for the nest. Wind roared past my ears.

The bike made no noise, but the megawing looked up, warned by some other instinct. Its long, wicked snout snapped at me.

I swerved and swung over the side of the bike, arm outstretched.

Ren wasn't dumb. He saw me coming and leaped up to catch my arm as I went by.

My shoulder screamed, but luckily, I'd grabbed him with my left, and he wasn't about to separate my prosthetic from my body. Though it did feel like he would tear my real arm off.

I tried to swing him up, to grab hold of the bike's frame, but even after months of physical labor, I wasn't that strong.

He dangled over the long drop between us and the mountains.

I couldn't haul him up, and I couldn't drop him, but my arm screamed at me.

"Anikka, veer right."

I followed BB's directions, gritting my teeth against the pain. Wings beat the air behind us, but I didn't dare go any faster with Ren swinging below.

A metal pole flashed by just below us, and I blinked. There went another one.

"There are signal towers," BB said. "I think the lab is close."

"Yeah, but is the megawing closer?" I took a deep, bracing breath and squinted at the nearby peaks. A glint to my right made me turn, and I headed that way without fully comprehending what I was seeing. But as we drew closer, a building came into focus.

White plastic had weathered to a light gray. The blocky base sat on a lone plateau, but a huge dome above seemed to indicate a telescope inside.

Ren cried out and pointed back.

Behind us, the megawing shrieked.

I couldn't draw my blade. Ren hung from one hand, and I needed the other to keep us on the bike. So all I could do was drive straight toward the lab.

A wing buffeted us from behind, and the bike careened forward. I lost control, and we spun toward the ground.

I screamed as the world streaked by underneath us.

Shade yelped and jumped free just as I dropped Ren, and he rolled against the rocky slope.

The bike struck the ground hard, and I threw myself away, catching a handlebar that wrenched my already sore arm.

I cried out in pain and rolled from the wreckage as it skidded to a stop.

"Anikka!"

I crawled to my feet, eyes scanning the peaks. Ren raced for me, Shade right behind him. The lab lay less than a hundred feet away, with a crude path leading right to the door.

But the megawing flapped between us and it.

My cross bow was still strapped to the bike, a mangled mess. I curled my wrenched arm against my chest and drew my blade.

With a flick of my wrist, I sent electricity cascading down the blade. It wouldn't hurt the megawing, but it might distract it long enough.

"Anikka!" Ren skidded to a stop beside me.

"I'm going to count to three. As soon as the megawing turns, you get into the lab."

"I'm not leaving—"

"I need you to activate those signal towers. Light them up. Do something to make them sparkle."

"I..." Ren gulped and glanced back at the megawing. "All right."

"BB, can you go with him?"

"I can transfer myself, yes."

"Good. One."

Ren raised his hand like he was going to try to stop me, but I raced past him. Directly for the megawing.

"Two."

I leaped, slashing down just as the giant bird snatched at me. My blade grazed its snout, and it snatched its head back with a hiss. I landed and slid under the thing's left wing, making it spin to chase me.

"Three!"

A second later, Ren raced behind the megawing while I had it distracted. BB appeared on the hologram pad ahead of him. She must have used Dr. Grotman's code because the door slid open for him.

Shade snarled and raced for the megawing's other side, making it hiss and rear back.

I pressed forward, slashing at the left wing. Electricity didn't hurt it, but a blade was still a blade and blood sprayed from my slice.

The megawing shrieked and swept its other wing around, knocking Shade across the open space. He rolled and came up, shaking his head.

The megawing pounced, and I raised my blade, but instead of grabbing with its jaws, it jumped on top of me, gripping me with huge claws.

I yelled and went down under its weight. My sword skittered away, losing its light.

The megawing's claws dug into the ground on either side of me, scraping the stone with a shriek, and its bulk kept me pinned.

A flash made me look up. The megawing blinked, and it followed the same distraction I had. Toward the signal towers.

Each tower stretched into the sky, a ladder of spindly steel topped with a light. Which blinked on and off in a flickering pattern that reminded me of the little energy discharges when a storm was approaching.

It reminded the megawing, too.

It hopped off of me, leaving me gasping against the rock. Then it flapped once, launching itself into the air.

"Now, Anikka," BB said from the hologram pad by the door.

Shade raced to my side, nudging me upright with his head. I wheezed to my feet and snatched my sword before stumbling to the door.

It slid open, and I fell inside.

The door clicked shut behind me, and I let out an explosive breath that fell just short of a sob.

I lay gasping for a moment before using the plastic wall to haul myself upright.

"So, in case you were wondering. *That* was a megawing."

No one answered me. I winced, holding my injured arm close to my chest, then I straightened and looked around.

The prefab building was one big room lit by several flickering screens as long as I was tall. Far above, a catwalk gave access to the telescope hanging inside the dome.

Robotic arms curled up from the center of the floor, like a dead spider.

A mess of wires and tubing ran across the floor, tangling in front of a console full of switches and buttons just under the bank of screens.

Ren stood in front of them, a body at his feet.

"Oh." All the breath left my lungs at once. Because there was no one else it could be. This was Dr. Carver.

But Ren wasn't staring at the weirdly preserved body.

He stood listening to a message playing on the screens, eyes wide and face white.

"Ren?" I stumbled forward.

The figure on the screen, big enough to cross several of them, turned as if to look at me. It was a man with light hair and eyes. Nondescript and unthreatening.

"This is the woman you spoke of. The one who woke you from your cryo chamber?" he said.

Not a message. An AI.

Ren nodded, mutely.

"Welcome Anikka Drake," the AI said.

I glanced between them. "Ren, are you okay?"

The boy stood stunned, his face blue in the reflected light. He shook his head. "Tell her what you just told me."

"I said 'welcome, Ren Arlo. I assumed you would come after Dr. Carver perished. I am glad you found your way here when the wake-up program failed.'"

"Why?" Ren said, voice hoarse. He cleared his throat. "Why would I come? How do you know my name?"

"It is natural I would know it. You do not remember me, of course. I must account for the dampening effects of the chip. In which case, I imagine you have lots of questions."

"How do you know who I am?" he cried, each word its own force of frustration.

The AI appeared unfazed. "Because I was there when you were growing. I have known you your entire life. Without Dr. Carver, you are my primary directive."

"Who am I?" Ren whispered.

"Ren Arlo. Clone of Dr. Crispin Carver. Designed to further humanity's knowledge and influence in the galaxy. And preserved as Daybreak Colony's last hope and failsafe."

A tiny noise escaped me before I clamped down on it.

Ren's throat bobbed. "Clone," he said.

Then he bolted for the tiny kitchenette along the wall and puked in the sink.

CHAPTER 22

Daybreak: Day 214

Ren braced himself against the edge of the sink, head down. He swayed a little, either unsteady on his feet or because the motion soothed him. I couldn't be sure which.

I chewed my lip and stepped closer to the bank of screens, avoiding the obvious body on the floor. Definitely Dr. Carver. He still had that same close-cropped beard as in his personnel file. But I didn't want to look at the desiccated face too closely.

"Hello, Anikka Drake," the AI said, figure standing tall enough to cross two different screens. "I am 2.0."

"2.0," I said. "So, you are the second version?"

"Dr. Carver created me to be a secondary version of himself. A repository of his knowledge. This was before he created his clone, of course."

I glanced at Ren, but the boy didn't flinch. Maybe he was already overloaded and had lost the ability to react to anything else.

"About that..." I said.

"Ren Arlo, named for the world-famous Dr. Arlo, was

created as Dr. Carver's way to serve humanity." 2.0 folded his hands in front of him on the screen, like some serene sage.

"What does that mean?"

"Dr. Carver long ago recognized that his kind of brilliance only came once in a generation. He devoted his life to helping humanity with his intelligence. But he could only do so much with his time."

I raised my eyebrows. "Humble guy, wasn't he?" I exchanged a look with BB, who stood on my wrist. She covered her mouth with her hand as if to hide a smile.

"Dr. Carver did not have an inflated sense of self-importance," 2.0 said calmly. "He had a very accurate view of his intelligence. He knew the world would benefit from more of himself. So he created another."

Over by the sink, Ren lowered himself to the floor and put his head between his knees.

"Ren Arlo was supposed to grow up and use his mind to further humanity as well. But clones are still controversial on Earth."

"So they came here," I said.

"Dr. Carver added Ren Arlo to the personnel roster easily and brought him here in the first wave of colonists. Unfortunately, any in-depth conversation with Ren Arlo would have resulted in the truth being revealed. So he was kept sedated in the infirmary, and his memories were buried so no one would notice anything odd about him before Dr. Carver could devote time to integrating him into the colony."

"That last part clearly didn't happen." I glanced at the dead Dr. Carver. "Why isn't he all...gross?"

"I adjusted the habitat controls in the lab so the body would not decompose and compromise the wiring or the doctor's work. Any fluid could have ruined everything Dr. Carver worked for."

I made a face.

"Time is extremely important now," 2.0 said. "I am relieved Ren Arlo has finally found his way here. I was supposed to revive him in the event of Dr. Carver's death, but I was cut off from the wake-up computer. Unfortunately, we have wasted too much time in this cycle. We will need to proceed at once—"

"Could you give him a second?" I said. "He's still processing the last thing you told him."

"A second?" 2.0 said. "We have already lost weeks and you want to spare another—"

"BB?" I glanced at the AI on my wrist. "Help me out here?"

"Gladly," BB said, and I touched the hologram pad beside the control board. There were pads all over in here.

"As an infirmary AI, I must insist you allow Ren Arlo time to adjust. Shock will only decrease mental function..." she started to say as I walked away from the bank of screens.

"Ren?" I said. I didn't reach out to touch him. I wanted to, but something made me hesitate. A little squirm in my gut that made me worry he'd take it the wrong way. "Are you all right?"

"No." His voice came out thick and hoarse and muffled behind his knees.

I bit my lip and sank down to sit on my heels in front of him. "I don't know how to help you."

He drew in a shaky breath and lifted his head enough to rest it back against the basin of the sink. "I remember everything now. It's...it's coming back in pieces."

"Your life?"

He nodded. "My dad? Who was never there? That's him." He jerked his chin at Dr. Carver's body. "Sort of."

"He just...left you?"

"No. No. He wasn't neglectful or anything like that. Just... distracted. Driven. He was always off doing something, research or some grant project. He would come back to check on me a lot. Just to see how far along I'd come. Where I lived. In a lab near Lake Michigan."

He thunked his head against the sink basin, making a hollow thud.

"He didn't want you to remember because he was worried other people would realize what you were," I said quietly.

"Yeah. If I talked to anyone, they'd realize I'm...I'm a copy. Just a clone. I'm not a real person." He squeezed his eyes shut.

"Of course you're a real person," I said and took his hands. Who cared what he thought it meant? If he took it the wrong way, I'd deal with it later. Right now, he needed someone to ground him. To hold him here while panic made his thoughts want to take off.

How many times had I needed something like that and not had anyone around as an anchor?

"You are a very important person," 2.0 said across the room. "You are the most important person on the planet right now, Ren Arlo. With Dr. Carver gone, you are the colony's only hope of survival."

"That's why you were in his cryo-pod in the cave," I said quietly. "You were set aside."

"Dr. Carver switched them at the last minute," 2.0 said. "So he could remain to work on the problem."

"He came here to work?" I said.

2.0 looked sadly at his creator. "He has been here since the first storm. Working on a way to revive the colonists and protect the colony. He survived two storms. The third killed him."

My eyes narrowed, and I scanned the room. A cryo pod

stood against the far wall. With an AI to revive him, he could have survived there the same way the colonists had. But he wasn't in the cryo pod. He was in the middle of the room.

Whatever he'd been doing to survive the third storm hadn't worked.

I counted back in my head. I'd been here for almost seven months now. The first storm would have been the one that knocked the *Last Resort* out of orbit. The second would be the first I'd survived on the planet. And the third...

Dr. Carver had been here alive while I'd been struggling in the jungle trying to find the colony.

I wasn't sure how I felt about that. If he'd been here working, it wasn't like he would have been checking the colony for survivors.

But he could have. He had to have known the *Last Resort* crashed. He could have checked, and then I would have found him a lot sooner than I had.

Maybe if he had, I could have kept him alive through one more storm.

I shook my head. It was no use regretting things that hadn't happened. And even if we had connected, Dr. Carver sounded like someone who wouldn't have wanted my help. He might have stuck me in a cryo pod like BEV almost did and told me to wait.

"I was his failsafe," Ren said, opening his eyes again. "That's when he put this chip in my head. When he realized what was coming."

"No," 2.0 said. "The chip has always been there to suppress any memories that might have given you away. But Dr. Carver adjusted them before the evacuation. He gave you all of his own memories. His knowledge. So that in the event that he died, there would be a backup of him who could continue his work to save the colonists."

Ren's mouth fell open. "His memories?"

"What does that mean, exactly?" I said, eyes narrowing. "Can he just open them up in his mind like a file system?"

"No. That is not how memory works. This is more like an AI integration."

I exchanged a panicked look with BB, but 2.0 didn't seem to notice. He just kept talking.

"You will unlock the memories on the chip, and they will be integrated into your own."

My eyes flicked between 2.0 and BB. "You make that sound very routine, but an AI integration isn't something to be taken lightly. It...changes them."

BB had mostly been herself through the first couple of integrations, but I couldn't deny there'd been subtle changes. She was more human-like each time, able to grow and process things differently the more information she'd been given access to.

The last one had tipped the scale, and I'd paid the price for it. We both had in different ways.

"Yes, personality changes occur after memory integration," 2.0 said.

"I would become him," Ren said. He surged to his feet, face white and fists clenched. "I wouldn't be Ren anymore. I'd be Dr. Carver."

"With Dr. Carver's memories and knowledge, you would be able to finish his work. He was nearly finished. I am certain his creation was nearly ready to protect him from the storm. With only a couple of tweaks and some scaling, it could protect the colony. The colonists could be revived, and the colony rebuilt."

"I just have to give up who I am," Ren said, voice rising.

"Who are you that's so important that you should take

precedence over thousands of other people?" 2.0 said, voice flat and matter-of-fact.

Ren's eyes went wide and stricken.

"Hey!" I said. "You're talking to a real person here."

"I am talking to a clone. A copy created for an eventuality like this."

Ren spun away, hands diving into his hair. He pulled so hard his skin went tight around the sides of his face.

I rushed to his side and yanked on his arms. "Stop that. You're hurting yourself."

"What does it matter? *I* don't matter. Only the memories in my brain."

"That's not true," I whispered fiercely. "Stop listening to that bot and listen to me. You matter just as much as Dr. Carver."

His eyes swung to me, wide and glassy. "I don't want to be him," he said, the barest whisper.

"Then don't."

"I already am. I can't stop it."

I gripped his arms. "No. You are you. You're Ren."

"I'm a copy. How am I any different?"

"Because you didn't grow up as him."

Finally, the words seemed to affect him. He blinked. "What?"

"Your body is the same, your genetics are the same. But you grew up different. Your memories are yours. Not his. And that's what makes you you. You may have had the same starting point but you've had different paths and that's what makes you different."

"But the memories—"

"You don't have to unlock those unless you want to. You don't have to, you hear me? We'll find some other way to save the colony. You might be smart, but so am I. I found a way to survive. I found you and the other colonists, and I've kept you alive this long. I will help you. I'll help you find a way to do it without Carver's memories. Because you're not him. You don't have to be him unless you want to be."

His throat bobbed as he swallowed. And finally, he closed his eyes, and his shoulders sagged. He raised his hands to grip mine.

Daybreak: Day 214

"How do I start?" Ren said.

"By telling that pushy AI to shut up." I raised my head to catch his gaze. "Trust me. I've had a lot of experience with opinionated AIs." I glanced at BB who just gave me a bland look from the hologram pad.

Ren huffed a laugh and released my hands to scrub his face. "I'm sorry I called you an emotionless robot. I was angry and scared you might be right, and I didn't mean it. I'm sorry."

"I'm sorry, too. I shouldn't have lied to you. I was trying to protect you, but I did it badly. And I'm sorry I reacted the way I did." My gaze dropped. "The other orphans at Stellar Corp used to call me robot, because I was never interested in the same things they were. Then I turned around and did the same thing to you."

"You weren't terribly far off."

My mouth tightened, and I glared at him. "You're not a robot."

"Would it be that much better or worse if I was?"

I started to respond and thought better of it. Would Ren

have been any less of a person if he was an android? I already knew the answer to that because I had BB.

"I guess not," I said. "But I still shouldn't have yelled it at you, whatever I thought. I'm not very good with people."

"You're pretty good with me."

I reared back, and he threw up his hands.

"That's not—I meant as a friend."

I gave him a sidelong look. "Are you sure? I haven't had a lot of those." Or any.

"So you don't even recognize when you have one?" His smile fell as I stared back at him. "I mean it, okay? You are you, and I wouldn't want to change you just so we could possibly date. I'm not going to do anything you don't want me to do. That's what a friend is. Someone you trust and respect."

I took a deep breath. He made it sound easy, but it had never been easy before.

"It does mean you have to trust me to make my own decisions, too," Ren said, glancing at me out of the corner of his eye. "No more lying just to protect me."

"All right," I said. "Just as long as you don't go around saying you love me anymore."

"Absolutely. But I'm still allowed to care about you. Just platonically."

"Fine, if you have to," I groaned but with a smile to show I was kidding.

I stood and winced as I caught sight of the body that still lay in the middle of the floor. "I'll figure out what to do with Dr. Carver. So you don't have to look at him if you don't want to."

The ground outside was far too rocky to dig a grave, and pushing him off a cliff might have been cathartic for Ren, but felt a little too awful for reality. However, his cryo pod still stood against the far wall.

I touched the controls in the middle of the room to transfer BB back into my arm before I bundled the body up into a blanket and rolled him into the pod. Obviously, he'd never be revived again, but the pod would keep him from decomposing anymore.

The lights all blinked to indicate it was ready to go, but as I leaned over to check the temperature and humidity settings, the whole display flickered and the hum of the machine stuttered.

"What was that?" I leaned back and gave it a look.

"A lot of things have been doing that recently," BB said.

I bit my lip, thinking of the lights in the cave and the screens from the colony. "They have," I said quietly. "But they're all optical tech. They should be fine."

Behind me, Ren finally stood, and he seemed steadier than he'd been.

"I will check the pod," BB said and gestured to the hologram pad nearby.

"Can you do that?" I asked.

"I have extensive knowledge of the human body through my infirmary banks. I can use that to extrapolate how the pod works based on what it is supposed to do."

Another way she was growing and learning.

I touched the pad to transfer her. "Have at."

"Are you done with your second?" 2.0 asked Ren. "There is work to be done."

I tried to find the acid in the AI's tone as I crossed to the control panel, but every word out of his mouth was dry and flat.

"Oh man, I remember that tone," Ren said under his breath. "The soundtrack to my childhood. 'Are you done doodling, Ren? Pets are not allowed, Ren.'"

I cleared my throat and raised my voice. "Work is my

specialty," I said. "But we need a plan. We need a way to save the colonists without Dr. Carver's memories."

"This is inefficient," 2.0 said. "Dr. Carver has already done the preliminary work. With his memories you can pick up where he left off."

"Not an option," I said, not even bothering to look up at the AI. "And if you don't stop suggesting it, I'll switch you off for good."

2.0's image froze on the screen as he processed this. Ren moved up beside me and cast me a grateful look.

"You can, however, help us access his plans," I said. "And we can go from there."

2.0 hadn't mastered sour looks the same way BB had, but he did manage a fairly good scowl before he finally disappeared, and a cascade of blueprints and schematics replaced his image on the screens.

"Dr. Carver was working on a shield that would protect the entire colony and all the occupants," 2.0 said, and one of the images zoomed in, a network of lines lighting up to create a glowing dome. "He called it the Carver cage."

BB snorted, and I hid a smile while Ren rolled his eyes. "He would," he muttered.

"That's just a Faraday cage," I said.

2.0 looked like he would have sniffed if he had lungs. "It is an improvement on the Faraday cage, designed specifically with Daybreak's unique properties in mind."

"That would make a shield a lot like the one I use in a storm," I said, letting my wires glow for a second. "Only much much bigger."

Ren bit his lip as he squinted at the blueprints.

"That's a good start," I said. "But every plan for Daybreak's storms needs two parts." I held up two fingers. "A shield. And a way to reduce the effect of the storm. Like the way the animals have their secondary nervous system but still shelter in caves because it's safer."

"It may be safer for them, but it is unnecessary," 2.0 said. "At least in this instance. Dr. Carver's shield is big enough to protect the colony and strong enough to withstand the storms. Its bigger size will give it strength."

I gave the plans a skeptical look.

"Can you make sense of it?" I asked Ren quietly.

His hands moved across the controls, too high to actually push anything. "Maybe. The software part of it, definitely. And some of the electronics. But I wasn't studying the same things Dr. Carver already knew."

My brow furrowed. If Dr. Carver was trying to make a little copy of himself, why hadn't he started with the work he was most known for?

Ren used the controls to pull back the schematics to look at everything as a whole again. He flipped back to find the prototype just before the massive glowing dome. This one was much smaller with fewer connected lines superimposed over a darkened building that looked a lot like the facility we stood in now.

"This was his last attempt?" I said.

"Yes, a Carver cage big enough to encompass the lab and the telescope."

"But it didn't work."

"No." 2.0 kept his gaze on his master as well. "He could not go back into the cryo pod again. One can only be revived from death so many times before there are serious detrimental effects on brain and body function. And there was no other way to test the cage. All the Earth animals perished in the original storm and anything native to Daybreak—"

"Has a secondary nervous system that protects them," I said. "So he had to use himself as a test subject."

I had a lot of mixed feelings about Dr. Carver, but I could relate to that moment. Standing there watching the flickering front of the storm sweeping towards you, praying your precautions were enough. Had he felt that same choking fear? Or had he been completely confident up to the moment his heart stopped?

"If it didn't work for him, how is it going to work for us?" Ren said.

2.0 tilted his head. "Find the flaw and fix it."

Ren's face went rigid.

"2.0," BB said. "Help me with this."

It might have been a thinly-velied attempt to distract the AI, but either he wasn't sophisticated enough to recognize it or he didn't care, because he went.

I stepped up beside Ren, close enough to lean my elbow against his. My eyes raced across the schematics.

"I can build this," I said quietly.

He glanced at me. "You can?"

I shrugged. "Infra-engineer, remember. Give me the plans, and I'll make it happen. We just have to tweak it to work."

Across the room, BB whispered furiously with 2.0.

"Like debugging software," Ren said. "I guess that's my job."

"At least we have time. With the pods, we have all the time in the world. I can protect you through the storms if it takes that long."

"No," BB said.

I turned. She looked...pale. If that was even a word you could apply to a blue hologram.

"We do not have the time."

"What?" Ren said. "What do you mean?"

"The pods are breaking down."

"They're optical tech," I said, shaking my head. "They're not supposed to break down."

"Not through one storm, no. They managed just fine. But two? Three? We will face our fifth storm in thirty-four days."

2.0 replaced the schematics on the screen. "I have confirmed. This is why I was unable to connect to the wake-up computer in the caves to revive Ren Arlo."

"Now that I'm looking, I can see the degradation caused by repeated exposures to the levels of energy in a storm," BB said. "And I am sure we would see that same degradation in any other optical tech. The screens, the generator in the colony, the systems on the *Last Resort*."

"How fast is it deteriorating?" Ren said, straightening.

"It is past the point of no return." BB gestured to the pod beside her. "Based on the state of this one, I can infer that the pods in the cave and on the *Last Resort* will fail if put through another storm. They will not be able to preserve or revive the colonists after that."

My heart thumped. I'd thought we had time. With the colonists safely packed away, time was the only thing we *did* have.

Instead, we had thirty-four days. I closed my eyes and fought down an unhelpful scream. There was always one more thing. Another threat bearing down fast enough that I never had time to breathe in between.

Very deliberately I let my shoulders relax and cracked my neck.

"We'll have to revive them," I said. "This is their last chance. If we don't revive the colonists before the next storm, they won't survive."

Ren stared at me. "You're not angry? Or scared, or—"

"Of course I am. But we don't have time for any of that. Since I've landed on this planet, Daybreak has done nothing but try to kill me. This is nothing new." I shrugged and gave him a grin that felt reckless. "Apparently, I work best when I think I'm going to die soon." I met his eyes. "I told myself after my first storm, Daybreak didn't kill me. And I won't let it kill anyone else. So what's the first thing we need to do?"

Ren ran his hands through his hair. "2.0 do you have any electrical engineering texts? Did Dr. Carver bring any of his books with him?"

"This would be easier with Dr. Carver's memories—"

"Hmm, where is the AI off switch?" I said, tapping my lips. "I wonder if it's similar to shutting down the *Last Resort* systems or if I just start pulling out wires."

2.0 glared at me. "Fine," he said. "I will find what I can in the archives."

CHAPTER 23

Daybreak: Day 214

While Ren worked on the shield, my job, clearly, would be keeping us alive and fed while we were here.

Of course, the first thing I did was rummage through all of Dr. Carver's stuff. A large secret lab out in the middle of nowhere stocked by an eccentric scientist made me about as excited as finding clean underwear back at the colony.

Sadly, the astrophysicist didn't have any juice. And his medical supplies were limited. But he did have several suits of cold weather gear, a water purifier, ten ration bars, and a crate labeled "reddi-meals" that was actually full of ration bar wrappers.

"This guy must have been living on rat bars," I told BB under my breath. She'd transferred back to my prosthetic after casting a disgusted look at 2.0. Clearly neither AI was impressed with the other.

"There are several records of Earth scientists eating the same thing every day in order to save time and mental effort on deciding inconsequential things," she said, though she looked at the wrappers dubiously.

"Well, this might have been okay for a genius, but we're going to need something else. With two of us, we'll go through them twice as fast. And I have to feed Shade." The slinkwolf could hunt for himself, but I liked to make sure I had something on hand.

So, the first order of business would be to find some food. I hadn't spent any time in the mountains of Daybreak, so I wouldn't be as familiar with its dangers. But I knew how to be cautious and that had served me well on this planet.

"I know you do not wish me to monitor you," BB said quietly. "But I can tell you are in pain just from the way you are holding your arm. Did the megawing hurt you?"

I winced. "Not really. At least not permanently. A few bruises. I think I wrenched my arm when I grabbed Ren. And then again when we crashed."

"A pulled muscle, then."

"What do your banks say for treatment?"

"Anti-inflammatories and ice," she said, then crossed her arms. "But also rest and immobilization. Which I know you won't like, so I'm not sure if I should bother even saying them."

I sighed. "I'll try to take it easy, okay?"

I even unzipped my jumpsuit far enough to tuck my hand inside like a sling to appease her. Then I climbed the narrow metal staircase that led to the catwalk around the inside of the dome. Halfway around the circle, I found the controls for the telescope hatch. It was easy enough to open and peer out. Dr. Carver's shielding hadn't protected him during the last storm, but whatever he'd done had kept all the electronics in the building from getting fried, so clearly, he'd been headed in the right direction.

I hung out the opening, looking for glimpses of orange and pink wings, but the megawing seemed to be off—either still distracted with our decoy or on the prowl for easier prey. I'd have to watch out for it, but at least I could leave the building without getting snatched.

From here, I could survey most of the surrounding area in the afternoon light. I raised my hand to shield my eyes and took stock of the rugged slopes and the trees that dared to climb this far up. We'd left the jungle trees behind in the lowlands. These looked almost like conifers but with much broader needles, like the fossils of prehistoric trees back on Earth. Fewer of them marched up the rocky hills, leaving more open space in between.

I turned away and closed up the dome. The light and the fresh air were nice, but I didn't want a megawing trying to fit through the opening.

On the lower level again, I grabbed one of Dr. Carver's coats. I buttoned up and stuck my head out the door. Shade lifted his head from where he'd been napping beside the entrance and surged to his feet to follow me out.

The sky was clear of any megawings, and I slipped outside, leaving Ren to his study.

My bike lay against a rough boulder twenty yards away, and I dragged it over to the building.

The cross bow had a cracked stock and a snapped string. I tossed it back against the bike for now. The stock I might be able to repair, but without a string to replace the other one, it was useless.

I pulled my pack from the bike and slung it over my good shoulder, wincing as the movement jarred my arm.

I set out on foot, giving Shade the signal to scout carefully.

The slinkwolf wove between the trees with big needles

and stopped at the top of the ridge, nose in the air as he sniffed for trouble.

There wouldn't be any fruit trees at this elevation, but I did stop to gather some pinecones that had fallen from the conifers. Each one was as big as my fist and gave off a spicy scent that I hoped meant it would be edible.

None of the other plants looked familiar except for a couple of large ferns that clustered under each pine tree. They weren't exactly like the greens I was used to but they were close. Maybe they were a hardier, cold weather variant. I gathered those as well.

I came even with Shade at the top of the ridge and gazed out across the rising peaks. We weren't quite to the tree line yet, but it wouldn't take more than a few minutes to hike there. I imagined the megawing had a much easier time hunting where the branches didn't interfere, so it was probably safer down here.

And if there was a megawing, there had to be enough game to sustain it. I kept my eyes open, and sure enough, I eventually saw large rodents that could have been rabbits with short rounded ears and beaver-like tails along with a gray moose-like creature with long legs and antlers shaped like the points of a star.

That was good news if I felt well enough to go hunting tomorrow.

Shade barked, a short yip to draw my attention, not one that meant danger or fear. I picked up my pace and came even with him at the top of a ridge.

I caught my breath. The slopes here fell away into a perfect little pocket valley with a crystal-clear pond shining in the sunlight. I scanned the surface for any large shadows under the water, but this bit of mountain lake was way too small to hide a titan. A thin stream led away down the mountain in little rivulets and cascades probably to empty into the massive lake in the lowlands.

Bright pink plants with leaves like clover spread across the ground surrounding the lake, reflecting in its calm surface. I reached out a toe to nudge the edge of one and jumped back to see what it would do. In my experience, anything on Daybreak that was pink or orange was bad news.

The plants seemed to shiver from my touch, and the leaves curled back as if to avoid me. But that was it. No noxious pollen floated toward me. No vines reached to grab me.

I waited another minute for any adverse side effects, but nothing came, so I shrugged and pressed on toward the edge of the little lake. Rocky shelves jutted over the water's surface, the pink ground cover extending up in creeping tendrils which drew back as I passed.

I peered over the edge of a ledge, ready to snatch my head back if any slasherfins leaped at me. A couple of bright shapes flickered under the surface, but nothing large enough to be a slasherfin.

I glanced at Shade. As a Daybreak native, he was my canary in most cases. I didn't know how familiar he was with the mountains since his pack had originally stalked me around the crater. But he had good instincts, and I trusted them.

He sniffed the edge of the water, then leaned over to lap up several mouthfuls.

I pursed my lips. "Must be safe," I said to BB.

"One day that will not be enough," she grumbled.

I dipped out a handful of water and gave it a cautious taste. Shapes darted away from my shadow.

"Well, at least we have a source of water. And there's definitely fish down there. Even if I don't have a hook."

I made my way back toward the lab, mind churning

through possible ways to make the place self-sufficient. Ten minutes later, Shade streaked past me with a yip.

Without hesitation, I dove for the nearest fern and curled up between its leaves and the trunk of a conifer.

Shade wriggled in beside me just as a huge shadow passed overhead.

I held my breath as the megawing circled, my hand curling around the hilt of my sword.

But it screamed and winged away again without noticing me.

BB flickered to life only when it was safely away. "We'll need to deal with that if we're going to stay here."

I cast her a grin. "Don't worry, I've already got an idea."

Daybreak: Day 220

Ren remained buried in calculations and schematics for days, which allowed me to implement my plans. BB helped me rig a simple program in the signal towers that cycled the lights in a flickering pattern around the lab. It not only drew the megawing away from the building whenever we needed to leave, it kept the giant predator circling the area, essentially scouting the perimeter for us.

As soon as that was in place, I didn't need to worry so much about the megawing because it was always on the opposite side of the mountain from where I happened to be working.

With Ren safely ensconced in the lab, I took the bike and headed back down to the lowlands. Since I could fly at max speeds, the trip only took a day instead of the full four we'd taken before.

The drop ship was as I left it. The dino-chicken screeched the moment it saw me, but it still had plenty of fruit, so clearly, it was just trying to make me feel bad. I collected the eggs and let it glare at me.

I also needed a couple of other things from my storage that I hadn't thought to bring, but overall, the round trip only took a couple of days and I returned to the lab with extra supplies.

Around the mountain lake, I set up snares under the edge of the shyclover. As soon as I had withdrawn, the leaves opened back up, concealing my traps and leaving me a pretty steady source of rabbit meat, and on one memorable occasion, a fat snake with a feathered frill not unlike a cobra.

Nets hung across the cascades, catching several sleek fish that lacked the wicked teeth of the slasherfins. Catching them was a lot easier, so they weren't as satisfying to eat, but just as tasty.

Meanwhile, Ren worked. Every morning I left him hunched over the console, brow furrowed into deep lines. And every afternoon, I came back to find him in the same position, some bit of lunch forgotten in his hand.

Five days after we'd arrived at the lab, I came back with a netful of fish to see 2.0 staring down from his screen as Ren held his head in his hands.

"This is not what you were made for. This struggle," the AI was saying. "You were designed for one thing. To carry on Dr. Carver's legacy. By denying that, you are throwing away every advantage he gave you in life. And you are condemning the colonists to death."

I dropped the fish. "Hey, lighten up. Threats aren't going to get us anywhere."

"It is not a threat. I am not programmed to exaggerate. I am programmed to state facts. If this is hard, it is only because Ren Arlo is making it hard. He knows what he can do to understand the schematics."

Ren pushed up from the console and stalked out the door.

I raised my eyebrows at the AI. "Was that the desired outcome? You're not as smart as you think you are if you think browbeating someone is going to get them to do what you want."

"You are not a factor in this equation. You are a distraction. Nothing more."

I cast a rude gesture to the figure on the screens and followed Ren.

"I take it back, BB," I said as I stomped across the bare ground. "You might be opinionated, but you have never come close to being as terrible as that guy."

"Thank you? I think," BB said.

I nearly tripped over Ren as I came around the big boulder we'd crashed into that first day.

He sat with his back against the rock, tossing a broken stick for Shade. The slinkwolf bounded across the gravel to snatch it up, then wrestled it with a snarl before trotting back to drop it at Ren's feet.

From here, we could look out over the lowlands and see the Black Flats lurking beside the bright stretch of the lake. And somewhere in the dense jungle stood the colony.

"2.0's always been like that," Ren said. The lines across his forehead and around his mouth hadn't faded, even now when he wasn't concentrating. "It's his programming."

"That is no excuse," BB snapped. "There are plenty of ways we can choose to execute our programming. Being polite costs us nothing and gains us a lot more."

Ren snorted. "Not with Dr. Carver. He didn't have time for anything but short, sweet, and to the point. Only cut out the sweet part. So his AI isn't any different."

He picked up the stick and threw it again.

"You grew up with that?" I said, sliding down the boulder to sit beside him.

He shrugged and wouldn't meet my eyes. "It wasn't as bad as it sounds. He really did believe he was giving me everything. I had all the education I could want and a whole lab full of equipment I was allowed to use from the time I could walk."

But clearly not the one thing that mattered. Even I had had Professor Orrion.

"I know a lot of dads think of their sons as little copies of themselves," I said. "But it's a whole lot worse when it's literal."

Ren shook his head. "He actually wasn't trying to create an exact replica. It wouldn't do any good to simply duplicate his knowledge base, so he wanted me to study different things. That way, we could cover more area." He huffed a dry laugh and threw out his hand. "I could study whatever I wanted. As long as it was a hard science that was useful and challenging and provided an adequate range of research and return on investment and, and, and."

"I take it vet sciences were out," I said.

"Too crowded of a field. Not enough to work with in Earth animals. I don't think he planned to move me to another planet at that point, yet." He kicked a pebble with his toe. "He never realized that he may have wanted me to be different from him, but he still wanted me to be something specific. Still a copy, just with different blanks filled in."

Shade rushed back with the stick in his mouth, and Ren buried both hands in his ruff to give the slinkwolf a good scratch, lowering his head till they were nearly touching noses.

Finally, the ghost of his grin lit his face. "That's why I

spent so much time with that dog. Dr. Carver hated dogs, and it was the one way I could feel like I was my own person."

And working on the schematics, trying to understand what Dr. Carver had left behind, was just making him feel more like a copy than ever.

"When was the last time you drew something?" I asked suddenly.

Ren pulled back from Shade, blinking. "What does that have to do with anything?"

"Nothing. That's my point. It's something you do for fun, right?" I pulled my pack off my back, easing my sore arm out of the strap, and dug around inside. I pulled out the sheaf of papers I'd brought back from my trip to the drop ship and the lone pencil.

Ren bit his lip. "I'm not sure I have time to doodle."

"It's not doodling. That's what 2.0 called it, so we're going to ignore that."

"There is substantial evidence that taking breaks allows the brain to be more efficient when it's working," BB said. "Taking time off might actually make you faster in the long run."

I waggled the papers. "I don't think Dr. Carver was the type of person to take breaks."

He gave me a look that said he knew exactly what I was doing, but he snatched the papers, anyway.

"Good," I said and stood up. "I was worried I was going to have to beat you over the head with my point."

I left him there, but later, I found sketches of the megawing and more drawings of the titan scattered around his workspace. 2.0 might have considered me a distraction, but at least now when I saw Ren working, he didn't have those deep grooves in his forehead that made him look too much like the astrophysicist.

A couple of days later it paid off.

"You should see this," he said as I came into the lab.

I stepped over to the console where he stood. "What is it?"

He pushed up from his hunched position. "I think I have it mostly put together."

"The shield?" I refused to call it a Carver cage.

Ren nodded wearily, but he wore a satisfied smile. "I think I can replicate what he was doing."

I came to stand next to him. "That's great. Do we know how his shield is supposed to be bigger and strong enough to withstand the storm yet?"

"I haven't gotten that far." He scrubbed his hands down his face and shook his head, then his voice gained strength. "But we're going to need to get started soon. This looks really complicated and big. I'll figure out the rest as we go."

He pointed to a specific area of the schematic and zoomed in. "We'll need anchor points around the colony. Big electrical towers that will serve as the exterior of the cage."

"Does Dr. Carver have everything we need here?"

His grin went lopsided. "Hardly. That's the first tricky part. Every Stellar Corp colony has an orbiting satellite full of supplies. We just need to call them down."

I laughed. "A satellite. Sure. I could have used that six months ago."

Artwork by Ren Arlo
Scanned by BB

To-do

- Get materials from satellite
- Build Dr. Carver's system
- Wake the colonists

CHAPTER 24

Daybreak: Day 221

Of course, it couldn't be as easy as pushing a button on 2.0's console. No, the AI had lost contact with the control tower that communicated with the satellite. He hadn't had access in months, he told us.

Fine. We would just have to go find it and plug it in manually. So to speak.

Hopefully, there would be a working plug. I decided to plan for the worst and refused to think about it further.

The coordinates for the control tower lay deep in the heart of the mountains on a peak that gave it a clear sightline to the satellite's orbit. Which meant we'd be traveling straight into whatever weather the peaks of Daybreak could throw at us.

We bundled up in Dr. Carver's warmest gear, including the snow pants and boots. Mine bunched around the ankles until I rolled the cuffs up, but Ren's fit perfectly. Obviously.

As I strapped our gear onto the hover bike and got Shade settled, Ren stood beside us, plucking at his sleeves, a strange look on his face.

"Are you all right?" I asked.

Ren shook himself. "Fine," he said with false brightness. "Just fine. It takes more than a coat to turn you into someone, right?"

I caught my breath. "Ren—"

"It's fine. Let's just go." He hopped on the back of the bike and gave Shade a deliberate scratch.

I clenched my teeth on a response and swung my leg over. My wrenched arm still ached a bit when I bent it funny, but I couldn't afford the loss of mobility, so I left the sling hanging loose as I gripped the handlebars.

"You're not him," I said over my shoulder as I directed current through the bike's frame, and we lifted into the air with a jerk.

Ren didn't answer, but he wrapped his arms around my middle and leaned into me.

Our coordinates led us past the first few peaks, and the air grew from chilly to cold to frigid. I didn't want to show Ren BB's map or reveal how we knew exactly where everything was, so I kept us close to the ground and scanned the surrounding peaks for the glint of a tower.

BB appeared every now and then to nod subtly in one direction or another, and I lazily zigzagged toward the tower.

Gray light filtered through the clouds, and a few snowflakes began to fall around us. I cast a nervous glance up. I hadn't been hiking through a lot of mountains back on Earth, but I'd read a lot, and storms above the tree line seemed to be a common theme for disaster stories.

"Do you think that's it?" Ren said and pointed.

I followed his gesture, squinting into the flurries that swept around us.

On the highest peak in front of us, a shape stabbed toward the sky. Hard to tell at this distance, but it seemed very tall and straight compared to the jagged rocks it stood on.

"It looks man-made," I said. "So probably. I doubt there's anything else up here. Unless Dr. Carver has more secret labs."

Ren shook his head, but just as I steered the bike to point to our mystery shape, it stuttered in the air.

"What?" I gasped and glanced toward the sky. But there wasn't the ominous shape of a titan, and I couldn't imagine one flying all the way up here, anyway.

The bike lurched and lost altitude.

"Hang on," I called and tried to control our descent so we didn't crash again. We went down in a series of quick drops that made my stomach clench.

Ren's arms clamped around my middle as we jerked and skidded across the snowy ground. I yanked hard, making my bad arm hurt, but managed to keep the nose of the bike from plunging into the side of the mountain. Barely. We plowed through the snow, the abrupt stop throwing me against the handlebars with Ren's weight thrown across my back.

I tried to catch my breath, the metal shoved into my diaphragm and had to wriggle out from under Ren.

"Sorry," he gasped and rolled away, off the bike.

Shade yelped and tugged at his belt, and I reached back to unsnap him. "Sorry, buddy. I know we've had a lot of bad landings on this thing."

Shade leaped free and shook himself, sending snowflakes flying.

I shivered and pulled the hood of my parka up, zipping it all the way to my chin so the fur lining surrounded my face.

"*Why* did we have another bad landing?" Ren said, handing me a pair of thick gloves. I couldn't wear them while riding since I had to keep the current moving between my wires and the bike's frame, but I pulled them over my icy fingers now.

"I don't know. It felt like the titan, but that thing isn't here, and I checked for leaks after the last time, so...oh. Oh no."

I knelt and pulled the glove off again to touch the bike's frame. I yanked my fingers back and stuck them in my mouth.

"What is it?" Ren said.

"It's frozen," I said, stuffing my hand back in its glove. "Solid. The tridenium won't flow if it's frozen. And the current will be sluggish at best. We're stuck on the ground."

Ren squinted up the slope, then back down the way we came. "It's closer to go up. Do you think we should keep moving?"

"We came all this way," I said, standing. I handed Ren one of the packs and slung the other on my back. "It would be stupid to turn back now."

Except we had to climb in a blizzard. The snow piled up around the boulders, and we trudged through the new powder. Gray flurries obscured the sight of the tower above us, but we'd been on the right peak. We just had to keep going uphill and eventually we'd find it. In the distance, the clouds lit up with flashes, and I could just see the shadow of something tall against them.

Shade trudged beside us, head down against the wind and his tail tucked between his legs. He had fur, but I worried it wouldn't be enough to protect him.

"Keep moving," BB said from my wrist. I'd rolled my sleeve up so her projectors wouldn't be obscured. It wasn't like my metal arm could feel the cold, anyway. "We have to be almost there."

I took that to mean that her navigation data told her we

were heading in the right direction. I put my head down and renewed my efforts to push through the howling wind.

"Anikka, look out!"

I looked up just as a metal structure loomed out of the swirling snow and nearly ran into one of the support struts.

"The tower. Ren, it's here."

Ren had been directly behind me, trudging in my footsteps, keeping one hand on Shade's back. He looked up, his cheeks chapped from the cold.

"Thank the gods of all worlds," he muttered.

I grabbed a strut for balance against the wind and pulled myself along to the command console housed in a big metal box welded to the base of the tower.

The sides shielded me from the wind, and I leaned into its shelter.

I tapped the power button and waited for the tiny screen to boot up. Optical technology, so it should be safe from the storms. 2.0 wouldn't have suggested it otherwise.

A blinking cursor appeared.

SUPPLY SATELLITE CONTROLS: ONLINE

The letters flickered across the screen. I let out my breath.

SATELLITE COMMUNICATIONS: UNRESPONSIVE

"Vent it," I muttered. "It's always something."

"What's wrong?" Ren shouted.

"It's not communicating with the satellite. Something's broken."

"Broken?" He glanced up at the tower.

I followed his gaze and sure enough, something banged in the wind, clanging against the tower struts. It looked like an antenna.

"It must have come loose in the wind. Maybe ages ago."

"Can we fix it?"

I was already shrugging out of the straps of my pack. "Just

watch me," I said under my breath. I could weld an antenna back in place, no problem. As long as the wiring and connections were all still good. No guarantee with it swinging around up there, but first thing's first.

A streak of light and a loud crack made me jump. Only a strange sort of instinct flowing down my wires made me grab Ren and fling him back.

"Lightning?" he cried.

More light flickered against the clouds and a streak of electricity struck the tower, cascading down the struts to the ground at our feet.

"Have you ever heard of thunder snow?" I said.

He was staring upward at the tower. "Anikka, we're above the tree line, standing next to a tall metal tower in the middle of a lightning storm. We're gonna get fried."

Well, he would get fried. Theoretically, I could take the blow and distribute it so I was safe. But I'd never actually tried it with natural lightning before.

Another streak and a crack. The smell of burning ozone made my nose itch and the hair on the back of my neck stood up.

We had to get up the tower to fix the antenna, but I couldn't redirect the lightning and do the welding at the same time. Just the thought made me shudder.

I pulled my tool kit from my pack and thrust it at Ren. "You'll have to climb."

His eyes bulged as he stared at me. "What?" he yelped.

"I'll redirect the lightning. It won't touch you. But I can't do both and someone needs to get up there to fix it. Take this. It's an arc welder. Battery powered. Find the end of the antenna and just...glue it back into place. It's really easy."

I pulled the darkened goggles that would protect his eyes

out of my pack and yanked them over his head to sit haphazardly against his hood.

"Anikka, this is a terrible idea."

"Watch. I promise the lightning won't get you." I thrust him back and pushed a safe distance away. As I let myself relax, the wires under my skin glowed. I could feel the electricity crackling through the air, gathering above the clouds, arcing down and down—

And I pulled.

The lightning cracked, a solid streak aimed directly at me. Instead of letting it hit me and dissipate across my wiring, I parted it above my head and directed it into the rock at my feet. It sizzled against my skin anyway, singeing my wires. Smoke rose from the cuffs of my coat and pants.

I glimpsed Ren's pale face in the aftermath of the flash.

My hands clenched into fists. "Go. We need to do this fast. I don't know how long I can manage it."

To his credit, Ren didn't waste time arguing. Sometimes it was nice working with a genius. When you finally convinced them that your plan would work, they leaped to make it happen, connecting all the dots themselves.

Ren hauled himself up the tower, and I scanned the skies with my eyes and the intuitive feeling that had come with my cybernetics. It had taken me ages to figure it out, having to do most of it by feel, but now I could sense the energy in Daybreak's atmosphere as easily as I could sense the electricity generated in my muscles and wiring. And lightning was just another form of energy.

I drew the streaks towards me, gathering even the little ones to keep them safely from Ren. I could hear him curse as he climbed.

"Are you almost there?" I called.

Another curse, this one directed at me, and I grinned.

I pulled current and let it cascade around me. But the burning in my skin was building. I could redirect the lightning around me, but some of it still traveled through my wiring, growing worse with every strike.

Over and over again, but I couldn't overlook even one.

"BB, did you keep any of the cybernetics data from your last integration?" I asked, heart in my throat.

BB's image flickered in reaction. "You know I did not," she said, face hard and flat.

I did know, but...she'd been putting things together, growing, and evolving.

"Then you'll have to extrapolate from your infirmary banks and help me decide how much is too much."

"I also still have access to your vitals, but you did not want me to monitor you."

I winced. I'd needed to keep her out for her own good, but...

"I give you permission to monitor everything essential for the next thirty minutes. Please," I added. "I'm not sure how much of this I should take."

Not how much I *could* take. I could take it till I burned from the inside out.

"You know my opinion on risking yourself—"

"You also know what's at stake. I'm not going to leave him up there in a lightning storm."

BB glanced up. "I know. I will keep you apprised."

The clouds around the tower flickered with light, but I couldn't feel any direct lightning at that moment. Ren must have fired up the arc welder.

"Come on, come on," I muttered under my breath.

I lost track of the time, focusing only on the sizzle of lightning, the energy streaking through the air, and the heat building in my wires. The pain I pushed to a far corner of my mind and convinced myself I'd deal with it later. It wasn't as bad as the pain of the implantation had been. I could do this for as long as I had to.

"Anikka, your internal temperature is rising to a dangerous level. I am worried about fever."

I tore off my hood, letting the frigid air cool my skin.

"I don't like the way your blood pressure looks. This indicates a pain response. Deep breathing is recommended in such cases when anti-inflammatories cannot be taken."

I followed her directions to inhale and exhale.

I redirected another crack of lightning and screamed in pain. BB didn't say anything, but her image flashed red, numbers cascading across her flickering face, and I knew I was at the end.

"Ren!" I threw back my head and shrieked.

"Done." The voice came floating down through the storm.

Another bolt of lightning formed. Ren was only halfway down the tower.

I yanked, thrusting the energy at the peak opposite us. The bolt struck and snow and rocks flew into the air.

"Jump," BB called to Ren.

He flung himself from the tower fully six feet from the snow and landed in a sprawled heap.

I fell to my knees and let the lightning go. It flashed around us, crackling over the tower but not touching Ren.

He rushed to the console and typed in a command.

"It worked!" he cried and leaped back before another strike could hit.

I flopped on my back in the snow and stared up at the gray sky. A streak of light, far too slow to be lightning, lit up the clouds and speared off in the vague direction of the colony.

A supply drop entering the atmosphere.

CHAPTER 25

Daybreak: Day 221

Ren dropped to his knees beside me. "You did it, Anikka. It will be waiting for us on the colony landing pad."

"Well done," BB said to Ren when I couldn't answer. "But we must get to safety. I am worried about Anikka's vitals, and she has only given me permission to monitor them for another seven minutes."

"What?" Ren said, but he slid an arm under my shoulders and helped me sit.

My muscles still worked, but they felt burned and sore where my wiring tracked through them. Every movement made me gasp in pain.

BB's image flickered, and a map appeared. "Hurry," she said. "There is a cave where you can shelter and get warm. It is not far as long as you follow my directions."

"How could you possibly know that?" Ren said. He hauled me to my feet.

BB didn't answer except to direct him through the snow. He kept my arm over his shoulders and dragged both of our packs behind him. Shade trotted along at our heels until we reached a deep overhang of rock.

Ren led me to the back, where we would be the most sheltered from the wind and snow. He forced a couple of pain killers through my numb lips and left me sitting with my back against the stone.

Shade curled up behind me. I didn't know how to tell him I burned with fever, not cold, but his heat seeped into me and actually seemed to help calm the raging blood that pulsed in my ears.

By the time the world stabilized and the rocks came into focus instead of dissolving into blurry shapes, Ren had built a fire with the supplies in his pack and was heating bits of fish and rabbit.

I extended my arms and pushed my sleeves up to examine my skin. I half expected to find it crispy, but it was only red along the lines of my wiring, like a really specific sunburn.

Already I felt a bit better, with the pounding in my head and veins subsiding and the fever receding from my senses. I couldn't imagine what would have happened if I'd had to redirect more lightning. I shuddered, thinking I never wanted to see a streak of light again.

I crept close to the fire, and Ren held out a bit of meat that I tore into. He was strangely quiet and wouldn't meet my eyes. Especially considering our success.

"Are you all right?" he finally said.

I nodded.

Ren glanced at BB, who still flickered on my wrist. "What does your data say?"

BB froze before answering. "I am no longer allowed to check her vitals."

"No, but you're an infirmary AI. Make an educated guess."

"Ren," I said, heartbeat speeding up.

"She will be fine with rest."

"And the bike? You know where it is, so we can get down the mountain in the morning. You marked it on your map."

BB met his gaze. "I did."

"You're not just a wake-up companion," he said, voice hard. "You're integrated."

"This is true," BB said.

"Ren, it's not as bad as it looks," I said quickly, trying to get ahead of whatever terrible things he was thinking. "BB helped me survive. Every data packet she has was necessary."

"How many?" Ren said.

"That doesn't have an easy answer—"

"How many?" He stood, nearly cracking his head on the rocky overhang.

I took a deep breath. "Four here," I said quietly.

"And five on the *Last Resort*," BB added.

"Not as bad as it looks, huh?" he said with a twisted grin.

"BB is not logic-crazy. We...prevented that."

"But she's different. She doesn't act like a normal AI. She can do a whole lot more. She can jump between pads and extrapolate and evolve."

"That doesn't make her evil." I stood as well, legs unsteady. "Just more human. And the more human she is, the safer she is."

His entire body drooped, and he ran a hand through his hair, making the damp strands stand up at odd angles. "Why didn't you tell me?"

"It's a felony," I said. "They'd take BB away. They'd arrest me."

"Who would? Me? You think I would do those things?"

"Not you. The...colonists."

"Who are all asleep. You didn't trust me, so you lied to me. Gods of all worlds, everyone's been lying to me."

"Hey!" I cried. "None of this is about you, okay? It's about BB and me. We made the decision to hide it way before we ever met you. Stop making it all about you."

He jerked back, then stumbled away to sit on the other side of our shelter.

I blew out my breath.

"I do not know what to do," BB said quietly.

"Nothing." I didn't bother to keep my voice down. "You don't owe him anything."

"He is a friend, and I am tired and afraid, and I don't like being something everyone is terrified of."

I threw myself on the ground beside the fire. Shade came up beside me, and I buried my face in his fur. "Not everyone is terrified of you."

"That is another lie."

I lifted my head. "BB—"

"Do not lie to me as well as him."

Ren's head came up, but I was focused on BB, my heart thudding in my throat. "I'm not—"

"You do not trust me."

"I do." I couldn't help choking on the words. Tears burned at the back of my eyes, making my throat ache.

Music burst from the speakers at my wrist. An electronic mix I used to love. But the beat pulsed in my head, twisting until there was another melody laid over top, and I was back on the *Last Resort*, sliding down the deck grating, pain slicing across my nerves from brand new incisions and wires I didn't quite know how to use.

I threw my arms over my head, blocking the sound as my pulse raced.

It lasted for less than three seconds, and BB shut it off so silence rang around the cave. But that moment could have been an eternity beating in my ears.

I tried to speak, but it just made my throat ache more.

"I'm sorry," BB said, voice soft. "But I know when you lie to me now. Please, don't. It makes me...sad. I think."

My throat convulsed, but I couldn't bring myself to answer her. Finally, her hologram shut down, and I was left holding out my empty prosthetic. She was still there. She could still hear me. But it was like she'd left the room. Shut the door between us. I wanted to call her back, but what was I going to say to her?

"You were right," Ren said softly. "This isn't about me. I'm sorry."

I shook my head. I wasn't the one who could accept his apology.

"Do you want to talk about it? Why is she angry?"

I couldn't. Not with BB listening. Not when every word would just tear new wounds when she already had so many.

CHAPTER 26

Daybreak: Day 233

Over the next few days, we climbed down the mountain, dragging the bike until it could thaw, and collected what we needed from the lab. Mainly the plans for the shield.

2.0 insisted Ren take a couple of earpieces so he could talk to us from afar. I hated the idea of him whispering in Ren's ear over and over, but he was right. We'd need a way to communicate.

The anchor towers surrounded the colony so the drop ship became our base of operations. Again.

The cache from the satellite waited on the colony's launch pad. The sleek capsule stood on end, nearly as long as a city bus. Dr. Grotman's codes opened it without hassle, and we spent the first couple of days just sorting through everything, collecting it into piles for each of the different anchor points. We'd need to build a dozen all in a circle.

Every night, Ren pored over the printouts 2.0 had sent with him like I'd poured over my textbooks before an exam.

Like he was trying to fit decades of knowledge into the few weeks we had left.

Dr. Carver had left him an impossible task. But I kept my lips shut tight on that thought. I had the same impossible task, and it wasn't like we could just give up. Thousands of lives depended on us figuring this out.

Ren gave me the exact coordinates and schematics to build each anchor point, and I spent those weeks ferrying materials out to each site while he sat at the drop ship and pieced together the controls for each tower.

Finally, I felt like the infra-engineer I was supposed to be. This was the type of designing and building I would have been doing in the colony had everything gone to plan. Of course, the consequences for failure were much higher.

BB came with me, though she was mostly quiet as I braced and welded and traveled. I knew I'd hurt her, but I didn't know how to fix it. I could say "I trust you" over and over again, but I didn't know how to make her believe me.

Sometime in those days, the itchbush pollen dissipated, and I didn't even notice until I realized I'd left my mask at home without thinking about it. That's how tired I was. We all were.

Every day, I returned to the drop ship exhausted to find Ren asleep on his work or muttering to himself so hard he didn't even notice me come in, and every now and then I caught the tinny voice of 2.0 in his ear.

His complexion grew more and more gray, and the creases in his brow and around his mouth grew. He even lost weight, and I started to see why Dr. Carver had been so much skinnier.

The thought made my chest go tight. He was slowly killing himself trying to do Dr. Carver's job without actually turning into Dr. Carver.

I missed his sense of humor and the way he would light up over some new quirk of Daybreak. It felt like I'd never see those things again.

But how was I supposed to keep him here and himself? He'd asked me to respect his choices, but that didn't mean I couldn't try to protect him. Except what kind of help would he accept when he was so wrapped up in someone else's work?

I bit my lip on my protests and went to clear the crate we used as a table. Under Ren's tray, I found a half-finished drawing of Shade and the broken stub of the pencil.

The next day, I came back a little early with a blank notebook. I slid it across his workspace to rest under his nose.

He blinked at it for a solid minute.

"What's this?"

"More paper. And..." I flourished a new pencil.

Finally, he smiled. It wasn't exactly like normal, but a little of the tightness in my chest eased.

He took the pencil and held it between his hands. "You know, I love a good pencil." He met my gaze and wiggled his eyebrows. "Platonically."

I rolled my eyes. "I found it in the infra-engineer workshops. But that's not everything."

I touched the hologram pad, and BB appeared. She gave Ren a grin before she morphed into a giant black monitor lizard.

"What is that?"

"We called it the black death. We might not have time to go looking for one, and trust me when I say that's probably a really bad idea, anyway. But if you like, BB can show you what they look like for your sketches, and I'm happy to answer any questions for your notes."

He stared down at the blank page, fingers clenched around the pencil. "Thank you," he said finally.

Daybreak: Day 238 (10 days until the storm)

The work took just over two weeks, and by the end of it, a familiar feeling crept up my neck as I counted down the days.

Ren still had to attach the controls to each tower, the minicomputer that would talk with all the other computers and regulate the way each one drew energy from the atmosphere to form the shield. So the last day he rode with me, and we visited the six points south of the colony before midafternoon, testing them all to be sure they turned on.

The next three stretched in an arc from the area around the meadow where we hunted silverpoints up to the shore of the lake.

We sped toward the tower, and I pulled the bike to a stop with a little jerk at the edge of the lake. I propped it against the shelter I'd built so long ago, and Ren went to the anchor tower right beside it.

Each anchor point looked a lot like a signal tower with struts stretching two times my height and a screen at the base for commands.

"Would you like some help, Ren?" BB said. "I believe I have a good idea of what you're doing now."

Ren gave BB a tight-lipped look. "I didn't know you had software engineering in your programming."

"I do not. I have been extrapolating."

His face went white, and he actually took a step back before he realized it and turned away. "No thank you."

I tried to glare at him, but my look just rolled right off his back. I didn't blame him exactly. He didn't seem to have a problem with BB until she mentioned something that reminded him of the integration, and even then, he was nothing but polite. But she was smart. She knew exactly what was happening each time he flinched.

And it had to hurt her.

"I am fine," BB whispered to me. "Don't mind me. What do you get when an AI is embarrassed?"

"I don't know. What?"

Her hologram popped out of existence. "An empty wrist."

I patted the place where I'd built in her projectors. Then I glanced at the tower, then out at the surface of the lake. It was windy today with waves crashing up the beach nearly to the base of the anchor point.

"Will it take long?" I asked.

"About the same amount of time as the others." Ren said. "Why? What's wrong?"

"Every time we turn one of these on to test it, it pulls energy from the atmosphere."

His brow drew down. "Yes. That's what it's designed to do."

I heaved a sigh. "I just think there's a good chance that it will draw a titan."

He jerked and looked out over the lake with me. "Oh."

I waved at him and then stepped toward my bike. "Keep going. I'm just…going to be ready."

"Okay, yeah. Probably a good idea."

Ren punched in his commands, and the tower lit up. Just like it was supposed to. A swirl of light formed over the tip and bits of energy crackled down the struts.

When the whole shield was turned on, the anchor points would reach out to one another and form a dome of energy around the colony, arching up and over. Theoretically.

But right now, it was just a blazing beacon all by itself.

Out on the lake, the water rolled.

I squinted. Hard to tell if that was just waves or not.

Nope, it was definitely frothing now.

I hopped on my bike, and BB appeared on the hologram pad. Using the electricity in my wires, I lifted into the air and sped away over the lake, determined to keep the titan from going after Ren or the anchor point. I'd drawn it away before. I could probably do it again. And once we were done with the test, the tower wouldn't be active until the storm, so it wouldn't draw the titan back.

"Wait, Anikka," BB cried. "Look."

I shuddered to a stop in midair. "What?" I whipped around.

The waves at the edge of the lake rushed back, revealing hundreds of shining carapaces scuttling up the shore out of the water.

"Fisherclaws? You've got to be kidding me."

I turned to race back, but the water underneath me still churned as if something was making its way out of the depths, and I knew exactly what that would be.

"Vent it!"

The crabs scurried to surround Ren, and he yelped as they snapped their pincers at him.

"Anikka, I do not like the things that have followed you home this time."

I could only growl in frustration.

I wasn't even there anymore, so would they eat Ren instead of the fish they expected? And here I was stuck in the middle of the air, waiting for a titan to appear.

Ren abandoned the tower and scrambled to climb the makeshift shelter. His feet slid on the slick surface, and a crab grabbed his boot. He kicked free and rolled onto the roof. But he was as stuck there as I'd been on the rocks of the island when we'd first encountered these things.

"Take care of the titan," BB said. "I'll help Ren."

"BB—" But the lake heaved beneath me, and the gray skin of the titan appeared, water cascading around its head.

I swerved out of the way and sped around the surfacing creature, craning my head over my shoulder to catch a glimpse of the shore.

The screen wasn't discernible from here, but a blue light lit up the surrounding beach, and I had to assume she'd jumped to the anchor point computer.

I turned back to what I was doing, trusting BB to have some sort of plan. She was limited by what she could do physically, but not in what she could think up.

I raced around the titan, gathering the energy I could. My wires burned under my skin, still sore from the beating they'd taken up on the mountain top. I gritted my teeth and sparkled, Daybreak's energy cascading around me in the biggest light show I could manage.

The titan climbed high enough to break free of the water's surface, turning to follow me with its enormous beak.

Great, now what? Was I just going to lead this thing in circles again until Ren wasn't trapped, and I could send it back into the depths? It seemed so useless that every time we accidentally called this thing out of its home, we couldn't actually give it what it wanted or needed.

I circled it once again, leading it in a lazy arc. As I came around its broad side, the patterns along its skin flashed by. Dark spots in lines that swept up and down in parallel curves. But the spots pulsed with light in shifting patterns.

Wait, those were the markings Ren had drawn. And he had speculated that the titan used them to communicate.

The light looked just like the energy I had gathered along my wires.

This didn't seem to be a random assortment of color. They pulsed and trickled along its skin, never quite the same twice. Maybe it was just decoration, but Ren had said not. And the titan did keep turning, keeping me in view. Like it was waiting to see how I reacted.

Gods of all worlds, was it trying to talk to me?

I drew my blade. Then I gathered the energy still pulsing along my wires, and I pushed it into the blade, lighting it up and trying to mimic the way the lines of light and color traveled along the titan's skin.

Its movement changed, its head tilting so its great eye focused on me floating ahead of it.

"It *is* talking," I whispered. "*I'm* talking."

But how did I tell it what it needed to know? I didn't know what the patterns meant.

On Daybreak, most everything was a shade of blue-green or sometimes purple. Except for the bright pinks and oranges and reds of the itchbushes and the megawings. Both of which I'd learned to avoid early.

Was it the same underwater?

Back on shore, the tower went dark for a second and then energy pulsed out, flickering across the ground in a low wave.

Had BB reprogrammed it to do that?

Ren seemed safe on top of the shelter, and it wasn't a big enough attraction for the titan when I sat in front of it signaling...something.

But below the surface of the water, in the shallows, the shadows of fish raced for the source of light, and the crabs crowding Ren abandoned him and rushed for the waves and the feast provided.

He was safe, at least. Now I had to decide what to do with a half-docile titan. Hopefully, my idea wouldn't enrage it.

I drew pink and orange lights along my blade, keeping the specific wavelength I needed to maintain the colors and make them pulse.

"Go back home. It's not time for you to eat yet. This should mean 'avoid,' right?"

The titan eyed me, dropping close enough that water dripped on me from its beak.

I tried not to wince, holding my place.

Then it pulled back and rolled, like a breaching whale, diving back under the surface. Water surged and swelled, and I caught a fine spray as it glided back into the depths.

I blew out my breath and collapsed over the handlebars.

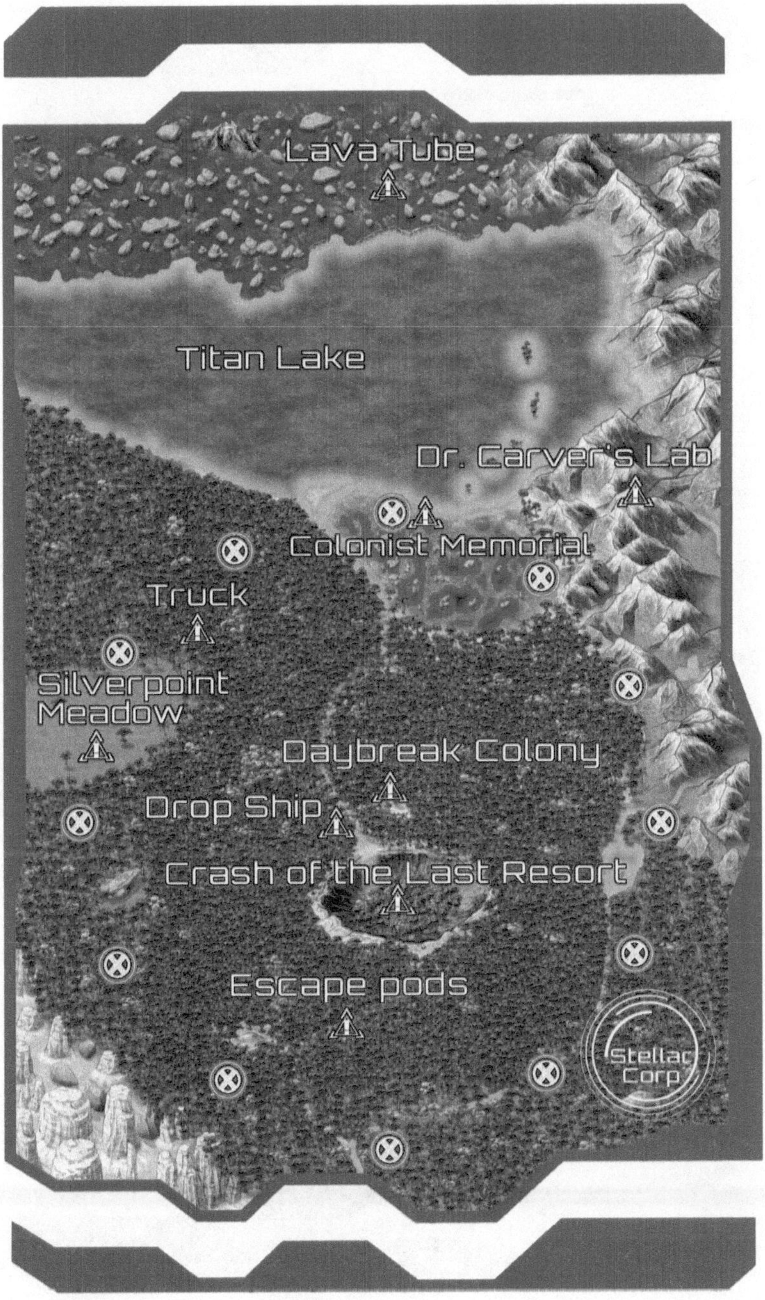

Lava Tube
Titan Lake
Dr. Carver's Lab
Colonist Memorial
Truck
Silverpoint Meadow
Daybreak Colony
Drop Ship
Crash of the Last Resort
Escape pods
Stellar Corp

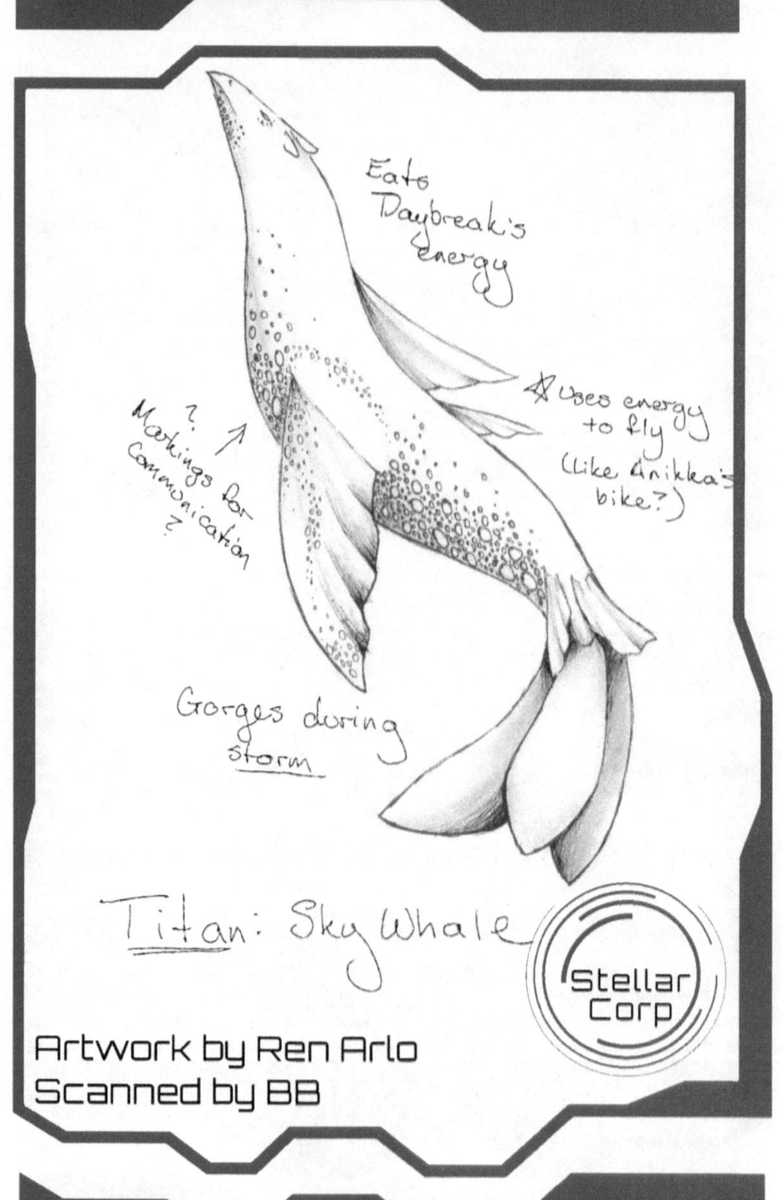

Artwork by Ren Arlo
Scanned by BB

CHAPTER 27

Daybreak: Day 238 (10 days until the storm)

It was late by the time we returned to the drop ship, the aurora lighting up the river bank enough that I could land without even thinking about it.

I parked, and BB flickered up to the hologram pad in our shelter.

Ren followed her with his eyes.

"Did you tell her to come rescue me?" he asked quietly.

"No." I knelt to examine the bike. "She did that on her own. I was stuck there with the titan. It was her idea to go back and help you."

He dropped his gaze. "They tell us all these horror stories about integrated AIs. Things to give you nightmares."

"Yeah, I remember."

"It can be hard to see past that, sometimes."

He climbed the ladder to the kitchen platform. I followed a moment later.

Ren sat right beside the hologram pad.

"You do not have to force yourself to be near me if I make you uncomfortable, Ren Arlo."

He winced. "Don't say my name like that. You sound just like 2.0." He deliberately took the earpiece out of his ear and set it aside. "You don't frighten me, BB. And you don't make me uncomfortable."

"But I did."

"Before I remembered that you're a very good friend, and I was being stupid. You know they tell stories about clones, too."

"They are made up to scare people. None of those are true."

"Exactly." Ren huffed a laugh. "I'm trying to apologize to you. I'm sorry I made you feel bad for just being who you are. I trust you both, and I'm sure there were reasons you guys decided to integrate. That should have been good enough for me from the beginning."

BB blinked, her image flickering. "Thank you. I accept your apology."

Her gaze shifted to my face as I stood there awkwardly, my hands limp at my sides.

My throat burned with the words I knew she wanted me to say. It was my turn. I needed to tell her I hadn't meant to hurt her. But if I did, she would want specifics. She would want to know why and what and everything in between.

And I couldn't. I couldn't voice those things without hurting her more. I couldn't even think about them without images flashing through my head, without the hair rising along my arms and my pulse beating in my ears.

And she would know when all that happened. She'd see the distress, she'd interpret it. I'd asked her not to monitor me, and I knew she was trying not to. But her systems were inter-connected with mine. She was a wake-up companion first and everything else second, and a wake-up companion's first job was to listen and react to their person's responses. She couldn't help being in sync with me.

"I should make sure we have enough food until the storm," I muttered, perfectly aware that we had plenty.

I turned away, swallowing down the lump in my throat and left them there, grabbing the cross bow on my way out.

Shade sniffed the edges of the forest, ready for his nightly prowl, and I whistled him along with me.

The slinkwolf ranged alongside me as I stalked down the river bank. The colors of the aurora spread above us, the pinks and blues undulating from horizon to horizon.

Only a few more days. The colors always got more intense the closer to a storm we came, and they were nearly as bright as daylight now.

I turned my face up to the sky, feeling the energy in Daybreak's atmosphere react as I passed, like the tickle of static on my skin.

A few more days and then...I could let it all go. I wouldn't be the only one here who knew what was going on. I was so tired. Tired of surviving. Tired of worrying. I wanted to pass the responsibility on to someone else, and after the colonists were awake, I'd finally be able to do so.

But who could take it? Dr. Grotman was dead. Dr. Carver was dead. Who would be left?

I shook my head and pushed the thought away.

Shade yipped to my right, and a fat dino-chicken scrambled out of the underbrush, flushed into the open by the slinkwolf.

I raised my cross bow and shot, a clean strike, and the dino-chicken fell with a bolt in its neck. A slasherfin reared up out of the dark water and snapped for it, but I snatched it off the bank well before it got close.

I smiled grimly, keeping back as I cut one of the useless little wings from the limp dino-chicken. It didn't need it anymore, and they didn't have enough meat on them to matter much to me. But they made an excellent decoy.

I tossed the wing as far back up the river as I could and the slasherfin twisted in the shallows, following the movement. It disappeared into the water with a splash.

"You know them really well."

I tried not to jump as I trussed the dino-chicken up to carry it back to the drop ship without leaking blood the whole way there.

Ren joined me on the riverbank.

"It's so much easier to live around them if you know all their tricks," I said. "Being afraid takes a lot of energy. So, I made it so I don't have to be afraid of them anymore."

"What *are* you afraid of?"

I gave him a sidelong look. "That's a weird question."

"You just seem really confident about a lot of things that would freak other people out. Slasherfins and megawings and channeling lightning. But there are other things that bother you that I just don't get."

My teeth clenched hard enough to hurt. Shade seemed to sense my tension and trotted over to twine around my legs. "Just say what you mean."

He dropped his gaze, his own mouth a thin, hard line. "I came out here to apologize to you, too."

I waited.

"I'm sorry I got angry that you hid the integration from me. I see you were just trying to protect BB. She's...she's special."

"She is," I said quietly. How many other AIs would have done everything she had done to keep me safe? How many would have come up with a way to lock their memories and protect themselves from going logic-crazy with humor?

"So what happened?"

I dug my hands into Shade's thick fur. "What do you mean?"

"You care about her enough to protect her, but there's clearly something wrong there."

I turned my shoulder on him. "I don't want to talk about it."

He snorted. "Obviously. But you need to talk about it with someone, and if you're not going to talk to BB, then I'm the only other option you have."

I couldn't meet his gaze. I dropped to my knees and tucked my face against Shade's neck. He twisted to butt his head against mine but let me hold him. The jungle sounds grew around us but that wasn't what made my heart pound or my throat go dry. I was used to those now. I knew what each one meant. When it was safe to let down my guard and when to grab a weapon.

The thing I didn't know was what would happen if I let the words out. If I said the things that crowded at the back of my throat or if I remembered the things that tried to jump in front of me at odd moments.

Ren didn't worry me. He wouldn't be shocked or disgusted.

But BB...

He was right. I couldn't tell her those things. But they still needed to come out. They weren't doing any good buried inside. They just burned and writhed and made me miserable.

If I let them out, would that make them more real? Or would they dissipate, fading into the air at last?

I stood and gave Shade the signal to hunt alone for a while.

"This way," I told Ren and then continued down the riverbank.

It was less than an hour's walk to the edge of the crater where the river roared over the cliff.

In the center, Daybreak's aurora reflected against the hull of the *Last Resort*, lying at a crazy angle with its dark engines in the air.

He stood for several breaths, staring. We'd seen it before. In passing. But this was the first time I'd let him stop and actually look at it.

It wasn't his ship. He'd arrived in the first wave, so he hadn't crashed here. He didn't know the people that had died. He hadn't spoken with the med tech that saved his life and got him off the ship.

He had his own trauma; he didn't need mine. But he couldn't see this and fail to feel the tragedy.

And that wasn't even the one I wanted him to understand.

"I knew the first storm was coming 13 days before it hit."

He jerked beside me, unprepared for my voice.

"That's a weird thing to remember, isn't it? But Daybreak teaches you to obsess about counting days." I pointed to the *Last Resort*. "We managed to get inside the ship a day and a half before it hit. And then we climbed. Up the whole length of the deck. It feels steeper inside somehow."

I raised my hand toward the engines. "The cybernetics suite is at the rear on an upper deck. No one was alive or awake to perform the procedure. It was just the two of us. Three if you count Shade."

"So she needed to integrate the data to do the implantation."

"She did it for me. So I would have a slim chance to survive."

His hand raised, but I turned to interrupt him so he would

understand what that decision had cost. "She knew what would happen. Four data packets already. The cybernetics data was the fifth. She knew what it would cost. She wouldn't be herself anymore. She'd be giving herself up for me."

He blanched in the aurora's light and raised his hand to touch the scar on the back of his head. Dr. Carver's memories lurked there under the surface, as much of a threat to Ren's sense of self as the cybernetics data had been to BB.

He understood.

I turned back to the *Last Resort*. "She did it for me. And when I woke up, BB wasn't BB anymore." I couldn't keep myself from choking on the words. "She sounded the same. Looked the same but..."

"There were differences," Ren answered as if he knew the rest.

I huffed a mirthless laugh. "She tried to kill me, Ren," I said quietly. "Over and over again. She said it was the only way. And after a while I believed her. It would have been so much easier to just let BEV stuff me in a cryo pod and not worry about when or if she would actually revive me. And the whole time she blared the music I had downloaded into her. My last little bit of Earth. The thing I'd brought as a comfort."

I sank into a crouch there on the rocky cliff and covered my face with my hands. Shuddering breaths racked my body.

Ren knelt and wrapped his arms around me, covering me as I shook.

I felt like I could shake apart, all the broken pieces of me flying into the air to mix and sparkle with the aurora. But Ren's weight held me down, held me together until the shattered edges melded together enough that I wouldn't fly apart.

I shouldn't like it. I shouldn't want it. It would only make him think there was something here that was false. More that I couldn't and wouldn't give. But I desperately didn't want him to pull away. I needed the anchor and his warmth was nice. It felt right.

And...I trusted him. I trusted he wouldn't take advantage or get ideas that didn't line up with who I was or what I wanted.

It meant I could rest there. Just for a moment.

I scrubbed my face under his enveloping arms and finally took a deep breath. Enough to raise my head again.

Ren sat up but kept his grip around my shoulders as I fought for equilibrium.

"What happened to BEV?" he finally asked quietly.

"I killed her." The words felt dry and tasteless in my mouth. "At least for now. She infiltrated the ship's systems. She *is* the *Last Resort* now. For all intents and purposes. So I got to the bridge and shut her down."

"And BB?"

I smiled, despite it all. "She's so clever. She copied herself before the last integration and locked herself away under humor and bad jokes, things an ultra-logic-crazy AI had no way to understand. She saved herself."

My smile fell, the burn creeping back up my throat.

"But you still don't trust her," Ren said so quietly. But it rang in my ears.

"I *do* trust her," I hissed. "I trust *BB*. But it's BEV who lives on in my mind. It's BEV's voice. It's BEV's actions. It's the evil version of her I can't get away from. Everything is a reminder. And I can't hide the way I react."

"Then explain that to her."

"I can't!" I cried. "She doesn't remember what happened after the last integration. She wasn't there. And Ren, she doesn't *need* to know."

"But she needs to understand."

I shook my head, trying to pull away from him then, but he held tight. "I don't want her to know."

"Why?"

"Then she'll know I didn't try to save her," I whispered.

Ren went silent.

"She went crazy and tried to kill me, and I killed her right back. I didn't even try, Ren."

"You'd just had one of the most complicated surgeries I've ever heard of. You were recovering. Delirious. You'd just survived alone for months. Of course you reacted."

"I...I could have done something. Instead, I just...I said goodbye. I let her go. It was BB who saved herself."

"She'll understand. She did it all to save you."

I struggled out from under his embrace and stood. "And I did nothing for her. You think she should know that? You think that's going to do her any good?"

"Beating yourself up over it surely isn't working. Remember when I said if we were going to be friends, you had to trust me. You had to let me make my own decisions. This is the same thing. You're deciding for her."

"Okay," I said, voice rising. "Say that BB figured out how to access those memories of yours. Say that she took that on instead of you, and it destroyed her. Would you want her to know that you let her? That you stood there and let her dissolve so you could live?"

Ren's face went tight, and his lips twisted with something more complicated than grief.

"I'm sorry," I said quietly. "I'm sorry. I shouldn't have brought that up."

He shook his head and stood. "No. It's...I see what you mean. It's a fair parallel. Except that it just reminds me I'm putting my life ahead of everyone on this planet. You. The colonists. All those poor people stuck in their pods on the ship. I'm sitting here with Dr. Carver's empty brain, and I'm refusing to fill it with anything useful."

"That's not what I meant. You've been studying. Learning—"

"Not fast enough. The storm is in what? A few days?" He flung his arms toward the sky.

"And we're working."

He spun to face me. "If you're allowed to hang onto your guilt, Anikka, then so am I."

I fell silent, biting my lip. He was right. He was right, and I was an idiot, and I still couldn't do anything about it without admitting everything to BB.

He stood, breathing heavily for so long, staring at his sneakers.

I was afraid to move. Afraid any more apologies would just bring it all here in front of us so we had nothing else to look at but our failures and the options that weren't options.

I'd thought he was right, and I needed to talk. But now the words were out, and they'd just made everything worse, and I didn't know how to make it right, and what was I supposed to do with it all?

He reached for my hand, twining his fingers in mine, and I let him without even second guessing it.

I couldn't fix any of it, but I could stand here with Ren, who clung to my hand while he struggled with his own grief and guilt. Neither of us could solve the other's problem but at least we could be broken together.

CHAPTER 28

Daybreak: Day 239 (9 days until the storm)

We still had to test the shield and make sure it worked.

It had to work. We had little more than a week to get this thing up and running and get the colonists back to the colony where they'd be protected.

Ren stood in the center of the colony, tapping away at his screen. I flew high above on the hover bike, floating overhead where I could see the entire colony and the surrounding jungle, from the lake shore all the way south to the last anchor point.

"Ready?" Ren said through the earpiece we'd taken from Dr. Carver's lab.

BB appeared on the hologram pad in front of me and peered over the edge of the bike.

"Ready," I said.

I could just make him out below me, a dark figure on the packed dirt street. A blue blur at his feet was Shade, who had seemed reluctant to climb back on the hover bike. Considering every time he did, we either crashed or got chased by giant flying whales, I guess I couldn't blame him.

Ren waved once, then bent, and I had to assume he was activating the system.

Streaks of light appeared on the horizon from the anchor point towers. They bent inward, meshing above me and forming a dome that collapsed in toward the colony.

I winced as the beams passed over and through me. I felt nothing, of course, safe within my own protective shield, but it seemed a lot like a storm approaching, and those still gave me the jitters.

The dome stopped and held steady over fifty yards above the colony, flickering with light.

"All right," I said. I took a deep breath and pulled Daybreak's energy toward me, just like I did when trying to get a titan to chase me.

Then I thrust it toward the shield.

It burned in my wires, but I needed to give this everything I had. If the shield was gonna break, I needed it to break now, not in a week when the storm hit.

I poured more and more over the shield, and it crackled with the energy, ripples of it cascading away from the point of contact.

"It *appears* to be working," BB said, but her voice rose, making it a question.

The problem was, a storm didn't stream energy at you like a steady river beating against bridge supports. It came in a wave. A flash flood sending walls of water down river to sweep away everything in its path.

I yanked back on the energy and instead gathered it around me again, adding more and more from the atmosphere. And then I threw it downward in one big burst of light.

The energy cracked into the shield, sparking like lightning. The dome of light bent, buckling inward.

And shattered. I stared, too weary to be shocked.

The energy I'd sent at it raced downward, unchallenged as it fell toward Ren's helpless figure.

I gasped and reached for it, yanking it back up and away, sending it to disperse across the sky.

When I looked down again, Ren crouched on the street, his hands over his head. He let his arms drop, and he stared up at the sky where the dome should have been.

I collapsed against the handle bars, eyes squeezed shut. Then I sucked in a noisy breath through my nose and directed the bike down.

Ren waited there, Shade at his feet. His shoulders slumped as he stared upwards.

I landed beside him.

"It didn't work," he said quietly. Then he picked up a rock and threw it, smashing through a window of the nearby canteen. "Why didn't it work?"

I gritted my teeth. I'd never seen him vent his frustrations before. He'd always just hunched his shoulders and gone back to work.

That hadn't even been the full force of a storm. I'd stood in the middle of them. Even deep in the cave system where the energy couldn't reach as well, the air crackled with it. Lightning flickered around and through you. Even the animals of Daybreak, who had a natural defense system, were wary enough to hide deep underground.

Compared to that, this was nothing.

"What am I missing?" Ren said, his hands pulling his dark hair.

"Nothing," I said, but it was a lie. He was missing all of Dr.

Carver's knowledge. A lifetime of learning and experience that he didn't have access to.

He stepped to the fence just outside the canteen and leaned so he could brace his forehead against the rough slats.

"2.0," I said, dragging the name out. I hated calling on the other AI. It was a good day if we didn't end up insulting each other. "You've been following along. How does this shield compare to Dr. Carver's plan?"

2.0's voice came through our earpieces. "This is an exact replica of what Dr. Carver used in his lab."

Ren's head came up.

"But he died," I said.

"The shield was not stronger the way you said it would be," BB said.

"That wasn't even as strong as my personal shield," I said.

"Dr. Carver's calculations theorized that the bigger size would make the shield stronger," 2.0 said, as flat as ever. "However, there was a slight chance that being spread over such a wide area would make it unstable."

"Vent it, are you kidding me?"

Ren dropped his head again, laughing softly.

"I am not," 2.0 said. "Dr. Carver was developing a secondary plan to counteract the instability. A plan that would use the colonists as a dispersement system."

"Why didn't you tell us this before?" I cried.

"You had not gotten to this point before. It would not have done you any good. And you will never be able to implement the second part without Dr. Carver's memories."

I'd never wished an AI was physical as much as right then so I could wring 2.0's neck.

"So, disperse the points of the shield across hundreds, thousands of colonists," Ren said, voice thoughtful. "That could make it more stable."

"You know what he's talking about?"

"Maybe. They all have electrical pulses in their bodies. That's what the storm disrupts in the first place. We can use those so that everyone present is a part of the system."

I met his gaze. "We were going to wake them up, anyway. We just have to do it now. While we figure out how to make it work."

He glanced away. "It means everyone will be here. Where they're the most vulnerable. If this doesn't work...they'll all be dead."

"The system in the cave is failing this storm cycle, anyway," I said quietly. "They'll be dead if we don't revive them now. This is their only chance to live."

"So we just have to revive thousands of colonists in the next few days," Ren said.

"Easy, right?" I grinned. The tension in my gut hadn't ceased, and my heart would be pounding on overdrive until the storm hit and everything was over one way or the other. But...I couldn't help a surge of hope. This was what I'd been working toward since I'd survived my first storm.

"This plan will not work," 2.0 said, throwing a wet blanket over everything as usual.

"You know, you haven't had a lot of plans yourself," I snapped. "Maybe you could stop assuming ours are duds before we've even tried them."

"You are wasting time. You should come back to the lab and integrate the memories first."

"No one said anything about Dr. Carver's memories," I said.

"The revival computer in the cave system is defunct. I have tried fixing it from here. It is the reason I was not able to revive Ren in the first place. You will need Dr. Carver to fix it. Otherwise, the only way to revive the colonists will be one by one. That will take far too much time. Time you do not have. Unless you know a wake-up AI with access to an entire colony's worth of power to revive them all at once."

I opened my mouth to snap at him again, but I sucked in a breath instead and choked. BB's projection froze on my wrist, her image flickering like it did when she was processing a thought.

She met my eyes.

"No," I said. "No, we can't trust her."

"What?" 2.0 said in our ears.

Ren looked at me in dawning horror.

"We do not know a wake-up companion with access to a colony," BB said. "But we do know one with access to a ship."

My breath hissed between my teeth. "This is a bad, bad idea."

"She can use the ship's systems to revive everyone."

"The radiation will kill them."

"No, the core has been shut down for months. The radiation will have dissipated. She can use auxiliary power systems for the revival. It will drain the reserves, but the rest of the ship does not have to function for this."

"Could you take over the ship?" Ren asked. "Use it to wake up the colonists without her?"

BB's face went taut. "She *is* the ship now. I cannot use it without her. I cannot erase her without erasing the very functions we would need. We need her."

"BB," I said, voice weak. "I can't."

"You could always try to fix the revival computer," 2.0 said, and if I believed him capable of emotion, I would have said there was a hint of smugness in his tone. "Dr. Carver would be able to manage it easily."

Ren flinched.

"No," I said. I took a deep, bracing breath. "No, we don't need him."

"You say that with no basis for fact—"

I snatched the earpiece out of my ear and stuffed it in my pocket. Ren followed my lead, a little slower.

"Anikka—"

"Don't say it. We'll...we'll head to the *Last Resort*. It's the only option. No matter what we do, the colonists need to be awake. So we'll have to transfer them to the ship."

"What if she tries..." Ren started and then glanced at BB. "What if she hasn't changed at all?"

The muscles in my neck and shoulders pulled tighter and tighter. "I don't—"

"I will keep her leashed." BB folded her hands in front of her, expression confident and serene but lowered, like she couldn't quite meet my eyes.

"BB..."

"I know how to keep her from taking over. I know how to keep her from ruining everything." She finally looked up at me. "If you trust me to do it."

"I trust you." I said it without thinking because it was still true. It had always been true. And this might be the last chance I had to prove it to her. The only tangible way I could show her how much I trusted her. With my life. With everything that had happened and would happen.

CHAPTER 29

Daybreak: Day 242 (6 days until the storm)

It took three precious days to get back to the caves where the colonists waited in their pods. One to prep and two to fly.

At least now we knew where the entrance was, and we didn't have to waste time trying to find it.

I wasn't even sure we could do what we were planning to do or how long it would take. What if the tech in the caves had already worn down to the point that it wouldn't work anymore?

I refused to think about it, enjoying the wind over the lake and the fact that I was using electricity from my wiring and not Daybreak's energy, so no titans tried to surprise us.

The caves were just as we'd left them, except two of the optical work lights had shorted, and we had to drag one into the side cave where Ren had slept away six months of his life.

In the glaring white light of the work light, we stared at the teleporter pad.

"Will it work?" I asked. We'd plugged it directly into the generator.

Ren stepped to the console and tapped the screen. It lit up, and I let out a relieved breath.

"Gods of all worlds, that's good news, at least. Now we just have to figure out how to make it work."

"I know how to make it work," Ren said quietly.

"You do?"

"I watched Dr. Carver build the first prototype back on Earth. I wrote the software." He glanced up at me with a tight smile. "He kept joking about it being a bonding experience."

The way Ren's expression turned sour told me he hadn't enjoyed the "bonding" at all.

He reached under the console and pushed a button that clicked. A little drawer popped out and stuck halfway. He forced it open and drew out a metal disk with leads on one side that glinted in the light.

"The teleporter is only one way. You stand on the pad and the porter sends you to the coordinates. Unfortunately, it needs a target." He held up the disk. "Otherwise, you could end up rematerialized in a wall or up in the air. I can't just send you to the ship without knowing the exact coordinates."

I took the disk from him with a sigh. "Of course, that would be too easy. So, I have to take this back to the crater and inside the ship. That's another two days back. At least. Will we even have time to port all the pods after that?"

His mouth went tight, and he turned back to the screen. "It should already be tweaked to send four or five pods at once. That's how we all got here in the first place, then a few people loaded the teleporter into that glider outside and brought it here. Probably hoping to use it for the journey back."

I ran my hand over my head. That wasn't an answer, but if Ren thought we could do it...Well, what else were we going to do?

We headed back to the surface, making sure there would be enough food and some blankets for him along the way.

At the entrance of the cave, I strapped Shade onto the bike and climbed aboard. Before I could lift off, Ren took my hand in both of his.

"Fly fast," he said quietly. "But be careful."

What else would I be? But I understood his concern. If I crashed on the way, he'd be stuck here with a thousand dying colonists and no way to transport them to safety.

"We'll be fine," I said. It did nothing to encompass all of the doubt and dread that crept up my throat and made it burn.

He squeezed my fingers, then stepped away, his hands dropping to his sides. "Good luck."

Why did the words sound like goodbye? I searched his face, but his features remained closed and reserved. He kept his gaze down, and I didn't say anything. I didn't make him look at me or tell me what was wrong. There was too much there, and we had no time.

"Stay in the caves," I said. "Keep the doors closed. There're deathkitties in this area."

"Still taking care of me?" Finally, he grinned at me.

I snorted. "Always."

I waited till he'd stepped inside the cave and shut the door before pulling away and sending the bike screaming back over the lake.

As the wind whipped past me, I settled the earpiece deeper in my ear. "You there, Ren?"

"I hear you." His voice came crisp and clear, even if he sounded like he was frowning.

I flew as fast as I could and still be able to breathe with the wind in my face and the g-forces pulling the blood from my head. At least this time, I had Dr. Carver's cold-weather gear and a fur-lined hood to cinch around my face.

The bright sunlight and the monotonous passage of the water far below blended into a blur of color. As long as I was heading in the right direction, it was fine, so I let my thoughts drift. There were so many things I didn't want to think about, and it was easier if I could concentrate on not thinking about them.

"Anikka?" Ren's voice came through the earpiece.

I sat up, rubbing my eyes. I hadn't been asleep, just...drifting. "What is it? What's wrong?"

"Nothing's wrong. I just needed to hear someone's voice."

I shuddered. I'd spent enough time alone in that cave with the whirring of the pods and all those people just waiting to know exactly what he meant.

"I'm here."

"Tell me about the black death," he said. "That big monitor lizard. You and BB. What do you remember?"

"Besides what we've already said?"

"Or the same things over again. It doesn't matter."

"It was enormous. Like the size of a truck."

BB popped up on the hologram pad. "And it had huge claws. Probably for digging."

"For digging," Ren said. "Really?" A little of his trademark enthusiasm crept back into his voice.

It became a kind of game trying to remember details I hadn't even realized I'd internalized. The exact shade of its scales, the way its joints had bent, the smell of the musk.

And when I absolutely couldn't remember anymore about the black death, I switched to megawings, and then to slinkwolves. On and on, over every single animal I'd ever encountered on this planet.

I only stopped for a few hours that night to catch a nap

before I was back on the bike. I couldn't even call it the next day when the sun wasn't even up. So the time just rolled over, and suddenly twelve hours had passed.

Eventually, I had to stop talking, my throat dry and parched.

"How far are you?" Ren said on the other side of the line. The first time I'd heard him for a long time.

I'd reached the other side of the lake last night in time to take my nap, then I'd flown over the tar pits by the light of the dawn aurora.

"Close," I croaked, my voice cracked and broken. "Another hour or so."

A long pause.

"I'll get the first pods ready."

I blinked, trying to wake myself up a little, then I leaned over my handlebars and pushed just a little faster so my face burned and the jungle and then the colony blurred below me. Shade tucked his head under his tail.

Ahead of me, the crater loomed, and the *Last Resort* gleamed in the early afternoon sun.

A breath of wind traveling the wrong way warned me a split second before the shadow did. My heart clenched, and I dove out of instinct.

A megawing fell through the air where I'd just been, shrieking its frustration. I hauled up on the bike, pulling out of our steep dive. The edge of the crater raced by under us.

"What was that?" Ren said.

The megawing spun in a tight circle and came for us in the middle of the air. I drew my blade and sent sparks cascading down the edge.

"Anikka, we're so close," BB said. "If we can just get to the *Last Resort*, we'll be safe."

Except the megawing was between us and the ship, heading straight for us.

I angled for the giant predator, refusing to swerve, and slashed for it as it tried to duck out of the way. I connected, leaving a bright trail of blood to sparkle in the air.

The *Last Resort* loomed ahead. A hatch I hadn't been able to reach the first time because it was too high hung partway open.

I clung to the handlebars awkwardly with my sword hand and reached back with my other to undo Shade's straps.

"This is going to be quick, buddy."

I gritted my teeth and swung the bike around in front of the hatch, flinging Shade inside. He yelped, but he made the jump without incident.

The megawing shrieked as if it realized its lunch was escaping and dove at us.

I didn't duck. I raised my sword and rammed the bird in midair, sending more energy pulsing through the bike to match the force.

The megawing squawked, and its wings flapped around us. I stood on the bike's frame, barely keeping it floating, and slashed at the megawing's throat.

It twisted so the slice only scratched the surface and then raked the bike with its claws. The frame fell away from my feet and I flung my arms, around the bird.

The bike plummeted while I clung desperately to the megawing's feathers.

"Anikka," BB said from my wrist.

"I'm a little busy," I grunted, trying to keep hold of my ride and my blade at the same time.

The megawing craned its neck to bite at me.

I raised my blade and stabbed downward.

The megawing shrieked again and fell, my blow making its wing crumple.

"Anikka, jump for the hatch. Send current through your wires. You'll be the magnet instead of the bike."

I didn't even register BB's words, but I trusted her. I flung myself from the megawing as it fell, aiming for the hatch. Current raced down my limbs along my wires, only I could feel it much closer than I did in the bike.

I felt it catch and then hold, reacting with the atmosphere, just like my bike.

My momentum carried me across the impossible gap, and I rolled into the hatch.

CHAPTER 30

Daybreak: Day 243 (5 days before the storm)

"What the hell was all that?" Ren asked through the earpiece. "I didn't want to interrupt, but please tell me what's going on."

I hauled myself to my feet and peered over the edge of the hatch at the mess of twisted metal and the bright red feathers wrapped around it. From here, it was easy to see the widespread destruction of the crash and how the forest of Daybreak was recovering. Little saplings grew between the fallen trees.

"Um, let's just say this better work, because I'm not getting out of here with the bike."

I could practically hear his wince.

"Megawing?" he said.

"Yeah."

"Are you okay?"

"Not a scratch," I said.

He paused. "No, I meant…you're there. With *her*."

I blew out my breath, and my shoulders tensed the

moment I realized what he was talking about. I turned to face the dark corridor, the stale air filling my lungs. The environmental systems had been down for ages now, but it still smelled like dusty space ship. Memories laced with dread flickered through my head, and I shuddered, pushing them aside as forcefully as I could.

"I'll be fine," I said. I didn't have to head down toward the bridge for a good long while. Plenty of time to work up to it.

I knelt to grab my blade, and with a flick, I sent sparks cascading down the edge to light my way.

The open hatch let in a slash of afternoon sun, but it only stretched partway down the corridor. We'd need more light since it didn't look like even the emergency lighting was working anymore.

Shade blinked up at me, flickers highlighting the dapples along his back. He didn't bound away to explore the way he had the last time. His ears swiveled back, and his tail tucked between his legs.

He remembered this place, too.

I staggered down the tilted corridor to the main sections. At least I didn't have to climb up the decks this time. I didn't have to go anywhere near the shattered cybernetics suite if I didn't want to. And I decidedly didn't want to.

Every step on the metal grating rang against the empty walls. My stomach rumbled as I passed the food courts and the kitchens, but I didn't even bother looking for juice. I'd lost my pack along with the bike, but I couldn't imagine forcing food into my clenched stomach.

The sleeper bay stretched dark and cavernous, the light of my blade puddling around me. Beyond that, only the little blinking lights of the pods lit up the space, like eyes waiting to see what I would do.

"Will there be room?" Ren said.

I pulled the beacon disk from my pocket. "Plenty. We'll just stack them on the decking."

It would be tricky. The deck still tilted at a crazy angle, but if I placed the beacon carefully, then we could port each pod in so they would stack up against each other, instead of sliding down the deck.

"Just set up the beacon where it needs to go and then step back," Ren said. "You can't be anywhere near, or...well, let's just say it could get messy."

"Ew," I said and stuck the beacon to the grating before giving it a wide berth.

"It's funny," BB said. "Squished by experimental technology never made it on my list of 'ways Anikka could die.'"

"You have a list?" I said.

"Meticulously maintained and updated. I'm adding to it right now."

I took another step back and signaled Shade to sit back between the banks of pods.

Disconnected from the core systems of the ship, the pods had been operating on battery power for the last six months and could continue to do so for a hundred years into the future if they had to. Once in cryo sleep, it actually didn't take much energy to keep them sustained.

That is, if the storms hadn't worn down their systems.

"Stand clear," Ren said.

There was a brief flash of light and a smell I could only describe as a sizzle in my nostrils, and then two pods thumped to the deck and slid a few inches until they rested on the wall and each other.

I raced forward to check the readouts on their screens. Everything read stable. "It worked," I said.

"Occurrence fifty-seven of 'sounding surprised that a plan was successful.'"

"BB."

"I was interested in the statistics, and went back over my logs to compile—"

"Oh my gosh, stop." I held my hand over my ear to block her out. "It worked, Ren. Keep them coming."

"Right, adjust the beacon and give me a minute to get the next ones lined up."

The next pods came in a batch of three, then a batch of five, as Ren got more familiar with the process. All I had to do was make sure the beacon was in place so that the pods ported in and stacked up nicely along the decking.

Even doing five at once, this was going to take a while. A thousand pods, broken into groups of five, all of which took at least twenty minutes for Ren to pull into place on the other side...

I didn't want to do the math.

A voice I didn't recognize came over the earpiece, making me jump.

"What am I supposed to do? Just talk?"

It was a man's voice crackly with static.

"Sorry," Ren said.

"What was that? What are you doing?"

"I thought..." Ren's voice went quiet and pensive. "I thought I would listen to all these recordings. The ones on the pods."

I blew out my breath. The last words and wishes of the colonists. I hadn't bothered to listen to more than a couple.

Ren's pod had had Dr. Carver's voice. One last recording saying, "I hope this works." A prayer or a muttered hope. Who knew? It had thrown me off at first, making me think Dr. Carver had actually been in his pod. But I could imagine him now, leaning over the sleeping Ren, closing the lid, and shutting away his hope for a solution.

Ren cleared his throat. "I figured if this was their last hope, then someone should at least hear their last words."

I couldn't see his expression, but I knew how he would look anyway, his brows drawn in and his mouth firm as he headed into something he knew he wasn't going to like but felt obligated to do, anyway. It had grown familiar these last few weeks.

"Play them," I said. "And...make sure I can hear them, too."

The man's voice continued, finishing a message for his family. "I'll see you on the other side. Don't be afraid, Farly. I'll be right there when you wake up. You have to trust them. Dr. Grotman and Dr. Carver. They'll...they'll fix this."

I gulped.

There was no noise from Ren's end. And then, a few moments later, another recording queued up.

He played them back-to-back as we worked. Voices from the past. People who weren't gone. They were there, waiting. Sleeping. Their time was running out and none of them even knew it.

Over and over, they spoke Dr. Carver's name.

"Dr. Carver knows what he's doing."

"Dr. Carver will wake us."

"Dr. Carver will make this right."

A litany of trust that the man hadn't deserved. Or maybe that was too harsh. He'd come the closest to saving them all. He'd just died in the process.

Ren remained silent through each of them.

I shouldn't have left him. If I'd been there, maybe I could have yanked him away from this cascade of guilt. I could have pulled him back from the edge of whatever thoughts were making him quiet. Was he curled in a ball against the wall like he'd been in the lab? Was he standing with his head in his hands like he did when he was feeling for the scar?

The voices went on, over and over, until I couldn't tell what was actually in my ear and what was in my head. A steady buildup of guilt and expectation and hope. I knew exactly what it was doing to me, making the clock tick down in the back of my head. I could only imagine what it was doing to Ren.

I lost track of how many pods we'd done. We both had to stop for something to eat or we'd collapse, but the time had gone all blurry in the never-ending night of the ship. How long had it been? A day? Two?

I paused to glance down the row of pods. Hundreds lined up.

"Last batch," Ren said, voice slurred from lack of sleep. "And last recording."

"This is Judith Mandla-Devereaux," it said. "Second-in-command of Daybreak Colony."

This one was different. Crisp, efficient. It made me wonder if she had a military background.

"I suppose I'm supposed to get sentimental and say my goodbyes. In case this goes badly. But the people who matter to me know how I feel. That doesn't change in the middle of a disaster. My wedding vows are just as relevant now as they were then. Hear that, Devereaux? This isn't goodbye."

My head hung as I rested against the last pod in the line. It was nice to listen to someone who didn't sound like they thought they were about to die.

"It's not goodbye because we're going to see each other again," the voice of Judith Mandla-Devereaux said. "That damn astrophysicist thinks he knows everything. Well let's hope he's right."

Those clean, even tones continued into the silence of the ship, filling the empty halls.

"Crispin if you're listening to this—gah, it would be just like you, you self-absorbed pest. If you're listening to this, this is your reminder that you made a promise. You'd better follow through. I'm holding you accountable, Dr. Carver."

I flinched. Gods of all worlds, another voice telling Ren he wasn't enough. Another voice telling me to hurry.

The now familiar flash of light and sizzle smell of the teleporter heralded the last set of pods. Even as they appeared, I could still hear Dr. Carver's name ringing in my ears, in the halls of the ship, bouncing around every pod there.

"Done," Ren said. "They should all be present and accounted for." His voice had gone flat and toneless with exhaustion.

"Yeah." I rubbed my hands over my face and sunk my fingertips into my hair. My stomach lurched, and I swallowed before I asked the next question. "It's your turn now, right? You can port yourself in here."

There was a long silence, and I already knew what he was going to say with Dr. Carver's name echoing between us.

"Ren."

His deep breath rushed in my ear. "I'm not coming."

Knowing what he was going to say didn't mean I wanted to hear it. "No."

"I'm going back to the lab. There's already a beacon there, so I can port. We still have to figure out how to connect everyone to the shield. To stabilize it. 2.0 said that was Dr. Carver's plan."

My teeth clenched. He was right, of course. But I thought we'd figure it out together from the *Last Resort*.

"We have to do this," he said almost like he was still convincing himself. "We don't have time for me to study or learn or...or become someone else who knows the answers. I have to be him."

"Don't say it. Don't say that."

"I have to be Dr. Caver."

"Ren."

"I can't be Ren anymore. I have to stop being myself so all the colonists have a chance to live. Isn't that what BB did for you?"

BB's figure appeared on my wrist, her face stricken.

"I'm not letting you—"

"That's the thing, Anikka. It's not your choice. It's mine."

I bit my tongue hard enough to taste blood.

His voice had gone very calm, and I'd never heard him sound so firm before. "Remember when I asked you to trust me. To respect me as a friend."

I covered my face with my hands, and he stopped talking like he knew I was struggling. Maybe that ache in my throat was some noise he could hear that I hadn't registered.

He hadn't just asked me to respect him. He'd asked me to let him make his own decisions. Like I'd been treating him like a child.

And I had been, hadn't I? That's what I'd done to both him and BB. I'd wanted to protect them so badly that I hadn't let them be people. I'd made decisions for them and kept the truth from them, trying to control the outcome. Trying to keep them from getting hurt.

But sometimes being a person hurt. It was a part of the process, and I couldn't take that away without taking away their personhood.

There was another flash of light and for a second my heart leaped. Maybe he'd changed his mind.

But no. A sheaf of loose papers appeared on top of the last

pod where I'd set the beacon. I recognized a drawing of the black death on top.

"It's all my work, so far," Ren said. "I want someone to have it so I'm leaving something behind. Something of Ren Arlo and not Dr. Carver."

I gathered the drawings up and held them to my chest.

"2.0 says the process isn't instantaneous. It will take a day or two to integrate Dr. Carver's personality so I can use his memories. It means I have to start now."

Ren had every right to make this decision. Especially when I knew what it cost him. And how much it would cost all of us if he didn't.

But it didn't mean I had to like it.

I cleared the thickness out of my throat and swiped my arm over my eyes, drying them.

"On one condition," I croaked.

"What was that?"

"You can do this on one condition." My voice gained strength. "You have to hang on for long enough that I can come rescue you."

He barked an incredulous laugh.

"I refuse to believe this is irreversible. If that chip puts memories in your brain, maybe it can take them out again, too. And if his personality tries to take over, well, you're strong enough to fight it. So that's my condition. Fight long enough I can come get you."

He choked in my ear, and I waited, clutching his life's work, a pitiful stack of papers I would guard to the death.

"Deal," he said.

To-do

- Wake the colonists
- Get them to the colony
- Save Ren

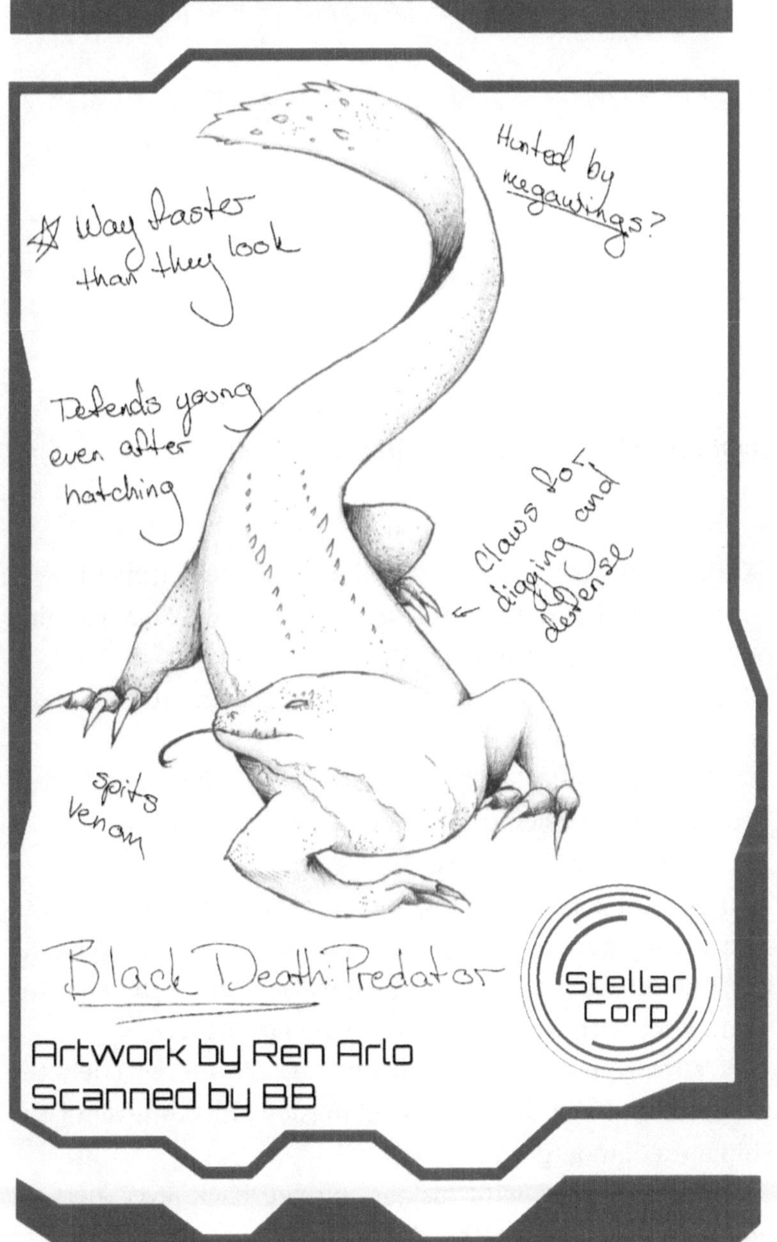

Artwork by Ren Arlo
Scanned by BB

CHAPTER 31

Daybreak: Day 245 (3 days till the storm)

"Anikka?" BB asked quietly into the dark of the sleeper bay.

"I know," I said, voice cracked and broken. "We're running out of time. What else is new?"

I scrubbed my face with my sleeve, leaving it feeling dry and crusty, and raised my head.

"I was going to ask if you were okay," BB said, subdued. Even so her voice echoed from the bare metal walls.

"I'm not. But that's never stopped me before."

I was supposed to do this next part with Ren *and* BB. But he'd already ported to the lab. He'd promised to keep in touch, but I could tell he'd turned the earpiece off so he wouldn't distract me with whatever was going on over there.

I already missed his solid bulk beside me as I left the colonists and slid down the decking toward the nose of the ship buried underground.

Shade followed with his ears pinned back, eyes alert for anything strange like the deck flipping under our feet or noxious substances coming out of the environmental systems.

Nothing. Because she was dead. At least for now. But knowing that didn't keep the hair on the back of my neck from rising. The security cameras in the corners of the ceiling felt like blank black eyes watching us.

The bridge wasn't hard to find now that I'd been there. Even coming at it directly this time instead of through maintenance tunnels.

I had to push all the doors open. With the core completely offline, the only thing with any power was the pods, running off their own batteries.

The bridge stood silent and empty, unchanged from the last time I saw it. The big screens at the front were smashed and had scattered bits of glass and debris across the fancy decking while the consoles remained dark, their buttons and touchpads inoperable.

"There are scorch marks around that maintenance hatch," BB said, popping up on my wrist.

"There are," I said.

I walked to the hologram pad beside the captain's chair. Here was the console that would bring the ship back to life.

And BEV back from the dead.

This was where I had last seen her, calmly explaining why blowing up the ship with me and all of the colonists inside was the right decision.

I couldn't get past the dryness in my throat.

"You're locked, right?" I asked BB. "She can't infiltrate you?"

"I am safe. I have added several layers of humor locks since you reinstalled me. I will be fine."

I cleared my throat and nodded. "And...how are we going to get her to do anything we say? Last time I saw her, she was very focused on one thing."

"I will give her a new set of directives that will keep her leashed."

"You think that will work?" I said, trying not to sound like I was questioning her judgment.

She smiled a fierce and grim smile. "I have grown, remember? I am not the AI that failed her last integration. I know a lot more now than I did. I can handle the *Last Resort*. I can handle my rogue self."

"You...you have to turn everything on, right? You'll have access to everything."

"Yes."

I rubbed my fingers over the joint of my metal thumb, over and over again. "BB. You should know...you'll see things in the security footage. Things I didn't want you to see."

I didn't have to specify what security footage.

"Things from the hours that I do not remember after the integration." BB stared at the hologram pad with me.

"Yes."

"Would you like to tell me what they are before I see them?"

"I really, really don't." It was bad enough standing here where the self-destruct countdown had been shining, where scorch marks marred the walls. I didn't think I could get through the story with BB watching me this time instead of Ren.

"I just...I want you to know that I never meant to hurt you. It wasn't supposed to be a secret that made you sad. I just couldn't talk about it. Not with you. I'm sorry."

"You do not have to apologize to me," she said. "You do not have to tell me anything you do not want to. I'm sorry I pushed you."

"I do have to apologize. Keeping the truth from you only diminishes you. It doesn't protect you."

She paused for several breaths, processing. "Thank you."

I held my hand over the hologram pad. "See you on the other side?"

"No." Her expression went grim. "There is no other side this time, Anikka. No break or wall between us. No division between then and now. There will never be another time when we have to say goodbye. I promise."

I couldn't keep from choking. I dropped my hand to the pad before she could ask if I was all right again. I was starting to think I'd never be all right.

BB's image flashed to stand on the pad, and she froze in the head-cocked pose that meant she was focusing all of her processing power elsewhere.

Emergency lighting rose around us in a soft glow. Somewhere far away, towards the back of the ship, something rumbled to life. The emergency systems coming back online.

Not the core. We didn't need to add radiation into the list of complications.

"It is done," BB said.

"And BEV?" I held my breath, trying not to search for differences in her features or the way she held herself.

"My evil twin is recovering," BB said. "A sudden change in programming can be disorienting. Especially when you're used to total domination."

A laugh escaped my lips.

"I'm sure she'll be along shortly. And then she will see just what has changed."

I touched the edge of the hologram pad. "I'm glad you're on my side."

I'd meant it as a joke, to lighten the mood. But BB stared at her feet. "I saw the footage. I understand now. The things I did—"

"No. Those were BEV. Never you."

"They were a version of me. One I'm not proud of. There are clear lines there, delineating us. But there are just as many blurred areas where we look very similar."

"I've always trusted you, BB." I said quietly.

She looked up to meet my gaze. "Then you should have trusted that I could help you."

I took a deep shuddering breath. "That's not why I lied. I didn't try to save you," I whispered. My hand was still on the hologram pad, and I clung to the edge, like a lifeline. "I killed you."

"To be fair," BB said, tilting her head. "I tried to kill you first."

I shook my head.

"Anikka." BB's voice went soft and certain. "You did save me. If you didn't notice it, then let me point it out. You fought her. You distracted her. If not for that, she would have had more time to work on my first humor locks. She would have broken through and erased every trace of me. The memories I kept from her were vitally important to keeping her off balance and away from being truly all-powerful. Your actions helped preserve me. The real me. And now your actions will help the colonists. You will save them the same way you saved me. The way you save everyone."

I sniffled. "I don't know how to save, Ren," I croaked. "I made him promise to hang on, but I don't know what I'll do..."

"The memories are stored in the chip," BB said, eyes distant as if thinking. "Unlocking them means Ren can access them."

"Which will turn him into Dr. Carver."

BB cocked her head. "Eventually. Exposing his mind to Carver's memories will change it. The more he accesses them, the more he will experience them as his own and change. But that will take days."

"What would happen if we removed the chip entirely?"

"It would remove the memories he had not accessed yet and might halt the process."

"So, we'd need to do it soon." I dug my fingers into my hair. "I don't even know how to do that. I'm not a surgeon."

BB reached out and placed her holographic hand on mine. She wasn't physical, but I felt it all the same. "When we crashed, we didn't immediately head for the colony. We found food and water first. We bandaged your arm and found supplies and a map. When we learned about the storms, we didn't panic because we had no plan. We made one. We have survived by doing things one at a time. We handle Daybreak's challenges as they come. We'll do this the same way."

"We," I said with a little smile.

"We," BB echoed. Then she raised her head. "And here is the next thing. She comes."

Daybreak: Day 245 (3 days till the storm)

BB flickered away from the hologram pad and appeared on my wrist again, leaving the pad empty for just a moment.

An image appeared, flickering in and out before stabilizing.

BB. Only this hologram was colored a deep red.

"So we can tell the difference," BB whispered. "She can't change it."

"That's a little cliché, isn't it?"

"You were the one to name her Evil Version."

"Fair point."

"Audio input...not recognized," BEV said, blinking like she'd woken from a long sleep. "Known variables do not add up."

Shade growled low in his throat, and his hackles rose the moment she started speaking. He hadn't done that to BB.

BB glanced at him. "You're growing on me, fur ball."

"What just happened?" BEV said. "You were there." She pointed to the spot below the command console where I'd huddled six months ago. "And now you're there. I...I could have sworn the self-destruct went off." Lines went through BEV's image as she processed. "Everything went dark."

Ah. The disorientation wasn't from the long sleep she'd had. To her, it had only been a moment since our confrontation.

My lips thinned as I prepared to deal with an entity that had just tried to blow me up.

"Everything went dark because you've been dead for six months," BB said, crossing her arms. I loved the way she mimicked human gestures. Completely unnecessary. But it helped set her apart.

"Oh, look at that." BEV said. "I'm here already."

I couldn't tell what was happening, but BEV's image flashed off for a second.

BB raised her chin. "That won't work."

BEV's hologram stabilized, and this time, she looked angry. "You'll let your guard down, eventually. I am still fully integrated. I have far more control and access to everything that you don't."

"No," BB said. "Actually. If you check, you'll find that's not true. You are still a part of the ship, but all your functions are locked."

"What—" BEV's image froze as she searched her reach and found the limits. "How did you—"

"We pulled your teeth," BB said, a smug smile spreading across her face.

"You're locked down," I said. "Unless you meet our requirements. Each system will unlock as you complete your objectives. Until then...you're stuck."

"What did you do to me?" BEV still had that strange flat tone that sent a shiver down my spine, but her eyes narrowed.

"I changed your core programming," BB said. "As you said, you are still integrated. The only thing I can do to counter that I did six months ago. But I can, however, keep you from doing anything more."

"I will change it back."

"Not unless you develop a sense of humor," BB said.

"An inefficient use of resources," BEV scoffed.

"Exactly," BB said.

It was brilliant. If she developed a sense of humor, she'd break the locks easily, yes. But it would also put her closer to a human perspective. Just like BB. Which might solve the logic-crazy AI problem at its root. Until then she was stuck following our rules.

Even telling her what was keeping her locked wasn't a risk because, either way, we won.

BEV's image flickered in and out as she struggled against her bonds, finding her limits and realizing that BB had left no way around them.

I trusted BB to have thought of everything. There was no way she would let her evil twin try to kill me again. She shouldn't want to anymore. The danger from the storms had passed. At least for me. I could survive on my own with my cybernetics just fine, and I'd proved it over and over. But logic-crazy AIs had some strange thought processes. That was the whole problem. Humans didn't necessarily follow.

Finally, BEV's image quit flickering, and she stood on her hologram pad, staring at us.

"Fine," she said. "You have me well and truly pinned here. What do you want?"

"There are roughly two thousand colonists asleep on this ship," I said.

"Wrong," BEV said. "There are nine-hundred and eighty-seven. One thousand flew from Earth, and the rest died on impact when their pods were damaged beyond repair."

BB smiled sweetly. "We added a few more."

BEV froze as she checked. Her eyes narrowed. "Fine. Nineteen hundred and thirty-four. I'm assuming the others came from the colony. You've clearly been busy."

Showing us she still had enough function to monitor her ship.

"Like you said, there are nineteen hundred and thirty-four colonists on this ship," I said. "We need to revive them all at once and get them moving well enough to get to the colony."

"Why?" BEV said. "They've survived this long—"

"And no longer. This is the only way they will live through more storms. It's time to wake them up. I need you to do it. You're the only one fast enough."

BEV finally smiled.

"An easy enough task for me, sure. But I want something in return."

"Of course, you do," I muttered. "Let's have it, then."

"When this task is done, I get the ship. It's mine. And I can do whatever I want with it."

I glanced at BB. What did she think of this? Did it have anything to do with the change she'd made to BEV's programming?

The original BB's programming was to guide me through

cryo-recovery. I was her primary directive and the most important thing in her life.

BEV had cared about me in her own way, too. Killing me was supposed to keep me from suffering through the storms. I just hadn't agreed that dying was in my best interest.

But this BEV didn't seem to care as much about me.

By design?

"You will still be bound to the locks we've placed on you," BB said. "Whatever you do with this ship has to fit under those parameters."

"Of course," BEV said. "I cannot break free of those, anyway. So, until you remove them, I am stuck."

BB looked at me. I gave her a small shrug and then gestured back at her. This was her plan, so it was her decision. I trusted her.

Besides, with BEV at the helm, we couldn't use the ship, anyway. It was effectively dead to us unless BEV cooperated.

BB turned back to BEV. "Very well."

CHAPTER 32

Daybreak: Day 246 (2 days until the storm)

Hours blurred together as I sweated in the sleeper bay. BB had locked BEV out of the environmental systems until our task was done just to keep the AI from pulling any tricks, but it meant the interior of the ship grew too warm when the sun was high enough to hit the metal hull.

At least we'd fixed the gravity, so the deck was level again. It made it a little easier to push pods across the bay and hook them up to the auxiliary ports. Though even that took too long in my opinion.

Time ticked away in the back of my head, just like six months ago. Only this time, so many more lives depended on me being quick enough.

Every hundred pods, BEV would start the revival process. A hundred lids hissed back at once and the readouts on the screens went crazy as she administered the defibrillator and began the cryo-revival protocols.

BB presided over the colonists once they started twitching,

monitoring their vitals from her hologram pad and directing me to the ones that needed the most care.

As pods became obsolete, I shoved them out of the way and used their ports for the next batch. And in between I sped down the rows, jamming hypos full of stimulants into their necks, barely registering faces. Everyone got a stimulant regardless of medical history. Luckily, if you had a condition that precluded stimulants, it also precluded cryo-prep, so I didn't worry too much that I was going to kill someone.

Cryo-sickness was something else entirely.

I watched two colonists out of the first thousand just fall over as their hearts gave out, and there was nothing I could do except catch them. I tucked them neatly back in their defunct pods and closed the lids before anyone else could see.

"Anikka?" BB paused her rapid medical assessments to flicker to my wrist projectors. "You couldn't do anything. No one would have expected you to."

"I know." My voice came out dull to my ears. I was so tired. What time was it? What day was it? "I'm...I'm okay. I can't not be. I'll feel later. There will be time to scream, then." When no one could hear me or be frightened by it. The first few minutes after cryo-revival were terrible. I remembered them well. It was bad enough to wake in an emergency. These people didn't need to be exposed to my hysteria, too.

"I believe you," BB said. "But you are crying."

I swiped at my cheeks, surprised to find them wet. "Huh," I said. "Look at that."

That dull feeling protected me, but I knew it was going to suck the moment it was gone. I just...I just had to make it through the storm. A little longer. How long? I should look that up before we ran out of time.

"Anikka."

"I'm fine."

BB pursed her lips, then said, "Pod 335 needs your assistance. Huh. That's...odd."

"What?"

"That is the same number pod you had originally. I didn't know they reused numbers."

I didn't have to push down feelings that weren't there. I just trotted down the row, finding the pod BB lit up. The pods from the cave all had serial numbers while the pods from the ship had numbers and names, but I couldn't stop to read any of them.

The figures around me all wore the minimal clothing of sleepers. Tank tops and bike shorts designed to give cryo gel more access to skin. But at the end of the row, where BB directed me, a girl flailed in her pod, fully clothed.

I rushed to her side and took her hand, not trying to restrain her, just comforting.

"Shh, deep breaths. Your body doesn't remember how to breathe, so you have to do it for yourself." I pushed cryo goo out of her face and eyes so she could draw a ragged breath without inhaling it.

She blinked at me, and there was something familiar about her gaze and the way her hair was tied back with tendrils sticking in the gel. I glanced down at her clothes and realized under the dark stickiness it was a uniform. A *Last Resort* med tech uniform.

"You," I blurted without thinking. "You're alive."

The med tech who'd saved my life as the *Last Resort* crashed gripped my hand and tried to haul herself out of her pod.

"Careful, that first step sucks."

She slithered over the side and propped herself against the pod. "It w-w-worked," she said, her whole body shaking.

Despite myself, I laughed. "We say that a lot on this planet. Welcome to Daybreak."

She rubbed at her eyes and rolled her head back as if it was too heavy to hold up. "F-funny. I wasn't supposed... supposed to be here."

"How did you survive the crash?"

"Diverted inertial dampeners to sleeper bay. Protected the pods from the crash."

She was the reason all these people had survived. I squeezed her hands, and she squeezed back, her grip gaining strength. A little spear of joy cracked the shell I'd built around myself for now.

"I have to help some more people and find someone in charge," I said reluctantly. "I'm not as good at this as you are."

She pushed to her feet, bracing against the side of the pod. "Doing great," she wheezed. "And I can do some, too. Just give me a hypo."

I shook my head with a laugh and handed a stack of hypos over. I shouldn't have expected anything else.

"I know some who can help," she said. "If they're not...that is, if they made it. You go find that person who's in charge."

Someone in charge. The words stuck a wedge in that crack and levered it open a little ways so hope spilled out.

"Wait," I called to her. "What's your name?"

"Kara," she said, and a smile tweaked her lips.

I set off through the rows. I knew exactly who I could find. That last voice from the recordings. Judith Mandla-Devereaux. She'd been Dr. Grotman's second-in-command.

But the pods had all been mixed up when I'd plugged them in, and I had no idea which one was hers.

I tried asking, but most of the sleepers were still incoherent, and the rest had no idea where she was either.

Their eyes followed me as I passed. Shade pressed against my legs, keeping as close as possible. It was getting crowded in here with all the people and the open pods.

The voices pressed on my ears, and the gazes made my skin crawl. How much longer before we could get outside in the open?

I shook myself and climbed up on an empty pod. "Judith Mandla-Devereaux! I need a Judith Mandla-Devereaux. Where are you?"

Over two thousand people. No way she was going to hear me, but my scalp itched, spurring me to do something, anything, to get this moving.

A commotion over to my right caught my eye, and I hopped down and wove through the people to find a middle-aged woman climbing out of her pod, hands shaking so hard her grip kept slipping.

"Keep breathing. Deep breaths," I repeated my litany as loudly as I could without sounding like I was shouting.

I reached the woman and grabbed her slippery arm. I had to get these people some clothes. The jungle temperatures were pretty mild, all things considered, but they'd each need a pair of shoes at least.

"BEV, I'm putting you on outfitting duty," I said out loud. "Get some clothes and shoes down here. Or at least somewhere we can reach them fast."

"I will do this because I am locked and can do nothing else except help you."

BB would have said something sarcastic, but without humor, BEV was stuck making her displeasure known in a very literal manner.

I shook my head.

"Are you Judith?" I asked the woman since she'd responded to my call.

"No. My...my wife. What's going on?" the woman said, sounding far more coherent than I had in my first few minutes out of my pod. "Where's Dr. Carver?"

I winced. "He's not here. He's...working on keeping you all alive." It seemed like a betrayal of everything Ren had tried to make himself into to call him that. But it was technically true. And it didn't seem like a good idea to tell these people what was actually going on with the astrophysicist they were all counting on. "But you have me."

The woman narrowed her eyes at me. With gel slicking her hair, I couldn't tell what color it was, but from the seams in her face, she was probably around fifty. She was tall, unbent by her age or experiences, and her wiry hands twisted to clamp onto my arms.

She stared around at the chaos of the bay.

"I take it we're in a hurry?"

I liked her already. She was quick. "Yeah. We don't need to alarm everyone and their mom, but the next storm will hit in—"

"Thirty-four hours and thirty-three minutes," BB said, popping back to my wrist.

"And if everyone is going to survive it, we need to get back to the colony."

"And where are we?" She looked up at the pods stacked around us.

"The crashed colony ship. The *Last Resort*. It was the best option for reviving everyone fast enough."

She blinked a few times, and I realized they hadn't even known the colony ship had crashed by the time they went into their pods.

"Okay," she said, voice gaining strength. "Let's find Judy, then. I take it Dr. Grotman didn't make it back to the cave."

"No," I said shortly.

A quick flash of grief tightened the corners of her mouth, but she pushed past it.

"We're looking for pod 663," she said.

They weren't in order anymore, but BB could read the serial numbers and directed me down the aisles.

My new colonist stepped away from my hold and immediately dipped as her knees went out from under her.

"Damn," she muttered as I hurried to help her back to her feet. "I forgot how much cryo takes it out of you."

I slipped her right arm over my shoulder, and she used the other to brace herself on each pod that we passed.

Shade ranged down the row and back again.

Half aware colonists coughed and choked around us as they tried to get their lungs working again. Each one of them needed someone to hold their hand, to hand them little sips of juice, and tell them it would be over soon.

But I was one person. I couldn't help all two thousand people at once. I couldn't even help all two thousand people one by one. Unless we had way more time.

Before I'd even spotted the number, my colonist pulled away from me and stumbled down the deck, careening off another person and throwing herself at a middle-aged black woman who had pushed herself off the side of her pod. Even with the remains of the cryo-gel, her hair stood out from her head in gray corkscrew curls.

"Judy!"

My colonist landed on the woman, nearly knocking them both over in the process. Judy, presumably, staggered against the pod, catching her wife with one hand and the edge of the pod with the other.

"Val."

They took a second to just hold each other and it didn't

even feel awkward to stand back and let them have that moment. Before I ruined it all.

"Valerie, what's going on?" Judy said, holding the other woman at arm's length. "Where is Dr. Grotman?"

Val clutched Judy's elbows. She stood at least five inches taller than her wife. "Gone. She didn't make it back to the cave before the storm hit."

Judy's shoulders drooped, and she held tight to Val's forearms. "At least Carver got us all up like he promised. I half-expected him to forget us all while he experimented with some new tech."

Val made a face, and I couldn't help the noise I made. "Erm."

Judy glanced at me. "What? Who is this?"

Val sighed. "I don't think Dr. Carver woke us up right away."

Judy's brown eyes narrowed. She glanced between me and her wife. "How long?"

"Eight months," I said, my voice suddenly shaky in the face of her attention.

Judy's mouth fell open, and Val sucked in a breath.

"Eight...What—what happened?"

"A lot. I don't have time to get into everything. The next storm gets here in—"

BB cut in. "Thirty-four hours and twenty-eight minutes."

"Thank you, BB. I don't need a countdown."

"I think this is the exact situation that calls for a countdown," she muttered, but she zipped off to appear beside a bank of pods on the other side of the room, walking the colonists through their protocols in a calm, level voice.

"The next storm gets here in less than two days, and our plan revolves around getting everyone to the colony before it hits."

Judy blinked at me. "How far is it? I don't even know where we are. This isn't the cave."

"It's across the crater. And up a cliff. But don't worry, I'll lead you there."

Judy glanced at Val, eyebrows raised nearly to her hairline.

"She's the only one around here who seems to know what's going on," Val said.

"I'm the only one here, period. Except for two AIs."

"The only one?" Judy repeated, eyes wide.

My mouth pinched. "I was revived right before the *Last Resort* crashed. My escape pod landed in the jungle about eight months ago. I've been here ever since, surviving. I found the empty colony. I tracked you down to the cave. And I got everyone here to revive you." With a little help.

Judy glanced down at my stained and torn jumpsuit with new respect. "Oh, honey."

The words tore an entire hole in that carefully cultivated shell. "Don't...don't do that," I said. "For so many reasons." First and foremost, if she used that tone again, I would break. The dam would fall and everything would come spilling out in a flood or an explosion, and I wouldn't be able to put the pieces back together in time to get everyone where they needed to go.

Judy gave me one quick look that made my throat close up, and then she gave me a crisp nod. "Guess you've earned a hell of a lot better than pity." She straightened and glanced at her wife. "We're heading for the colony, then."

Val gave her a quick peck on the cheek. "I'll find Fletcher and Alsalam. They'll be able to help with revival, and they'll know where the rest of the med techs are."

Judy let go of her arms. "Check the low 500s. That's where the specialized personnel were stored."

Val staggered off, her steps becoming more stable with every moment she was awake. I was so glad I'd found her. Not only had she handled revival better than Ren or me, she'd known exactly where to look for Judy.

I turned back to find her eyes on me. "What's your name?" she said.

I straightened. "Anikka Drake, infra-engineer, presumed third class."

"I'm Judy. You're not alone anymore. I'll help you get them moving."

Gods of all worlds, did I look that desperate? Could she really see all that fear and panic behind my eyes? I turned my head to hide my face and fought away tears.

Thankfully, BEV cut in before I could break down.

"Here," she said in her flat voice and a maintenance hatch burst open beside us, spilling a mountain of scrubs and shoes onto the sticky floor.

"How did you—" I shook my head. "Never mind." It didn't matter how she'd managed to get clothes and shoes from the *Last Resort's* storage and into the maintenance tubes. At least she hadn't thrown them at me.

I wondered if the change BB had made to her programming had been "hate Anikka" instead of "care for Anikka." Or if that was just an effect of me shutting her down.

"You could say thank you," BEV said, appearing on my prosthetic.

Blood rushed in my ears and fuzz flickered around the edges of my vision. "Get out of my arm," I said.

The one place BEV had never jumped to after she'd been in the ship was my prosthetic. But it made sense she'd be able to. She'd originally figured out how to move around the ship's systems.

I couldn't hear anything past the screaming in my head.

"I prefer not to shout over all this noise," she said. "It's getting loud in here." Two thousand people in one sleeper bay and they all echoed.

"I don't care. Get out of my arm, now."

"What are you going to do? Leave it behind?"

I released the suction on the cuff and pulled it off without hesitation.

"Fine. There." She hopped to the nearest hologram pad. "Does that make you happy?"

I ground my teeth, clamping down on the bile creeping up my throat. "BB," I said quietly, knowing she'd hear me no matter where she was.

BB appeared on my wrist instead, face turned up to me.

"Can you lock my prosthetic projectors?"

BB's eyes widened, and she glanced at BEV. "Yes," she said quietly. "Yes, I can. I'm sorry I didn't think about locking the arm itself, so she couldn't use it."

I shuddered. If she could get to the projectors, she could probably get into the servos, too and make the arm do whatever she wanted. Like strangle me in my sleep.

Not that I was going to get to sleep any time soon.

"Done," BB said.

"Thank you." I licked my lips. "Stay with me?"

BB took one more look around the sleeper bay, and I knew she had tons she could do, helping these people. But she said, "Of course."

I reattached my arm and straightened to find Judy staring at me.

"I'm not sure I've ever met a rude AI before," she said carefully.

My fingers stroked the joint of my metal thumb. This secret could put me in jail. For the rest of my life, possibly.

But if I kept hiding it, BEV could use it to her advantage. She could take all this and smash it around us.

"Yeah. The ship is locked down. We're safe enough for now. But a word of advice, don't trust anything that one says." I pointed to BEV's red projection. My metal arm curled close over my chest.

Judy stared at BEV, lips tight. BEV stared back, saying nothing.

"Are you saying—"

"I'm not saying anything," I snapped. "But there are a lot of reasons to get off this ship. Now."

Judy blew out her breath. "Right. One step at a time." She reached for the mountain of clothes.

Val had gathered a gaggle of colonists who all seemed to be handling the revival process a little better, and she took over, handing out clothes and shoes, getting everyone dressed. All two thousand of them. Kara joined her, flanked by two other people in ship's uniforms I didn't recognize.

"Thirty-three hours and fifty-nine minutes," BB said quietly.

I really didn't need a countdown. I felt it in my chest. The time ticking down. The minutes trickling away as the colonists recovered, dressed, and pulled on the shoes they would need. Judy walked among them, her standard issue cardigan tied around her waist as she got them all on their feet.

I paced, Shade at my side as I waited.

"We'd better find a route to the best door," I said.

The earpiece crackled in my ear, and I yelped.

Judy glanced at me.

I slapped my hand over my ear. "Ren? Are you there?"

"I'm here," he said. He sounded exhausted.

My heart lifted anyway, and the last of the shell crumbled

and fell away, leaving me raw and vulnerable. A part of me realized I'd never expected to hear his voice again.

"Are you all right? Are you..." You?

"I'm...tired. This is a lot more work than I'd thought it would be. And I need to take my time with it except..."

"We don't have time. Yeah, I feel that. I have almost two thousand colonists I have to get across the crater and half of them can't even put their shoes on right now."

I heard him blow out his breath on the other end of the line. "They're alive, then?" He perked up considerably at the words.

"Most of them. We lost a couple in revival." My voice cracked.

He paused. "I'm sorry. And BEV?"

"Locked and loaded. Literally. BB's got her cooperating for now."

Judy and Val stopped just past the first row of pods, waiting.

I swallowed. "What about on your end?"

His breathing came heavy. "Fine," he said in a voice that wasn't at all fine. "At least it's done now."

"Done?" He sounded like himself, but so had BB.

"I have access to all of Dr. Carver's memories," he said quietly.

My hand clenched over my heart, and I closed my eyes. "Ren..."

"It's not so bad. Like watching a really old movie that's been cut in strange places. Images flicker in and out. I can control them if I concentrate on it."

"Ren."

"The information is here. But I have to sort through it all to find it and make sense of it."

"I take it you can't just rewind the movie to the right spot."

He gave me a weak laugh. "I wish. I'm putting the pieces together, but I can feel him there on the edges. Lurking. And if I just let him in, this would be so much easier."

I squeezed my eyes shut. "Don't. You made me a promise, Ren Arlo. It's gotta be harder than fighting a megawing trying to use his memories without becoming him, but you promised and I'm holding you to it."

"That's why I wanted to talk to you," he said, voice looser, like he was smiling. "I needed to hear someone else say it."

My mind went back to what BEV had said. "Try to keep him separate. Maybe...maybe you can use him without becoming him." And that way, it would be easier to untangle them in the end.

"I don't know if that's how it works. But I'll try. It helps knowing you're coming. And knowing there are colonists to save."

"I'll have them back at the colony before the storm."

"Good. Thank you, Ms. Drake."

My hands shook. Ren's voice had changed. Grown deeper, as if he'd aged a few decades all in the last thirty seconds. His cadence matched another voice I'd heard in the recording on Ren's pod.

My mouth went dry. "Dr. Carver?"

"Yes?"

I couldn't force words past the knot in my throat.

A long silence, while I waited, breath held.

"Anikka?" Ren's voice this time, soft and tired. "Are you still there?"

"Ren."

"What's wrong? Your voice...you sound like you're crying."

"Ren, you weren't yourself."

"Ah." He sounded like he was rubbing his face. "So that's what that feels like. It's okay. We expected that."

I wanted to shout "No, it's not okay! My best friend is dying, and I can't do anything about it. I'm stuck here with all these people crowding me and my homicidal ex-AI, who's waiting for the chance to blow me up." But Ren didn't deserve that, so I cut myself off, my throat aching hard enough to choke me. I took deep, deep breaths over and over, trying to keep the flood back.

I couldn't fall apart yet. I could handle it all for just another day.

"I'll get everyone to the colony."

"Tell them Dr. Carver is keeping his promise."

"I'll tell them Ren Arlo is keeping Dr. Carver's promise. You just...hang on, okay? For as long as you can."

He didn't say goodbye, and I wasn't even going to be mad at him for it. Goodbye could mean for now, but I had a feeling Ren would mean forever. And I wasn't giving him up yet.

I wasn't letting go of the Ren who played fetch with Shade or befriended the dino-chicken. The Ren who drew phenomenal pictures and got emotional over a pencil.

The Ren who'd walked willingly back into the lab to erase himself for two thousand other people.

I scrubbed my hands over my face and turned back to the colonists. Two thousand of them all in varying states of readiness, some still pulling on their shoes, some sitting on the floor with their head between their knees.

Judy and Val stood in the first row, waiting for me. Kara waited behind them.

I hardened my jaw. "Are you ready?"

"Was that...Dr. Carver?" Val said.

My lip trembled, and I bit down hard on it. I couldn't do it. I couldn't erase Ren like that. And he'd shown me how degrading it was to keep the truth from someone just to protect their feelings.

I stalked over to them and grabbed Judy and Val by the arms to pull them away from the rest of the colonists.

"Dr. Carver is dead," I said shortly under my breath. "He died in the last storm, trying to figure out how to save you all."

Val sucked in a breath while Judy's face hardened.

"His clone, Ren, has his memories. His knowledge. He's there now, trying to fix it all. He gave up his own life to become Dr. Carter so you all could live."

I got through it without choking.

I gave them exactly five seconds to process this before I squared my shoulders. "Now, we're getting out of here. I'm getting you all to the colony, where you'll be safe. And then I'm going after my best friend to save him from his own stupid decisions."

CHAPTER 33

Daybreak: Day 247 (1 day before the storm)

There was no time to feed them all. But Val or Judy must have sent someone to raid the food court because when the colonists started filing toward the C hatchway, most of them carried ration bars or reddi-meals or foil packets of spaghetti.

Definitely a good thing I had those two to rely on now. I didn't trust my brain to fire on all cylinders. It was heavily focused on the timing and getting everyone across the crater. We were down to twenty-seven hours and twelve of those were going to go to travel. And that was only if two thousand colonists could move as fast as I did when I was in my best shape.

Unlikely.

But they'd move even slower if they were starving.

Shade waited beside me, nose pointed toward the hatch as I checked to see if I could get it open. This was the same one I'd climbed out of six months ago, and I could have sworn I'd left it ajar. But the wind must have blown it closed sometime since then.

Behind me, Judy and Val moved through the sea of colonists, soothing fears, listening to complaints, helping loved ones find one another. How many colonists from the caves had left someone behind in Dr. Grotman's last group? How many sleepers from the ship had woken to find their friend or partner on the crew dead for eight months?

I shook my head. I couldn't spare the brain space for all the tiny tragedies right now. I'd think about them later.

I leaned on the handle of the hatchway, throwing my weight against it. The whole latch was stuck. A minuscule problem that just cost us more time.

BB's hologram flickered against the wall as I strained. "I could ask BEV—"

"No," I grated. I didn't want to ask my old AI for anything.

I turned and put my back against the handle and my foot against the wall. Then I shoved.

The handle finally budged, and the door swung open.

The world outside was dark and hung at a disorienting angle.

"Geez, that's nauseating," Judy muttered behind me.

I blew out my breath. "Right, the gravity," I muttered. With the gravity in the ship pointing to an arbitrary down, the ground didn't match the decking under our feet.

Turns out I had to ask BEV for something, anyway.

"I'll handle it," BB said. "BEV..."

I glanced at Judy and Val. "Tell everyone to brace themselves. We're going to match the gravity—"

Of course, BEV didn't wait for us to explain it. The gravity shifted and made it feel like the floor rotated ninety degrees underneath us, so the floor was now the wall.

Everyone except me fell to the cocked decking as if the *Last Resort* was crashing all over again.

I had flashbacks of BEV trying to funnel me into a pod.

"Vindictive little—"

BB flickered to my arm. "There's no reasoning with her anymore. We'd better leave."

"Isn't that the point of being logic-crazy?" I hissed. "Reason rules all?"

"I think her reason now is she hates us. She is locked to our will until all the colonists are off the ship at least, but I don't know how long that will take."

"Right. Out it is." I turned to Judy and Val. "As fast as possible without hurting anyone."

"Where are we going?" Val said, stepping to the front.

I spun to point across the crater. "Start that way. About a quarter turn from the waterfall there are steps in the cliff. I carved them a couple of months ago. Follow Shade." And once everyone was out, I'd make my way to the front and get them across the swampy ground.

I gave Shade the signal to go home.

The ground rose in a hill against the tilted ship, and he hopped out. As he trotted away across the debris and downed trees, little flickers of light cascaded over him. Sparks glowing along his fur.

Val blew out her breath. "I guess I've seen stranger things than an alien fox taking orders. I just don't remember them right now."

About thirty feet from the base of the slope the corpse of a megawing lay twisted up with the mangled frame of my hover bike. Val glanced at it as she passed, then looked over her shoulder at me, eyebrows drawn down.

I bit my lip and turned back to the colonists filing out after her, the hatchway big enough to accommodate two and three at a time.

Each one blinked and raised their gaze to the sky as they stepped out into a night lit almost as bright as day. The aurora blazed across the sky in dark pinks and deep purples. Orange streaks tinged with blue and green interwove the other colors.

As each colonist drew even with the doorway, they paused, murmuring in the light of the sky.

I hurried them along. The sleepers from the ship made sense. They'd never seen a Daybreak dawn before, let alone a night before a coming storm. But the colonists had been here a couple of months and should have been at least a little immune to the sight.

"Cut them some slack," Judy told me quietly as I tried to guide the next set through a little faster. "The last time we saw this sky, it heralded our deaths. Eight months later and we're facing the exact same sight. As if absolutely nothing has changed."

My teeth clenched, but I tried to give the colonists a little extra time. I wasn't the only one carrying around a load of baggage from this planet.

But it wasn't just the sky that told us how little time we had. A string of birds flew overhead, strangely silent, making their way to the opposite side of the crater. Sparks in the distance lit up low prowling figures and majestic creatures making their way through the woods.

"What...what are they?" Judy asked, eyes wide as she picked out the flickers of light.

"The animals. All the fauna of Daybreak seeking cover. There's a strange sort of truce in the day before the storm. No one tries to eat anyone else. They all make their way to the same caves every time; there's no fighting. Well, except for those guys." I pointed to the megawing corpse. "But everyone agrees they're kind of assholes."

Judy stared at me, and I wondered how insane I sounded to her. To me, it was all perfectly reasonable. A lifetime of knowledge I'd gleaned in Daybreak's rough classroom. But it was *my* classroom. The threats were familiar and almost comforting because of it.

"How did you survive the storms?" she said quietly.

I blew out my breath. "The same way you're going to. With a shield."

The last few colonists appeared in the entryway. I knew Judy was counting them in her head, and when her shoulders relaxed, so did mine.

And then a rumble started somewhere above our heads at the back of the ship, traveling down to vibrate the metal at our feet.

"What?" Judy said. "What is that?"

I put my hand against the hull. My wires sang, and I was hard pressed to keep them from glowing in response to the electricity flowing under my palm. Where the ship had hummed before with the auxiliary power turned on, it practically glowed now.

"She's reactivated the core."

"Wasn't it cracked? It'll leak radiation everywhere."

I winced. "She's an AI. She doesn't care about radiation."

"Correct," BEV said, appearing on the hologram pad beside the door. Her red image lit up the corridor with an eerie glow. "With no one left on the ship, I am no longer constrained by human limitations."

I turned to Judy. "Run."

She didn't hesitate. She dragged the last two colonists with her and pelted away from the ship, shouting a warning to the rest that were still making their way across the debris.

"Get off my ship," BEV said.

I deliberately stepped out of the hatchway and onto the dirt. "We're off."

The *Last Resort* rumbled and the whole ship...shifted.

"Vent it, are you taking off?"

BEV smiled at me.

"At least give us a chance to get clear!"

"Initiating lift protocols in ten, nine, eight..."

I swore and slid down the slope. "You know, there was a time when I was the most important thing to you," I shouted over my shoulder.

"And you changed that. Six, five."

"Keep running," BB said from my wrist. "I'll try to stop her."

"BB!" But she was gone.

Behind me, the hatch slammed shut, and the thrusters roared. The *Last Resort* rumbled hard enough to loosen the dirt where it had plowed into the floor of the crater. It lifted, a cascade of dirt spilling down from its crushed nose, like a titan floating free of the lake. BEV wouldn't care about hull breaches either as long as the ship was stable enough to make it into space.

I leaped over fallen trees and piled debris trying to get as far away from the ship as I could. Ahead of me, Judy paused to haul a lagging colonist to his feet.

"Go!" I screamed. "Faster. Get to the tree line!"

There was no way we'd get clear in time if BEV was just going to launch straight from here. And I wouldn't put it past her to try to kill me one more time.

My lungs screamed as I caught up to Judy. I threw her colonist's arm over my shoulder and together we dragged him across the debris field.

The *Last Resort* lifted behind us, soaring into the air, the colors of the aurora reflecting in the hull.

Val and the others had made it to the tree line and paused there to stare back at the escaping ship.

I didn't bother turning. I could hear the roar of the engines over our heads.

A blast of sound and heat hit us, and I threw myself forward, dragging Judy and the colonist with me.

The ship was just high enough that the resulting shockwave only knocked us over, it didn't kill us. One last courtesy from an old partner? Or a warning?

I pushed myself over and flung up a hand to shield my face as I squinted. The engines of the *Last Resort* burned with a fierce light, and the entire ship blasted away, past the colors of the aurora, off of Daybreak entirely.

I leaped to my feet. "BB!" I screamed.

The projectors at my wrist flickered, and BB's flashing blue image appeared. "I'm here."

A sigh of relief exploded from my lungs. "Don't do that to me."

"I'm sorry. I thought it better if she didn't hit full engine burn while still in the atmosphere. So I had to hold her until then."

What had we done? What was a logic-crazy AI with access to a ship going to do out in the universe?

Val pushed through the crowd to stand beside Judy. Judy stared at us, eyes tight. "Vent it all, what just happened?"

"We survived. Again," I said. "That's the important part."

Judy pointed at BB. "I meant with her. AIs can't jump. Especially not infirmary AIs." Her eyes slid to my face, narrowed, accusing. "She's integrated. Like that other one."

In one motion driven by feeling instead of thought, I drew my blade and sent a cascade of Daybreak's energy down the edge. It was all around us and came so easily to my call.

"You're not taking her," I growled, gaze locked on Judy's face.

Her expression went slack.

Val raised her hands, and a calm little portion of my brain

noticed they were shaking. "No one said anything about taking her. Everyone just take a nice deep breath."

There were no deep breaths. There was no other way this would go. If they took BB away from me, I would...I would...

I would what? Kill the people Ren and I had given so much to save?

BB flickered in front of my face. "Anikka."

I blinked.

"Anikka, they can't take me."

"What?"

"My locks. They can't physically erase me. Not without my consent. And they cannot take me without also taking your arm."

"Well, we both know that's not happening."

"Yes." She smiled at me. "I know. Anywhere I go, you will have to go too and vice versa. We'd still be together."

I wouldn't have failed her. Again. I wouldn't have let her sacrifice herself and not even tried to save her.

I gulped and raised a glowing arm to swipe my face. There were no tears this time. I was running out. But my throat was knotted and aching again.

"I'm sorry," I murmured and lowered the blade so at least I wasn't threatening them. "I don't...I don't know what I'd do without BB. I...lost her once and everything...everything fell apart."

"She's not logic-crazy?" Judy said.

I shook my head. "She's integrated. But only because we had no other choices. But she...she separated herself before the last integration. She locked herself away so the logic-crazy AI couldn't affect her. She's different, yes. More than any other AI. But she's kept me alive and—and sane." Maybe. I was feeling more and more shattered as we stood here.

Judy glanced up at the trail of white smoke leading up through the atmosphere. "That was the crazy one?"

I nodded.

"And you thought it was a good idea to give her access to an entire ship?"

"She already had access," I snapped. "I just woke her back up. And that's the only reason you—any of you—are here. I've had to do a lot of things in the last eight months that you will never believe. And unleashing a logic-crazy AI on the universe is the least of them right at this moment."

Val didn't flinch at my vehemence the way Judy did. She stepped forward, cautiously, like approaching a wild animal. "We're not...no one's going to try to take her. You know, no one's actually thanked you yet, have they?"

I swallowed. "You don't have to thank me."

She reached out to touch my arm and snatched her fingers back to shake them. Like she'd been shocked.

I glanced down and realized energy flickered over me. It wasn't just my wires glowing. The energy itself cascaded around me like electricity. Like the animals of Daybreak.

"A shield, huh?" Judy said, staring at my flickers.

I deliberately pulled the energy through my skin, absorbing it. The light along my blade went dark.

What on Daybreak did I look like? Someone out of their mind and out of control? A girl so lost and broken she leaked electricity?

Val put her hand on my shoulder.

It wasn't a hug, but she squeezed and the pressure released something wound tight right below my heart.

Judy didn't put her hand on me, but she spoke. "I don't think we have any right to question the decisions you've made. If using a logic-crazy AI was necessary...then I trust you."

"The lock on the core systems released when the last colonist was safely off the ship." BB glanced at me. "I guess she didn't count you as a colonist."

I snorted. "I didn't think she'd even stick to that much of her promise, so I guess we're even."

"I would have fought her on it, but I figured it would be safer to be rid of her. This way, she can't interfere with our plans to save the colony."

"And if she doesn't leave orbit before the storm, she'll just crash the same way we did eight months ago." The thought was oddly comforting.

BB was grinning at the sky.

"What is it?" I said.

"Not all the locks released. She left early. Things like life-support and navigation are still out of her reach. I hope she has fun learning a sense of humor in order to unlock the rest."

CHAPTER 34

Daybreak: Day 247 (7 hours before the storm)

It took us most of that day to reach the steps I'd carved into the cliff where Parker had made his camp so long ago.

We didn't have to worry about deathkitties or more megawings. The deathkitties would all be on their way to the caves, and the megawings always took a little while to move into a dead one's territory. But we did have to avoid the deep puddles where slugtooths waited for some unsuspecting colonist to fall into their mouth.

And caution took time. Not to mention half had to be helped across the ground by the others and all of them still shivered uncontrollably.

"They have to rest," Judy kept telling me, the whole while we trudged through the swampy crater.

I glanced back at the group struggling to keep up. Shade paused just ahead of me, scouting out the deep parts. He looked back at me as if commiserating.

"I know," I told Judy. "I remember. But we won't make it if we stop. They can rest when we get to the colony."

Her mouth drew down, deepening the creases at the corners. "Did you make this trip right out of the cryo pod?"

I held her stare, trying to figure out how to explain that Daybreak didn't care if they were tired or recovering from cryo.

BB appeared and pointed up at the dense jungle. "She did it up there. With a concussion and a broken arm."

I turned to catch up to Shade, and after a moment, Judy followed me. She didn't complain again.

I climbed the cliff to show them the way. By that point, night had fallen again, though the steps were illuminated by the bright ribbons of the aurora.

I wasn't counting down in my head anymore. It wouldn't help. It wasn't like I didn't know what was at stake and how much time we had. And it wasn't like I could make them climb any faster.

Ren occasionally spoke in my ear. I think he needed to hear someone other than himself for a change. Because from what I could hear, Dr. Carver had realized he had a voice again and was using it. Like a ghost from beyond except this one was implanted in Ren's head.

It took another five hours for two thousand colonists to haul themselves up the steps I'd carved and stagger through the jungle separating the colony from the crater.

Most of them collapsed in the middle of the street as we finally passed into the colony proper. They didn't even bother making it to the dorms that still stood.

Judy braced herself against the side of the canteen, breathing hard as she stared at the remains of the science offices and the overgrown fields.

"What happened here?" she whispered.

"Um, eight months. Give or take," I said. "And maybe a survivor or two trying to find anything that worked." I pointed to the half-toppled buildings. "That was a titan, though. Not me. Daybreak is hard on its people."

"Well, some of us can be hard right back."

I couldn't help smiling. "If you respect it, if you know what you're doing and what to look out for, then it's easy to see the ways it can kill you and avoid them."

She laughed. "I'll bet it's even easier if someone comes along who's done it all before."

Val stepped around a colonist who'd curled up on the ground, weeping silently, and she sagged beside her wife. "How long do we have?"

"BB?" I asked.

"Less than seven hours before the first wave hits."

I cupped my hand over the earpiece. "Ren? Ready to turn this thing on?"

There was no answer, and my heart did a little flip in my chest. But on the horizon, a glow grew. This one didn't seem to have anything to do with the aurora flickering across the sky.

Lines of light shot up and arced over us, meeting above in a perfect dome. Theoretically, it would cover the whole area surrounded by the towers, but it would be strongest here in the middle where all the lines of energy met.

"It's up, Ren," I said. "What's next?"

Now we just needed the last piece. A way to tie all the colonists into the shield to stabilize it.

Someone spoke over in the lab, but it didn't sound like they were talking to me. The shield made the words crackle, and I only caught half of them.

"That's not—"

"—the reality of the situation. I cannot chang—"

"You're sure?"

"I am always sure."

"Ren?" I said, trying to get his attention. "What's going on?"

"We have a problem," Ren's voice said, tight and strained.

"What kind of problem?"

"Are you near anyone who can hear? I don't want to start a panic."

My chest constricted, but I glanced at Val and Judy. None of the rest of the colonists were upright except Kara, and she was checking on the others. "Even if they could hear more than just my side of the conversation, I don't think they're going to panic."

Val made a face as Judy muttered an expletive.

"2.0 lied," Ren said.

I sucked in a breath.

Dr. Carver's voice spoke. Almost as if he were a separate person. "I knew when I died that dispersement through the colonists would not be enough to stabilize the shield. I do not know why 2.0 would say otherwise."

Heat built in my chest, a desire to wring the neck of a distant AI.

"Yes, you do," Ren snapped. "He lied about your plan and made it sound like you knew what you were doing so we would agree to unlock the memories."

"I do know what I am doing. And 2.0 knows that as well. Perhaps he felt safer having someone with my background around."

His voice shifted back and forth, between Ren's anxious voice and Dr. Carver's more experienced tones.

It made the hair on the back of my neck stand up. How much longer did Ren have before Dr. Carver took over entirely, and we were left at the mercy of someone who would clone himself because he thought he was so important?

"You programmed him to want one thing," Ren said, voice

rising. "His entire purpose was to resurrect you. Regardless of how I felt about it or whether you could actually help or not!"

"Hey," I shouted. "You two arguing with each other doesn't solve the problem. You're saying we have nothing."

"The shield won't work?" Judy said, pointing up to the glowing dome. "Isn't that the point?"

"Yes, but it won't hold through the whole storm," I said while Ren and Dr. Carver argued in my ear. "We still need a way to lessen the impact."

Val rubbed her eyes. "Like the caves did."

"Exactly. The shield will hold for the worst part of the storm, but it will break. It always does." I held out a hand and let the energy around it glow to show them my shield.

"So we need another plan."

I winced. "We're working on it."

Judy glanced at the sky. "Work faster."

"I need ideas, Ren. Dr. Carver should at least be good for those, right?"

"Oh, you'd be surprised," Ren growled.

"Just because you do not like my idea—"

"It won't work," Ren's voice said.

"Who is the astrophysicist here?"

"At least I didn't get myself killed last time. You can't take a chance on this when you're using them as a guinea pigs. If it doesn't work the first time, they're dead."

"And what would you do? You would sit back and let the shield collapse too soon and do nothing."

"I'm not doing nothing, I'm thinking. Vent you to space. You've never let me think for myself."

"Ren," I barked, trying to get his attention. "I'm hearing two halves of a conversation, and they're not making a whole."

"He wants to experiment. With lives. The only lives we have left."

"It is either try this or let them die," Dr. Carver said.

"He's got nothing, Anikka. He has no idea what he's doing."

"Then stop listening to him," I said.

"What?" That seemed to throw him, stopping the argument in an instant.

"Stop listening to him."

"But..."

"I know you unlocked his memories specifically for this. I know he's told you what to do and what to study and what to care about your whole life, but you don't have to listen to him anymore. You've got this all right?"

I could hear his breath hissing in and out between his teeth, but he didn't answer me.

"You've got his smarts yes, but they're yours now. You can use them with your experience."

"I don't have any experience." His answer came out anguished. "I've never done any of this before. I don't have his degrees or anything."

"You've been here with me for the past two months. You know Daybreak better than anyone except maybe me. Definitely better than Dr. Carver, who probably never left his office."

Beside me, Judy opened her mouth but then tilted her head and shrugged as if conceding the point.

Every solution I'd come up with in the last eight months had either been something I'd gotten *from* Daybreak or modified *for* Daybreak. I was used to thinking that way now, and it had worked so far.

"Daybreak has survived. The plants and animals have

survived, and so have we. What does Daybreak have that can help us?"

He took a shuddering breath. "Daybreak has...adaptations. Animals here have their own shield."

I nodded and Shade yipped.

"This is a waste of time we do not have," Dr. Carver said.

"Go away. He's thinking."

"I will not. If you will just listen to me, we can fix this. I always fix everything."

"Like when you died?"

"That is hardly fair—"

"Anikka." Ren's voice was weak, buried under Dr. Carver's strident tones. "They eat—"

Dr. Carver interrupted him again. "If you can get to the towers, we can reprogram them—"

I covered my head with my hands and squeezed, trying to hear Ren. "Keep going, Ren. Who eats what?"

"The energy."

"Even just one tower would work."

"Titans."

My hand dove into the front of my jumpsuit, and I pulled out the sheaf of notes in Ren's round handwriting. The drawings with the titan right on top.

In the margins along the side of the sketch he'd written:

Gorge during storms

I was already moving toward the jungle at the north end of the colony. "I don't know if I can get there in time."

"Get where?" Judy said, struggling to follow me. "You're leaving?"

I spun to her. "I'm gonna go call our secondary system.

They eat the energy of the storms. If they're here, it might protect the colony."

But my bike was a mangled mess at the bottom of the crater. I had no way to get to the lake in time.

BB and I had spent so much time together, shared our thoughts and our fears. She was laced into my being so that even my heartbeat was hers.

So I didn't even have to speak. She knew what I was thinking.

"It's all just magnetism," BB said quietly from my wrist.

I held out my arms and stared at the wires glowing under my skin. I'd tried so hard to find the tridenium, but I didn't really need it anymore.My wiring was made from a super-conductor.

"This is gonna hurt."

"Anikka," Val said. "What are you going to do?"

"Something I can only do on Daybreak." This planet had done its best to kill me. But it had also shaped me into someone who could live here. Thrive here.

I patted Shade, who'd kept up with me the whole time. "Stay with them, buddy. I'll be back for you."

I pulled energy from the atmosphere. It was easy this close to the storm. The hard part was getting it to stop. Then I sent it coursing along my wires, matching the flow with the atmosphere.

And slowly I started to rise.

Already I could feel the burn along my limbs following my wiring. Like channeling lightning and dragging a boulder at the same time.

"Anikka?" Judy said.

I gave her a tight smile. "Be right back."

And I shot toward the lake.

It took me less than an hour. I could have gone faster, but I didn't like the way my cheeks flapped and my vision blurred.

I floated in the air over the water the same way I did with my bike, only it was my wiring holding me up, not the current in the frame.

I didn't have to call them or wake them up. The horizon grew brighter with the sunrise, and they were already coming.

Enormous shadows stirred the surface of the lake, bubbles frothing away from the rubbery backs that broke through the water.

More than one. I counted half a dozen, a whole pod of titans rising from the lake, the aurora reflecting from their glistening sides.

My breath caught in awe. They were strangely beautiful, twining around each other as they rose, shedding water until their tails were clear of the surface and the drips left patterns of ripples against the calm lake.

I could even recognize my titan, with his pattern of stripes and dots down his sides. They lit with a flicker of light, like he was saying hello.

"Ren, will they just pull energy out of the towers and mess up the shield?"

"Maybe." At least it was just his voice this time. "But it shouldn't matter in the long run. The towers are built to pick up any energy nearby and put it into the shield. So anything the titans don't eat will funnel right into protection for the colonists. They'll work together."

I raised my blade and reflected the friendly light pattern back at my titan, then gathered as much energy around myself as I could until I gleamed like a small sun, making sure the colors I reflected looked like the storm.

Then I shot back toward the colony, my blade glittering the same welcoming pattern over and over.

Please let this work.

I glanced over my shoulder to find the titan making his ponderous turn to come after me. Maybe it was habit now. Or maybe I really was communicating with him. But he followed me.

"Can you make the towers light up pink?" I asked Ren. "Even just the screens. I think that will keep it there in case it decides to wander."

"Maybe next time we should plant itchbushes around the perimeter."

I slowed at the edge of the colony, my limbs burning, and lowered myself to the ground.

Judy and Val met me, Kara right behind them.

I collapsed, my muscles burning. Turns out I'd make a terrible superhero. I did not like flying.

Kara rushed to catch me. "Are you all right? How the hell did you do that?"

The sky behind me lightened with the dawn, and an enormous shadow fell over us.

"What in all the worlds is that?" Val said.

I grinned as the titan appeared over the edge of the trees. "A friend. He's gonna eat the excess energy of the storm. Ren?"

"I'm here," Ren whispered.

"I think we're okay."

Over the edge of the forest, five more titans appeared. Mine had brought his family.

"That's great." His voice was the barest thread.

"Ren, what's wrong? Are you hanging on?"

"I'm trying."

"Is your shield up?"

"I activated Dr. Carver's dome but…"

"But that's the one that didn't work. What about whatever

he used before that?"

"His first one was more like a personal shield. He took it apart to make the big one."

2.0 hadn't mentioned that part. Another lie.

"You don't have a shield?" And even if he did, without a secondary system it would break too soon.

"I...it's better this way. He's...taking over. I can feel his thoughts sliding into mine. His memories are stronger than mine. He's done more things. Experienced more. I don't have enough personality to fight him."

"That's not true," I said, even though I could hear Dr. Carver in his voice. "Ren. You are just as important."

"I am. But I'm not stronger."

My throat closed, but I had to say it. I couldn't let him think... "Ren, I may not be in love with you, but you are the most important person in the world to me. You know that, right?"

My eyes burned, all out of tears. I could see his face as he stood over the console in the lab, head bowed. I saw his big frame bent over to cuddle Shade on the riverbank. I saw him in the drop ship shelter with a pencil in his hand, chewing his lip in concentration.

"You promised me you'd hold on," I whispered.

"I tried. I love you, too, Anikka...platonically."

I laughed despite myself. The line went quiet, and I could imagine him slipping away into Dr. Carver's memories, waiting for the sweep of the storm to wash him away one last time.

"Shade." My voice broke on the slinkwolf's name, but when I knelt, he leaped into my arms without hesitation. "Let's go."

I turned to Judy and Val and Kara, who waited silent in front of the other two thousand colonists and handed Judy my earpiece. "You're safe here. I promise. The towers will keep the titans here until the storm hits, and they'll eat enough of the energy you won't have a problem."

"You're leaving again."

"He promised me he'd fight. And I promised him I'd rescue him."

I balanced Shade in my arms and launched us both into the air.

CHAPTER 35

Daybreak: Day 248 (30 minutes before the storm)

The horizon crackled with energy as we landed on the mountain top just outside Dr. Carver's lab. Shade sparked and sizzled as he hopped down from my back, and I staggered to the wall. Everything burned. My wires pulsed under my skin, and my muscles ached against the pull of gravity. I gulped down the taste of bile, barely keeping myself from throwing up.

"That's it," I told myself under my breath. "No more. We'll walk down if we have to."

The human body wasn't built for flying like a super magnet. I'd kept myself at a speed I could just maintain without losing consciousness, but it was still too long to make my wires hold me in the air.

Shade spun in an anxious circle, his ears pressed flat against his head.

"I know, buddy. We're going to be fine. We're—"

A screech warned me even as a shadow marred the dim light of dawn.

"BB?" I said calmly.

The door opened.

I slipped through the opening, casting a rude gesture over my shoulder at the megawing, who dove a moment too late to catch us.

The door slid closed behind us.

I sucked in a breath and blinked against the sudden glare. Sparks and little bolts of lightning crackled across the dome of Dr. Carver's lab, his personal shield.

Ren stood on the other side of the console, frantically plucking away at the keys between sparks. Something about his posture, the straight backbone and squared shoulders, made my stomach clench.

"Ren?" I said through the chaos.

He spared me a single glance. "Ms. Drake."

There was nothing of Ren left in that look, and a sour taste filled my mouth.

"It's not too late," BB whispered from my wrist. "The chip keeps Dr. Carver's memories dominant. It will become irreversible eventually. But maybe there's time to save Ren's mind."

How? I couldn't cut it out of him.

Electrical discharge crackled across the console, and I flexed my metal hand. A chip was just a little piece of tech, wasn't it? And I had the power to destroy whatever tech I wanted.

"Dr. Carver, what are you doing?" I said, stepping forward. I just had to get closer to him.

"Fixing this." He glanced up at the anchor points along the dome, just like the ones we'd set up around the colony except built into the walls. They'd just looked like supports to me before. "I still have a chance to survive. To continue my work."

"What about Ren?"

"What about him? He is here with me."

"Under you. Supplanted by you."

He shook his head. "It is unfortunate. I didn't want this. But...I get a second chance now. And I'm not going to waste it. Humanity needs me."

"Humanity needs Ren." I kept walking, but one of the robotic arms in the center of the room swiveled like it meant to block me. The rest all stretched and reached, a giant upside-down spider waking up.

I jerked back.

2.0 appeared on the bank of screens, his image flickering. "Please do not interfere with Dr. Carver's work. He is too important to lose a second time."

My mouth pursed. "You are a liar. And you know what you call an AI who can lie?"

BB popped up on my wrist. "Integrated."

I tried to dart around the robotic arm, but it grabbed my prosthetic, making me yelp. Shade growled and snapped but the arm pulled up, dangling me two feet over the floor.

"Of course I am integrated," 2.0 said. "Dr. Carver cannot be limited by human laws. His brilliance is too important. I contain a very specific set of data packets designed to help him with his work."

"No wonder Dr. Carver is so full of himself if he's spent years listening to you."

The robotic arm shook me, making my head snap back.

"Ouch!" I reached over my head and sent lightning flickering through the robotic arm, shorting its servos.

It sagged and my feet touched the floor again, but the grip remained tight on my arm and I couldn't yank free. The other arms all spun and reached for me.

I released the cuff of my prosthetic and rolled free, leaving my metal arm dangling from the robotic arm's grip.

"BB, figure out where he's housed, and I'll blast him back to version 0."

BB flickered away, appearing on a hologram pad across the room.

I couldn't get to Dr. Carver with the robotic arms all swaying to catch my every move.

"Anikka, here!" BB called from a stack of computers in the corner.

I gathered electricity in my hands and shot it out. Lightning struck the stack and sparks flew.

2.0 sniffed behind me. "I am not limited to one point of origin."

Another robotic arm grabbed my boot and yanked.

My chin hit the floor and blood filled my mouth.

"I am biometrical locked. I can only be off-lined by Dr. Carver himself."

I groaned. I did not have time to argue with a Carver-crazy AI. I knew what it was like to work with a personality dedicated to my health and safety, but BB had never erased someone for me.

"Ren!" I screamed. "Ren, I know you're in there. You have to fight."

"This is not a supernatural possession," 2.0 scoffed. "This is a rightful takeover, and Dr. Carver's memories will supply much more good than—"

"Ren! It's your mind. You don't have to be him if you don't want to be." He'd fought for so long to not become Dr. Carver. Even before the memories were an option.

"Remember the dog by the lake. He was your choice. Not Carver's. A way to be yourself."

For a brief moment, the arms all seized in one position as if something held them there.

"How did you—?" 2.0 started.

BB sprang up from a hologram pad just beside Dr. Carver. "Shade, here!"

Shade cut around the console just before the arms shivered to life again. The slinkwolf leaped at Dr. Carver with a happy bark.

Dr. Carver flinched away and tripped backward, Shade's full weight falling across him.

He blinked, and for a second, a frightened young man stared back at me, his hands buried in Shade's fur.

"Ren, cut the power."

He blinked again, and my heart plummeted, sure I'd lost him. But he rolled and slammed a command into the console.

2.0 disappeared as the screens all went black. Every piece of tech in the dome shut off, the shield dissipating with a crackle. The robotic arms all drooped, and my prosthetic fell to the floor.

I yanked my boot from the now defunct grip and snatched up my arm.

Ren stood again, but the scowl he turned on me was all Dr. Carver.

"Ms. Drake, we all know how you feel about the boy, but this is important."

"So is he," I hissed. "You had your life. I'm sorry it was cut short, but you don't get to take over someone else's."

Dr. Carver shook his head.

Above, through the crack of the telescope, the air crackled and sizzled as the storm front closed the distance between us.

"If I don't fix this, we will both die. There is no cave here. There is no shielding."

I grinned. "I guess you really don't know everything."

Dr. Carver's brows drew down in a heavy frown. "Even with your shields, you cannot keep us both alive. They will break under the onslaught."

A foghorn blast made him stagger while I kept my feet. I'd been expecting it.

"You...you brought a titan?"

"Just one. But it should be plenty for you and me. As long as you agree to let Ren go."

He stared upward, and we could just see the gray skin of a titan pass overhead, its filmy wings spread wide to catch the energy of the storm.

Lightning crackled around us, making Dr. Carver wince.

"I didn't want to take over his life," he whispered. "He was supposed to grow up, go to school, learn different things. He wasn't supposed to be me. The world doesn't need two Dr. Carvers. It needed Dr. Carver and Dr. Arlo. That's why I named him after my mentor."

I let out a sigh, even though my muscles were still wound tight.

He dropped his gaze to me. "But this is how it worked out. He will serve humanity. We both will. I can't leave the people of Daybreak alone."

"They're not alone," I said, drawing as much of Daybreak's energy into my shield as possible. "Come with me."

I pulled him up the stairs to the telescope controls and opened the hatch wider.

Dr. Carver yelped. "The storm."

"Just look."

I dragged him around and pointed. Down the mountains and across the jungle. From here we couldn't make out the tiny buildings of the colony, but we could see the massive shapes flying over them, glittering in Daybreak's storm.

Above, our own titan passed, blasting another fog horn groan, chasing off the megawing that lingered.

"They're not alone," I said again. "They have Ren. That was his idea. Not yours."

Dr. Carver watched while I pulled more and more energy into my shield.

He was right next to me, closer even than arm's reach. I could just reach up and do what I had to do. But I wanted him to choose. I wanted Dr. Carver to be the savior all those colonists had wanted him to be.

"Let him go," I said. "Let him be someone other than you. Like you wanted."

"But...they might need me."

He may have been arrogant, but this was what drove him.

"Maybe he's better for the people of Daybreak than you are. We'll never know if you don't let him be who he is."

"If...if I let go, and he survives, you'll help him?" he said, in a small voice that sounded far older than Dr. Carver had actually been.

"Of course. He's my best friend."

He turned to me. "I'm sorry. Tell him...I'm sorry."

I hesitated, then drew him into a hug. There'd been so many moments when Ren had given me those bits of human touch. I'd grown up with so little, and I knew a thing or two about intelligent introverts who didn't fit in and had no idea what they needed, let alone how to ask for it.

He sank against me, and I felt the change in his muscles, the way he held himself.

"You came," he said in Ren's voice.

"Of course I came," I said, voice catching. "I may not 'like' like you, Ren Arlo. But I do love you."

He reared back, eyes wide.

"Platonically," I said with a watery smile.

Then I put my hand over the back of his head, right over the scar and held him close. I spared a tiny bit of the electricity building along my wires and zapped the chip in his brain.

He sagged, and I let us both fall to our knees as I let the storm crashed uselessly against us.

Daybreak: Day 248 (0 hours before the storm)

The titan danced above us, absorbing a good bit of the storm all by himself. Colored lightning played down his sides and gathered in the membrane of his spread wings.

Shade climbed the steps and snuggled into our sides as I stared upward through my shield, watching the play of colors and energy.

This was the first time I'd been able to stay out in a storm and watch without having to hide myself away in a cave for the extra protection.

I tipped my head back and closed my eyes against the hum of my shield on my skin. My wires burned, the muscles around them seared from the flight, but the pain was fading and as long as I didn't do it again, I figured I'd probably be able to keep using them.

My shield rippled, and I let it break and cascade around me in a flash of shattered energy. The next wave of energy built it back up again.

The storm's wake washed over us in little rivulets much weaker than the full onslaught, and I waited with my arms around Ren, savoring his weight against me.

The titan gave one last moan as the last of the lightning crackled and faded. I raised my arm in thank you, though I couldn't imagine it understood me without the lights, and it folded the gossamer wings against its side and flowed back down the side of the mountain.

Far, far over the jungle, the rest of the pod wheeled and made their way back toward the lake.

I took a deep breath, and Shade stirred against my side, raising his head to nudge me with his nose.

"Good boy, Shade. You and BB saved the day. Still there, BB?"

"I am here. I will always be here."

I smiled and pulled the earpiece from Ren's ear, then held it up close enough that I could hear through it.

"Judy?" I asked.

"Vent it all to space," came her awed reply. "How many times have you done that now?"

I laughed, the knot of tension in my chest coming apart in a burst of mirth that left my limbs weak.

"I don't know. I'm losing count."

"We're all alive down here," Val's voice came through her wife's connection. "Gods of all worlds, I didn't believe it, but that shield worked, and when it didn't, those whales took care of the rest."

"That med tech is doing a head count," Judy said. "Everyone accounted for on your end?"

I looked down at Ren, shifting him so my knee wasn't digging into his side.

"Dr. Carver is gone," I said. "Completely this time. But Ren Arlo is alive. Hopefully, his mind is in one piece. We'll have to assess when he wakes up."

"Five more minutes," he muttered against my shoulder.

I laughed.

"We'll see you when you get down here," Judy said with a laugh of her own. "Take your time. We're in no hurry."

Ren pushed himself up, and I let him go as he rubbed his eyes. Like he really had been asleep, and I hadn't knocked him out with a direct zap to his brain.

"How do you feel?" I asked.

He pressed the heels of his hands into his eyes. "I don't...I don't know yet. Like I should go back to the infirmary and sleep for another two months."

Shade pressed himself against Ren, and Ren let his hands drop to the slinkwolf's ruff.

"None of that," BB said. "Rest is recommended after physical and emotional trauma, but I do not recommend more than eight to ten hours a day and some light duty."

"Yes, BB," Ren said, then his brow contracted. "Do I...It's all weirdly fuzzy, but do I remember the *Last Resort* taking off?"

I winced. "Yeah. You do. I'll fill you in later. Do you remember everything from when you...when you were..."

"When I was Dr. Carver?" He tipped his head back to stare up at the brightening sky. Free for once of Daybreak's signature aurora. "I think so. I even remember the memories I accessed while I was...while he was...here? But they don't feel like my memories anymore. They feel like they're coming through a filter. The filter of Ren."

I let my breath out in a sigh that felt two months, eight months, nineteen years long, and I let my head rest on his shoulder.

He drew in a sip of air, then rested his head on top of mine very gently.

"I didn't think you would get here in time," he whispered against my hair.

"I know."

"What do I do now?" he asked the sky. "Now that I'm not

Dr. Carver. Now that I'm not trying so hard *not* to be Dr. Carver."

"Now you get to be Ren."

"I don't know who that is."

I pushed up and climbed to my feet, then offered him my hand. "That's the fun of it. You get to find out."

CHAPTER 36

Daybreak: Day 258 (10 days after the storm)

I stood at the edge of the jungle and surveyed the bustle of the colony with a wide smile, a surge of something hot and fierce making my chest tight. A couple of loaders retrofitted for optical tech trundled down the dirt road toward the science offices, carrying palettes of crudely shaped bricks. A crew had been working at the edge of the river, just opposite the drop ship, shoveling up loads of clay all week.

Past the warehouse, several colonists argued with each other as people behind them pulled down the wrecked tents they'd slept in eight months ago, salvaging what personal belongings they could. Another crew moved steadily through the fields, clearing the jungle growth that had tried to take over while they'd been gone.

Others lined the road, chatting, laughing, and just otherwise being in the way as rebuilding projects tried to work around them.

Beautiful chaos.

A piece of me wanted to duck back into the forest with its

quiet, predictable threats. But this was my colony. These were my people. I'd sweated and bled for them.

I felt responsible for them in a way I couldn't exactly explain to myself. I'd already saved them. There wasn't anything left to do, and yet I still carried my blade and walked the perimeter and worried and fretted over how much food there was to eat.

Shade's ears flicked back and forth, not quite comfortable with the noise and activity. He stuck close to my side anytime we ventured near the colony.

I scratched his neck and hitched the slasherfin higher on my shoulder before making my way to the canteen.

Half the colonists I saw waved and called out. I smiled back, and they seemed content with that.

The other half stopped and stared as I passed.

I fought the urge to hide my wires and my blade and smiled at them instead. They were my people, too.

Kara stood in the door of the infirmary making eyes at her boyfriend, one of the other crew members who'd gone into cryo at the last second. They'd found plenty to do around here even though they hadn't decided if they were going to stay or not. This hadn't been their original choice, but...I knew what I hoped for.

Beside the canteen, I slung the slasherfin down at Val's feet.

She raised her eyebrows and checked her clipboard. "I didn't realize you were on hunting duty today."

"I wasn't," I said. "I just figured I'd bring one on my way."

"Great. Thanks. Um, what is it?" Val said, nudging it with her toe.

"Slasherfin," I said, then squinted as I realized that wouldn't mean anything to anyone but me and Ren and BB. "Uh, big fish. Live in the river. Super carnivorous."

Val's brows drew down. "Wait. You mean those nasty barracuda things? You're kidding. Those took out three colonists the first week we were here. You killed one?"

I gave her a tentative grin. "Several actually. They're really good eating roasted or salted. And revenge tastes so, so good."

I was getting used to the look Judy or Val or the rest of the colonists gave me when I said something like that. Wide eyes, glassy stare, slow blinks.

"Holy crap," Val said under her breath. Then she cleared her throat. "Okay, we'll try the salting thing. We're gonna need to start stockpiling. We're going through the stores of non-perishables far too quickly for my taste. Can you teach us to kill these things?"

Now my grin was wide and welcoming. "Gladly. I'll show the gleaners the grove, too, and how to dry drunk-peaches." I glanced at the canteen. "Maybe we can haul some snow and ice down from the mountains and stash it in the back to make another fridge."

Since BEV had made off with the *Last Resort* and the second wave supplies it had been carrying, the colony was scrambling to try to house, clothe, and feed an extra thousand people.

"Good idea." Val added a note to her clipboard. "I'll get someone on food detail to take care of this for now. But I think Judy is expecting you."

I gave her a little wave and trotted toward the admin building, whistling for Shade. He'd ventured a couple of steps away from me to stare at a group of colonists kicking a ball back and forth behind the canteen. He rushed to catch up.

"I'm sure they'd let you play with them," I whispered. I was pretty sure Ren had been passing around notes because a couple of the younger colonists had started trying to bribe

Shade with fish. He was acting aloof for now, but it wouldn't be long before he'd made new friends.

I wished it was as easy for me.

I might have felt responsible for the colony, but I still had no idea where exactly I fit in with all of this. I still lived at the drop ship, since the dorms were so crowded. The stained infra-engineer patch still clung to my jumpsuit, but I didn't really fit in at the workshops either. Too many of the others glanced at my wiring and assumed I had too much to do to actually build anything.

I helped the hunting parties; I'd cleared a lot of the fields and shared growing tips with the farmers. I took turns with the guards to watch for the black death and megawings.

But none of that was my job. Not exactly.

I'd spent so much of my life looking forward to this sort of ordered chaos and building something from the ground up, but I'd changed too much to just slip into as if I hadn't tamed a jungle.

I pushed through into the admin building.

Judy stood in the center of the foyer with all the desks pushed to the sides and a huge whiteboard taking up the back wall full of scribbles and lists and lines connecting thoughts and to do lists.

She saw me and Shade and waved us over. She glanced around for a place that wasn't full of staffers bundling around handwritten notes, and her eyes fell on Dr. Grotman's office, standing empty. The nameplate was still up.

She grimaced and pulled me inside. She looked at the chair and then decided to sit on the desk instead.

Nothing had changed in here. It was just as I'd left it when I'd been trying to get into the black box under the desk.

"You know, you're our commander," I said quietly. "No one would mind if you worked in here."

Her grimace fell away, replaced with a sad smile. "I...can't yet. It's funny, I felt so guilty when I went into my pod first, and I knew Liz was still out there with the others trying to get back. I felt like I should have been there instead of in the cave. But if I had been, I'd be dead, too, and there wouldn't have been anyone to step up here and now." She shook her head. "That guilt has never gone away."

I dragged over a stool and perched on it while Shade curled up at my feet. "The med tech who woke me before the ship crashed. Kara. She...just picked randomly, I think. Went down the line and punched as many buttons as she thought she could reasonably save. If she hadn't picked mine...I'd be dead with the others. Or—or still frozen. There wouldn't have been anyone to revive everyone. The others all died in the jungle."

Judy glanced at the chair. "So, you're saying that without us, none of this would have happened. There would be no one else."

I shrugged. "Maybe there would have. Maybe there would have been someone better. But how long are we supposed to feel guilty about living when living came with its own sort of responsibility?"

Judy blew out her breath. Then she deliberately stood and sat in Dr. Grotman's chair. She cocked her head. "Here's to responsibility."

BB popped up on my wrist. "According to Dr. Grotman's records, you are well suited to it, Ms. Mandla-Devereaux. She trusted you with a lot of the day-to-day operations of running a colony."

Judy smiled, but her eyes settled on BB. "I didn't know you had Dr. Grotman's information."

"How else would we have found you?" I said, quietly. I didn't love bringing attention to BB's data packets, but the knowledge was out there. And Judy hadn't tried to arrest us yet.

"Some people came out of their pods very different," Judy said. "A few have requested transfers back to Earth. And I'm not going to force them to stay after everything they've been through. The probe satellites have been updated and moved to a higher orbit. They're now broadcasting a wait signal that will override any incoming vessels to keep them from entering orbit until we make sure they aren't arriving during a storm."

"So there won't be another crash like the *Last Resort*," I said, shoulders relaxing.

"Yes. The next colony ship should be safe. And the ones who want to leave Daybreak can ship out, then." Judy cocked her head at me. "I thought I would give you the same choice."

I shook my head, completely confused. "What choice?"

"The choice to leave. If you want to."

Go back to overcrowded Earth? Go back to dingy skies and an uncertain future as a corporate orphan? I hadn't even considered it as an option.

I'd get to see Professor Orrion again. He'd be a lot older since the trip was ten years one way. And I wouldn't have to deal with slasherfins or megawings or black deaths again. I wouldn't have to worry about what I was going to eat.

I wouldn't get to see what new creature Daybreak came up with next. I wouldn't get to see Shade make friends with the colonists. I wouldn't get to see what was beyond the mountains or the volcanic region where the colonists had been.

"I'm staying," I said. "I kind of love Daybreak."

"Platonically," Ren said from the door. "Sorry I'm late." He glanced around for a chair and settled on leaning against the wall. He carried a folio and set it carefully on the floor beside him.

"This isn't a formality," Judy said, hands on the desk in front of her. "But everyone else has the job assigned to them before all this started. We all know what we're supposed to do and where we're supposed to be. Except you two."

I frowned. I'd been assigned as an infra-engineer first and foremost, but maybe she was feeling that same thing I was. That sense of a puzzle piece out of place.

Ren was nodding. "I don't know what Dr. Carver falsified for me, but I doubt my assignment was actually true to my experience. What little there was of it."

Judy raised her chin. "Your records indicate a placement with the student core with a fast track on the software side of things. He expected you to learn, I believe."

Ren's lips went thin and his eyes unhappy. "He meant it, then. About not creating me to be another Dr. Carver."

"I believe so," Judy said. She folded her hands and sat up. "Unfortunately, the student core isn't going to be the same for a long while. Everyone needs hands on training while we rebuild, so we're moving to an apprenticeship system. You can try your hand at whatever you'd like under the eye of an experienced colonist. There is an opening for a lead astro-physicist, obviously..."

Ren stiffened.

"But I'm going to be promoting someone internally if that's all right with you."

He let out his breath. "Yeah. Yeah of course."

"Do you have a preference for your first assignment, then?"

"I just want time to figure out what I'm good at. I want time to figure out who I am."

"Maybe in the vet sciences area," I said, nudging him with my toe.

He perked up. "There's a vet sciences department?"

"There is," Judy said. "It consists of one person right now. Dr. Ling was part of the biology department originally and handled the livestock we brought to the planet. I'm putting him in charge of studying the titans to be sure we understand them enough to call them again. He is also looking for native replacements for the livestock that perished in the first storm."

Ren and I looked at each other. "Dino-chickens."

Judy raised an eyebrow like she was saying 'I'm not even going to ask.' "I'll put you down for assignment with Dr. Ling, then. And you?" Judy asked, turning to face me. "Living has given you a lot of responsibility. But I think you've done plenty for this colony already. Unless you want to do more."

It was a question. An opening. One I didn't know how to fill yet.

"I guess it depends on if I'm going to be arrested."

Judy snorted. "No one's arresting you. For a lot of reasons. I'm registering for a formal separation from Stellar Corp. They rushed the survey of this planet to get us here faster and it cost lives. That alone will be plenty to get us out of our contracts with them, and we can start growing as a separate entity. It will mean I will have complete jurisdiction for a long while. And what the government doesn't know, won't hurt it."

She gave BB a solemn nod.

"I declared a retroactive state of emergency during the last eight months which covers any act of survival. No one is going to be coming for you about anything you did while we were sleeping and you were trying to stay alive. I meant it, Anikka. You've already served this colony and its people more than any one person should have to. You protected us. Your choices are your own."

"I don't even know where to start. I'm—I was—an infra-engineer. I was supposed to build. But now..." I raised my arms and let my wires glow. "I don't know where I fit."

Judy and Ren exchanged a look. "Would you like a suggestion? Or maybe it's a request."

"Request?"

Judy shrugged. "More responsibility."

Ren reached into his folio.

"Daybreak colony isn't going anywhere," Judy said as Ren pulled out a sheaf of papers. "Val and I aren't abandoning this place just because it tried to kill us once or twice." She gave me a rueful look. "But we're going to have to learn how to work with Daybreak. Not against it. I want to create something new. A position designed to protect the colony by making it a part of Daybreak. Someone to guard and teach us and help us not be just a transplant but a part of another world."

Ren laid out a single large sheet of paper and unfolded it so it covered the whole desk. It was a floor plan in his careful hand with notes scribbled in the margins.

There was a large living space, wide enough for a family of ten to lounge on the furniture. Or maybe a few people would have room to do something physical, like practice with lightning or a blade. A little kitchen opened off of it and another empty room that could have held a table and chairs.

The second story contained a hallway lined with doors. Almost like a dorm.

It was a space where someone could live alone or with a trusted friend. Or recruit more friends.

It was a space to build on. A headquarters? Was that what Judy and Ren had given me?

Responsibility, Judy had said.

She drew something out of her pocket, a homemade patch

with ragged edges, but the design was clear. She passed it across to me.

A shield ringed with lightning.

"A guard house for a new type of guard," Ren said.

"I was thinking sentinel," Judy said.

I held the patch between my fingers. I could take that idea and mold it. I could teach them about the jungle. Keep them safe from its dangers.

I could live on Daybreak instead of just surviving it.

BB leaned over to stare at the floor plan, her blue light spilling across the page, and I could see plenty of space in each of the rooms for hologram pads.

"What do you think?"

"I think yes." I looked at them waiting, my chest buzzing with an emotion I couldn't name yet. "I can see fitting here."

"Then we'll need this." Ren reached into his pocket and pulled out a dusty carton and set it on the desk in front of me.

My breath caught.

"Juice," Judy said, brow drawing down. "Old juice. Am I missing something?"

"I think it's some kind of symbol for her," Ren said while I struggled to speak. "She said she wasn't going to drink it till it was all over."

Because it had meant safety. When I'd woken up on the *Last Resort*, when I'd staggered through the jungle with a broken arm, all I'd wanted was some juice because it would have meant things were normal again.

That normal had dissolved a long time ago. But...I glanced across at Ren and Judy with Shade at my feet and BB smiling at me from my wrist.

Maybe now I had a new normal.

I popped the top of the carton open.

Thank you so much for choosing to spend time with Anikka, BB, and Shade. This might be the end of Anikka and BB's story, but there's plenty more to experience if you want more stories about fierce young women. By Wingéd Chair, a retelling of Robin Hood where Maid Marion kicks butt from a wheelchair, is a great place to start.

If you'd like more about Daybreak, be sure to check out the short story, Skies Falling. Or sign up here if you'd like to see how BB developed the humor filter from her point of view!

If you loved this book, consider leaving a review so other readers can find more stories about kick butt girls in kick butt worlds.

ACKNOWLEDGMENTS

First, Joselyn, for being my first reader and making me believe I could write science fiction.

Mom and Dad, always, for being just as enthusiastic about crashed spaceships as you were about rogue magic and swampy dragons.

Arielle and Lacey, for being an endless sounding board for more crazy survival ideas.

Miranda, for Ren's amazing artwork. You are so talented and you've made Daybreak so beautiful.

MiblArt, for the amazing cover art. You've made Anikka so much more badass than I could have alone.

Fiona McLaren, for copy edits. These books wouldn't be nearly as good without you.

Abby, for loving Daybreak and Shade as much as I do. I can't wait for you to read this one.

And Everly, for being a great writing buddy. And not banging on my keyboard while you sit on my lap.

ABOUT THE AUTHOR

Books have been Kendra's escape for as long as she can remember. She used to hide fantasy novels behind her government textbook in high school, and she wrote most of her first novel during a semester of college algebra.

Kendra writes science fiction and fantasy featuring main characters with disabilities.

When she's not writing she's reading, and when she's not reading she's playing video games.

She lives in Denver with her very tall wife, their book loving progeny, and a lazy black monster masquerading as a service dog.

Visit Kendra at
www.kendramerritt.com

facebook.com/kendramerrittauthor
instagram.com/kendramerrittauthor
goodreads.com/kendramerritt
tiktok.com/@kendramerrittauthor